The Russian Tapestry

ALSO BY BANAFSHEH SEROV

Under a Starless Sky

The Russian Tapestry

BANAFSHEH SEROV

First published in Australia and New Zealand in 2013
by Hachette Australia
(an imprint of Hachette Australia Pty Limited)
Level 17, 207 Kent Street, Sydney NSW 2000
www.hachette.com.au

10 9 8 7 6 5 4 3 2 1

This edition published in 2015

National Library of Australia
Cataloguing-in-Publication data:

Serov, Banafsheh.
The Russian Tapestry / Banafsheh Serov.

978 0 7336 3380 5 (pbk.)

Historical fiction, Russian.
Love stories, Russian.
Soviet Union – History – Revolution, 1917–1921 – Fiction.
Romance fiction.

A823.4

Author photograph by Lorrie Graham
Map by MAPgraphics
Cover photographs: woman courtesy of Getty Images, gates and trees courtesy of Trevillion, St Basil's Cathedral courtesy of iStockphoto
Cover design by Ellie Exarchos
Text design by Bookhouse, Sydney
Typeset in 11/15.75 pt Sabon LT Pro
Printed and bound in Australia by Griffin Press, Adelaide, an Accredited ISO AS/NZS 14001:2009 Environmental Management System printer

The paper this book is printed on is certified against the Forest Stewardship Council® Standards. Griffin Press holds FSC chain of custody certification SGS-COC-005088. FSC promotes environmentally responsible, socially beneficial and economically viable management of the world's forests.

For Mark

Tallinn
Tsarskoe Selo
Narva
Alexander Palace
ESTONIA
Pskov
Riga
LATVIA
Baltic Sea
Battle of Tannenburg
Battle of the Mazurian Lakes
POLAND
Warsaw
GERMAN EMPIRE
NETHERLANDS
BELGIUM
Carpathian Mountains
AUSTRO-HUNGARIAN EMPIRE
FRANCE
ROMANIA
ITALY
SERBIA

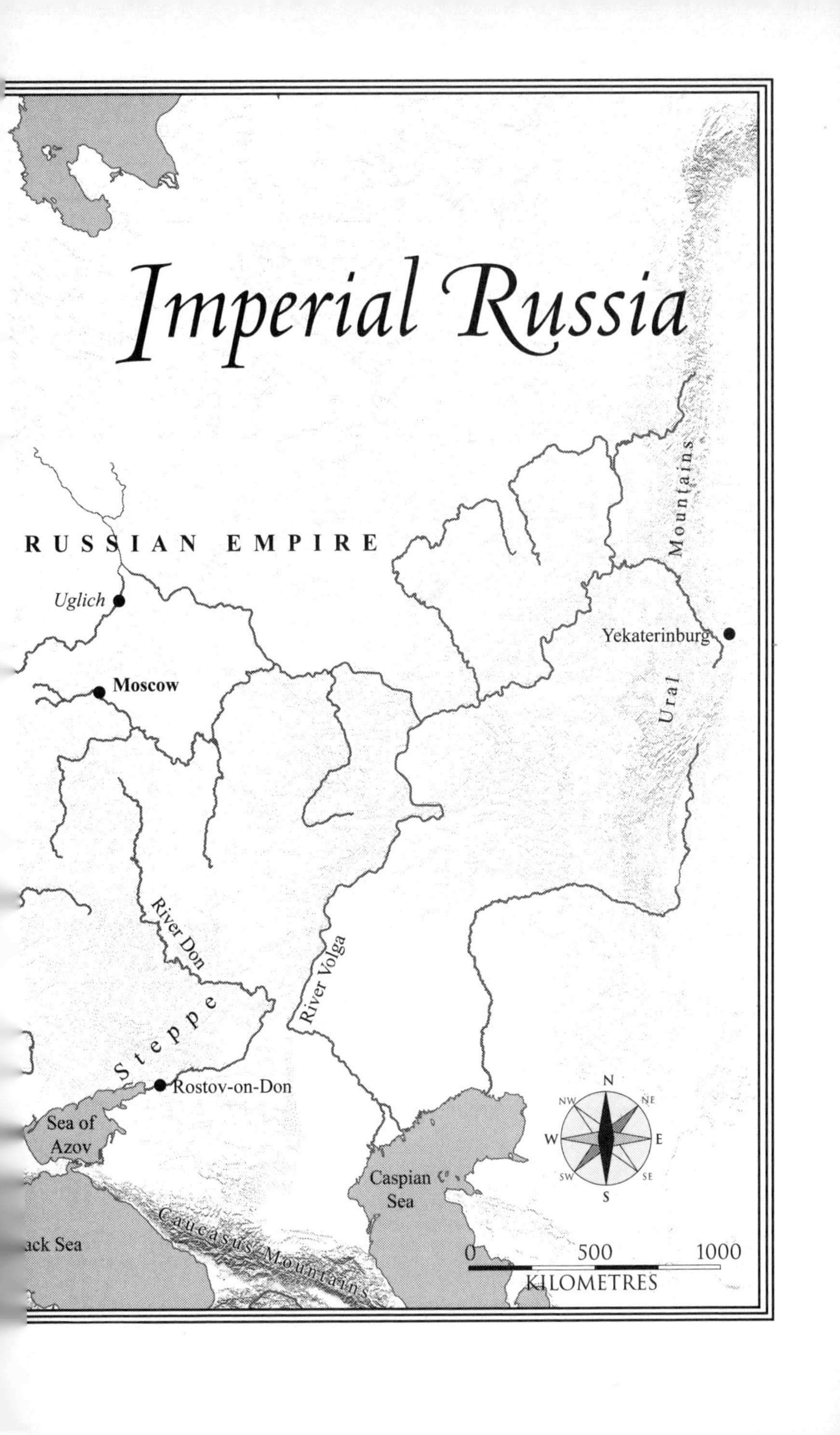
Imperial Russia
RUSSIAN EMPIRE
Uglich
Moscow
Yekaterinburg
Ural Mountains
River Don
River Volga
Steppe
Rostov-on-Don
Sea of Azov
ack Sea
Caucasus Mountains
Caspian Sea
N
NE
E
SE
S
SW
W
NW
0
500
1000
KILOMETRES

'And only now, when his head was grey, had he really fallen in love as one ought to.'

Anton Chekhov, *The Lady with the Little Dog*

I

St Petersburg, September 1913

The carriage moved slowly along the cobbled streets towards the Mariinsky Theatre. Marie Kulbas drew back the curtain to gaze at the starlit sky and the moon, suspended above the baroque buildings like a perfect pearl.

'Close the curtain, Marie,' Pauline Kulbas instructed. 'There is nothing so unbecoming as a young lady staring out the window with a dazed expression in her eyes.'

'That's unfair, Mama.' Marie moved away from the window, but continued to peek out from the corner. 'It's my first visit to St Petersburg, after all.'

'Mama is right.' Nikolai leant forward and pulled the curtain closed. 'You need to make the right impression if you want your first season to be a success,' he teased.

'Never mind, dear child.' Monsieur Kulbas, looking uncomfortable in his evening suit, patted Marie lightly on the knee. 'You'll get the hang of society soon enough.'

Every September Marie's parents visited St Petersburg from Narva for the start of the season, and this year Marie, who had just graduated from school, was joining them for the first time. Ahead of her was a month of invitations to gala balls, festivals and masquerades. Marie had spent the past weeks attending fittings for gowns and commissioning feathered hats from the best dressmakers and milliners in the city. Tonight, dressed in a full-length amber-beaded gown and a bejewelled Roman headdress, Marie was making her debut. As a graduation present for his sister, Nikolai had secured a box at the Mariinsky Theatre to watch the Imperial Russian Ballet.

Their coach came to a stop outside the entry and the coachman opened the door, offering his hand for Madame Kulbas. Stepping down after her mother, Marie looked in wonder at the pale green building with white trim before her eyes were drawn to the finely dressed crowd lingering in front of the Romanesque facade.

'Look, Kolya, that's the former prima ballerina Mathilde Kschessinska,' Marie whispered to her brother. 'I've heard so much about her.'

'So have I.' Nikolai leant closer. 'It's rumoured that your prima ballerina was the Emperor's mistress before he was married.'

'I don't believe you!' Marie said, scandalised.

Nikolai shrugged. 'Believe what you like, but he did buy her a mansion.'

As they approached the red carpet leading to the vestibule, Nikolai offered his arm to his sister. 'May I?'

'Oh, Kolya, I never imagined it to be so wonderful,' Marie said when they walked inside.

Dazzling chandeliers, dripping with crystals, hung from the ornate ceiling and bouquets of large flowers stood in huge urns. Women with long feathers in their hair and high-waist fitted dresses walked arm in arm with men in evening jackets, their hair carefully pomaded.

'Why, Masha, I do believe you are swooning,' Nikolai said with a laugh.

They followed their parents to the second level, where an usher led the family to their box at the right of the stage.

Marie drew in her breath and squeezed her brother's arm as she gazed around at the ornate walls and row upon row of dark velvet seats.

'See over there?' Nikolai pointed to the large gilded box at the back of the theatre, facing the stage. 'That's the imperial box.'

'Why is it empty?'

'Apparently the Empress doesn't enjoy society. Last time she attended the theatre she walked out halfway through the performance. It caused quite a stir!'

The lights dimmed and the conductor led the orchestra into the chords of the overture. Latecomers hurried to their seats and a hush fell across boxes and stalls. Marie's heart beat faster as she turned to the stage.

Ballerinas in white hooped skirts and jewelled bodices glided with effortless grace, their every leap and turn a cause of wonder and admiration to Marie. Mesmerised, she soon forgot her nervousness about making a good impression. Slightly leaning forward in her seat, she immersed herself in the full drama of the unfolding love affair.

At the conclusion of the final act, when the spirits of Prince Siegfried and Odette ascend into the heavens above Swan Lake, Marie joined the crowds in applauding the dancers. Afterwards, waiting outside with her parents for their carriage, she felt slightly light-headed, as if stepping out of a dream. Before them, there was a long row of carriages and automobiles waiting to pick up the patrons.

'What's keeping that blasted driver?' Monsieur Kulbas paced the footpath, stopping every once in a while to check along the queue for their carriage. 'May the devil take him! We are going to be late.'

'Herman, please.' Madame Kulbas looked about her to see if anyone had noticed her husband's blasphemy. 'If you must curse, at least try to keep your voice down.'

Pulling out his pocket watch, Monsieur Kulbas checked the time. 'We should have been at my cousin's home ten minutes ago.'

'I'm sure he will not mind if we are a little late. He knows there is always a wait for carriages following the ballet,' said Nikolai.

A car tooted its horn, startling Madame Kulbas. 'Those horrible, noisy things!' She turned to Marie. 'You know Nikolai has convinced your father to order one. Personally, I can't see the attraction. I've already told your father I refuse to ride in them.'

Marie smiled. 'You'll soon be used to them, Mama.' She looked at the crowd milling at the front of the theatre. The whole evening was like a fairy tale and she did not want it to end. She started when Nikolai touched her on the elbow.

'Marie, I want you to meet a friend of mine, Pyotr Arkadyich.'

Turning, Marie saw a young man with wavy flaxen hair and round glasses.

'*Enchanté,* Mademoiselle.' Clicking his heels, he bent to kiss Marie's gloved hand. Straightening, Pyotr opened his mouth to say something more when they were interrupted by the Kulbas's carriage pulling in at the kerb.

Nikolai turned to his friend. 'Do you wish to ride with us to Mostovsky's?'

Pyotr's eyes flicked to Marie's, then back to Nikolai. 'Thank you, but my mother's carriage should be here any moment.' Turning to Marie, he clicked his heels once again. 'I shall look forward to meeting you again shortly, Mademoiselle.'

At the Mostovsky mansion, the hosts stood at the entrance greeting their guests.

'How are you enjoying your first season, Masha?' Madame Mostovsky enquired, giving Marie a warm smile.

'I'm enjoying it enormously, Madame.'

'We are very much looking forward to having you stay with us while you're studying in St Petersburg, Darya especially.'

'Madame is very kind.' Marie curtsied.

She followed her parents and brother up the wide curving staircase, past the full-length mirrors and bouquets of colourful flowers, to the ballroom. Inside the large rectangular room, chandeliers bathed the scene in dazzling brightness. Fires in the marble hearths kept the room at a pleasant temperature and an orchestra played softly in one corner. Fashionably dressed women sipped champagne while openly scrutinising one another's appearance.

As Marie made her way through the crowd to where her cousin

Darya was standing, she saw Pyotr talking with a group of young men who called to her brother.

'You seem to have caught Pyotr's eye.' Darya fanned herself lazily with a large ostrich-plume fan.

Glancing over her shoulder, Marie saw that Pyotr was watching them. 'Don't be ridiculous, Dasha. It must be you he's looking at.' With green eyes and a tall slender figure, Darya was never short of admirers.

Darya laughed. 'I have known Pyotr for a long time, Masha, and he has never looked at me that way.'

Marie turned again and saw Pyotr lean towards Nikolai and whisper something. She hurriedly turned to her cousin again as the pair left their group and headed in the girls' direction.

'Good evening, gentlemen,' Darya said, fluttering her fan coquettishly.

'My dearest cousin.' Nikolai kissed Darya's hand. 'You look charming tonight.'

Marie rolled her eyes at her brother's honeyed tone then caught Pyotr staring at her, his lips curled in a bemused smile. Embarrassed, she dropped her eyes.

They chatted idly, with Darya and Nikolai doing most of the talking. Around them, waiters in bow ties carried trays of food to long tables in the adjoining dining room.

'I'm famished,' Nikolai said, looking longingly at the passing trays. 'Shall we get something to eat?' He offered his arm to Darya, who took it demurely.

Pyotr held out his arm to Marie. 'Mademoiselle?'

Copying her cousin's manners, she took Pyotr's arm and they followed Nikolai and Darya to the dining room. Around them, the other guests made their way to the tables, conversing in subdued tones.

Long tables arranged with elaborate and exotic dishes lined the room. Vases of flowers decorated each end of the tables, while a pair of stuffed white swans took pride of place in the centre.

'Did you enjoy the ballet?' Pyotr asked as they moved along one of the tables.

'Yes, very much. Thank you.' Marie held her plate out to a waiter in white coat and gloves who served her a slice of lamb. 'Tchaikovsky is a genius.'

'Was this your first ballet?'

Marie felt her cheeks grow hot. Surely he must know this was her first season. 'Yes, it was,' she replied with as much grace as she could muster.

'And what did you think of our ballerinas?'

'They are extremely talented. I especially enjoyed Karsavina's performance. But of course, this being my first season, I have little to go by. How did you find the performance?'

'I confess, I don't know enough about ballet to comment. I tend to favour the written word over performance.'

He paused as another waiter put food on their plates.

'Nikolai tells me you intend to study law,' Pyotr continued.

So, they had been discussing her. 'I start next May. My uncle has been kind enough to invite me to stay here while I'm in St Petersburg.'

'Law is an unusual choice for a woman.'

'Not according to the women's emancipationists. They believe women should have the right to vote and run for office. Finland already has women in its parliament.'

'Are you going on about women's suffrage again?' Nikolai interrupted as he and Darya joined them. 'Hope she's not boring you, Pyotr.'

'We're not going to spend the rest of the evening talking about politics, are we?' Darya said with a pout.

Nikolai stopped a waiter who was carrying a tray of champagne flutes. 'No more talk of politics.' Placing his plate on a nearby table, he passed them each a glass. 'Let's drink a toast.'

'To what?' Darya asked.

'To a long and happy life.'

The five-piece English orchestra struck up a waltz. A murmur ran through the crowd and, led by the host and hostess, couples started to move back to the ballroom.

Marie saw Darya's eyes seek out Nikolai's.

Obliging her, Nikolai bowed deeply. 'Would you give me the honour of this dance?'

Leaving their plates and glasses for the waiters to collect, they made their way to the edge of the circle. Taking a firm hold of Darya's waist Nikolai guided her confidently into smooth gliding movements.

'They make a handsome pair,' Pyotr observed as he and Marie followed them out.

'They do,' Marie replied absently. She was growing increasingly eager to join the dancing, yet Pyotr seemed not to notice that all around them couples were taking to the floor.

'Do you enjoy dancing?' She regretted the words as soon as they left her lips. First she had lectured him about women's suffrage, now he would think she was inviting him to dance. He must find her dreadfully forward.

Turning to face her, Pyotr bowed stiffly. 'If you'll excuse me, please.' And without waiting for her reply, he withdrew in the direction of the drawing room.

Marie's eyes stung with tears of shame. She hurried out of the ballroom, not looking to her left or right for fear she might meet with a familiar face.

'Marie!' It was Nikolai. 'What's wrong? I saw Pyotr leave and then you rushed away . . .'

'I've never felt so humiliated,' Marie said.

Nikolai shook his head sympathetically. 'Poor Masha.' He offered her a handkerchief. 'This is very uncharacteristic of him. I have known Pyotr for a long time and never have I seen him behave like this.'

'He is proud and snobbish,' Marie retorted. 'I never want to see him again.'

'Don't be so quick to judge,' Nikolai advised. 'Stop these tears.

How do you expect to make a success of your first ball with red-rimmed eyes?'

'I think I'd rather go home.'

'Nonsense! Now go dry your eyes and then I will have my first dance with my sister.'

Marie agreed and a few minutes later, having reapplied powder and lipstick, she entered the ballroom. Escorted by her brother, she moved to the centre of the floor.

Following her dance with Nikolai, other young men approached. Occasionally, as she was whirled about the room, she saw Pyotr standing to one side, staring fixedly at the dance floor with a pained expression. When her eye caught his she quickly looked away, determined to avoid all contact with him.

It was not till many hours later, when the family was waiting for their carriage, that Marie was forced to face him again.

'I trust you enjoyed your evening?' he asked politely.

'I did, thank you,' Marie said tersely.

'You seem fond of dancing,' Pyotr persevered.

Marie, who had been avoiding his gaze, turned to look at him. What a curious character he was. After humiliating her before the whole of St Petersburg society, he now had the gall to engage her in conversation.

'It's Marie's first season,' Madame Kulbas offered when it became apparent Marie was not going to respond.

Pyotr opened his mouth then closed it, as if unsure of what to say. Clearing his throat, he asked, 'May I call on you during your stay?'

'I'm afraid we have a very busy schedule, which leaves little time for other activities,' Marie said coldly.

'Marie,' her mother hissed in her ear, 'what has come over you?'

'Maybe at a later stage,' Pyotr persisted, 'when you have settled at your cousin's place.'

To Marie's surprise, Pyotr's expression seemed to hover somewhere between despair and regret. She felt her resolve waver.

'She would be glad to receive you,' Nikolai broke in as their carriage arrived.

'Of course.' Marie glared at her brother.

'Why did you say that?' she demanded as the carriage pulled away. 'You saw how he treated me. Why did you make me promise to receive him?'

Nikolai took her hand. 'Masha, Pyotr did not mean to offend you. It is just that his shyness makes him awkward around women. Give him another chance.'

'I don't see why I should,' Marie argued.

Her brother smiled. 'Do it for me.'

Marie moved into her uncle's mansion the following May, accompanied by her maid, Anna Radzinsky. Her quarters, with views of the fashionable Nevsky Prospect, included two bedrooms, a living room and a lavatory. The living room, with a set of bay windows leading to a small balcony, had views of the Winter Palace and the golden dome of St Isaac's Cathedral.

'How do you like your rooms?' Darya asked over dinner on Marie's first evening in her new home.

'They're charming. I know I'll be very happy here.'

'I saw Pyotr today,' Darya said, a coy smile lifting the corners of her mouth. 'He asked after you.'

'Really? I find that surprising.' All these months later Marie still felt the sting of his rejection.

'Pyotr is rather unusual,' Darya continued, as if she hadn't heard the scorn in Marie's voice. 'He's not at all like the other young men in St Petersburg. I've never seen him dance once at any ball. He's always in some quiet corner, with his nose in a book.'

'Dasha's right.' Monsieur Mostovsky looked up from eating. 'You and Pyotr –' he pointed to Marie with his fork '– have a lot in common. I remember you as a little girl, always with a book in your hands.' He let out a throaty laugh. 'Whilst Darya and your brothers chased one another, you sat quietly in the library reading the books.'

Marie was about to object to her uncle's assessment when Darya interrupted.

'That's settled then.' She clapped excitedly. 'I shall call him after dinner to organise a visit.'

Marie groaned inwardly.

'A marvellous invention, the telephone.' Monsieur Mostovsky beamed. 'Herman should get one.'

'Papa was quite taken by them on his last visit to St Petersburg.' Marie was grateful for the change of subject. 'Mama is less convinced, but I think Papa will manage to persuade her.'

Two days later, having forgotten Darya's intention to invite Pyotr to call, Marie was reading in her rooms when the footman announced Pyotr Arkadyich had arrived.

'Please show the gentleman to the drawing room,' Marie instructed the footman, irritated that Darya was not home to receive him herself.

Calling Anna, Marie changed from the pale blue dress she had been wearing, into a silk dress with a high lace collar.

Anna fastened the last of the pearl buttons down Marie's back and then stood back to scrutinise the result in the mirror. 'Don't you think this dress is a little conservative to receive a gentleman caller?' she asked.

'No, it's perfect,' said Marie. 'Now help me tame these curls, will you?'

When Anna had finished with her hair, Marie hurried down to greet her guest.

'I took the liberty of buying you a small present,' Pyotr said almost immediately upon Marie's arrival into the drawing room.

Surprised, Marie undid the wrapping and gasped when she discovered it held a copy of Chekhov's *The Lady with the Little Dog*. Opening the book to the first page, she read a few lines.

> *It was said that a new person had appeared on the sea-front: a lady with a little dog. Dmitri Dmitritch Gurov, who*

> *had by then been a fortnight at Yalta, and so was fairly at home there, had begun to take an interest in new arrivals.*

'Nikolai said you are fond of reading.' Pyotr looked anxious. 'I thought you might enjoy Chekhov.'

'Thank you. That's very thoughtful.' She smiled at him and saw his face relax.

'Shall we have some tea?' She rang the bell for the house maid.

'I know you are busy and I shan't demand any more of your time,' Pyotr said. 'I simply came to welcome you and offer you this gift.'

'Won't you please stay?' The words slipped out spontaneously before she had a chance to stop them.

Pyotr too appeared surprised by the invitation. 'Are you sure, Mademoiselle?'

'Darya should be back shortly. She would be disappointed to hear she has missed you. And please call me Marie.' She motioned for him to take a seat. 'I'd like to hear more about your favourite books.'

Over the summer, Pyotr became a regular visitor to the house, bringing with him armfuls of books. He read aloud to Marie his favourite passages, and she found she looked forward to his visits more and more. In a letter to Nikolai, she wrote: *I have grown fond of Pyotr. He is such a dear friend. We can discuss our views openly with one another without fear of causing offence. So far our only argument has been over the merits of Hugo as compared to Tolstoy . . .*

'Do you seriously believe Hugo is a better writer than Tolstoy?' Marie demanded.

Taking advantage of the white nights, Pyotr had suggested they take a stroll through the Summer Garden. A light breeze rustled through the branches, scattering leaves onto the footpath.

'Tolstoy is a genius and I deeply admire Levin's philosophical ideals in *Anna Karenina*,' Pyotr explained, 'but I found *Les Miserables* rich and lyrical. The story of Jean Valjean is very powerful.' He gave a passing glance at the pair of statues flanking the path. 'It is simply my opinion.'

'So you disagree with Chekhov and Dostoevsky when they say that Tolstoy is the greatest of all novelists?'

'I told you, I do not dispute Tolstoy's genius.' Pyotr laughed. 'No one depicts Russian society as realistically as he does.' He shrugged. 'I just happen to enjoy Hugo more.'

'You are being absurd.' Marie pretended to be indignant.

'I shall miss our discussions when you return to Narva.' Pyotr's voice was serious now. 'I've grown extremely fond of them.' Stopping abruptly, he turned to face her. He looked nervous as he took her hand. 'It's not just our discussions I've grown fond of.' He swallowed.

Marie's pulse began to race as she lifted her gaze to meet his. 'Yes?' she prompted, her heart filling with joy.

He opened his mouth to speak, but then changed his mind. 'Forgive me, I do not dare.'

'Please, speak freely, Pyotr,' she whispered.

He turned his head away, dropping her hand. 'It is nothing.' Then, looking to the sky, he added, 'It is getting late. We should head back.'

She felt her hand slip through his, disappointment replacing her joy. She studied his face a moment longer, noting the lines of strain at the corners of his eyes. There was more to what he was telling her.

She nodded. 'Yes, we'd better go back or I'll be late getting ready for dinner.'

2

St Petersburg, 30 July 1914

'Your Excellency.' The maître d', a short stout man with a perfectly waxed moustache, bowed deeply. 'How wonderful to see you again.' He motioned for the valet to help their guest with his hat and coat. 'Countess Volkonsky is already here,' he added quietly.

'Thank you, Mikhail.'

Dressed in his dark blue military uniform, the colonel checked his reflection in the mirror. At thirty-seven, Alexei Basilivich Serov's hair was just beginning to recede at the temples. The touch of grey above his ears blended well with the blond hair and made him look distinguished. Fluent in German and speaking a little French, he was a fine horseman, a superb dancer and an excellent shot. Though of medium build and height, Alexei nevertheless struck an imposing figure through the grace and manner in which he held himself. He nodded at his reflection, satisfied, then addressed the maître d' once more.

'Have you seen to our usual arrangements?'

'Of course, Excellency,' Mikail replied. 'This way, please.'

Alexei followed him through the crowded room, nodding and smiling at familiar faces. The most fashionable restaurant in St Petersburg, the Donon was famous for its high-ranking clientele as well as its exquisite food.

At the back of the restaurant, Mikail drew open a set of heavy crimson curtains, which led to a narrow corridor with dim lighting and doors to private rooms. A Tartar waiter stepped aside when the two men approached. Rapping lightly on one of the doors, Mikail waited for permission to enter then stopped to let Alexei pass before him.

'Enjoy your evening, Excellency,' he murmured, before withdrawing discreetly.

'Alexei Basilivich! I have a good mind to send you packing.'

Countess Natalya stood in the middle of the room in a close-fitting white gown that accentuated her narrow waist and full breasts. 'What time do you call this? The champagne has grown warm.'

'Forgive me, Natalya.' Taking her hand in his, he drew it to his lips but at the last moment, turned her palm upwards and kissed the sensitive centre of her wrist. 'You look divine.'

'You are a cad, Alexei.' Natalya pursed her lips, then smiled. 'What kept you? Was it your wife?'

'I had some business that required my attention.' He rang the bell to summon the waiter standing outside the door. 'Bring us a new bottle of champagne,' he ordered.

When they were alone once more, Alexei hooked an arm around Natalya's waist, drawing her to him. 'I've missed you.' He kissed her on the neck.

'Not so fast.' She pushed him away. 'You have not even explained what business was so important that you kept me waiting for almost an hour.'

'Surely you understand the consequences of the assassination on relationships between the Serbs and the Austro-Hungarians,' he countered.

'Omph! The assassination!' She turned to the table where a cold supper was laid out. 'I'm tired of hearing about the Archduke and his mousy wife. It seems all of St Petersburg is obsessed by it.'

'My dear countess, the Archduke was after all the heir to the Austro-Hungarian throne.'

'So, what of it? What do the Serbs and Austrians have to do with us?'

'Austria, backed by Germany, has declared war on Serbia, in which case Russia must step in to defend the Orthodox Serbs.'

She shrugged. 'I'm bored by it all.' The countess spread a small dollop of caviar on crispbread and popped it in her mouth.

'In that case, let us hear no more about the subject.' Alexei grabbed her hand and pulled her towards a sofa in the corner of the room.

'No.' She snatched her hand away. 'I have not forgiven you yet.' Moving to a chair on the other side of the dining table, she leant forward, presenting Alexei with a view of her ample cleavage.

The waiter entered carrying a tray bearing a bottle of champagne and two glasses.

'Will there be anything else, Excellency?'

'No thank you.' Tipping the man, Alexei whispered, 'Make sure we are not disturbed.'

'Yes, Excellency.'

Alexei filled the glasses and offered one to the countess.

'I'm still waiting for your explanation.' She fixed him with a stern look. 'I thought you had forgotten me,' she added in a hurt voice.

'Forgotten you? My dearest Natalya, you are the most ravishing creature in all of St Petersburg. How could I forget you?'

Clearly pleased by Alexei's response, Natalya beamed. The sternness disappeared from her eyes and, taking Alexei's hand, she drew him down into a seat beside her.

'Will you stay tonight?'

His face grew serious. 'I'm afraid I cannot.'

She stiffened. 'Is it your wife?' She stood abruptly and moved away from him. 'You never showed such concern for her in the past.'

'This has nothing to do with Emily. I must know if Russia will enter the war. My regiment might be called to the front any day.' Alexei went to her and took her in his arms. At first she shrugged him off but then relented and allowed him to draw her into his chest. 'I'm a professional soldier,' he whispered into her hair. 'This is what I've trained for all my life.'

'Oh, Alyosha, is there really going to be a war?' Turning to him, she looked up at his face with concern. 'What if . . . what if you are hurt, or worse, what if you . . .' The words were choked by a sob.

Alexei felt a surge of affection for her. He kissed her, brushing his lips down her cheek to her smooth jawline. It pleased him to hear her breathing slow and deepen with every kiss. Travelling lower, his lips found her throat and he felt a stirring in his groin when a moan escaped her lips. Returning to her mouth, Natalya's lips parted. He kissed her hard then, stopping to catch his breath, he looked into her eyes. Confident of the answer to his unspoken question, he took her hand and led her to the sofa.

Two hours later, Alexei quickly climbed the stairs to the officers' club. At the top of the steps, he was met by a valet who helped him with his hat and cloak.

'General Tatistchev still here?'

'Yes, Excellency. The general is in the smoking room.'

'And Foreign Minister Sazonov?'

'I'm afraid the foreign minister has already left.' Moving quietly behind him, the valet brushed lint from Alexei's coat. 'Does Your Excellency require supper?'

Alexei gave a small wave of his hand. 'That will be all, thank you.'

As he walked briskly to the end of the corridor, Alexei heard the swelling of voices from behind heavy double doors.

'Good evening, Excellency.' Opening the door for him, the footman gave a short bow.

Silvery blue smoke hung in clouds above clusters of uniformed men. A waiter offered Alexei a drink. Choosing brandy, he took a large sip and surveyed the room. He found the general by a set of windows, surrounded by a group of officers.

'The Emperor needed a lot of convincing,' Tatistchev was telling the men. 'He kept saying he wanted more time to think.'

'It's that *Nemka*, that German woman, whispering in his ear,' a lieutenant said hotly. 'I always thought her behaviour was odd but now . . .' He spread his arms theatrically. 'Now that she has brought that holy man of hers to the court – that . . . that Rasputin . . . well, the Emperor doesn't seem to be able to make a decision without discussing it with her first.'

'Don't be so hasty to judge the Emperor, Lieutenant,' Tatistchev advised. 'After all, he has the weight of the nation pressing on him, not to mention the fact that the Kaiser is his cousin.'

'The Emperor is nothing like his late father,' a captain close to Alexei mumbled. 'This one is better suited to writing poetry than leading us into battle.'

'I remind you,' said an elderly major, glaring at the captain from under bushy brows, 'you are speaking of the Emperor.'

The captain bowed. 'My apologies.' He gave the major a rueful smile. 'I meant no offence.'

Alexei returned his attention to Tatistchev. Taking another sip from his brandy, he enjoyed the feeling of the liquid flame travelling down his throat.

The lieutenant was impatient to learn more. 'Has the Emperor reached a decision?'

'Well . . .' Tatistchev took a long pull on his cigar. 'The foreign minister was pleading with him to mobilise our troops, while the Tsar shouted that he didn't want to bear the awful responsibility of sending thousands of men to their deaths.' Tatistchev paused as waiters circled the group with fresh rounds of drinks. 'When I saw how troubled the Emperor was, I stepped forward to commiserate with him on the difficulty of his decision. I didn't mean anything by it, but it enraged the Emperor. He declared, "I will decide," and he signed the order forthwith.' Tatistchev held out his glass to be refilled. 'As we speak, gentlemen, wires are being sent all over Russia, summoning our troops.'

The group fell silent as each man absorbed the news. Then, after a long moment, the lieutenant raised his glass above his head. 'To the motherland.'

And then the drinking started in earnest.

A few hours later, Alexei stumbled out of the carriage, almost losing his footing.

'I'm fine,' he said brusquely to the coachman who was climbing down to help him. Reaching into his vest pocket, Alexei pulled out a few coins.

'Thank you, sir,' the driver beamed. 'God bless you.'

Alexei dismissed him with a wave then made his way unsteadily up the stairs to the door. A triangle of light from gas lamps lit the entrance. Alexei checked his watch. Four o'clock. The staff would not rise for another hour. Patting his pockets, he searched for his key.

'*Chert Poberi!* Dammit!'

He thought back to his movements during the evening, trying to remember where he might have misplaced the key. But his memory of events following Tatistchev's announcement were hazy.

'*Chert Poberi*,' he cursed again.

He lifted the large brass knocker and rapped on the oak doors. After a few minutes, he heard the sound of shuffling slippers approaching.

'Who is it?'

'Open the door, Anton.'

The door opened a crack. Upon seeing Alexei, the butler pulled the door wide and straightened his back.

'Terribly sorry, Excellency, for my oversight; I thought you had your key. I would have made sure someone had stayed up to let you in.'

Ignoring the apology, Alexei headed for the stairs, grasping the rail to steady himself. 'Tell Grigory I need to speak to him first thing in the morning.'

Hesitating a moment, the butler asked, 'Doesn't Your Excellency wish to sleep in, considering the late hour you're retiring, sir?'

'In the morning,' Alexei repeated, dropping his hat and cloak over the railing.

'As you wish, sir. I shall be up directly to help with your uniform.'

'Yes, fine, fine,' Alexei replied irritably.

A few minutes later, the butler – having dressed in his trousers, waistcoat and jacket – joined Alexei in his room to help him change from his uniform into his nightdress. Afterwards, Alexei, his urges spiked once more by alcohol, tried the door of his wife's bedroom and was irritated to find it locked. He knocked and called her name several times, but there was no response. At last, disgruntled by her rejection, he went to bed.

Despite his best efforts to remain discreet, Emily most likely had heard the rumours of his private rendezvous with Natalya, whom he had met the previous year at a ball held by the Empress for her two eldest daughters. Alexei's eyes travelled to the studio photograph of his own daughters that sat on his bedside table. He gazed fondly at the three faces; at the big, bright, shining eyes looking straight into the lens. Irena's raven hair, held back by a silk ribbon, reminded Alexei of Emily when they had met. He had been a young lieutenant then, stationed in Narva.

Although charming and from a good family, Emily provided little intellectual stimulation and soon after their marriage, Alexei had grown bored. He started his first affair when Emily was pregnant with Irena. If Emily suspected anything, she never let on, and busied herself with their newborn.

Two years later, they had a second daughter, Vera. Alexei, who had hoped for an heir, was disappointed. A brief affair with the daughter of a low-ranking officer ended badly with the young woman falling pregnant. The family hid the pregnancy but privately demanded compensation from Alexei. To her credit, Emily stepped forward and took in the illegitimate child, raising Tonya, who was now ten, as one of her own. She never spoke of the affair but took to spending more time in her private chambers with the door locked. He sighed. It was his own fault that she rejected him now, Alexei admitted to himself drowsily . . .

When he next opened his eyes it was morning, and the room was flooded with warm sunlight. The maid must have been in to draw back the curtains while he slept. Rising, he pushed open the windows and took a deep breath, filling his lungs with the morning air. Across the street, a crowd had gathered around a red poster which had been affixed to the wall. Alexei watched as a man with a cane and a top hat tapped one of the men in the crowd on the shoulder.

'What is going on? What does the notice say?'

'Haven't you heard?' another man replied. 'We're at war! The posters are call-up notices.'

The bedroom door opened behind Alexei and Grigory entered with a breakfast tray and the morning paper.

'Good morning, Excellency. Did you have a pleasant evening?'

'Have you seen the posters?' Alexei asked.

'Yes, sir. They've been putting them up all over the city since seven this morning.'

Alexei's aide-de-camp since graduating from military school, Grigory Alexandrivich had proved to be both capable and loyal. With a mop of curly black hair and brown eyes, he was never short of female admirers. Yet despite an abundance of willing young women, Grigory had yet to marry.

Alexei picked up the newspaper. The front page announced the mobilisation of the troops in large, bold letters.

'Shall I take your boots to be polished?'

'Yes,' Alexei replied absently.

'Will there be anything else, Excellency?'

'Is Madame Serova awake?'

'Madame and the young ladies left an hour ago to visit their seamstress.'

Alexei massaged his eye where a pain pulsed. 'Make sure my trunk is packed. We could receive a telegram to join the regiment at any moment.'

Once Grigory had gone, Alexei sat at a small table, sipping his tea as he scanned the news. On the inside pages, he read that the trial of the six assassins of the Archduke continued in Sarajevo.

He folded the paper and pushed aside his breakfast tray. War was upon them. Unlike the other men at the officers' club, he felt no thrill or sense of joyous anticipation at what lay ahead. He knew Russia was not ready for war. The military could boast of its gallantry and courage all it liked, but the fact was the Germans were better equipped and more efficient at mobilising troops than the Russians could ever hope to be.

Tsar Nicholas II was a private man who had never wanted to become Emperor. Pacing in the library, his thoughts were clouded and confused. Outside the sky was grey and it looked as if it would rain. Yesterday he had signed an order to mobilise millions of Russians for war. An hour ago, he had received a call from his foreign minister to tell him that the Germans had declared war on Russia for her refusal to call off the mobilisation. There was no question; war was imminent. In the past week, he had sent his cousin Wilhelm numerous telegrams pleading for the Kaiser to mediate between the Austrians and Serbs, but to no avail.

He wished desperately to be with his family at Tsarskoe Selo, rather than stuck in the Winter Palace surrounded by men hungry for war. Earlier in the day, he had stood on the balcony with Alexandra and waved to the crowds carrying Russian flags and shouting, 'Long live the Emperor.' Now, alone in his study, he ached for the company of his wife.

Alexandra never liked the Winter Palace, preferring their fairy-tale compound in Tsarskoe Selo, twenty-five kilometres south of St Petersburg. Nicholas smiled at the memory of their first dance there during her winter visit to Russia in 1889. His smile slipped as he recalled the behaviour of Russian society, especially the women, who continued to shun his wife and spread vicious rumours.

He sighed. Alexandra was as misunderstood as he was.

He wished for his subjects to respect him as they had his late father. Yet despite the strength and leadership he had shown by dismissing the call for constitutional reform in 1895, he sensed that many in the palace considered him weak and indecisive.

In truth, he cared little for affairs of state. If not for the promise he had made to his father when the old Emperor was on his deathbed, he would have gladly relinquished his responsibilities in favour of spending his days with his family.

Sitting behind his desk, Nicholas pulled out his diary from the top drawer and opened to a new page.

July 31st, 1914
A grey day, in keeping with my mood . . .

3

Narva, Estonia, August 1914

On one side of the two-storey manor house, the fields on the Marinsky estate stretched as far as the eye could see. The rising sun slowly burnt the low mist that had crept over the fields, making them shine like emeralds.

Over one hundred kilometres south-west of St Petersburg, Narva was on the most eastern point of Estonia. Part of the Russian Empire, the Estonians took up the call for mobilisation with similar enthusiasm to their Russian counterparts.

Marie stood at the heavy iron gates separating the house from the road heading into the town centre, waving to the column of cars, wagons and people. The cars' headlamps blurred in the mist and she could not make out any faces. She was sure no one could see her either, yet she continued to wave. The travellers were in high spirits. Even above the throaty rumble of the engines, Marie could hear the men singing, their voices rising and falling in unison to patriotic tunes. She watched the road for a little longer before walking back to the house.

Nikolai had enlisted the moment war was declared. At fifteen, her younger brother Valentin was too young and moped around the house at the injustice of his age. Hearing of her elder son's decision,

Pauline Kulbas was quiet at first, but on the following day had called the family tailor to the house to measure Nikolai for his uniform.

Back in her bedroom, Marie wondered how the war would affect her. Would her classes be suspended or would they continue uninterrupted? Pyotr had telegrammed to let her know that he had enlisted and had asked if he could visit her in Narva before joining his regiment. Marie smiled, imagining Pyotr in his uniform.

There was a knock on her door and Anna entered.

'This came for you with the afternoon mail.'

Marie recognised the handwriting on the envelope. 'Thank you, Anna,' she said, taking the letter hurriedly, eager to be alone. 'I'll call you when I'm ready to be dressed for dinner.'

Marie waited for Anna to close the door behind her before she ripped open the envelope.

> *My darling Marie,*
>
> *Knowing you, being with you, brightens my world. I have never felt such joy as I have in the moments we share. On the afternoon your train pulled away from the station, I thought my heart would stop. I felt empty, and when I looked at the sky, it too had lost its brightness and grown lonely and cold.*
>
> *You are my light. Without you, I am lost. I only need to know that you feel a fraction of the affection I hold for you to be a happy man. Have pity on my poor soul and tell me you feel as I do.*
>
> *Forever yours. P*

Marie pressed the letter to her breast. The secret sadness she had harboured since their separation had vanished, replaced by a happiness that radiated through her body. She read the letter twice more, each time experiencing the same joy.

'He loves me,' she whispered aloud. 'Petya loves me.'

'Masha!'

She could hear Nikolai's footsteps racing up the stairs.

'Marie, you lazy thing, are you in bed?'

Jumping to her feet, Marie ran to the door and flung it open. She stopped short when she saw her brother in his uniform.

Nikolai did a turn. 'Well?'

'You look so – different,' she said, taking a step back. Then she flung her arms around him. 'You look magnificent.'

'I have joined the Hussars. We've been busy all morning organising the transport of our horses on the trains.'

'When will you be leaving?' she asked, her heart suddenly contracting.

'I'll go to the officers' training camp in a week.' He frowned. 'Why such a sad face, Masha?'

She looked at him seriously. 'Will you promise to come back?'

'Stop your sulking, you foolish girl,' he said with a laugh. 'Those Germans are no match for our bravery and numbers. I'll be surprised if the war lasts more than a few weeks.'

Marie smiled but she couldn't shake the trepidation she had felt at the sight of her brother in uniform. 'I hope so. I could not bear to lose you.'

'Cheer up.' Nikolai squeezed her shoulders. 'I don't want my memory of the last couple of days at home to be of my sister sulking like an old *babushka*. Have you heard from Pyotr?'

'Yes, he'll be here this afternoon.' Even to her own ears her voice sounded worried. 'He can only stay one night before having to join his regiment.'

All afternoon Marie waited restlessly for Pyotr's arrival. Nikolai had left some time ago in the motor car to meet him at the station. Several times, imagining she had heard the sound of wheels crunching over the gravel, she rushed to a window, only to come away disappointed.

She carried Pyotr's letter in her pocket, intermittently placing a hand over the envelope, and feeling renewed joy at the words he'd written. Nervous and unable to focus, she had changed several outfits.

Finally, she heard the car coming up the driveway.

'They are here!' Marie shouted over the upstairs railings. 'Anna, quick, my dress!'

Anna hurried up the stairs, carrying another of Marie's dresses over one arm.

'Quickly, Anna. They'll be here at any moment.'

Slightly out of breath, Anna met Marie at the top of the stairs. 'You must promise there will be no more changing of outfits. This is the third dress Zoya has ironed for you today. The poor thing is run off her feet pressing your clothes as well as all the extra things she has to do for dinner tonight.'

'Oh, Anna, please don't be cross. If you only knew what I'm going through; how jangled my nerves are . . .' She stopped herself from revealing too much.

'Nerves and excitement aside, there will be no more changing of outfits.'

'I promise.'

Throwing her arms around Anna, Marie impulsively kissed her hard on the cheek.

Lifting the dress over Marie's head, Anna carefully let it slip over her shoulders and hips. Marie fretted the entire time, turning left and right to look at her reflection in the mirror.

'Hold still.' Anna fed the tiny buttons through the narrow slits.

They heard the front door open and Nikolai's voice speaking to his valet. 'Bring us a bottle of vodka in the parlour.'

'My curls have come loose,' Marie fretted.

Anna pinned back the strands and, as a final touch, fastened a Grecian headdress over the top, then stood back to appraise her handiwork.

'How do I look?' Marie did a spin.

'Breathtaking!' Stepping closer, Anna smiled affectionately. 'Pyotr Arkadyich would be a fool not to fall helplessly in love with you.'

Marie blushed. 'So you know – as to Pyotr and I.'

Anna started to pick up the discarded garments from the arm of the chair. 'I had guessed.' Straightening, she smiled. 'Your behaviour today only confirmed what I had been suspecting for some time.'

Marie stood with a rigid back before the parlour door. As the footman opened it, she drew a deep breath before exhaling in a long sigh when her eyes fell on Pyotr.

'Ah Masha,' Nikolai greeted her with a kiss.

She looked shyly at Pyotr, who was standing slightly apart from them. 'Hello, Pyotr.' She held out her hand for him to kiss. 'You look so different dressed in your uniform.'

'I confess, I feel different,' he replied stiffly. 'I trust you are well?'

Slightly confused by the formal greeting, she did not answer straight away.

'I am, thank you,' she said eventually. An ache squeezed her chest at the lack of warmth in his tone.

At that moment, her parents joined them in the parlour and Pyotr moved to greet them. Watching his back, Marie wondered as to the reasons behind his mood. Questions flooded her thoughts. Had she misunderstood his letter? Was he no longer in love with her? Had he changed his mind so soon after declaring his love? No, she could not believe any of those things. There must be another explanation for his behaviour. Still, as she continued to debate with herself, the hurt pressed at her, digging in its sharp claws.

'Let us all sit down,' Monsieur Kulbas said and motioned to the sofas.

Choosing a double seat, Marie was disappointed to find Pyotr moving to the chair furthest away from her. Again, she felt the heavy weight of confusion on her heart. Around her, they had started talking about the mobilisation, but Marie understood little of what was being said.

'You are very quiet, Masha,' her father observed. 'Is everything alright?'

'Yes, Papa.' She managed a smile. Her eyes sought and found Pyotr, who returned her look briefly before turning away.

During dinner, the main topic of conversation was the Archduke's assassination and the imminent war. But Marie was hardly listening. She played with her food, unable to swallow past the lump in her throat.

Seated beside Monsieur Kulbas at the head of the table, Pyotr stole several glances in her direction, only to turn away quickly whenever their eyes met. Each gaze added to her misery and made her wish for a speedy end to the evening.

Following dinner, the men excused themselves to the parlour for cigars and spirits.

'May I too be excused, Mama?' Marie asked.

'Are you unwell? You hardly touched your dinner.'

Marie faltered. 'It's nothing serious. I have a slight headache and wish to retire early.'

In the vestibule, she spied her father ushering Pyotr into the library. Just before they disappeared behind the door, her father turned and, seeing her, smiled at her from over his shoulder. Surprised Nikolai was not with them, she sought him out and found him in the parlour, where he was reading the evening papers with a cigarette smouldering between his fingers.

'Why have you not joined Papa and Pyotr?'

Nikolai turned in his chair to face her. 'Come in,' he said. 'Close the door behind you.'

Marie did as he said and moved to stand by his seat.

'Papa wanted to speak privately with Pyotr.'

She gave him a questioning look. 'Why?'

Nikolai shrugged but his smile told her he knew more than he was letting on.

'Kolya, stop teasing. You must tell me why Papa wants to see Pyotr.'

'Why should I tell you anything? You have been acting miserable all evening.' He pretended to go back to reading his article.

She gave his arm a hard pinch. 'Tell me!'

'Alright, I will tell you.' He laughed. Stubbing out his cigarette, he led her to the sofa. 'Now, I cannot be certain, but earlier today

Papa received a telegram from St Petersburg. Shortly after that, he called me to the library.'

'Who was the telegram from?'

'It was from Pyotr.'

Marie's stomach lurched. 'What did it say?'

'He did not tell me. But he asked me what I knew of Pyotr.'

She reached for his hand, squeezing it hard between both of hers. 'And what did you say?'

'I told him the truth. I told him Pyotr is the son of a lowly princess and a gambling father who over the years has whittled down the family fortune to almost nothing.'

Her hands dropped away. 'Kolya, how could you? Pyotr is nothing like his father!'

Nikolai held out a hand. 'Let me finish.'

'You mean to tell me you had more to say? After what you told him, I'm surprised Papa has not thrown Pyotr out already.' She turned her back to him, fighting her emotions.

He turned her by the shoulders. 'It's important for you also to hear this, Masha. All Pyotr's family has left is the city mansion belonging to the princess and the land in the Urals, which was managed by Pyotr's father and his foreman until Pyotr came of age.'

'I care nothing for his financial situation. I love him regardless.' She moved to leave, but Nikolai touched her arm.

'I also told him that I cannot think of a nobler man, that Pyotr has taken over the management of the estate and it has started to earn him a profit. I told Papa that I have no doubt Pyotr will make you very happy.'

Marie blinked back at her brother in surprise. Her face softened. 'You said all that?'

He smiled. 'You two were born for one another.'

After dinner, Pyotr and Marie walked arm in arm through the orchard. A warm breeze in the trees stirred the branches, heavy with fruit. Shadows danced around them. But even now that they were finally alone, Pyotr seemed agitated and preoccupied. Marie desperately searched for a topic to begin a conversation, but all her attempts were met with monosyllabic answers.

'I can't stand this, Petya,' she said at last. 'You are leaving tomorrow and I may not see you for a long time. In your letter you said that you loved me, yet you have hardly spoken a word to me since you arrived.'

'Don't reproach me.' Pyotr took Marie's face in his hands. 'I'd rather die than be the cause of your unhappiness.'

His hands were smooth and warm against her skin, making it tingle. They had stopped in front of the rose bushes at the far end of the garden and the air was alive with the scent of blossoms. Marie could not be sure whether it was their perfume or Pyotr's touch that had made her suddenly dizzy. Her disorientation must have shown on her face, for Pyotr dropped his hands.

'I'm sorry.'

'Petya.' Marie took both his hands in her own. Dressed in his uniform, he looked different from the bookish young man who had visited her every Sunday in St Petersburg. 'Please tell me why you are being so distant.'

'The truth is,' he began uncertainly, 'I came to Narva with the intention of asking for your hand in marriage. I am in . . . in love with you,' he stammered. 'But I'm afraid I will not be a worthy husband.'

'No, Petya, you are wrong.' Marie suddenly felt breathless. She looked into his eyes, desperate to assure him of her love. 'You are so, so very wrong.'

Pyotr pulled her tight against him and pressed his lips to hers. She moved deeper into his arms, wishing they could be joined like this forever.

After the kiss neither could speak for a time. Holding hands, they stole glances at one another and then laughed and dropped their heads self-consciously when their eyes met.

'There is something I need to tell you,' Pyotr said finally, 'and I'm not sure if you're going to like it.'

'Shhh.' Marie placed a finger on his lips. 'If you are about to confess to previous affairs, I am happy for them all to remain buried in the past.'

'No, it is not that.' He kissed her hand. 'I cannot believe my good fortune to find someone as wonderful as you.'

Marie smiled at the words and the modesty with which Pyotr had spoken them. 'What is it, my darling?' Then, struck by a new thought, she asked with alarm, 'Did Papa refuse to give his consent?'

Pyotr shook his head. 'No, it's not that either.' He gently pulled her into his arms again. 'Your father has given his consent on the condition that I make you fully aware of my circumstances before you accept my hand in marriage.'

Leading her to a nearby bench, he took a deep breath, then began to tell her of his father's gambling, his mistresses and the shame of having to sell their assets and his mother's jewels to pay for his father's debts.

'Marie, I have my mother's good name but little else. My grandfather, aware of my father's weaknesses, established a trust fund that pays me seven hundred rubles a year. It is not a large sum compared to what other men can provide, but over the past few years, I've managed to save enough to buy myself a small parcel of land and hope to buy another after the war. In time, I am confident I can provide you with a lifestyle similar to the one you've been accustomed to.'

Marie listened, kissing his face when he told of his humiliation and imagined herself sharing his dreams. After he finished speaking they continued to sit, the light slowly growing dim around them. Finally she said, 'I love you. I will always love you. Money and land mean nothing to me as long as you continue to love me. I promise to wait for you, Petya, and you must promise to return to me.'

Then, for the second time that sultry evening, they kissed with the intensity of lovers who, having recently declared their feelings, must again be forced apart.

4

The German Front, 27 August 1914

The thick smell of tobacco greeted Alexei as he entered the windowless room. General Alexander Samsonov, the commander of the Russian Second Army, had called a meeting at the officers' hut to discuss strategy. A large military map spread across the mahogany table marked the positions of the Russian and German armies.

'Gentlemen,' Samsonov's deep voice bounced off the bare walls, 'we have just been informed that the Russian First Army has defeated the Germans in Gumbinnen.' He pointed to a spot in the top right-hand corner of the map, close to the Russian border. 'They are scurrying like rats into the surrounding forests.'

The men let out a loud cheer.

'It looks like we'll be home before winter,' a colonel said, twisting the end of his moustache.

'We'll send the Germans packing with their tails between their legs,' called a voice from the back. 'There is no way any army could match the might and gallantry of the Imperial Russian Army.'

'What do you think of that, my friend?' A boisterous major general clapped Alexei on the shoulder. 'We'll show those Germans a thing or two by the time we're through with them.'

'Long live, Tsar Nicholas!' came the cry.

Alexei said nothing. Moving closer to the map, he studied the layout of the two armies' positions.

Samsonov raised a hand to quieten the room. 'Gumbinnen is a decisive victory for our country. Our regiment also needs a decisive victory to prove our gallantry.' Around the room, heads nodded in agreement. 'We move from here and here –' Samsonov pointed to positions on the map '– towards the German army to cut off its retreat.'

Alexei leant in. The Germans would have the advantage of fighting on their own land, he noted.

'How big is the army we will be facing?' Alexei asked.

'The German army has lost a large number of men and a great deal of artillery. They will not pose a threat.'

'Then our men should be given a day of rest.'

Samsonov looked around. 'Who said that?'

All heads turned towards a young lieutenant with an angular face and pale blue eyes, who had risen from his seat.

'Many of them have been fighting for days,' the officer explained nervously as Samsonov's eyes bored into him. 'Our supply lines are stretched and the men hardly have enough bread or soup to sustain them. We need at least a day to rest the men and allow for fresh supplies to reach us.'

'The men can rest after they beat the Germans,' Samsonov said dismissively. 'As for food, I'm told there is an adequate amount for each division.'

The lieutenant registered the reproof and gave a clipped bow. 'Of course, General.'

And with that the meeting drew to a close.

Following supper, a group of the officers gathered for a game of cards. In the thin yellow light, the lieutenant's eyes blazed in anger. 'It is madness to insist on sending wave after wave of men to be slaughtered,' he declared. 'We must pull back, regroup and draw up a new plan.'

Alexei agreed with the young man's objections, however his suggestion that the army retreat like cowards was unthinkable.

'We've had numerous victories over the past few days,' he said in a measured tone. 'I am confident that if the cavalry has a chance to show its skills, the Germans can be pushed further back into their territory. What we need is for the infantry to make headway into enemy territory, and then the cavalry will be able to finish the job properly.'

The lieutenant snorted. 'With all due respect, the cavalry puts on a great show of handling horses and swordsmanship, which is all very romantic and idealistic, but I am yet to see a horse that can stop a bullet and not be killed in the process.'

Grigory rose abruptly. 'Sir, need I remind you that you are addressing a superior officer?'

The lieutenant lowered his head in apology. 'I have caused you offence,' he said to Alexei politely. 'It was unintentional. I merely wanted to illustrate the folly of using horses against German guns.'

Alexei raised a hand to acknowledge the apology. 'I assure you, we are all just as eager to defeat the Kaiser as you are. However, it is unthinkable for General Samsonov to concede at this stage, just as his old rival in the First Army has had a victory. To place himself in favour with the Russian people, the general needs a victory.'

'But at what cost? Our men are hungry and exhausted.'

'We are told our reinforcements are a day's march away. The increase in the first line of men will help protect our flanks and allow us to press forward in the centre.' Alexei scanned the faces to make sure all were in agreement with him. 'Gentlemen,' he motioned for Grigory to grab his coat, 'it's been a long day. I suggest we retire for the evening.'

Lieutenant Sergei Bogoleev stepped out into the cool night air, angry with himself. Speaking out against his superiors could jeopardise his career.

The son of a schoolteacher, Bogoleev had risen through the infantry ranks hoping to escape his humble beginnings and join the inner circle of men with power. Ambitious, he had his sights set on a great deal more than what his wealthy colleagues were willing to concede. Since volunteering, he had more than once been overlooked for promotion while less capable men from the upper classes advanced.

Every rejection was fuel for the fire in his belly. And Bogoleev had plenty of fire to sustain him. He seethed at the arrogance of his commanders. The army had enough men and artillery to overpower the Germans yet the commanders doggedly kept to outdated strategies. Stationed safely behind the lines, Samsonov and his fellow commanders held countless meetings, sent out coded messages no one understood and argued over whose fault it was when things went badly.

Patience, Bogoleev reminded himself. He had to remain patient and bide his time. One day, his chance would come and *he* would be in the position of power. One day he would gain the respect he deserved.

Bogoleev walked quickly past grey tents lit in hues of rose and bronze by the setting sun. The soldiers resting from fighting in the trenches sat outside their tents. Everywhere he looked he saw the tense expressions of men strained to the limit. It frustrated Bogoleev to see the exhausted faces, the deadened eyes. How did Samsonov expect these men to win battles when they barely had enough energy to keep themselves upright?

He made his way to a group of soldiers gathered around a campfire. Men carrying buckets of water filled canteens, sometimes placing a consoling hand on the shoulder of a man who had lost a brother or a close friend.

'May the devil take them.' The soldier sitting beside Bogoleev spat into the fire. He saw Bogoleev watching and apologised. 'Forgive me, Lieutenant. I forgot myself.'

'You can speak freely,' Bogoleev assured him.

'I am a simple man. I know little as to tactics of war. All I know is that all day German cannons fire at us, sending bodies flying in every direction. And yet our commanders order more men to charge against them. They bunch us together, making us an easy target for German machine guns.' He shook his head. 'It just seems hopeless.'

Bogoleev nodded in agreement. His eyes moved to where the wounded lay on rows of stretchers, their uniforms, soaked in blood, stuck to their limbs. Grimy faces grimaced in pain.

Rising to his feet, Bogoleev knew he must say something to boost the men's spirits. 'I understand your anguish and share your frustration,' he began, then paused. 'We must fight to protect our women and children. To protect Mother Russia. It is our duty to keep those tyrants away from our borders.'

Looking at the faces around the fire, Bogoleev knew his speech was not having the desired effect; while some nodded as he spoke, most stared into the fire with fixed gazes and clenched jaws. But for the life of him he could not summon the words to inspire them. He knew that most of the men under his command faced the battlefield with fear, not gallantry.

The next morning he woke to a thick fog. The two hundred men he commanded stood to attention, their stares hollow. Inspecting the troops it surprised him that, only a month into the war, they already resembled an army of old men.

The Germans did not wait for the fog to lift before unleashing their first wave of fury. The Russian guns responded, filling the air with silver trails of smoke. Shells whistled, screamed and burst, drowning out the shouting.

As Bogoleev entered the battle, he thought little of heroism. He simply prayed he would survive the fighting long enough to see the end of war.

5

Tannenberg, 28 August 1914

Alexei watched the battle unfolding through his binoculars. The shadowy figures of Russian soldiers ran across cratered earth only to be mown down by machine-gun fire that came from the heavily wooded terrain.

The horses, unable to move through the crush of bodies and fallen trees, stamped and reared. A group of cavalrymen with their sabres drawn charged from the left. A German machine gun cut down three. One man, his foot still in his horse's stirrup, was dragged along the ground for several hundred metres before he fell, hit by shrapnel.

Alexei's horse neighed and shook its head. Leaning forward in the saddle, Alexei patted its neck.

After an hour of continuous bombardments, an uneasy silence settled over the battlefield. Guns fell quiet, allowing the breeze to disperse the mix of smoke and dust.

At the sound of approaching hooves, Alexei turned to find Grigory galloping towards him.

'Any news?' The words had barely left Alexei's lips when he heard shouts from the men: 'It's an aeroplane!'

The guttural rumble of the engine was faint but unmistakable.

'Your Excellency, look there, above the treeline.'

Alexei followed Grigory's finger to the dark shape of a German reconnaissance plane.

'Men, get the guns!' he shouted. 'Where are our gunners? Why is no one firing at the bastard?' Unlatching his rifle, he fired twice at the black shape.

Men ran every which way. Some, taking their cue from Alexei, dropped to one knee and fired their rifles. Undeterred, the German plane circled the trenches.

'Shoot them down!'

Finally, two gunners towed a Russian Pulemyot Maxima gun into position. Precious time was wasted as men rushed to secure the cart and load the ammunition.

Dismounting, Alexei hastened to join the group.

'Your Excellency?'

'Not now, Grigory.' He reached the group in a few long strides. 'You there,' he called to the gunners, 'what's taking you so long?'

'It's overheated. It hasn't had time to cool, Excellency.'

Alexei looked anxiously at the sky. The plane made another turn further into their territory. Sporadic gunfire followed it wherever it went.

'You're a fool, Leshev,' a voice called out. 'You are lazy. You have not been looking after your gun. That's why it keeps overheating.'

'Watch your tongue, you viper!' Leshev reached for his knife. 'Or I'll cut it off.'

'Enough!' Alexei yelled. 'How long before it is ready to be used?'

Leshev looked to the other gunner, who nodded. 'It should be cool enough to use now.'

'You're too late, Leshev. Look, the plane is leaving.'

Shading his eyes against the sun, Alexei saw the plane fly towards the horizon.

'You imbecile!' a sub-lieutenant shouted at Leshev. 'Even with these trees our enemies probably now know our position.' He turned to Alexei. 'With Your Excellency's permission, I will personally see to it that the gunner is punished for his incompetence.'

'Please, it's not my fault,' Leshev protested. 'Your Excellency saw for himself the gun was overheated.'

'Keep your silence, you –'

'Leave him,' Alexei interrupted.

'But, Excellency, this gunner has clearly neglected to take proper care of his equipment. We need to make an example of him.'

Alexei shook his head. 'You know as well as any man that these guns regularly overheat. I have personally witnessed men urinating over the guns in the middle of battle to keep them cool.'

A ripple of laughter rose from the crowd.

'Your Excellency, I must object.'

'To what? Guns overheating or men urinating over them?'

There was more laughter from the crowd. The sub-lieutenant's face turned beet red.

'This is highly unorthodox. The gunner must be punished.'

'You there.' Alexei pointed to a corporal.

The man stepped forward. 'Yes, Excellency?'

'Check the gun to see if it's well maintained.'

In the distance, German gunners woke from their temporary slumber to renew their assault.

The sub-lieutenant seethed beside Alexei as the corporal inspected the gun, then said, 'Your Excellency, the gun is well maintained.'

Alexei turned to the sub-lieutenant. 'It appears that you may have made an error of judgment.'

Barely able to contain his rage, the sub-lieutenant clicked his heels and gave Alexei a stiff salute. Holding a firm grip over his sword, he did an about-face and shouldered his way through the crowd.

The men dispersed, falling silently into ranks to prepare for the next wave of battle. As they did, Alexei recognised the young lieutenant from the previous evening. What was his name? Bogoleev? He had a bemused look on his face. Their eyes met and held for a moment. Then, smiling, Bogoleev straightened his shoulders and saluted.

Tannenberg, 29 August

'The Second Army is being attacked on both flanks.' Grigory handed Alexei an envelope. 'This telegram came directly from HQ.'

Mounted on his horse, Alexei stood at the head of his company of men. He ripped open the envelope. His brows knitted over the coded words.

'What is this?'

'I believe it's a coded message from General Samsonov.'

'It is still coded,' Alexei said, frustrated. 'How am I supposed to know in which direction my men are to attack?'

'I'm afraid the telex operator is not familiar with this coding, sir.'

Alexei thrust the piece of paper back into Grigory's hand. 'Take this back to the operator and tell him to ask for the decoded message. And while you're there, telex a request to send the reserves to the front.'

'But, Excellency, if the Germans intercept the signal they'll be able to anticipate our tactics.'

'If you can think of a better alternative,' Alexei retorted, 'I'll be happy to consider it. Now hurry!'

Alexei hoped headquarters would agree to his request for reinforcements. Although the reserves, who were mainly conscripts, lacked the ability and competence of the professional soldiers, the army was in desperate need of manpower.

Lifting his binoculars, Alexei turned his attention back to the battle. Through the gauzy smoke, he watched with a sense of helplessness as bodies buckled in cries and screams.

Along the lines, whistles sounded another wave of attack.

'Lances and swords ready.' Alexei drew his own sword. Behind him, he heard the metallic swish of weaponry as his men followed his lead and he waited for the signal.

Whistles shrilled.

'Charge!'

Thousands of men on horseback and foot rushed down the hills into the woods. The first wave fell quickly to machine-gun fire and

Alexei had to manoeuvre his horse around the bodies. Leaning forward over his horse's neck, he urged it to go faster.

Through the haze of fire and smoke, he saw a German soldier stand and aim his rifle. Unhooking the strap on his own rifle Alexei straightened and, placing his sabre across his lap, drew aim.

Pain as sharp as razor blades ripped through his right shoulder, and a dark sticky liquid sprayed across his face. A second bullet hit him in the upper-left thigh, throwing him off his horse.

He fell hard, rolling a few times before coming to a stop. In the moment before he lost consciousness, he was dimly aware of a pair of hands lifting him.

6

South of Tannenberg, East Prussia, 30 August 1914

Villagers ordered to evacuate snaked along the road in an endless procession of carts. After days of rain, the sky was clear and bright, white clouds floating in a brilliant blue expanse.

The Russian army was in retreat following the defeat at Tannenberg, with orders to leave nothing behind to feed or shelter the enemy. Most of the villagers, fearing attack by the advancing German troops, joined the exodus without protest. Those who refused were forced out.

Nikolai, walking with his valet, watched with alarm as an old woman screamed and clung to her doorframe, lashing out at the soldiers in a feeble attempt to save her house. They pulled her away, and she shrieked as her home went up in flames. Sinking to her knees in the mud and with no fight left in her, she stared at the burning ruins.

Nikolai picked up the shawl that had dropped from her shoulders and offered it to her. The old woman looked up. Seeing his uniform, her eyes suddenly blazed with fury and she slapped his hand away. Nikolai left the shawl close to her feet and retreated.

His valet, outraged by the insult, started towards the woman, but Nikolai held him back.

'She has lost everything. She has a right to be angry.'

'What's that?' his valet asked suddenly.

Looking up at the sky, Nikolai saw a German plane. At the sound of the engines, people on the street scattered. Within seconds, shells were exploding around them. Spotting an upturned cart, Nikolai ran towards it. Behind the cart he found a young woman and a child huddled together. The child, a boy of nine or ten, looked at Nikolai with wild, frightened eyes.

A shell exploded close by, showering them with rocks and debris, and Nikolai instinctively dived forward to shield the pair. They stayed like that for what seemed to Nikolai like hours, though it was probably only minutes.

Once he was sure the shelling had stopped, he drew back, slightly embarrassed by the intimacy of such closeness to strangers.

He stood and began to brush the dirt from his uniform, his ears still ringing from the sound of explosions. Extending a hand to help the woman, Nikolai noticed her leathery skin and calloused palms, telltale signs of hours spent working outdoors.

The three of them slowly emerged from behind the cart and looked around. Nikolai's breath caught in dismay at seeing the town reduced to rubble. Bodies were strewn everywhere. Smoke hung low over the scene like a thick blanket.

He spied the bloodied corpse of his valet thrown against a charred wall. Kneeling beside him, Nikolai closed the lids over the glassy eyes. A lump as hard as a rock lodged in his chest. Remembering the old woman, he turned to where she had sat moments ago, only to discover nothing remained but a large hole.

Returning to the woman and boy, he helped them to turn the cart upright, then the boy climbed into it. Nikolai placed the pair's meagre belongings by the boy's feet.

'Thank you.' The woman glanced in Nikolai's direction and he was struck by her clear green eyes. She hesitated briefly, as if wanting to add something more, but then seemed to change her mind. Without a second look at Nikolai or the village, the woman picked up the shafts of the cart and wheeled it away.

Nikolai stayed to help the few remaining villagers bury their dead. The local priest, his church reduced to blackened walls, walked among the fresh graves, his lips moving silently in a private conversation with the dead. With nothing more to be done, Nikolai left the village with what remained of the regiment. As they merged with refugees heading east, low clouds gathered in grim masses, hiding the sun. Travelling at the head of the procession, Nikolai listened to soldiers start up a marching song, though their voices seemed listless.

It wasn't long before a rumble rippled through the clouds. Nikolai pulled his cap low as the first light raindrops fell from the sky. Soon there was no escaping the downpour as it soaked the earth.

At dusk, the regiment reached the outskirts of another village. Nikolai followed a captain to a barn where, exhausted, he bedded down on warm hay. Despite not having eaten all day, he fell immediately to sleep, still wearing his wet boots and coat. It felt like only a few minutes had passed before he was startled awake by an explosion, followed immediately by a second. Disoriented and still dazed from slumber, Nikolai scrambled to his feet.

'Fire!' someone shouted and Nikolai turned to see flames engulfing part of the barn. Grabbing his pack, he ran outside after the other men.

The night sky was lit with flames. Dark silhouettes carrying pails of water ran back and forth between the village well and the burning barn. A screaming soldier with his uniform on fire ran out, trying to hit at the flames across his back. Another two tackled him to the ground, rolling him in the mud. The soldier continued to thrash his arms and legs until eventually he fell unconscious. One of the other soldiers removed his coat and together the pair lifted the injured man. As they passed Nikolai, he peered at the figure. There was something familiar about him. Dressed in an officer's infantry uniform, his once flaxen hair now singed black, Nikolai gasped in recognition. Pyotr!

Needing to be sure, Nikolai ran after the two soldiers. He shouted, 'You there, stop!'

The field hospital was in a nearby hut that had escaped the enemy bombs.

'Did you see an infantry officer with severe burns brought in a moment ago?' Nikolai asked a civilian who was bandaging a soldier's wounded arm. Next to her, a child held a gas lamp and she occasionally moved the child's hand to where she needed the light.

'Take your pick.' She gestured at the crowd of wounded without looking up.

Nikolai grabbed the woman's arm. 'This one only just arrived, carried by two soldiers.'

The woman showed no sign of resentment at being handled roughly.

'I have seen and bandaged more wounded soldiers than I care to count,' she said wearily. 'Your friend is just one of many.' She rested a sympathetic hand over his. 'I'm sorry.'

Pulling her arm from Nikolai's grasp, she moved to her next patient, applying fresh ointments and bandages.

Finding a gas lamp Nikolai walked carefully between the bodies, occasionally bringing the light close to a face.

A soldier grabbed at Nikolai's boot. 'Water,' he moaned.

Nikolai knelt by the man and wet his lips with water from his canteen. Almost immediately, others around him cried out for water. Everywhere he looked, hot, feverish eyes begged for relief. He passed his canteen from one set of lips to another until it was nearly empty then continued his search.

Finally he spotted the infantry officer stretched across a bed of straw. His uniform was tattered and burnt.

'Pyotr!' Nikolai cried and dropped to his knees beside him.

Pyotr's lashes parted slightly on hearing his name. The whites of his eyes stood out against his burnt skin. Where it had peeled away, raw pink flesh glistened. He moved his lips but no sound came out. Nikolai cradled his friend's head in his lap and poured his last few drops of water over his cracked lips.

'Don't worry, Pyotr.' Tears pricked the back of his eyes. 'I will look after you.' He looked around for help but could see no one in the thin light.

Pyotr moaned and moved his lips again.

'Don't try to speak, Pyotr. Save your energy.'

'Marie,' Pyotr croaked.

'You will be with her shortly. Soon you'll be transported to St Petersburg and she will visit you at the hospital and read to you from those silly novels you both enjoy so much.'

A faint smile touched Pyotr's lips. The tension eased from his limbs and he closed his eyes. Then he began to tremble.

'What is it, Pyotr? Are you cold?' Nikolai took off his coat and placed it over him. Again he looked around for help.

A group of soldiers headed by an officer was moving along the rows of patients, stopping to speak briefly to each group.

'We have orders to move out immediately,' the officer told Nikolai when they reached him.

Nikolai scanned the dark interior. Only those injured who were still able to walk were being evacuated, he noted.

'What's going to happen to the casualties?'

The officer's eyes dropped to where Pyotr lay trembling on the ground. 'All lorries are already packed with artillery. Anyone who cannot walk will be left behind.' He spoke into the darkness, reluctant to look Nikolai in the eye.

'He is like a brother,' Nikolai said desperately. 'I cannot leave him. Please, I beg you, help me to find room for him on one of the vehicles.'

'They are being used for the cannons and telexes.' The officer started to walk away. 'There's nothing I can do.'

'What about sulkies or carts?'

The officer shook his head. 'There are no horses or ox to pull them.'

'Surely there is something we can use.'

'I'm sorry.'

'But the Germans . . .'

'Our reserves are moving to hold them back. We hope to regroup with other corps and stage an offensive.'

Nikolai shook his head. 'What will happen to all these men?'

But his question went unanswered as the men hurried away to repeat the orders to others.

Nikolai hesitated, torn. Should he evacuate with the others, as ordered, or stay with Pyotr? He felt a light tug on his shirt and looked down to see Pyotr's feverish eyes looking up at him.

'You . . . must . . . go.'

'But I can't leave you,' Nikolai protested.

Pyotr grabbed feebly at Nikolai's open collar. 'You . . . must.'

Tears filled Nikolai's eyes. 'I will not leave you like this.'

Sensing a presence at his elbow, Nikolai turned to find the woman and child who had been applying bandages standing beside him.

'You must hurry, your regiment is leaving.' She placed a hand on Nikolai's shoulder.

Nikolai just shook his head wordlessly.

The woman brought her gas lamp closer to take a better look at Pyotr.

'Is this the man you were looking for?'

Tears rolled down Nikolai's face as he nodded.

'I will look after him.' She spoke Russian with a thick accent. 'I promise to stay with him.'

Nikolai looked up and, in the light of the lamp, saw a flash of green eyes. 'I remember you!' he exclaimed. 'I saw you earlier in a village down the road when the Germans attacked. You are the woman with the wagon.'

'Yes. I recognised you as soon as I saw you.'

'Do you still have the wagon?' he asked hopefully.

The woman shook her head. 'It was destroyed in the fire.'

Nikolai looked at the child clinging to the woman's skirt.

'Don't you want to save yourself and your boy?'

The woman gave him a sad smile. 'The child is not mine. I found him lost and hungry under an elm tree a few days ago.' She looked down at the child, whose face was in the shadow beyond the circle of light cast by the lamp. 'I've tried asking where his parents are but he does not talk, even though he seems to hear and understand well enough.' She looked back at Nikolai. 'I fed him, and since then he follows me everywhere.' She motioned to the men leaving. 'You must hurry.' She squeezed his arm. 'They have almost finished evacuating.'

Nikolai closed his eyes, knowing he must leave but not able to abandon Pyotr. Outside, it had started to rain again. Heavy drops thudded against the thatched roof, masking the moans of the men.

'Kolya!' Pyotr's pleading eyes searched for Nikolai.

Nikolai leant closer. 'I am still here.'

'Promise me one thing.'

'Anything.' He replied, touching Pyotr's shoulder. Pyotr winced with pain. Nikolai, realising his mistake, quickly removed his hand. 'Maybe you should not be speaking, Pyotr.'

Pyotr shook his head. 'You must promise to tell Marie I always loved her.'

'Don't speak like that, Pyotr. You two will soon be reunited.'

Exhausted, Pyotr closed his eyes. 'She must know. Please, tell her I wanted to spend the rest of my life loving only her.'

'I will,' Nikolai said in a choked voice. 'I promise.'

7

The River Don, South-West Russia, July 1914

Leo Nicholaevich Ivanov blinked at shafts of warm sunlight spilling through the open curtains. He yawned and rubbed his eyes. From outside, he could hear Marina instructing the girls on feeding the chickens. His head felt as heavy as a sack of wheat.

'May the devil take that Mikhail Andreyavich! I have never known such a hangover.'

'Good morning, sleepyhead.' Marina entered the room, wearing an apron over a simple printed dress. She sat on the edge of the bed and began to plait her hair.

'I slept in.'

Marina smiled. 'It's alright. The girls and I managed.' She twisted the plait and pinned it in place. 'Did you enjoy yourself last night?'

'Mikhail had made apple vodka for the wedding. Things got a bit rowdy after the third round.'

'That reminds me . . .' Marina went to her trunk. 'Where is it?' She looked under neatly folded scarves, shirts and shawls. 'Aha!' She pulled out a shirt in pale blue, decorated with vines of darker blue flowers. 'I've made Tanya a new shirt to wear to the wedding.' She held it against herself. 'I wanted to surprise her so I kept having to come up with errands and tasks to keep her out of the house while I was sewing it. Well, what do you think?'

'The colours will bring out the blue in her eyes,' Ivanov said. 'I will have to be doubly vigilant today. All the young Cossacks will want to dance with our daughter.'

'Speaking of which, the matchmaker stopped me yesterday outside the store. She complimented Tanya and said she could find her a good match.'

'Tanya is too young.' Pushing back the covers, Ivanov sat up. 'What would that old goat know about when is a good time for our daughter to marry?'

'Don't get angry, she was only suggesting that with the war there are fewer suitable boys.'

'The war will be over in a few months.'

'God be willing.' Kneeling before the icon on the wall, Marina crossed herself.

Lifting her to her feet, Ivanov wrapped his arms around her waist. 'Let's not talk about it now.' He pressed her close against him. 'I can think of more pleasurable ways we could spend our time.' He pressed his palm against the rounded mound of her belly. 'I hope this one is a boy.'

'Maybe then you would leave me alone.' She laughed and attempted to wriggle free, but Ivanov tightened his grip around her. She slapped him on the arm. 'I have to help Tamara with her wedding dress and then hurry back to plait the girls' hair.'

'They can wait.' He inched her towards the bed. 'I'm your husband. And I need you now.' He kissed her neck then sucked gently on her earlobe.

'Lyova, please.' But despite her protests, he felt her body grow soft under his kisses.

He pulled her down to the bed and Marina straddled him, easing herself down, her warmth enveloping him. Thrusting rhythmically, they moved as one with the familiarity of old lovers. Running his hands the length of her legs, he gripped her buttocks, pressing her harder against him. He climaxed almost immediately with a shudder that made both their bodies tremble and go limp.

As they lay side by side, Ivanov held his wife against his chest.

'I hear Dmitry and Tamara are moving to Moscow after the wedding.'

'They leave first thing tomorrow. Dmitry has a job as a machine operator in a munitions factory.'

'That coward! Enlisting in the munitions factory excuses him from serving at the front. Dmitry is an insult to the Cossacks.'

'You're a fine one to speak.'

'Should I go off to war then?' He tried to pull her towards him again.

Smiling, she batted his hand away and sat up. 'Russia needs men like you and Dmitry to stay home and keep the country running.' Buttoning the front of her shirt, Marina walked over to a hook on the wall to fetch her white lace scarf.

'Marishka –' Ivanov propped himself up on one elbow '– there's something I need to tell you.'

'It will have to wait. I'm already late.' She wrapped the scarf around her head. 'Oh, and don't forget, the thatch on the barn roof needs fixing.'

'I'll get to it straight after breakfast.'

'Make sure you do it before you take a bath. I don't want you dirty at my sister's wedding.' She hurried out with a final wave.

When Ivanov emerged from the bedroom, he found Tanya at the stove, stirring the contents of a pot.

'I have your breakfast ready, Papa.' Taking a wooden bowl, she spooned in a generous amount of *kasha* and placed it before him with a thick slice of bread.

'*Spacibo*, Taneshka.' She had inherited her mother's cheekbones and skin so fair it was almost translucent. 'You are growing into a fine young woman any Cossack would be proud to have as a wife.'

'Thank you, Papa.' A blush spread across her cheeks.

'Where is your sister?'

'Olga has gone to the river to fetch water.'

'Will she manage on her own?'

'It's a bit heavy for her but she should manage.' Tanya placed a hot cup of tea next to him.

'Looking forward to the wedding today?' Blowing his tea, Ivanov was about to take a sip when he noticed the red, blooming across Tanya's neck and cheeks. 'You hoping to see someone you like, perhaps a boy?' he asked, smiling.

'Stepan Sergeiavich asked if I would dance with him today.'

'Did he?' Leaning back on his chair, Ivanov hooked one arm over the back. 'And what was your reply?'

'Stop teasing, Papa.' Kissing him on the top of his head, she took his empty bowl and began to wash it.

They arrived at Marina's parents' home ahead of the groomsmen. Ivanov could hear the singing coming from the village.

'What time do you call this, Marishka?' His mother-in-law greeted them at the door. 'Dima will be here any minute to take Toma to the church. Did you remember the bread and salt?'

'I have everything right here.' Marina kissed her mother three times. 'Is Toma ready?'

'Your sister looks like an angel.' His mother-in-law beamed. 'Hurry, get inside. I can hear them. They are almost here.'

Dressed in white, Tamara sat perched on the edge of a seat in the centre of the room. Her face brightened when she saw her sister.

'Oh, thank God. I thought you might not make it in time.'

'I arrived home to find Tanya was still in the bathtub and Olga's feet were covered in grime. By the time I got them ready, I barely had any time for myself.'

'Never mind, you're here now.' Holding both her hands out, she beckoned her sister to her. 'I'm so nervous, Marishka. Feel my hands; they're as cold as ice and I'm shaking like a leaf.'

'It will pass.' Marina pressed her sister's hands to her face. 'You'll be alright.'

'And what will I do afterwards, in Moscow? I know nothing of city life.'

'Don't worry, Toma. You are a capable girl. You'll manage somehow.'

'At least Dima is not going to the front. I don't know how I would cope without him. How will you cope without Lyova, and a new baby arriving in a few months?'

'What do you mean?' Marina stared at her sister.

'I mean how will you cope without your husband? Who will plough the fields?'

'Lyova will look after the fields.'

Tamara looked from her sister to Ivanov.

'Dima told me the Cossack men are leaving tomorrow on a special train to the front.' She was looking questioningly at Ivanov, who stared at his feet. 'They are part of several cavalry regiments. What's wrong, Marishka? Why are you looking at me like that? You've gone as white as a ghost. Lyova, quick! Help me take her to the bedroom.'

Outside the bridegroom had reached the house and was waiting with the guests at the gates.

'Oh God, there's no time. They're here!' Tamara cried.

At that moment, their mother entered the room. 'What's keeping you, Tamara?' When she saw Marina's face, she stopped. 'What's happened to my daughter?' she asked accusingly. 'What's happened?'

'Marina has just had a turn.' Ivanov stood between Marina and his mother-in-law. 'With all the excitement of the wedding and the baby, she's overtired. You go with Tamara.' He ushered mother and daughter towards the door. 'You can't keep everyone waiting; they will think you're being disrespectful. I will look after Marishka.'

'Don't worry about coming to the church,' Tamara whispered. 'Let Marina rest.'

Through the open windows, Ivanov heard the crowd cheer loudly when Tamara emerged from the house.

'What beauty! What radiance!' they shouted.

Ivanov stood at the window and watched as the wedding procession made its way down the streets towards the church. He heard his mother-in-law explain to their guests that Marina had been taken ill and Ivanov was staying behind with her.

'When?' Marina's voice was strangled. 'When were you planning to tell me?'

Ivanov turned slowly away from the window. 'I tried this morning.'

'When?' she screamed at him.

'Marishka, please.' He knelt beside her. 'We are Cossacks. Our ancestors have been protecting our borders for centuries.' He took her cold hand between both of his. 'I will only be gone for a few short months and the girls are old enough to help you in the fields.'

Wiping her tears with her scarf, Marina turned her face away from him. 'What if you never come back? What if you are killed? What will become of us then? Have you given any thought to how we will manage without you?'

'Marishka, my darling, what kind of talk is this? Please, look at me.'

'I cannot. You have broken my heart.'

'This is our last night together, Marishka. And your sister's wedding! Have I sinned so terribly that you are willing to forsake me on my last night with you?' When she turned to face him, he saw her eyes were still brimming with tears.

Throwing her arms around his neck, she kissed him on the lips. 'Lyova! I am so afraid.'

'Don't be. Everyone says the war will be over soon. And while I'm away, I will write to you. I will write every day.'

It was a sombre crowd that accompanied the Cossack men to their train the next morning. Dressed in their military clothes, with sabres hanging from their belts, they embraced family members, kissing each one hard on the lips. On board the train, the men jostled by the windows for a chance to see their loved ones a final time before the train took them away.

'Have you got everything you need?' Marina asked.

Ivanov nodded. 'Tanya packed me some bread and cheese for the journey.'

Silence, heavy with anguish, settled between them. They were startled as the train gave a hiss and shuddered into life. The conductor blew his whistle, warning the last of the passengers to board.

'I must go.' Turning to Marina, he lifted her chin and kissed her on the lips.

'Lyova.' Their heads bent close, the words drifted into the air and hung there trembling, before finding their way. 'Remember that I love you.'

8

Petrograd, September 1914

The bell at the front of the tram clanked loudly. Marie waited as a mother and daughter, both dressed in heavy coats, climbed aboard before she disembarked. A cold breeze hinting of early snow blew at her face and neck. Turning up her collar, she quickened her step. Under one arm, she carried her textbooks and in the other hand she carried a letter from her mother which had arrived that morning.

Stepping into a café, she chose a seat at a small table. Breaking the seal, she pulled the letter from the envelope.

It was dated late August.

> *Dearest Masha,*
>
> *I trust you are in good health and are continuing with your studies. Your father and Valentin are both well and send you their love.*
>
> *After a month of no news, we finally received a letter from Nikolai last week. He was still in good spirits, but of course the letter was dated before Tannenberg. Lord only knows how far his spirits have plunged after witnessing so much devastation. I pray this war will end soon, and your brother and Pyotr return home safely.*

So many of our friends and neighbours have already lost sons and loved ones. The list of dead, wounded and missing fills several pages of the daily paper. My dearest friend Ekaterina Antonava's youngest son Andrei is among those who were killed in Tannenberg. I've spent every day at her house since hearing the news. Poor Kitty! She is a shell of her former self. I am at a loss to know how to comfort her. She looks as if all life has deserted her. She barely eats or drinks and simply sits in her chair all day with deadened eyes. It's enough to break your heart.

Your father and I will be leaving shortly to light candles for the dead.

You must write soon and tell me the news from Petrograd.

We miss you terribly.

Your loving mother,
P.
P.S. Are you still planning on visiting this autumn?

Folding the letter Marie replaced it in the envelope with a heavy heart. She ordered wine and drank it slowly, feeling its warmth gradually seep through her. Spying a newspaper on a nearby table, she politely asked the owner if she might borrow it. Poring over the list of the dead, the missing and the prisoners of war, Marie held her breath while scanning the names. As usual the list ran over several pages. Row after row, the names blended into one another. She let the air out of her lungs in a slow sigh when she got to the end without reading a single name she recognised. She tried not to think about how each name represented the loss of someone's brother, husband, son or father, a man with hopes and dreams.

News of the Russian army's defeat at Tannenberg and the Masurian Lakes had come as a shock. Everywhere, Marie heard talk of it and the flood of casualties that arrived daily at the hospitals.

Some blamed the commanders, others the superior German artillery. She had even heard rumours that the Tsarina had been passing army secrets to her former homeland. The Tsar, in a patriotic move, had changed the name of German-sounding St Petersburg to Petrograd.

Marie returned the paper to the neighbouring table, then looked around the café restlessly. She was suddenly overwhelmed by a feeling of guilt and powerlessness. Sitting in a warm café, she reflected on all the men who were cold and hungry, ready to sacrifice their lives for their country. Her eyes fell on a poster advertising the women's corp. She knew a number of women who had already joined. Her thoughts turned to Nikolai and Pyotr and the horrors they must be facing. Marie resolved that she, too, must fulfil her patriotic duty. Paying for her wine, she decided she would go directly to the hospital.

'And what am I to say to your parents when they find out?' Anna said as she struggled with Marie's thick curls before the mirror.

Marie, watching Anna's efforts with growing impatience, replied, 'Tell them I would not be able to look Nikolai and Pyotr in the eye knowing that while they fought, I did nothing.'

'What about your studies?' Anna fastened a broad-brimmed hat with a feather into place with hatpins.

Marie fixed her gaze on the uniform she had been issued: a grey dress in a rough material with white apron and matching veil. 'I can work my shifts around my studies. Besides, in times of war, one must remember one's responsibility is to the motherland.'

'Oh, Marie.' Marie looked up to see Anna's compassionate eyes in the mirror's reflection. 'I know you better than that. You are thinking that should Pyotr or Nikolai be sent to the hospital, you want to be there to look after them.'

'I can't bear it,' Marie's voice choked, 'to think of either of them wounded, suffering, while I sit back and do nothing.'

When Marie reported to the hospital that evening to begin her training, she was assigned to a young doctor who introduced himself as Mikhail Leskov.

'Most arrive traumatised, suffering from head lice and influenza,' he told Marie as she followed him through the wards. He spoke with the weariness of someone who had worked for days without rest. He stopped by the beds of several patients, his tired eyes hovering briefly over the faces. 'These men were encircled by the enemy near the swamps of the Masurian Lakes.' Dr Leskov lowered his voice. 'The lucky ones managed to escape by hiding in the forest. They had to listen to the cries and pleading of thousands who drowned.' He shook his head. 'It drove some of them mad.'

Marie soon fell into a routine that involved waking early, going to the hospital before her classes, then working another shift starting in the late afternoon. Anna packed her lunch and then brought her dinner to the hospital where they ate together in the small kitchen. Once Anna had left, Marie would walk through the ward checking on patients and making them comfortable. She read to them from the newspaper and wrote letters which they dictated. Sometimes she just sat by the soldiers' beds to keep them company.

Having grown up surrounded by servants, Marie was awkward at first with simple domestic tasks. After a few weeks, however, she discovered to her surprise that she had capable hands and was often asked to accompany the doctors on their rounds. As her responsibilities in the hospital grew, she began to decline invitations to the theatre and dinner parties in favour of long night shifts.

To keep up with her studies, she read aloud from her textbooks to dozing patients. On those nights when she found herself unable to concentrate, she would pick up her copy of *The Lady with the Little Dog*, which she carried with her everywhere like a talisman.

Imagining she was reading to Pyotr, her voice grew warm, secretly hoping someone, somewhere, was doing the same for Pyotr.

9

East Prussia, September 1914

Alexei opened his eyes to the sight of towering elm trees and the scent of brewing tea.

'Welcome back, Your Excellency.' A soldier smiled down at him. 'We were not sure you were going to make it through. I'll tell the lieutenant that you are awake.'

A few minutes later Lieutenant Bogoleev was by his side with a crust of bread and a hot drink. His face, shadowed by stubble, looked older. While Alexei chewed his bread, dipping it in his tea to soften it, Bogoleev filled him in on their situation.

'We are cut off from the rest of the regiment. I stole into a nearby village to gather news, but so far I haven't managed to get any solid information.'

'You speak Polish?'

'My Polish grandmother was from these parts and she taught me how to speak the language.' Bogoleev gave a shrug. 'We were poor and sometimes my parents sent me to spend the summer with my grandmother just so they didn't have an extra mouth to feed.' He smiled. 'I didn't mind. I loved my grandmother.' His face darkened. 'The First Army suffered a catastrophic defeat at the Masurian

Lakes. Thousands drowned, stuck in the swamps.' He dropped his head for a moment, then returned his gaze to Alexei.

'We can't stay here much longer. The German army is advancing fast. We need to join our troops behind the lines to have any chance of escaping capture.' He moved closer, his voice brisk. 'Do you feel well enough to travel, Excellency?'

Alexei nodded.

Hooking a hand under Alexei's good arm, he helped him to his feet.

Sharp pain seared through Alexei's injured thigh. He put a hand against Bogoleev to lessen the weight on his leg.

'You'd best take my horse,' Bogoleev offered. 'I'll walk with the men.'

For the next few days they marched through the forests by night. By day, they rested in abandoned barns or in the woods. At times when sleep eluded him, Alexei lay awake watching the orange and purple leaves dance on the wind until they fluttered to the ground.

As he watched, he thought of the changing weather. Soon the temperature would drop and the ground would freeze. With conditions worsening, the supply lines would be further stretched. He closed his eyes, letting out a sigh. How in the world would the army cope through winter?

'We have located the troops at a fortress, a day's travel from here,' said Bogoleev, dipping his bread into his tea. 'Your aide is with them. I sent one of my men with a message to him. He saw you get shot on the battlefield and was relieved to hear you are alive.' The lieutenant refilled Alexei's cup with steaming tea. 'He said to tell you he has arranged for your return to Petrograd on the hospital train.'

'I am grateful for your help, Lieutenant. In my report I'll be sure to mention your gallantry and recommend you for a medal.'

Bogoleev snorted. 'I didn't do it to get a medal. I would be grateful, however, if you could convince *Stavka* to overlook my humble background and make me a captain.'

Alexei noted the sarcasm in Bogoleev's voice but chose not to comment on it. 'I will do my best.'

Bogoleev gave Alexei a sidelong look. 'There are not many commanders like you in the army. The way you defended that young gunner . . .' His shoulders gave a small shrug. 'Every other officer I've ever met would have made an example out of him without a second thought.'

'We all must do what we think is right.'

Bogoleev nodded. 'I suppose so. By the way, there's something else you should know.' He started to collect their empty cups. 'General Samsonov is dead.'

'What? How?'

Bogoleev pressed two fingers against his temple. 'He shot himself.'

Alexei could not be certain but he thought he detected a hint of a smile on the other man's lips.

Bogoleev looked at him, his eyes cold and pale as winter skies. 'It appears our general couldn't accept the defeat in Tannenberg.'

At Petrograd station, men resting on stretchers were lined along the platform. From his carriage window, Alexei saw volunteer nurses following at the heels of a handful of doctors examining the injured men.

'Why are these men not being taken to the hospital?' he asked a nurse who accompanied an orderly into his carriage.

The nurse looked at the men through the small window. 'There are not enough beds, Excellency.' She dropped her gaze as if ashamed by the admission. 'There will be another hospital train arriving in a few days to take them to Moscow.'

'You need not worry, sir,' the orderly assured Alexei. 'We'll be taking you to the officers' hospital where you will be well looked after.'

Grigory and the orderly helped Alexei off the train to where a wheelchair waited on the platform. Soldiers and lower ranking officers shuffled out of the way to allow him to pass. Alexei caught the hatred in the eyes of a soldier, his face badly injured, when he was told to step aside. Ahead of them a corporal flung the end of his cigarette on the ground. Two soldiers immediately pounced on the discarded stub and began fighting for it. The orderlies standing nearby pulled them apart roughly.

'I'm sorry you had to see that, Excellency,' the orderly apologised. 'The war seems to make animals out of some men.'

Alexei said nothing. He motioned Grigory over and whispered in his ear. Grigory nodded and, reaching into a satchel, pulled out Alexei's cigarette case. Walking over to one of the nurses, he handed her the cigarettes.

'Please ensure these are distributed among the men.' He cast a long look across the mass of bodies. 'I'm afraid it won't be enough for all of them, but it might bring comfort to some.'

Taking over from the orderly, Grigory pushed Alexei's wheelchair to the end of the platform, where Emily and the girls waited in two open-topped cars. As soon as the girls saw their father, they jumped out and ran towards him, their golden hair fanning behind them.

'Papa!' they called. Irena was first to reach him and she threw her arms around him.

Alexei winced as the force of her embrace jarred his shoulder.

'Careful, ladies, remember your papa has been injured,' Grigory cautioned.

'Papa, are you badly hurt?' Irena asked. 'Mama said you were shot twice.'

'I was.' Alexei laughed and gestured to the two younger girls to come forward. He cupped their faces, kissing each one three times. 'And till I'm well enough to move about with a cane, it's your job to wheel me everywhere.'

'As the eldest,' Irena declared, 'I shall be the first.' She walked behind the wheelchair and Grigory, with an amused smile, stepped away, bowing respectfully.

'With Mademoiselle's permission, I shall see to the trunks.'

Irena began to push the wheelchair towards the waiting cars. Her younger sisters, forgetting their shyness, walked on either side of Alexei with the youngest, Tonya, clinging tightly to her father's hand.

'Did the Russian men fight gallantly?' she asked.

'That is a stupid question, Tonya,' Irena retorted from behind Alexei. 'Have you not been listening to the governess each morning when she reads from the paper?'

Alexei squeezed his daughter's hand. 'Yes, we fought gallantly, my little Tonya, but at times the Germans' guns were far superior to ours.'

Tonya took a tentative look at the platform full of men behind her. 'Are these all the men whose names are printed in the paper?'

'Some of them.' Alexei sighed. 'Others were not so lucky.'

'What was battle like, Papa?' Vera looked down at him with serious eyes.

Alexei was not sure how to answer his daughter and was almost glad when they reached the cars so he didn't have to respond. The driver opened the passenger door and Emily, dressed in an elegant wool suit, stepped out to greet him.

The girls helped their father to his feet. Pulling himself to his full height, Alexei took Emily's gloved hand and pressed it to his lips.

'You look radiant, Madame.'

Emily gave a relieved smile. 'We were so worried about you, Alyosha.' Her smile slipped and her lips started to quiver. Fumbling in her handbag for her handkerchief, she pressed it to her nose, turning her face away as a sob escaped her.

'Madame, please . . .' Alexei took a step towards her but a sharp pain stopped him in mid stride.

'We'd better get you to the car,' Grigory said, stepping quickly to Alexei's side. 'It is still too soon to put any weight on your leg.'

Alexei, too overcome with pain to speak, allowed Grigory to help him into the car. Emily sat beside him and Grigory slipped into the front with the driver. The girls climbed into the second car and together they drove through the streets to the hospital.

By order of the Empress, several of the city's palaces had been converted into makeshift hospital wards. Orderlies pushed Alexei's wheelchair through a hall with high ceilings, gold-embossed pillars and three-tiered chandeliers. Men lay between sheets of crisp white linen in rows of beds. Alexei's bed was in a curtained-off area at the far end of the hall, which was recently converted to cope with the influx of wounded men. Several icons sat on a small writing table next to a porcelain washing basin and water jug.

The Empress and her two eldest daughters, dressed in nursing habits, visited him on his first day. The grand duchesses, training to become qualified nurses, cleaned and sterilised his wounds while their mother looked on. Although Alexei had met the Empress before, it was always on official occasions, where she had often appeared stern and unsmiling. Standing beside her daughters now, her face showed none of its usual rigidity. She made light conversation, enquiring after his family and health. As Tatiana finished reapplying his bandages, the Empress looked approvingly at her work. She gave her daughter a light pat on the arm that made the grand duchess beam with pride.

'Thank you, Your Highness.' Alexei bowed his head. It was an uncomfortable experience to disrobe and have his wound attended to by the grand duchesses. He felt further embarrassed that he could not move out of his bed to show them the respect the royal family deserved.

The next day, Alexei was relieved when, instead of the Empress and her daughters, he was tended to by a young physician. Pressing a stethoscope to Alexei's back, the doctor asked him to take deep breaths.

'Your lungs are clear.' The doctor straightened. 'There is still a slight infection around the wound on your leg. Once that's healed you are free to spend the rest of your recuperation at home.'

A nurse walked around the curtain, then, seeing a high-ranking officer in a state of undress, stepped back hurriedly, murmuring an apology.

'Come back, nurse,' the doctor called after her as Alexei dressed. 'We have finished.'

'I'm sorry to disturb you.' The nurse's grey eyes slipped from the doctor to Alexei. 'I was sent to take the patient's temperature.'

'Come in, my examination is done.' Nodding to Alexei, the doctor took his leave. 'I'll be in again tomorrow, Excellency.'

'Thank you, doctor,' Alexei replied absently, his gaze fixed on the nurse. Her eyes were a most unusual colour, he thought, and her heart-shaped, Slavic face was soft and appealing.

Her manner, he noted, was measured and assured, her movements full of grace and confidence. She was from a high rank, he deduced.

'Keep this steady between your tongue and jaw, please,' she instructed, placing a thermometer under his tongue.

She took his pulse, frowning slightly as she counted the beats. He thought the creases between her finely shaped brows extremely charming. He found himself longing to learn her name and was impatient to be rid of the thermometer.

'Not long now.' She looked up from her watch and smiled as if she'd read his thoughts. 'Your pulse is normal.' Taking the thermometer, she checked the reading. 'You have a slight temperature, but nothing to worry about.'

'You are very thorough with your examination,' Alexei complimented her. 'Have you been volunteering for long?'

She inclined her head graciously. 'You are too kind. I've only been a volunteer at the hospital for a few weeks and still have a lot to learn.'

'Is Mademoiselle betrothed?'

'Yes.' An uneasy look entered the grey eyes, turning them a shade darker. 'We plan to marry after the war.' She looked away, busying herself with packing her instruments. His eyes lingered on her, following her movements from under his brows.

'Is your fiancé fighting in the war?'

'Yes,' she said in a hoarse voice. 'I think my job is done here,' she said abruptly. 'Is there anything else I can do for Your Excellency before I leave?'

'Would you mind handing me my cane? I wish to take some air.'

The nurse found the cane leaning at the end of the bed and held it out for him. 'If you wouldn't mind helping?' Alexei said. Holding on to her shoulder, he lifted himself out of bed. When he took his cane, his fingers brushed over her hand. She pulled it away, her face colouring.

'Will there be anything else?'

'Would you care to accompany me for a short stroll?'

'I'm needed elsewhere. Perhaps some other time.'

'In that case I shall not detain you any longer.' The nurse was about to leave when he added, 'Except . . .'

She looked at him expectantly.

'May I enquire as to your name, Mademoiselle?'

'Kulbas.' A small smile curved her lips. 'Marie.'

'A befittingly beautiful name.' He bowed his head before her. 'It was a pleasure meeting you, Mademoiselle. Your fiancé is a lucky man to have you waiting for him.'

'Thank you.' Ducking her head, she hurried away.

Alexei woke up in the middle of the night, panting. He looked around in confusion in the dark, unsure as to where he was, until his eyes adjusted and he realised he recognised his hospital surroundings. He must have called out in his dream because a nurse carrying a candle pulled back the curtain to check on him. Alexei shook his head when she asked if he needed something and she nodded, closing the curtain behind her.

Getting out of bed, he limped to the small table. Pouring water into the basin, he splashed it over his face.

His dream came back to him; Bogoleev knelt beside him, his hands streaked with mud and blood, working feverishly to rip strips from his shirt and wrap them around Alexei's wounds.

Becoming aware of a glow, Alexei lifted his head and saw a light at the end of the hall and heard the soft padding of footsteps. Through a slight opening in the curtain, he saw the flame move closer, hover briefly at the foot of beds, then move again. As the footsteps drew nearer, he saw it was the young nurse, Marie. Her face, only partially visible, glowed golden in the candlelight and her movements seemed as light as air, giving the impression that she was floating over the parquet floors.

As if sensing his gaze, she turned to him.

'Your Excellency, why are you out of bed?' She moved towards him, her eyes shining brightly, reflecting the flame. 'Do you need anything? I have finished my shift but will be happy to get you whatever you need before I go.'

'No need to trouble yourself. I noticed the light and . . . I'm afraid I was caught spying to see who it belonged to.' He laughed, cringing inwardly at the nervousness in his voice.

She pressed a finger to her lips 'We'd best move away from the other beds. We might wake the patients.'

'You seem to be carrying a few books with you,' he remarked, noticing she was balancing several volumes in the crook of one arm.

'Oh, these are my textbooks. Sometimes I come here straight after classes. I'm studying at the Smolny Institute.'

'How will you get home at this hour?'

'My uncle sends a carriage for me.' She checked her watch. 'It should be here by now.'

'May I?' he asked, reaching for the books.

She let him study the titles.

'You study law?'

'I'm in my first year.'

'And how are you finding it?' He handed back the books.

'Very interesting. I hope to join the district attorney's office in Tallinn when I finish.'

Tilting his head, Alexei regarded the young nurse with renewed interest. There was something unique about her. The women he knew from society or those he had met at court rarely appeared interested in the world beyond their salons and dressmakers.

'A civil servant is an unusual choice of career for a woman,' he said. 'What prompted you to choose this field?'

'I want to help people, to help our society,' she replied simply.

'Really?'

She gave a shrug that seemed a little self-conscious. 'In Sweden, Finland and Britain, women already participate actively in the running of society. I don't see a reason why we can't have the same in Russia.'

Alexei smiled. It was refreshing to meet a woman who not only held strong opinions, but was not afraid to voice them. 'You are obviously very passionate about this topic.' He was about to add something else when he was cut short by a throbbing in his leg. Wincing, he tried to shift his weight to alleviate it.

'How thoughtless of me to keep you standing for so long.' Placing her books on the floor, Marie took Alexei's arm. 'Let me help you back to your bed.'

'I enjoyed our brief talk,' he said as he slipped between the sheets. 'I hope we will have a chance to continue our conversation.'

She smiled. 'I would like that, but right now, you must rest. Goodnight, Excellency.' She drew the curtain behind her.

Listening to the fading sound of her footsteps, Alexei thought about their conversation. Despite her youth, she spoke with confidence and passion. His thoughts then turned to Natalya, who showed no interest in any talk outside society gossip. The young nurse may not have Natalya's celebrated beauty, but she possessed a certain grace and intelligence that outweighed that of other women he had met. Closing his eyes, Alexei soon fell to sleep, a small smile creeping across his lips.

Driving in the carriage, Marie rested her head against the plush padding. She thought back over her day and the intriguing new patient she had met. She was sure he was much older than her but she could not guess by how much. His olive skin and pale hair made him appear youthful but his rank and the confidence with which he engaged her spoke of a maturity that was only gained with age. He had surprised her when she had come across him in the dark. His manner earlier in the day had been flirtatious, but in their night-time encounter he had seemed genuinely interested in her studies and her ideas . . .

Marie yawned, weariness pressing against her eyelids. The last thing she recalled before she fell asleep was the smiling face of the commander as she wished him goodnight.

10

Petrograd, September 1914

All day Alexei had been in a state of inward turmoil. He had called for a nurse several times in the hope that Marie would come and was disappointed when each time a different nurse appeared.

He was still preoccupied with thoughts of how he might arrange a meeting with her when Grigory announced that Countess Natalya had arrived to visit him.

'Darling!' Natalya leant over to plant a kiss on Alexei's temple. 'So glad to hear the infection on your leg wound has cleared.'

Grigory offered her a chair, then excused himself.

'When will you be going home?' Natalya peeled off her lace gloves.

'I'm being released tomorrow to the care of Emily and her physician.'

'I'm sure between the two of them they will take good care of you.' Her voice was leaden with sarcasm.

'Emily's physician is an irritating fool,' Alexei groaned. 'To your good health!' he said, mimicking the physician's favourite phrase.

Undoing the clasp of her fox stole, Natalya folded it neatly on her lap. 'I'm surprised Emily has not organised for a priest to visit as well.'

'I am *not* dead.'

'Priests are not merely for the dead.' Natalya raised an eyebrow. 'When was the last time you took communion?'

'We had a priest in our regiment who said Mass every morning.'

Natalya leant forward. He smelt her perfume, floral and expensive. 'And are you forgiven all your sins?' She laughed, pleased with herself. 'Why, Your Excellency, I do believe you are blushing.'

Sitting back, she asked, 'Have the Empress and her daughters come to visit you since your arrival?'

'Only the one time. They tend to spend most of their time at Tsarskoe Selo.'

'If you ask me, the Empress's behaviour is undignified. I have it on good authority that she and the two eldest daughters have been assisting in medical operations and amputations.' She pursed her lips in distaste.

'Perhaps they wish to make a contribution to the war effort,' Alexei said mildly. He became aware of a movement by the curtain and looked up to see Marie.

'Good morning, Excellency. I'm here to change your bandages.' Marie ducked her head in greeting. 'But I can come back later if you wish.'

'No,' Alexei said, a little too hurriedly. 'Now is a perfect time.' He was aware of the countess giving him a quizzical look. He returned her look with a smile. 'You don't mind, do you?'

'Not at all,' she replied stiffly. 'I shall wait on the other side of the partition.' She stood, throwing Marie a measuring glance before stepping behind the curtain.

'I was beginning to think you had forgotten your promise to visit me,' he whispered when Marie was at his side.

Marie kept her eyes downcast, but he noticed a smile tugging at her lips. 'I've been very busy.'

Encouraged by her smile, he turned his head towards her as she peeled back the bandage on his shoulder.

'I'm going home tomorrow,' he murmured. Impulsively, he touched her hand.

Startled, Marie stepped back, knocking the bedside table and spilling a bottle of iodine.

'Let me help you.' He took out his handkerchief, but she shied away.

'I can manage,' she said in a trembling voice.

Glancing up Alexei saw that Natalya had been watching the exchange with narrowed eyes.

'It's good to see you are so well looked after,' she said waspishly.

Beside him, Marie stiffened. 'I will let the doctor know I have changed your bandages, Excellency.' And she turned away from his bed without meeting his eyes.

'You have wasted little time in charming the nurses,' Natalya said once Marie had gone.

'You are mistaken, Natalya,' he said impatiently, suddenly wishing to be rid of her.

Snatching up her stole, she fastened it around her shoulders. 'I am not blind, Alyosha.' She picked up her silk bag and made to leave. 'Any fool can see you are very much taken by her.'

Feeling mortified, Marie walked quickly to the end of the hall, and from there escaped into the garden. Once outside, she drew in large gulps of air. Finding a secluded bench, she sat down. Clutching the small cross she wore around her neck, she attempted to calm herself.

It was her fault, of course. She should have known better. Having felt an initial attraction, she should have extinguished it. Instead, she had behaved like a foolish schoolgirl, smiling openly into his face.

When he leant into her, a furnace had flared in the pit of her stomach, cutting the air in her lungs.

Closing her eyes, she let out a slow, deliberate breath. He would be leaving tomorrow, she thought, and she would forget her silly behaviour. After all, she was an engaged woman, she chastised herself.

'Marie.'

She looked up and seeing the colonel, immediately straightened in her seat.

'I'm sorry if I upset you,' he said.

She felt his eyes on her, heard the pleading in his voice, but still didn't dare to return his look.

'I behaved inappropriately. Forgive me. May I join you?'

She shifted, making room for him to sit beside her. They sat side by side for a long while, neither one speaking.

He broke the silence. 'I understand my action was rash and unexpected.'

She opened her mouth to interrupt him but he stopped her. 'Please, let me continue. You have every right to feel insulted. I . . .' he faltered, 'I meant no dishonour.'

She stared out into the distance.

'I wish I could take back my actions,' he continued. 'I know you are engaged.'

'And you are a married man,' she snapped, putting emphasis on the word married.

'Yes, of course.' His chin dropped to his chest. 'Will you forgive me?'

She turned to face him. 'What is it exactly you want from me?'

He hesitated. 'I've never met a woman like you. I think I'm . . .'

'No, please stop.' She held out a hand. 'I don't think I want to know.'

He was about to speak again when a voice called, 'Marie!' It was Anna, waving an envelope.

Marie jumped to her feet as Anna ran towards her.

'What is it, Anna? What's happened?'

Anna was breathing hard. 'I came as soon as this arrived.' She handed Marie the envelope. 'It's from Pyotr's mother.'

Marie tore open the letter. 'Maybe they've received news from the front.'

But as she scanned the letter, Marie felt her body grow cold. 'It's Pyotr! He's . . . he's . . .' Suddenly the trees around her began to spin. She put out a hand to steady herself but the strength in her had weakened. Her vision went blank at the same time as her body collapsed to the ground.

The train jolted and knocked, and every once in a while let out a long mournful whistle. Slumped against the window, Marie stared at the fields. Outside, women in colourful scarves toiled on small plots and carried water from the river. Children ran barefoot alongside the train. The only thing missing from the picturesque setting was the absence of men working beside the women.

Marie unfolded the letter from Princess Sonya which she held in her hand and read it again, as if somehow this time the words would carry a different meaning. But every time it was the same: Pyotr was missing, presumed dead.

Valentin met Marie and Anna at the station. Pale and tall with a dusting of hair above his lip, he no longer resembled the little boy who used to follow his big sister everywhere.

Marie embraced him, holding him tight against her. When they pulled apart, her eyes were moist.

'You are growing into such a handsome young man,' she said, smiling through her tears.

Valentin blushed, but didn't respond. When they reached their carriage, he helped first Marie then Anna into the cab. He made sure the porter had secured the trunks at the back and, after tipping him, climbed in too.

'How's Mama?' Marie asked.

'She's devastated. So many of our friends' sons who went off to war have been killed or are missing. We have lost many, many men.' Valentin's voice was grave. 'Any news of Pyotr?'

Marie bit down on her lips and handed him the letter from Princess Sonya. 'There's been no further news.'

They passed the rest of the ride in silence.

Marie's parents met her at the top of the front steps. She flew into her mother's embrace, burying her face in the crook of Madame Kulbas's neck.

'Child, the Lord has His ways of testing our faith. Be strong.' She kissed Marie's face. 'You must be tired from the trip. Go upstairs. I've had Zoya prepare your room.'

The footman carried Marie's trunk to her room, where Anna started to unpack the clothes.

'I wonder if you can do that later, Anna?' Marie suggested. 'I'd like to lie down for a while.'

Once Anna had left, Marie went to her trunk. Between folds of silk dresses and woollen shawls, she found the small diary which had been returned by the army along with Pyotr's other possessions. Before leaving for Narva, Marie had visited her fiancé's mother. The princess had pressed the diary into Marie's hands.

'He wrote about you.'

Marie ran her fingers along the smooth leather cover. Some of the pages, singed at the corners, fell apart at her touch. Opening it to the first entry, she read of weekend hunting parties in the country and picnics by the lake. He wrote candidly of his shame at having to borrow money to satisfy his father's creditors and gambling losses.

He wrote, too, of meeting Marie, the instant attraction he had felt and, later, his growing love for her. He shared her excitement at the announcement of their engagement and dreamt of marrying her after the war and raising a family.

Later, he had written of his experiences at the front, his growing dissatisfaction with the endless bloodshed. In the corner of his last entry, there was a smudged print of Pyotr's left thumb, where he had pressed the page to keep it from closing. Marie traced the edges of the print with her own thumb. A tear rolled down her face and landed on the page, mixing with the ink.

The small thrill of victory at downing an enemy soldier is followed immediately by the realisation that I have taken a man's life. We live and breathe alongside corpses. Indifferent to death, we step over the fallen to get to their guns, wiping the blood-speckled rifles against our breeches.

There is nothing magnificent or gallant in war. Everyone around me wears the same face of defeat I feel in my heart. I do not look into my brothers' eyes for the fear I might find the souls behind them already dead.

I feel no pain other than the pain of being away from Marie.

I have no fear other than the fear of never seeing her sweet face again.

I have no desire other than to spend a single moment with my arms wrapped around her.

Dear Lord, another order has come to retreat. I am to leave immediately. Will there ever be an end to this madness?

There were no more entries. Hidden between the pages, she found a letter addressed to her, but never sent. Unfolding it with trembling fingers, she read the few short lines.

My beloved heart,

As I write, an eerie silence descends over the fields after the day's battle. I watch a flock of birds fly in a V-shaped formation across a blood red sky. And I can't help but feel jealous of their freedom to fly in any direction they choose. If I had that freedom, I would not waste it on exploring faraway places. Instead, I would fly straight to you. Upon reaching you, I would perch on your balcony and sing tirelessly until you finally came to me.

Together again, we would never part. I beg you to wait for me.

Forever yours,

Petya

How the diary and the letter survived the fire, no one could explain. It seemed someone hoping to find food had pulled Pyotr's pack out of the rubble and among the charred blankets and tins of food inside had came across the diary. She wondered if they had looked through the pages, read his entries and then pitied him enough to hand the diary to authorities. Whatever the reason, she was grateful for this small act, this kindness that returned part of Pyotr to her.

The following Sunday, Marie joined her family at a special service held at the Lutheran church at Narva. Sitting in the pews, she looked at the familiar walls she had known ever since she was a little girl. A pair of stained-glass windows and a simple painting of mother and son, their faces lit by a halo of light, were the sole adornments in the otherwise austere stone church. The Lutheran pastor, standing before the congregation, reminded the patrons of the necessity of sacrifice during the war.

'*O God, listen to my prayer,*' the pastor read from the Book of Psalms. '*From the ends of the earth I call to you, I call as my heart grows faint.*'

Pressure built in Marie's heart as she listened to the words. Had God forsaken her, deserted her in her hour of need? Why did He not answer her prayers and send Pyotr home?

'*Lead me to the rock that is higher than I. For you have been my refuge, a strong tower against the foe. I long to dwell in your tent forever and take refuge in the shelter of your wings.*'

Following the reading, the pastor led the congregation in prayer for the departed. He then asked God for the safe return of those still fighting.

At the conclusion of the service, the Kulbas family stood with the pastor outside the church, exchanging condolences with other families who had lost loved ones.

'Thank you for including Pyotr in your prayers,' Marie said, her voice hoarse from crying.

Patting Marie's hand, the pastor's smile was sad. 'Put your faith in the Lord, my child. At such difficult times, our faith in God is the only anchor we have to hold on to.'

II

East Prussia, October 1914

At five in the morning, it was still dark. Nikolai stood up and stretched. The muscles in his back and shoulders ached from the heavy pack he carried. Despite his exhaustion, he had not slept well. He decided to step outside in search of a warm fire.

Millions of stars studded the sky. Not far from him, the last embers of an old campfire glowed red. Men gathering firewood fed broken branches to the dying flames. As the fire gathered momentum and its warmth reached them, the men relaxed and started to talk among themselves.

Seeing Nikolai approach, the enlisted men stood and saluted.

'At ease.'

The soldiers returned to their seats, but they were clearly made wary by the presence of an officer among them.

Pulling out his silver case, Nikolai removed a cigarette. Striking a match, he inhaled deeply then exhaled, the plumes of smoke dissolving into the darkness. Sensing the watchful eyes of the other men on him, he offered his cigarettes to those sitting around him.

'Take one,' he urged when they shook their heads. 'We are all brothers here.'

'It's not right for us to be taking an officer's cigarettes,' a heavy-set Cossack replied.

'But I insist.' Nikolai still held out his open case. For a long moment no one moved, then the Cossack stood and, stepping forward, took one.

Lighting the cigarette with a stick from the fire, he nodded at Nikolai.

'May I speak freely, Your Honour?' he asked.

'Of course.'

'You don't act like the other officers. Most of them –' the Cossack motioned with his chin towards the officers' hut '– don't even look at us.'

Secretly pleased by the compliment, Nikolai shrugged. 'I'm aware how many of my class view the working classes,' he said, not taking his eyes off the fire. 'The Bible, however, teaches us differently.' Lifting his eyes, he looked directly at the Cossack. 'It tells us we are all born equal before God.'

The Cossack held Nikolai's gaze, a smile lifting his lips.

Around them, the light changed from black to steely grey and the rounded silhouettes of the surrounding hills came into view. A snowflake twirled and landed on Nikolai's jacket, melting quickly. Soon large flakes were falling steadily and around the campfire, men blew into their hands and moved closer to the flames. Finishing his cigarette, Nikolai threw the butt into the fire.

'Lieutenant Kulbas.'

Hearing his name, Nikolai snapped to attention. He turned to see the captain, accompanied by a regimental clerk, walking towards him. The men saluted.

'The treasury needs someone who's versed in European languages. How many languages can you speak besides Russian?'

'I am fluent in French, Estonian, Latvian and German, sir,' Nikolai replied.

The captain looked at the treasury clerk, who nodded.

'That will do. Fetch your belongings and follow me,' the captain ordered.

'Where am I going?'

'You'll be leaving for the military headquarters north of Warsaw. There is a station twelve kilometres from here. A train will take you to the fortress.'

Nikolai could hardly believe his ears. A clerical position would not only save him from the front but might also enable him to find out the whereabouts of Pyotr. He saluted his senior officer, resisting the temptation to thank him profusely.

The captain turned to the other men gathered around the campfire. 'Who among you can read and write?'

Several heads turned to the Cossack.

'I can, Your Honour.'

The captain regarded the Cossack with suspicion. 'How many years of schooling?'

'Six, Your Honour. My father insisted all us children should learn our letters so we could read to him from the Bible.'

'Grab your pack,' the captain instructed. 'We'll leave in an hour.'

Waiting in line, Nikolai stamped his feet to keep warm. Low clouds continued to shake out their load of snow. Aside from Nikolai and the Cossack, the other men were older soldiers, legs slightly bowed from the weight of their packs. The regimental clerk checked the list he had on his clipboard then, satisfied, led the party on their march away from the front. The snow fell gently, dusting the fur on their *papakhi* hats with white flakes. If seen from a distance, Nikolai thought, the group might have been mistaken for old men out for a walk in the woods.

'What great luck to be selected for clerical duties.' The Cossack smiled broadly.

Nikolai nodded, pulling his fur hat lower against the cold.

'Do you think they'll have some *kasha* for us?' The man's dark eyes glinted in the thin daylight.

'I hope so,' Nikolai said.

'I've not had anything but dry biscuits and muddy tea for weeks. I could do with a hot meal.'

Nikolai nodded. He felt guilty that his income, supplemented by what his parents sent him, allowed him to buy food from the locals. He had seen other soldiers with little or no money raid villagers' homes, demanding food at the point of their bayonets.

'Leo Nicholaevich Ivanov.' The Cossack held out a large pink hand.

'Nikolai Hermanovich Kulbas.' They shook and fell into step.

A man ahead of them started singing an old folk song that recalled long Russian winters. Slowly other men joined in, their steps moving in time with the tune.

Coachman do not whip the horses.
It was all just lies and deceit . . .
Farewell, and dreams and peace.
And the pain did not close the wounds,
Will remain forever with me.
Coachman, do not whip the horses.

Nikolai knew the lyrics well, having sung them many times with his family. Hearing them made him ache to be with them again.

Ivanov glanced sideways at the lieutenant walking just ahead of him. Not big in stature, he carried his pack over slightly rounded shoulders, his frame struggling under its weight.

Ivanov scoffed. Typical officer, he thought. He's probably never known a hard day's work in his life. And yet this one seemed different, he admitted. At first he had been suspicious when the lieutenant had joined them by the fire. And when he said *We are all brothers here*, Ivanov had to restrain himself from laughing aloud. Brothers! Bah!

No other officer would express such a sentiment. They treated the men like cattle. But this lieutenant – what did he say his name was? Nikolai Kulbas – he seemed genuine. His eyes had held no mockery when he declared that they were all equal before God. He had meant what he had said.

Ivanov regarded Nikolai more closely. It seemed to him the rounded shoulders were weighed down by something more than the weight of his pack. Oh well, he thought. What did it matter? Whatever was troubling the lieutenant, it was not his concern. The important thing was that he was being transferred behind the lines. Away from the trenches and the relentless German shelling. It was obvious, despite all the promises, that the war would not end soon. The Russian army was not winning and Ivanov must do everything in his power to save himself.

For Marina.

He had been back once since joining. Meeting him at the station, Marina had looked radiant, as if lit by an internal flame. Seven months' pregnant, her stomach stood out like a small mountain. When she had first told him she was pregnant, his immediate thoughts were that this time it would be a boy. What he would give to be holding her now, to nuzzle his face into her hair and inhale her scent.

'Oh, Marina,' he whispered into the icy air. 'I will do anything to be back with you.'

At that moment, Ivanov knew with absolute certainty that he would stop at nothing to return.

To his home.

To his family.

To Marina.

12

Petrograd, October 1914

Entering his study after breakfast, Alexei rang the bell for Grigory to bring him the day's correspondence.

'Good morning, Your Excellency,' Grigory greeted him upon entering the room.

'Good morning. What do you have for me today?'

'The regular invitations to suppers and card games, and one from the countess to join her in her box at the theatre.' Grigory handed Alexei the pile of envelopes. 'There is also a telegram from the war ministry,' he added, pointing to a large envelope. 'It was delivered to the door a few minutes ago.'

Ripping the seal, Alexei read the contents.

'I'm being promoted to the rank of major general,' he told his aide. 'I will be commanding a regiment at the Austro-Hungarian Front.'

'Congratulations, Your Excellency,' said Grigory. 'What a great honour.'

'Thank you,' Alexei said. For a moment, he wondered if Marie would be impressed by his promotion. He stole a glance at his reflection in the glass cabinet and tried to imagine himself through her eyes, dressed in his uniform, the medals across his chest. He sat a little straighter, pushing back his shoulders. What was it about her that preoccupied him so? She had smiled at him. A smile that had travelled all the way to her warm grey eyes and, through them, straight to his heart.

Looking at the telegram again, he cast it on top of his papers. Part of him was glad to be leaving Petrograd. He was tired of the endless pastimes; the frivolous card games, suppers and visits to the theatre. What he wanted was to return to his regiment, to be among soldiers, where he belonged. He needed to be back at the front; back fighting for his motherland.

Emily's physician, a bespectacled man of around sixty, bent over Alexei's leg to examine the wound. His young assistant stood behind him holding the medical bag with an impassive face.

'To your good health, sir, your leg is healing well.' The doctor straightened and smiled, revealing several gold teeth. 'You will be back on your horse in no time. Now let's take a look at your shoulder.' He shuffled around to the other side of the bed.

Sitting poised and stiff on a chair at the end of the bed, Emily was watching the examination closely, too eager, in Alexei's opinion, to jump in with a comment or to answer the doctor's queries regarding his health.

'Has he been exercising?' the doctor asked her.

'He walks every day. I tell him he shouldn't exert himself too much but he doesn't listen to me.'

'To your good health, Madame.' The doctor chuckled. 'As far back as Adam and Eve, men and women have never listened to one another. What do you think, Ivan?'

The young assistant snapped to attention. 'I . . . I'm afraid I've had too little experience in this field to offer an opinion,' he stammered.

The old doctor chuckled again. 'To your good health, young man. There will come a time when you look back on your early days of inexperience with a great deal of nostalgic affection.'

Alexei rolled his eyes and saw Emily give him a sharp look.

The doctor manipulated Alexei's arm, observing his reaction with every movement. Alexei gritted his teeth and pretended to feel no pain, but the doctor wasn't fooled.

'I'm afraid your shoulder is not doing quite as well as your leg, Excellency.'

'Both wounds are healing well,' Alexei insisted, rising from the bed and pulling his shirt over his shoulder. 'I plan to rejoin my regiment in the next few weeks.'

'Please tell him he will not pass the medical,' Emily begged of the physician.

'My dear wife, your concern is very touching.' Alexei reached for Emily's hand. 'But I'm afraid our motherland needs me and it's my duty as a commander to return to the front.'

'To your good health, Major General.' The doctor moved towards the door, followed by his assistant. 'In my opinion, if not left to heal properly, your shoulder will continue to ail you for quite some time. Having said that, we are at war and our motherland needs every one of her brave sons to help protect her borders.'

Emily went to see the two men out then returned to Alexei's bedroom. 'I would like a private word with my husband,' she told Grigory.

'Of course, Madame.' Grigory gave a low bow and left the room.

When the door had closed behind him she turned to Alexei.

'I don't think you should be in such a hurry to return to the front.'

Alexei buttoned his shirt, keeping his back to his wife. He was in no mood for a scene. 'I am a professional soldier. You knew that when you married me.'

'Have you grown tired of me?' She asked in a sudden burst. 'Is that why you are so eager to leave?'

Alexei let out an exasperated breath. 'I have a responsibility to my men.'

'Look at me.'

Alexei stood and turned abruptly to face her. The sudden movement sent a stabbing pain through his leg. He winced and, clutching his thigh, dropped to the bed.

'See?' Emily cried. 'You are still not fit enough.' She began to sob. 'Why are you so eager to leave?'

Alexei considered going to her and gathering her in his arms, to comfort her. Lifting himself, he wavered for a moment, undecided whether he should go to Emily, but in the end decided to leave the room without offering a consolatory word.

Three weeks later, Alexei sat behind his large desk in the library. His leg was almost completely healed and his shoulder, while still painful, was moving more easily. He was ready to take up his new commission, he decided. He had already dictated letters to this effect and they had been sent to the relevant authorities. The final two letters he planned to write in his own hand.

My dearest Countess,

I regret I will be leaving immediately to join my regiment in Poland. During our close friendship, I have admired your charm and beauty. I shall forever look back on our time together with great fondness.

I remain your most humble servant.

Alexei

The note, brief and formal, would leave no doubt in Natalya's mind that the affair was over. Since her visit to the hospital, they had met only twice, and each time Alexei had made excuses to leave early. The high spirits he once found so alluring had grown tiresome. Her charm and beauty, celebrated by all Petrograd society, seemed somehow diminished in his eyes. He reasoned the affair had simply run its course; that the countess, bored by their routines, would soon have sought the attentions of a new admirer. In his heart, however, Alexei knew the truth. A shift had occurred in him. Although not certain as to the implications, he was sure of its source: Marie.

He recalled her face at the moment before she fainted. She had uttered a name with such longing, such sadness, Alexei had felt his own heart pierced.

That was the last time he had seen her. A few days after he was discharged, he visited the hospital in the hope of seeing her, only to learn she had returned to Narva to be with her family.

'It was her fiancé,' the nurse behind the desk informed him. 'He's been listed as missing, presumed dead.'

Taking a fresh piece of paper, Alexei wrote his second letter.

Dearest Marie,

I cannot begin to describe the effect of seeing you distraught. It pains me deeply to know you are suffering. How I wish I could comfort you, could fold you in my arms and soothe away your cares, but I know this is an impossible dream, the mere infatuations of a foolish man. You were wise to reject my attentions. I am far too old for you. And you are in love with another man. How I wish I was ten years younger. I would have fought to win your affections.

Alas, it is not to be. I am leaving for the front to take immediate command of a new regiment. If the Lord sees fit that we should never meet again, I want you to know that you have made a great impression upon my soul.

A.

He stared absently out the window, wondering how Marie was faring. In his imagination, he saw himself visiting the hospital on leave, perhaps surprising her with a large bouquet of flowers. He imagined them dining at the Donon – not in the private rooms, but out in the main hall where all of Petrograd could see them.

Alexei sighed. It was all a dream, a foolish, hopeless dream. For a moment, he considered tearing up his letter to Marie. Changing his mind, he reached for the brass bell and rang it.

'See to it these letters are delivered to the post office,' he told his butler. 'And have Grigory prepare my trunks. I wish to leave for the front tomorrow morning.'

13

Russian Headquarters, Warsaw, December 1914

'Post.'

A dozen pairs of eyes looked up expectantly. Surrounded by the horrors of war, the men's salvation came from the sharing of a bottle, a game of cards and the letters that arrived by post.

'Lieutenant Kulbas.'

Nikolai's chair scraped loudly against the bare floor. He walked quickly to the soldier, his eyes fixed on the bundle of letters held out to him.

Returning to his desk, Nikolai sifted through the envelopes. Three were from Marie, two from his father and one from Valentin. Anxious for news from home, he ripped open one of Marie's letters and read it quickly. It was dated three months ago. In it, his sister wrote about her volunteering and the difficulty of juggling study and work. He frowned. She still had no news of Pyotr.

'Good news from home?'

Nikolai lifted his eyes and saw Ivanov, who tapped an envelope against his fingers. 'I got one too.' He was beaming. 'It's from my wife.'

'What does she say?' Nikolai asked.

'I have not read it yet.' The Cossack folded the envelope and put it in his pocket, giving it a light pat. 'I'm saving it for later.'

A warrant officer dropped a pile of folders on Nikolai's desk with a thump. He gave Ivanov a sharp look. 'Don't you have some work to do?'

Ivanov stepped back and saluted, pushing out his chest in an exaggerated manner. 'Yes, Your Excellency. On my way.' Doing an about-face, Ivanov marched back to his desk with stiff legs.

Around the room, men stifled their laughter. Frowning, the officer left, banging the door behind him.

Nikolai put Marie's letter away with the rest in his drawer and turned his attention to the files.

The hours till the end of his shift seemed interminable. It was dusk when at last he rushed to the barracks, impatient to read his letters. Ignoring the men playing cards in the corner, he flung himself onto his bunk. Pressing each letter to his nose, he inhaled deeply, imagining he could detect a faint scent from home. After rereading Marie's letter, he opened one from his father. A sharp pain ripped through him upon learning that several of his friends had been killed. Sitting up, he leant closer to the light and read the sad words a second time. Crushing the paper against his chest, he fell back on his mattress with a cry.

He felt a hand on his shoulder.

'What is it?' Ivanov's voice was full of concern.

'My friends . . .' Nikolai held out the letter.

Ivanov gently prised it from Nikolai's fingers and read it. Crossing himself, he handed it back. 'May they rest in peace,' he said simply.

Nikolai looked up. 'Peace, you say? Yes, perhaps you are right. Perhaps the peace of death is preferable to the hell of the living.'

Picking up his letters, Nikolai pushed past Ivanov and ran out of the barracks. The icy air greeted him with a sharp slap across his body. Small fires were burning in front of tents, with men huddled around them for warmth.

He headed towards the closest one, and the soldiers gathered around shuffled aside to make room for him.

He ripped open the remaining letters and read them, each one adding to his grief. The last he read was one of Marie's, dated just two and a half months earlier. Her handwriting was scratchy and hurried, as if the letter had been written without her usual care.

> *My dearest Kolya,*
>
> *I have received the most awful news from Princess Sonya: Pyotr has been declared missing in action, presumed dead.*
>
> *Please, my darling Kolya, tell me you know where Pyotr is. Tell me he is injured and being looked after until he is well enough to be transported to one of our hospitals. Tell me that you will find him and bring him home.*
>
> *Forever yours,*
>
> *M.*

A gust of icy air caused him to shiver and he moved closer to the flames. A pair of large hands placed Nikolai's coat over his shoulders. He did not need to lift his head to know the hands belonged to Ivanov. Wordlessly, he shifted to make room for the Cossack.

The two men sat side by side in silence. Someone added another log to the fire and the flames stretched around it.

'I have become a father for the third time,' Ivanov said after a while. 'My wife wrote to tell me I have my first son. She named him Leo Leonovich.'

Pulling out his cigarette case, Nikolai offered one to Ivanov. Smoothing the cigarette between his fingers, Ivanov lit it, inhaling the smoke into his lungs.

Nikolai knew he should congratulate Ivanov, find some vodka and toast his friend, but his throat was tight and he could not speak. I have failed my sister, he thought. I should never have left Pyotr. Dropping his head to his chest, Nikolai covered his face with his hands and wept.

14

Petrograd, December 1914

Marie stared at the wall, rubbing the small gold cross between her thumb and index finger. On her table was the letter from Nikolai, sitting where she had left it. From time to time, she picked it up, read the words then returned it to the same spot. Nikolai described how he had last seen Pyotr.

> *Pyotr and the woman I left him with have both disappeared without a trace. At times I question myself, think I may have the wrong village. Yet no matter which village I go to or who I ask, I am always met with the same shrug of the shoulder and the same blank stare.*

Since receiving Nikolai's letter, Marie had no will to leave her bed. She spent whole days and most of the night lying on her side staring dry-eyed at the shadows passing on the wall.

I am in hell, she thought. And I'm being punished for my sins. For she had sinned, she knew, in mind if not in body. And still one name resonated within her, together with a mixture of shame, joy and regret.

Alexei.

His attentions had filled her with rapture and longing, had touched a part of her she had thought was Pyotr's alone. She had received Alexei's letter upon her return to Petrograd and her body had flushed with pleasure at reading his words. Tormented by guilt, Marie couldn't help but feel God was punishing her for her weakness. Pyotr's fate was *her* fault.

There was a gentle knock on the door, and Marie heard it open.

'Masha?' It was Anna. 'I've made tea.'

Marie, her gaze still fixed on the wall, did not turn.

'Please, Marie. You haven't had anything to eat or drink for two days.'

Anna's dress rustled as she moved to the bed. Marie heard the clink of the tray and smelt the strong brewed tea.

'Marie?' Anna's voice faltered. 'Marie, please, look at me.'

Marie felt Anna's weight sink onto the mattress and her soft hand touch her shoulder. Unable to speak, she simply shook her head and buried it deeper into the pillow.

'Darling Masha.' Anna's fingers stroked Marie's tangled locks. 'I wish I could take away your pain.'

'You can't.' Marie's voice, muffled by the pillow, was strained. 'No one can.'

'You must keep going, we all must . . . for Nikolai's and Pyotr's sakes.'

At the mention of Pyotr, Marie's body shuddered as if hit by a blow. She twisted around to face Anna.

'I know you are worried about Pyotr,' Anna continued, pouring the tea into a tall crystal *estekan*. 'But no one knows for sure what has happened to him. He could still be safe.' Anna held out the delicate glass on a saucer.

'Why has he not written?' Marie demanded, ignoring the proffered tea. 'Why does no one know where he is?' She could hear her voice growing hysterical.

'Please have some tea,' Anna urged. 'It will help to calm you.'

Marie did not want the tea. She did not want to be calmed. She wanted to scream and kick and howl at the unfairness of it all.

Shutting her eyes tight, she let out a scream so shrill with despair and so loud that it burnt the back of her throat. She heard a crash as Anna dropped the *estekan*, shattering the glass. Pounding the mattress with her fists, Marie screamed and screamed until she had no more breath left.

'Have mercy on my soul, dear Lord,' she croaked in a hoarse whisper. 'Let Pyotr live.'

15

East Prussia, March 1915

The roads were choked with throngs of people and wagons piled high with possessions. Every so often, the crowds were forced to move aside to allow trucks and buses to rush reserves to the front.

Perched on a wagon, a silent child dressed in an oversized jacket sat close to a young woman. His fingers, pink from the cold, were clasped in his lap to stop them from shaking. The woman wore a threadbare coat, patched in several places. Earlier in the day, she had traded her last two apples for a blanket she now had draped over her head and shoulders. In the back of the wagon, also wrapped in a blanket, a third passenger lay hidden among the woman's few possessions, moaning gently.

When the army had retreated from the burnt-out village, the woman and boy had slipped away too, carrying the wounded soldier between them in a rug. But the boy was too small to carry such a heavy weight for any distance and the woman, in despair, had looked around for help.

'Please,' she begged of the men rushing past. 'Help us.' She grabbed at their sleeves but they brushed her hand off without even looking at her. Feeling a tug at her skirt she glanced down to see the boy pointing at a wheelbarrow half hidden under the rubble of a fallen wall. 'Good boy!' She ran to it and dug through the debris to free it. Grabbing the handles, she wheeled it back to where the boy knelt beside the soldier.

'Help me lift him.'

Together they lifted the soldier into the wheelbarrow and hastened out of the village on a small dirt road that led into the forest.

Protected by the night's veil, they travelled in darkness, the woman relying on her instinct and memory to reach the hut that had belonged to her grandmother. Close to a sandy swamp, the hut was surrounded by thick pine and beech trees. When they reached it, the woman was relieved to find it stood untouched by war. Here, they could spend the days undetected and in relative safety. Few people inhabited the area, which could only be reached by narrow, difficult roads.

Inside the hut, she lit a candle and, with the help of the boy, moved the soldier onto the bed in the corner of the room.

Even before she cut open his uniform, she smelt the infection. The flickering light from her candle threw distorted shadows across the blistered skin. Although she had seen infections before, the sight of the soldier's wounds made her stomach twist. From a pile of logs in the corner, she made a fire and boiled water in a pot. Dried herbs hung in aromatic clusters above the window where the woman had suspended them during her last visit a month before. Taking a handful of chamomile leaves, she threw them in the pot to brew. Next, she grabbed the small jar of sea-buckthorn oil made from the shrubs growing behind the hut. As a young girl, she had collected the orange berries for her grandmother and stood by her side as she extracted the oil.

She ripped away the soldier's uniform and smeared a generous amount of oil over his burns to reduce the inflammation and help close the wound.

The soldier moaned and called out.

She leant forward, placing one ear close to his lips.

'Marie,' he whispered.

'I am Katya,' she told him. 'I will look after you.'

A small crease formed above the soldier's brow. 'Marie,' he repeated. 'Marie!' He was growing agitated.

'Shhhh, do not call out. I am here.' What would it hurt to let the soldier think she was Marie? Katya reasoned.

Soaking strips of material in cooled chamomile tea, she laid them over the wounds. The uniform, now no more than a charred rag, she burnt in the fire, making the flames glow a little brighter and warming the room. The boy sat on a stool staring at the hearth, shivering with exhaustion and from a rush of adrenalin. Katya gave him a mug of hot tea sweetened with honey and a handful of the dried orange berries to strengthen his immune system. Then she folded some old blankets and arranged a bed for them.

'It's not much, I'm afraid,' Katya said to the boy and, when he hesitated, added, 'we don't have any other blankets and once the fire dies it will get cold.'

The boy took off his boots and shyly laid next to her, curling his body into a foetal position.

Together they passed a fitful night: the soldier coughing and wheezing on the bed, Katya and the child huddled together.

Checking the soldier's wounds in the morning, Katya was relieved to find they were not as bad as she had thought. The skin, pink and blistered, would heal. She applied more oil, then covered the wounds again with fresh strips of cloth soaked in cooled chamomile tea. Now they needed to eat. Katya stepped outside. She would forage for berries or find an animal to trap. She was surprised to find the boy at the edge of the forest standing over a grave, his eyes fixed on the headstone. He turned when he heard the sound of her boots approaching.

'She was my grandmother.' Katya placed a hand on his shoulder. 'We are staying in her hut.'

The boy nodded and placed a hand over his chest.

'Yes, I loved her very much. And I was very sad when she died. Since then, I come here regularly on my own. Each spring, I plant small flowers around her grave, sweep the cobwebs from her hut and tend to her small plot of herbs. In winter, I dry and bottle the herbs the way my grandmother taught me, and store them away.' Inhaling deeply, Katya bent to clear the dead branches from the grave. 'Still, I'm glad she's not alive to see this miserable war. It would have broken her heart.'

The boy looked up at her with clear blue eyes and then, to her surprise, he slipped his fingers through hers. Never having had children of her own, she was unsure how to react.

'Would you like to find some berries?'

The boy nodded and together they walked into the woods. Stopping to pull berries off branches, she collected them in her skirt. On the way back to the hut, the boy suddenly stopped and, grabbing a stick, wrote something in the dirt. Katya stared at the letters.

Having only had a few years of schooling, she sounded out the letters one at a time. 'Fyodor,' she read. She looked at the boy and he smiled back. 'Is that your name?'

The boy nodded.

Katya crouched so her face was level with his. 'Do you know where your parents are Fyodor?'

The boy shook his head. A tear snaked down his face.

A year after her grandmother's death, Katya lost her parents to a plague that swept through the countryside like a storm. Her brother joined the army and was fighting somewhere in Galicia. She had hoped to join her sister in Warsaw when the war reached the village, trapping her.

'I've lost my parents too,' Katya said, her throat closing over the words. 'Right now, you and the soldier are the only family I have.'

The boy looked up at Katya, his eyes brimming with tears. Impulsively she hugged him, pressing his thin frame against hers.

Ding.

They froze.

Ding.

The sound came from behind a stand of beech trees. Katya pulled Fyodor down to lie flat on the ground. Through the trees, she could make out a small movement. Scared it might be Germans, she motioned for the boy to follow and crawled behind the trunk of one of the old beech trees. Katya held her breath, afraid that the tiniest of movements might give away their hiding place.

Ding. Ding.

The sound moved closer to their left. Katya slowly looked around from behind the tree, then burst out laughing. The sound that had startled them had come from a bell around a goat's neck.

'It's alright, Fyodor, it's only a goat.'

Fyodor stepped out and smiled when he saw the goat. Half starved and exhausted, the goat put up no resistance when Katya approached with a handful of leaves then grabbed it by the collar to lead it back to the hut.

She tried hard to milk it, but it was too thin to give them any milk. In the end she had no choice but to kill it. Boiling some of the meat, she served it with potatoes she had stored in the hut and fed the soldier the broth.

Each day Katya and Fyodor went out into the forest, checking on the traps they had laid and picking berries. On their walks, she told him stories of her childhood, recalling her regular visits to her grandmother and her fond memories of the place. She told him of how she had learnt about the medicinal plants growing wild in the thicket, and described the healing properties of the herbs they gathered, showing him how to dry the leaves and extract the oil.

'Some are for eating and some are for healing,' she said, repeating the words of her grandmother.

Fyodor, still silent, helped her with the chores. In the mornings, he built the fire and fetched water. He helped her change the soldier's bandages, washing them and leaving them by the fire to dry while she made breakfast.

Other than the few words he occasionally scratched in the dirt, Fyodor did not speak. Katya asked him questions, hoping he would reveal something of his past, but he simply stared at her with his clear blue eyes.

At night, she woke to the sound of his screams. 'Mama! . . . Mama!'

She would draw him into her arms, stroking his face. 'Shhh.' She rocked his small frame, murmuring soothing words until he was calm again.

They lived quietly in her grandmother's hut through autumn and winter, but spring brought the war closer. They heard bursts of gunfire and artillery in the distance. Katya decided they had no choice but to leave, and head east.

The wheels of the wagon sank in the mud. When Katya had bartered some of her valuable herbal extract for the ox, she had hoped it would take them all the way to Warsaw. But now the beast, weak and old, had stopped in the middle of the road and was refusing to go any further.

'*Tso!*' She whipped the animal, bringing down the strap on its back. From behind them came curses and yells as other refugees urged them to get moving. Katya was about to bring down the strap again when Fyodor grabbed her hand. Jumping out of the wagon, he moved to stand in front of the ox and, fishing in his pocket, pulled out a piece of bread he had saved from breakfast. The ox took the whole piece in its mouth, his jaw working around it. Clucking his tongue, Fyodor pulled gently on the reins. The ox shook its head and flared its nostrils and Katya was sure it would refuse to move. The boy pulled more firmly, making the same clucking noise. This time the wagon jolted forward. Pleased, Katya smiled and held out her hand to help Fyodor back onto the wagon. Patting the ox on its rump, Fyodor shook his head and smiled back at her. The sweetness of his smile ignited a warm maternal glow in Katya that surprised and delighted her in equal measures.

Turning in her seat, she looked at the soldier lying on his back. His skin, though scarred and wrinkled, had started to heal. To strengthen his lungs, she had been giving him chamomile tea brewed with mint and daisies. Yet still his breath rattled obstinately in his chest. He had lost more weight, too, and his ribs protruded above a hollowed stomach.

He moaned and moved his lips but Katya could not hear the words. She suspected he was once more uttering his longing for the woman whose name he kept repeating. 'Marie . . . Marie.'

They had only moved a few metres when the air was splintered with the sound of mortar shells exploding in the woods close by, shaking the ground. Women screamed and children wailed for their mothers. A second shell exploded, closer this time, igniting in a ball of fire. Shocked, Katya was slow to react. She looked to where Fyodor had stood only a moment ago, but he was no longer there.

'Fyodor!' she shouted, looking frantically about her.

She spotted him standing by the side of the road, his eyes glazed with shock. In front of them a man running for shelter cried in pain and dropped to the ground holding his knee. Blood ribboned from between his fingers. Fyodor stared at the injured man, his lips parted in a silent scream.

'Fyodor!'

The boy looked up at her with a blank expression.

'Fyodor, run to the trees!'

Fresh bursts of gunfire drowned Katya's words.

As she leapt from the wagon, her ankle twisted under her weight and she fell hard on the ground. Pain shot up one side of her body like an arrow. Struggling to her feet, she again screamed at Fyodor to run to the trees. Still the boy stood frozen, staring blindly. Limping over to him, she grabbed his hand but he resisted, pointing to the wagon.

'There's no time.' She hastened towards the woods, pulling him behind her. She could do nothing to help the wounded soldier. People pushed past them in a panic to reach safety. Forcing Fyodor behind a fallen tree, Katya threw herself on top of him, shielding him with her body. Around them, bullets thumped and ripped into the trees. *Thump. Thump. Thump.*

A woman fell on Katya, splattering the side of her face and her back with warm, sticky blood.

'We are unarmed,' a man shouted. 'For the love of God, we have women and children with us.'

Under Katya, Fyodor's body trembled. She buried her face in the back of his neck.

When at last the guns fell quiet, no one moved or spoke. Tentatively, a few emerged from their hiding places and walked back to the road. Katya pushed the dead weight off her back and the woman rolled away, her eyes fixed on the sky. Katya struggled to her feet, her ankle throbbing. Looking down, she could see it was starting to swell. She helped Fyodor to his feet, and wiped the mud and tears from his face with the hem of her skirt.

'Are you hurt?' she asked, searching him for any injury. He shook his head. Looking to where the wagon stood on the road, he pointed to it.

'We'd better take a look,' Katya agreed. She took a step, stumbled and nearly fell. Fyodor rushed to help her.

'It's only a sprain,' Katya assured him. 'I'll be alright in a few days.' Propping an arm under her shoulder, Fyodor helped her hobble back to the wagon. Climbing into the back, he turned his attention to the soldier. When he looked up, his face was deathly white.

'What is it? How is he?'

Fyodor held up his palm. It was soaked red.

16

Mostovsky Mansion, Petrograd, March 1915

The rooms echoed with the sound of girlish laughter and Marie recognised her cousin Darya's laugh pealing through the adjoining room. Marie sat close to the window on a plush couch, playing absent-mindedly with the fringes of the velvet-roped curtains.

Suddenly her cousin's voice was close. 'Look at you!' she exclaimed, walking towards Marie with outstretched arms. 'What a bore you've been lately, keeping to yourself.' Darya leant forward and lightly kissed Marie on each cheek. 'You look ghastly. *Pas du tout jolie.*' She pinched Marie's cheeks. 'What you need is to add a little colour to that pale skin.' Pulling a lipstick from her purse, Darya tried to dab a little red on Marie's lips.

'Darya, please. I'm not in the mood.' Marie pulled her face away.

Darya sank onto a chair and edged it close to Marie.

'Darling, you are not doing anyone any favours by looking and acting like a crow. When are you going to stop wearing these awful black clothes and join society?' Leaning back in the chair, she proceeded to remove her gloves, one finger at a time. 'Lord knows there are enough black-clad women these days without you adding to them.'

'How can you be uncaring like this when so many families are mourning the loss of their sons?' Marie demanded.

Darya's green eyes grew serious. 'Is that how you see me? As uncaring? There's not a day goes by that I don't think about Russia's dead and missing. I'm not cold-hearted, Marie. I'm aware men are losing their lives and limbs in this horrid war.' She looked at her cousin, lips pursed. 'I know what you must be thinking: empty-headed rich girls with little interest other than filling up their social calendars with endless dinner parties and balls. Well let me tell you this . . .' Darya straightened in her seat. 'If I seem cheerful it is not because I am blind to what's happening but because my heart can only stand a certain amount of pain before it is broken for good. If not for these gay gatherings, what do our men have to look forward to when they are on leave?'

Marie shook her head. 'I'm not ready to rejoin society.' She clutched at the small gold cross at her throat. 'I feel I am betraying . . .'

'Pyotr.' Darya finished Marie's sentence for her. She gave her hand a gentle squeeze. 'Don't lose heart, *cherie*, Pyotr might still come home.' Checking her watch, Darya rose from her chair. 'I must be going, I still have a million things to do before dinner tonight.'

'You have guests tonight?'

'Just a little gathering.' Darya gathered her gloves. 'I've invited Tamara Karsavina.'

'The ballerina?'

'Yes. I simply adore her. The Grand Duchess Vladimir will also be there. She has just come back from the front. Her dedication to the wounded soldiers is amazing.' Marie made a move to rise from her seat. 'No, don't get up, *cherie*.' Darya leant close and kissed Marie's cheeks again. 'I came to plead with you to join us. There will be an interesting crowd and you never know –' she winked '– you might even enjoy yourself.'

Marie doubted that. 'I'll think about it,' she said.

Later that evening, having decided to attend the dinner, Marie stood nervously at the top of the stairs dressed in a blue silk dress that hugged her waist and hips. Over her shoulders, she wore a mink stole, a present from her parents. Her heels hardly made a sound as she stepped lightly down the stairs to the grand entrance. Usually punctual, she was running late after spending most of the afternoon fretting over what to wear. In the end, she had settled on a dress with a modest neckline and sleeves that covered her arms.

The footman met her at the bottom of the stairs. 'If Mademoiselle cares to follow me, the guests are having champagne in the parlour.'

Opening the double doors, the footman announced Marie.

Darya rushed to greet her. 'Masha! I'm so glad you decided to come.' Taking Marie's hand, she led her to a group gathered around a proud elderly lady with a long narrow nose and a black feather fastened to her coiffure. Marie recognised her as the Grand Duchess Vladimir.

'Your Highness, may I present Mademoiselle Marie Kulbas.'

Marie gave a low bow. 'Your Highness.'

'Marie is my dearest cousin and she's staying with us while she studies law at the university,' Darya told the group, adding proudly, 'She also does volunteer work at the hospital.'

'What a charming girl,' the grand duchess said approvingly. 'Tell me, Mademoiselle, how do you find the time to juggle studies with volunteering?'

'I do my best, Your Highness.'

The grand duchess gave Marie an appraising look. 'You know, I was the first to start a hospital train. It was during the war with Japan. Since then the Empress and her daughters have started a few of their own but I was the very first. I'm sure you have heard of it. It regularly brings casualties from the front. I have many students helping me when the trains pull in with the wounded. You should come down to Warsaw station. I could use a capable girl like you.'

'Your Highness is extremely kind,' Marie said, shyly.

During dinner, Marie sat between the famous prima ballerina and an English gentleman who spoke very little Russian but adequate

French. Prince Dimitry, an officer on leave from the front, was describing the trenches.

'It's the most horrendous situation. With the thawing of the ice, the whole place has turned into a marshland. Our boots sink right up to our knees. It is almost impossible to transport heavy artillery as everything gets bogged.' He took a sip of his wine. Everyone waited for him to continue. 'Men are just as likely to leave the front because of trench foot or typhus as they are due to a bullet or shrapnel wound.'

Marie had seen the effects of trench foot at the hospital. Doctors regularly amputated soldiers' black, gangrenous toes, throwing them in buckets placed beside surgery beds.

'With the Germans transporting troops from the western front to the east,' a diplomat with a bushy moustache added, 'Russia faces a dire situation unless we quickly get more supplies to the front.'

'I've heard the Tsar is planning on replacing his uncle as the Supreme Commander,' Karsavina said.

'Why in the heavens would he do that?' the grand duchess said irritably.

Karsavina leant forward. 'Apparently the Tsarina is not pleased with the grand duke. Rumour has it that the priest of hers, Rasputin, has been advising her as to the course the Emperor needs to take to win the war.'

A murmur rippled among the guests as they absorbed this new piece of gossip.

'Surely even the Empress would not go so far as to allow that . . . holy man of hers to dictate military decisions,' the grand duchess said, her tone horrified.

Before anyone could respond, Darya rang a bell at her elbow and the dinner plates were replaced with crystal goblets of brandied dried fruits. The mood at the table changed at the arrival of this favourite dessert and the conversation turned to theatre and ballet.

Using the pretext of early classes, Marie excused herself before coffee was served.

'Remember what I said about coming down to Warsaw station,'

the grand duchess reminded her. 'You are exactly the type of girl we need.'

As Marie approached her room the door swung open. Anna stood shivering in her nightgown, her hair braided loosely for bed.

'Anna, what is it?' Marie asked. Her gaze fell to the yellow envelope Anna clutched in her hand and she felt a tremor of apprehension at the sight of the telegram.

Anna handed the envelope to Marie. 'It's from the front.'

Marie's knees were weak as she tore open the envelope and scanned its contents.

'It's Nikolai.' She covered her mouth to prevent the laugh from becoming a sob. 'He's coming home on leave.'

17

Galicia, Poland, May 1915

Alexei blinked in the gaslight and looked around at the unfamiliar dugout. Still dressed in his breeches, he seemed to have spent the night on a thin mattress with no sheets.

He wondered how he had ended up here rather than in his own bed in the officers' quarters. Swinging his legs off the cot, he tried to sit up, but immediately his head swam and he fell back on the bed. Rolling over, he closed his eyes and waited for the nausea to pass.

With the war at a stalemate on the western front, the Germans had started to move their troops to the east to fortify the Austrian lines. The Russians, in turn, had received orders to pull back from their positions.

Last night, following dinner, the officers had passed around bottles of vodka to drink over card games. Within hours there were several empty bottles lining the table.

Sitting up more slowly this time, Alexei rubbed at his stiff neck. His head, hazy with details of the previous night's events, throbbed relentlessly.

Looking around the room, he found his boots and his holster under the bed. When he pulled out the holster, though, he saw it did not hold his revolver. He thought maybe Grigory had taken it to be cleaned and oiled, but when he reached for his boots, something heavy and shiny fell on the floor. He picked it up and gaped at it.

In his hand, he held a German Luger he had never seen before. He stared at the gun with growing uneasiness, then started as the flaps of the dugout pulled back and a captain's frame filled the entrance. On seeing Alexei, the man saluted and removed his cap.

Alexei stared at the captain, recognition dawning.

'Bogoleev!' He got to his feet and they shook hands. 'When did you get here? I see they have made you a captain at last.'

'I arrived late last night from the front.'

'And what news do you bring?' Alexei asked, returning to his seat on the bed.

Bogoleev shook his head. 'None good I'm afraid. I lost over half my men.'

'I'm sorry to hear that,' Alexei said, then, struck by a new thought, he asked, 'How did you know to find me here?'

'I saw Grigory bring you here last night.' Bogoleev added hesitantly, 'You looked . . . unwell.'

Alexei looked down at the Luger. That solved the mystery of how he had got here, but it didn't explain the gun.

'That's a beautiful pistol,' said Bogoleev. 'May I?'

Alexei handed him the gun. Bogoleev weighed it in one hand, then stroked his fingers over the carvings on the handle. 'It's well crafted.' He handed it back.

'Yes, except it's not mine. I found it under the bed.'

Just then, Grigory appeared carrying a freshly laundered uniform for Alexei.

'Maybe your aide could shed some light on the mystery,' Bogoleev suggested.

'What mystery, Captain?' Grigory hung the uniform on a nail before turning to Bogoleev.

'Do you know who this gun belongs to?'

Grigory glanced at the gun Alexei held out. 'I'm not sure, Excellency.'

'I shall leave you to solve the origin of the gun, Major General.'

Clicking his heels, Bogoleev saluted. 'I am to leave today to join the forces defending Warsaw.'

'I wish you every success. Warsaw is the last line of defence between the advancing armies and Petrograd. We must defend it at all costs.'

Bogoleev's eyes flashed with something close to fury. 'At all costs?' A shadow crossed his pale eyes. 'Our men are already hungry and exhausted. They are stretched to their limits. Many are worried about their families.' Then, as if remembering he was speaking to a superior officer, Bogoleev's expression changed and his tone softened. 'They have little will to fight.'

'You must make them. The army needs a victory against the Germans to strengthen the morale of the Russian people.'

'How can I make them? By turning my gun on them?'

'Warsaw must be defended with every last drop of blood!'

Bogoleev's eyes fixed on Alexei's. 'Is this what you believe, Major General?'

'It's of no consequence what I believe. It is the will of the Tsar.'

'Then he has condemned us to death,' Bogoleev said hotly. Replacing his cap, he saluted Alexei once again and, making an about-turn, marched out.

Alexei stared after him. 'A strange character.'

'If I may speak freely, Your Excellency,' Grigory said, 'this is what happens when the middle classes are permitted to join the rank of officers.'

Alexei shook his head. 'The captain is a good soldier.'

'And yet he speaks like one of those rebels . . . those Bolsheviks who speak against the war.'

'Perhaps,' Alexei said absently. His gaze fell on the pistol he still carried. 'I wish someone could shed some light on how I came to be in possession of such a gun.' He turned it in his hand. 'A silver Luger is not the type of weapon one simply discards. It must have an owner.'

'It certainly is very puzzling. When Your Excellency failed to return from the outhouse last night, I became worried. In your condition . . . well . . . it would have been easy to take a wrong turn and end up arrested by an enemy patrol.'

'Did you come after me?'

'I intended to, but the enemy started shelling the trenches. When it stopped I saw you stumbling out of the woods. There were dark stains on your shirtsleeve and jacket, which I first mistook as mud. It was only when I took them to be laundered that I discovered their origin.'

'And? What was it?'

'Blood, Your Excellency.' Taking the clean jacket from its hook, Grigory carefully laid it across the cot.

'Blood?' Alexei repeated, mystified.

'Your face was ghostly white, Excellency, and I feared you may be ill,' Grigory continued. 'You refused to let me take you to your quarters so I brought you here.' Scanning the room, he added, 'I apologise for the accommodation.'

'Where's my revolver?' Alexei asked.

Grigory hesitated. 'Your holster was empty.' He pointed to the silver Luger. 'And you were carrying that. Your revolver has since been found, Excellency. I took the liberty of having it cleaned and oiled for you.'

Alexei sat up straight on the bed. 'Where was it?'

'It was found beside the body of an Austrian soldier.'

Alexei felt a chill pass through him. He moved a hand to steady himself as he got up from the mattress. 'Take me to him.'

Emerging from the dugout, details from the previous night's events came rushing back. He had stepped out to relieve himself, but had failed to find the outhouse in his drunken state, and decided to empty his bladder behind some bushes. The icy wind carried the rumbling sound of the shells exploding on the frontline. Above him, the full moon coloured the landscape in a metallic blue–grey. He was buttoning his trousers when he sensed a movement to his right. Alert now, he drew out his gun and released the safety catch.

Standing still, he listened.

There it was again: the sound of mud slurping and sticking to boots. Blood rushed to his head, clearing the fog left by the vodka. The boots were half dragging, as if their owner was too tired to lift his feet. Crouching low, Alexei saw a shadow pass, a lone soldier perhaps, moving between the stumps of burnt trees. Not sure if the soldier was Russian or an enemy spy, Alexei kept close to the shadows and followed him. The soldier's steps were unsteady, careless of where his feet landed. Aiming his revolver, Alexei straightened and yelled in Russian, 'Who goes there?'

The figure spun and Alexei caught the flash of something metallic in his hand. Taking no chances, he fired two shots. The figure twisted, hitting the ground hard as it fell. Alexei circled it, ready to fire again. Moving closer, he turned the body over with his boot and recognised the Austrian second lieutenant stripes on the shoulder. Clutching his chest, the officer stared up at the sky with frightened eyes, taking sharp, shallow breaths. Blood oozed from between his fingers.

Realising the Austrian might have been leading a group of men on a mission, Alexei dropped to the ground, looking for signs of other movements in the shadows. But all was still.

Along the road, stretcher-bearers raced back and forth to the front carrying away the wounded. Kneeling beside the Austrian, Alexei checked his pulse.

'Man down!' he yelled.

Two men carrying a stretcher heard his cry and ran towards him.

'He must have got separated from his regiment,' Alexei told the men.

One of them lifted the Austrian's hand to look at his chest wound. He shook his head. 'There's nothing we can do for him.'

Picking up their stretcher, they ran back in the direction of the trenches.

The Austrian moved his mouth, and then pointed to his chest. Searching the pockets, Alexei found a letter, one corner splattered with blood. Folded between the pages was a family photo. Standing behind a grave-looking man and plump woman, the Austrian soldier smiled at the camera.

He's only a boy, thought Alexei, and suddenly felt light-headed. Alcohol and adrenalin mixed and swirled in his head, making him nauseous. Rising to his feet, he tripped and fell, his vision and memory going blank.

A simple wooden cross marked the final resting place of the Austrian soldier.

Alexei crossed himself. Remembering the silver Luger in his pocket, he pulled it out. Turning it in his hands, he admired the fine craftsmanship. The gun was most likely a parting gift from the soldier's parents. Engraved on the handle were the initials A.S. The boy's background might not have been so different from his own, Alexei thought, noting that they even shared the same initials.

Opening the gun's barrel, he saw that it was empty. Something hard turned and sank deep inside him.

His fingers traced over the initials.

He returned the gun to his pocket and turned towards the camp.

Behind him, the sun hovered briefly over the grave, then settled into the horizon like a molten ball.

18

Petrograd, May 1915

The train belched gusts of steam, swathing the platform in clouds of vapour.

'Nikolai!' Marie's voice was lost in the noise of the station. 'Kolya!' She ran towards her brother, pushing through crowds in her haste to meet him. She threw her arms around his neck.

'Masha!' Nikolai swung her in an arc then put her down and held her at arm's length. 'Let me take a good look at you.' He ran a critical eye over her and frowned. 'You've lost weight.'

'Enough of me.' Marie waved a dismissive hand. Smiling broadly, she linked one arm through his and led him to the gates. 'Is this all you carry?' she asked pointing to the small pack.

'Yes.' He held out his pack to a porter, who hurried over to take it.

Squeezing her brother's arm, Marie said, 'I can't tell you how much your telegram cheered us. It was the tonic we needed.'

They walked arm in arm to a group of cars parked in a long row.

'I borrowed Uncle's motorcar.' Marie pointed to a shiny black vehicle. 'It's so kind of him to let us use it considering how hard it is to find the fuel. We are to dine with them this evening and afterwards Dasha has invited us to join her at the ballet.'

'It seems you have my stay planned out.' Nikolai kissed his sister affectionately on the forehead.

Marie smiled back warmly before her smile slipped. She stopped walking and, after hesitating a moment, asked, 'Have you any news of Pyotr?'

Nikolai ran a hand over his face. There was hardness around his eyes and Marie sensed he was thinking of lies he could tell to ease her suffering. In the end, he replied, 'I've heard nothing.'

A sob escaped Marie's lips and she bit down on her knuckles before more could follow.

'I wish I had better news for you.'

'I know you have tried your best.' She took his hand and they walked the last few metres to the car in silence, the initial joy of their reunion overlaid with sadness.

Marie did her best to keep Nikolai in good cheer but although outwardly he was charming, she sensed a change in him. His boyish looks had been replaced with the careworn visage of a man with the weight of the world on his shoulders. He was quiet and pensive through dinner, playing with his food.

'You've hardly touched the duckling,' Darya remarked, pouting.

Nikolai stared at Darya as if not comprehending what she had said.

'It's so strange,' he responded in a faraway voice. 'I was just thinking I had not seen or tasted such food for a very long time. I'm almost afraid to touch it, for the fear this might all be a dream.'

'The cook has been having such an awful time finding ingredients,' complained their aunt. 'There's a shortage of everything.'

'Tell us about the front,' Darya interrupted. 'What's it like to fire a gun at a man?'

'Darya!' her father interjected sternly. 'Please excuse her, Nikolai. At times my daughter takes leave of her senses.'

Marie regarded her brother, noting how his jaw tensed and eyes darkened. Nevertheless he smiled obligingly to show he had taken no offence. His hand moved to his breast pocket and he pulled out his cigarettes.

Marie cleared her throat. 'There are still ladies at the table,' she whispered from behind her serviette.

He looked at her distractedly, and she motioned to his cigarette case.

'I apologise,' he mumbled, putting the case back in his pocket.

'Perhaps you are tired,' Marie said, concern for her brother rising. 'Would you like to skip the ballet tonight?'

'Skip the ballet?' Darya protested. 'But everything is already arranged.'

Nikolai gave a defeated smile. 'I would not dream of disappointing you, my dear cousin.'

'That's settled then.' Darya smiled triumphantly.

The brass bell was rung, the last of the dinner plates were cleared and the guests were treated to ramekins of crème brûlée.

'Are you sure you want to go to the ballet, Kolya?' Marie murmured to Nikolai following dinner. 'It's not too late to excuse yourself.'

'What are you whispering about, Marie?' Darya asked suspiciously. 'I hope you are not encouraging him to stay behind.'

The servants helped Nikolai and Marie into their coats. Smiling, Nikolai offered an arm to his sister. 'I'll be fine,' he assured her, and together they descended the stairs to the waiting carriages.

Later that night, Marie woke to the sound of feet pacing outside her bedroom. Rubbing her eyes, she sat up in bed and turned on the lamp. Throwing a woollen shawl over her shoulders she opened the door leading to her living room.

'What are you doing up at this hour?'

Nikolai turned. A cigarette burnt between his fingers. 'I couldn't sleep.'

'What's the matter, Kolya?'

Nikolai's lips tightened. 'It's not something you would understand.'

Not wishing to provoke him, Marie did not insist. 'I am here if you need me.'

Nikolai stared at her for a long moment, then dropped to his knees, burying his face in his hands.

'Forgive me, Masha,' he wept. 'I failed you.'

'What are you talking about?'

'I did not save Petya. I did not find him.'

Marie knelt and took his hands in her own. 'It's not your fault, Kolya,' she said, feeling the tears welling in her own eyes. 'I know you would have done your best.'

They had organised to spend the second half of Nikolai's leave in Narva. Entering the first-class carriage, Marie chose a seat close to the window and Nikolai sat opposite her. Removing their hats and gloves, Anna and Marie talked softly between themselves. Travelling in the same carriage was a factory owner who complained bitterly to Nikolai about the lack of coal to run his machinery.

Their driver met them at the station and, taking their luggage, led them to the waiting motorcar.

Nikolai ran his hand along the smooth curves.

'So Mama relented and let Papa buy a car?'

'She refuses to drive in it, says the noise upsets her nerves. She still gets them to bring the carriage for her whenever she travels into town.'

Pauline Kulbas, dressed in a simple navy-blue dress, which made her appear unnaturally gaunt and grey, greeted her children at the front stairs, Herman and Valentin by her side.

'My boy . . . my darling Kolya,' she said, her voice breaking with emotion. Holding out her arms, she embraced him warmly. 'Oh, my son.' She raised her face and arms to the sky. 'Thank the Lord for giving me this moment.' Taking Nikolai's face in her fleshy hands, she kissed him four times, before her husband demanded his turn. Taking his son's hand between his, he shook it heartily and then drew him into his embrace and kissed him.

'I'm so very, very happy.' He looked at his son through wet eyes. 'Never mind me,' he said, clearly embarrassed by his tears. 'I'm just a silly old fool. Come in to the drawing room, we must celebrate the safe arrival of our son.'

In the drawing room, Pauline Kulbas sat in her usual chair close to her husband, while Marie sat by her mother, holding her hand. Nikolai and Valentin shared a sofa. Marie noted Valentin stole admiring glances at her brother in his uniform.

'Tell me, son,' Monsieur Kulbas was first to speak. 'What news do you bring from the front?'

'Please, Herman,' Madame Kulbas protested. 'The boy has barely had time to catch his breath and you're already bombarding him with talk of the war.'

'I don't mind, Mama,' Nikolai assured her. Leaning forward, he reached for one of the freshly baked pastries. 'As you know, I have not been in the trenches since the beginning of the year. In Warsaw there is a lot of discontent over allegations the English are shipping to their own troops munitions that were intended for the Russian army.'

'I always knew the English could not be trusted.'

'Papa,' Marie berated him. 'That is surely just a rumour.'

'I'm not sure if I agree with you, Marie,' Nikolai said. 'There is a massive shortage of guns and ammunition. Our supply lines are continuously compromised and the reserves have to wait for someone to be killed before they are given their guns.'

'Oh dear.' Pauline Kulbas leant back in her seat, breathing heavily.

'Mama!' Marie rang the bell. 'Let's leave talk of war till later. Mama is in no condition to hear it.'

The door opened and a maid in a white apron and matching cap entered.

'Zoya, help me take my mother to her bedroom,' Marie requested. 'And bring me her smelling salts.'

❦

Alone, father and son sat in silence staring alternately at their hands and at the fields beyond the bay windows. Finally, unable to contain his curiosity, Herman Kulbas asked, 'Is it true what the papers say about Warsaw being in danger of falling to the Germans?'

Nikolai's face, already pale, contorted and an uneasy look crossed his features. 'The Allied offensive is at a standstill in France, and the Germans are taking the opportunity to send troops to strengthen their lines on the eastern front. If Warsaw falls –' Nikolai lifted his palms '– then there is every possibility Russia could lose the war.'

Monsieur Kulbas dragged a hand through his hair. 'And where does that leave Estonia?'

'I'm not sure, Papa, but the situation is not good. If the Germans break through our defences in Poland and East Prussia – and there is every indication that they could – there is nothing to stop them taking the Baltic states. Narva could fall into German hands.'

Monsieur Kulbas sighed and pulled out his cigarette case. Nikolai too took a cigarette from a box on the table. Smelling it, he smoothed it with his fingers and placed it between his lips. Taking the lighter, he cupped a hand over the flame and lit his father's cigarette and then his own.

'Germans or Russians . . .' Herman Kulbas exhaled smoke, 'what I dearly want is to live long enough to see Estonia independent from foreign powers.'

19

The Carpathian Mountains, May 1915

The lonely light of dawn crept over the land, gradually bringing into view a group of men kneeling around a priest holding an icon. Quiet and reflective, the men accepted their blessings with bowed heads, then crossed themselves and rose to their feet, adjusting the weight of their ammunition packs across their shoulders.

Behind the lines, soldiers with tense backs waited for the order that would send them into battle. When the order finally sounded, no great cheer went up. As the marching band struck a military tune, weary bodies, heads hung slightly with lingering thoughts of loved ones, filed away, keeping in step with the boots of the men in front of them.

Ahead of them, the rumble of guns waking in the distance signalled the first wave of the attack.

Standing at the head of the line, Alexei drew his sword. Trickles of sweat rolled down his arms.

At the sharp wail of the bugle sounding the start of the attack, his muscles, tense with anticipation, released with a collective sigh.

Everywhere, men climbed over parapets and ran across no-man's-land. Shouts came from all directions, mixing with the tearing screams of shells. His men, having won an enemy trench, frantically secured it against a counterattack, shovelling and packing dirt against the damaged trench walls.

'Your Excellency.' The infantry soldier saluted. 'We have secured the trench with five prisoners and two machine guns.'

'Escort the prisoners to the camp,' Alexei instructed, 'then send a runner to ask for further orders.'

'Yes, Your Excellency.'

Alexei, followed closely by Grigory, headed to the far end of the trench where men were inspecting damaged machine guns. The body of a soldier cut almost in half was slumped at the foot of a gun.

'That was our machine-gunner,' Grigory shouted above the gunfire.

Alexei beckoned to a young soldier. 'You there, get behind the gun.'

'Y-yes, Excellency.' Scrambling to his feet, the soldier ran to the machine gun and started shooting into the trees. Each burst of gunfire slammed the machine against his body, bouncing him backwards.

Click. Click.

The gun coughed, jumped and fell silent.

'I think it's jammed.' The soldier shook the handles.

A mortar shell screeched low over their heads. Frightened, the soldier threw himself on the ground, covering his head with his hands.

Without thinking, Alexei ran to drag him to safety. The whistling sound of a second mortar sliced the air and exploded close by. Bright yellow light warmed one side of Alexei's body as he was lifted off the ground and flung hard onto his back. Sharp pain shot through his neck and leg as fountains of dirt rained down on him. He heard muffled screams before everything around him turned dark.

When Alexei next opened his eyes, his vision was flooded by brilliant white light. His first thought was that he had entered heaven.

In the distance he could hear the faint echo of artillery fire and, closer, the flapping of canvas in the wind. As his surroundings came into focus, he realised the bright light was the sun streaming through the white canvas walls of the field hospital. Brushing a hand over his head, he felt bandages. He patted them tentatively, then his probing fingers moved down his neck to where a dull ache pulsed. Touching the spot, he swiftly withdrew as agonising pain seared the base of his throat.

'Water, General?' A soldier with a weathered face and kind eyes held out a wooden cup to him and helped him lift his head.

'You have been asleep for some time.' The soldier spoke with a strong Ural accent. 'Your aide will be pleased to see you awake. He carried you to the infirmary on his back.' Cradling Alexei's head in the crook of one arm, he tilted the cup, wetting Alexei's lips.

Alexei coughed, spluttering water over the sheets. The water, though cool on his lips, did little to put out the fire in his throat. Adding to his discomfort, the tightness in his lungs made every breath wheeze inside his bruised ribcage.

'I'm such an old fool. Your injuries must make it difficult for you to drink.'

Alexei opened his mouth to speak, but instead of words, a garbled sound escaped him.

'You rest, Major General.' The soldier eased Alexei's head back onto the pillow. 'I'll go find your aide.'

So Grigory had rescued him, had carried him on his back according to the old soldier. Alexei had a faint memory of seeing the earth rush beneath him but he could not be sure if it was a real memory or just a trick of his feverish mind. The effort of trying to piece together his last moments exhausted him. He closed his eyes and drifted into a troubled sleep.

When he awoke the brightness of the sun had faded into the grey light of the afternoon. Feeling stiff, he shifted his weight but at once regretted it as his muscles screamed in protest. Turning his head carefully he saw Grigory asleep on a chair. His normally meticulously presented uniform was dishevelled and his hair, uncombed, stood at odd angles. Grigory looked up and, seeing Alexei awake, fell to his knees beside the bed.

'Your Excellency.' He kissed Alexei's hand. 'It is a relief to see you awake.'

Alexei wanted to say something but was again halted by harsh primitive sounds that escaped from his throat.

A nurse appeared carrying fresh bandages. Grigory jumped to his feet and, stepping aside, made room for her to tend to Alexei. Stout, with deep-set brown eyes, the nurse worked with great efficiency and few words.

'You've suffered partial suffocation, broken ribs and a shrapnel wound to your neck,' she said, straightening the sheets. She tucked them firmly under the mattress, then stood back to inspect her work. 'The doctor will call on you on his rounds,' she stated matter-of-factly.

After the nurse had left, Grigory helped Alexei take a sip of water. Alexei coughed, his chest burning as if branded with hot coals. Though his throat was still dry, he refused another sip. Running his tongue across his dry lips, he eased his head back on the pillow and closed his eyes.

In the days that followed, Grigory rarely left Alexei's side. Alexei often woke to find him sleeping on a wooden chair by his bed and in the mornings Grigory woke early to serve Alexei soup and lukewarm tea, refusing the nurse's help to serve breakfast.

Each night, the doctors made their rounds, checking on patients, dismissing some back to the front and organising for the transfer of others to Petrograd or Moscow hospitals. Long hours of work without sleep or proper nourishment showed in the dark circles around their eyes.

With three broken ribs, Alexei's chest felt as if it were wrapped in a tight coil. His breath wheezed in short, sharp bursts. Blinking in the darkness, he heard the doctors moving about in the late hours of the night. Thinking their patients were all asleep, they talked candidly among themselves. The endless stream of wounded and lack of resources gnawed at their resolve and sapped their energy, as Alexei learnt.

Occasionally other officers, some on crutches, others in

wheelchairs, came to sit by Alexei's bed during the day. It didn't seem to bother them that he couldn't talk. On the contrary, his silence encouraged many to speak openly, finding in him a patient and sympathetic listener. One officer, a very young staff captain with fine aristocratic features and an easy smile, visited Alexei daily with news and reports he'd learnt from other officers. He'd been shot in the shoulder and had his arm in a sling.

'I have heard that the Emperor will be visiting the hospital next week,' that staff captain informed him. 'It is rumoured you and your aide are to receive the Order of St George for heroism during battle.'

Alexei smiled. The Order of St George was the highest honour of the Russian army.

The Emperor is very generous, he wrote on the chalkboard he used to communicate.

A week later, the Tsar visited the hospital with the young Tsarevich.

'For gallantry in battle.' Tsar Nicholas looked genuinely pleased to be awarding the medal. 'You have done well, General.' He draped the sash across Alexei's shoulder and, as Alexei stood to attention, pinned the medal to his chest.

Alexei winced only slightly from pain when he saluted, his chest swelling with pride.

Moving on, the Tsar removed a medal from the box handed to him by his assistant and pinned it to Grigory's chest.

'Take a good look at these brave men,' he told his son. 'They do our country proud.'

20

Poland, May 1915

Foraging at dusk in the ruins of a nearby village, Katya came across a cellar beneath a collapsed wall. Using her kerosene lamp, she searched through the debris for something they could eat. It was only by chance she found the handful of potatoes. Rubbing the soot and dirt from them, she saw that they were old and shrivelled but still edible. Putting them in her hessian bag, she scrounged for more. She had left Fyodor asleep in a nearby barn and was anxious to get back before he woke and found her missing. Turning over the bricks, she hastened her search but when she found nothing more and was about to crawl out of the cellar she heard voices. Realising they were headed towards her, she quickly put out the lamp.

'I would give anything right now for a bottle of vodka and a hearty meal,' a voice said in Russian.

'I'd rather have a night between clean sheets wrapped in the warm limbs of a woman,' the other replied, and they both laughed.

Katya pressed her body against the wall of the cellar, hardly daring to breathe. For the next few hours, she stayed hidden as the soldiers moved through the village, her senses alert to the sound of their feet as they dragged and lifted rocks to build barricades and hide artillery.

'Remind me again why we have to do all this digging,' one complained as they dug a trench a few metres from Katya.

'If we have to fall back, we'll use this village as our next line of defence.'

'And why do we need to do this while it's dark?'

They had stopped digging. Katya heard a match strike against a hard surface.

'You're a fresh recruit, right?'

'What's that got to do with anything?' the first soldier replied testily.

'Only a fresh recruit or an idiot would ask such a question.'

Metal clanked as a shovel hit a rock. 'You dare call me an idiot?'

'Easy, comrade, I meant no disrepect. Anyone who has served at the front knows if the Germans get a whiff of what we're doing here, they'll send their planes to pound it into smithereens. Now pick up your shovel and get digging or we'll never finish this trench before daylight.'

Katya lost track of how much time passed. She suspected she had fallen asleep at one stage because the next thing she knew a thin grey light was shining through the cracks in the wall. Remaining hidden, she listened until she was sure the men had gone, then she cautiously crawled out of the cellar.

The air was crisp and cool. She stretched her back to loosen the stiffness then, sticking to the shadows, hurried back to the barn.

The hinges opened with a reluctant groan. A triangle of sunlight filled the small interior and quickly disappeared again. Katya stood at the doorway and waited for her eyes to adjust to the darkness.

'Fyodor?'

Detecting a stirring in the corner, she turned to see the boy step out of the shadows. When he came closer, she saw his eyes were wet.

'I'm sorry I took so long.' She ran her hand tenderly over his face. Lifting her bag, she said brightly, 'I found some potatoes.'

Fyodor's lips lifted into a weak smile.

'What? You're not hungry?' Katya asked jokingly.

Fyodor's smile stretched and he nodded.

'Then hurry and fetch some water from the river.' Katya ruffled his hair.

Fyodor picked up the bucket and ran out of the barn. Katya turned to the figure lying on the ground. It was nothing short of a miracle that the soldier had survived this long. Shot in the arm, the bullet had narrowly missed an artery.

Kneeling beside him, Katya could hardly believe the withered body belonged to a living man. So many times she had considered abandoning him. She and the boy could have made their way much quicker without him. The ox, killed in the crossfire, had been left at the side of the road along with most of their belongings. They had pulled the wagon and the man in it for kilometres before they'd found the abandoned barn. But neither she nor Fyodor had the strength to pull the heavy wagon any further. Even if they had, the soldier would not have survived the trip. The barn offered shelter and a place to rest for a few days.

She looked into the soldier's face. His eyes, hot and burning with fever, stared straight up. His breath struggled in and out of his lungs in wet rasping gasps.

'How are you feeling this morning?' Katya smoothed back his hair. She regretted the words almost as soon as they parted her lips. 'I have found some potatoes. I can make soup.'

The soldier showed no sign he understood. She took the cold bony fingers between her own. 'I don't know how else to help you,' she said, a lump growing hard in her throat.

The wheezing chest, barely able to hold on to life, expelled air in irregular bursts. His feverish eyes stared confusedly at Katya. She made the sign of the cross on his forehead. Through her own tears, she thought she saw the soldier's eyes brimming.

'Go,' she whispered. 'Fly to the arms of Lord Jesus.' Tears rolled down her face. She wiped at her face with the back of her hand. 'Go now and stop your suffering. You'll be reunited with Marie when she eventually joins you in the next life.'

The soldier turned his head slightly and looked directly at her. His eyes were full of gratitude. 'Marie.'

Katya hesitated a moment then leant forward. 'I'm here. I'm with you now.'

'Masha . . . You came.'

Katya gave him a reassuring smile. 'Yes, I came and I will never leave you.'

'I'm sorry.' His breath wheezed and struggled.

'You have nothing to be sorry for.' Overcome with grief and helplessness, Katya dropped her head into her hands. When she looked at him again, a faint smile played beneath his matted moustache. He took a breath and, as he exhaled, the eyes became lifeless.

Katya felt a hand on her shoulder and turned to see Fyodor.

'He's gone,' she said simply. 'He's no longer suffering.'

She wrapped the soldier's body in a sheet she had taken from her grandmother's hut in preparation for his death, then they carried him outside. Using their hands and breaking up the soil with some strong sticks, they dug a shallow grave, placed the ragged body in it and covered it with earth and rocks. At the head of the grave, Fyodor planted a wooden cross he had made from fallen branches. Covered in sweat, Katya said a prayer. Stumbling over the words, she ended the prayer with a few words of her own.

'Dear Lord, here lies a soldier, his body buried far from his family and homeland. We entrust him to your arms.'

They both stood for a moment, looking down at the grave.

'He was smiling.'

It took a moment for Katya to register the boy had spoken. She turned and looked at him in disbelief.

'The soldier,' he said again. 'He was smiling at you when I came in.'

At the sound of his voice, the wall Katya had built inside to protect herself collapsed and she held the boy tight against her. Releasing him, she said, 'I don't understand. How is it you are speaking?'

He shrugged and dropped his gaze.

'What happened to you, Fedya? Why did you stop talking?'

He looked up shyly. Tears filled his eyes. 'When the Germans attacked, I remember holding my mother's hand. She screamed at me to hold on tight. I was scared. There was so much smoke and people ran everywhere. I fell and lost my grip. I could hear my mother screaming my name, but I could not see her.' Tears finally streamed down his face. He wiped at them with the back of his sleeve. 'I screamed and screamed till I had no voice left.'

'Oh, Fedya.' She pressed him against her. 'Do you remember where I found you?' She rubbed his shoulders. 'You looked so frightened, it broke my heart to see you.'

'I thought she would come.'

'Your mother?'

He nodded. 'I thought she would come back for me.'

'Didn't anyone stop for you?'

Fyodor shook his head. 'You were the first.' Fresh tears began to flow. 'I wanted to tell you I had a mother, a family, that I was lost. But nothing would come out.'

'What made you come with me?'

'Your eyes reminded me of her. They made me feel safe.'

She touched his face. 'We are orphans, you and I. But as long as we have each other, we will never be alone.'

21

The Carpathian Mountains, Austrian Front, May 1915

As the light faded, orders came to mount a fresh assault. With the aid of spotlights, the German machine guns shredded the attacking lines, littering the fields with bodies. At dawn, with the sun hanging like a ball of fire, stretcher-bearers crawled among the prone figures, searching for survivors.

Alexei, unable to stand for long, watched as the wounded men arrived at the field hospital. Grigory worked tirelessly alongside the nurses, applying iodine to wounds and bandaging them with quick, efficient hands. His lips, stained brown from biting the caps off the iodine bottles, pursed tightly over his teeth, and he wiped continuously at his brow.

The men, too weak to swat at the flies hovering around their wounds, lay motionless on the grass. A priest in a black cassock threaded between them, waving incense and giving Communion.

Those with minor wounds squatted in tight circles, watching the scene with detached looks that told of defeated spirits. Doctors moving among the men gave urgent instructions to the nurses who followed closely behind. Those they could save they operated on immediately; those beyond saving, they left for the priest.

As Alexei watched, a wounded man in a delirious state mistook a nurse for his beloved and grabbed at her skirt. 'Anushka, don't you recognise your Shura?'

'Of course.' The nurse gently disentangled herself from the man's grip. 'You must rest,' she said. 'I'll be back as soon as I finish my rounds.'

'Don't leave me, Anushka.'

'I'll be back, Shura.' She squeezed his hand. 'I promise.'

Reassured by this, the soldier rested his head back on the ground.

One of the nurses said something and Alexei turned stiffly to face her.

'I brought you a nice mug of tea.' She placed the steaming cup by his elbow. 'Lunch will be served in an hour in the officers' tent.'

Alexei thanked her with a small nod. He tried smiling but it was hard to move his face with the bandages covering it. Bringing the mug to his lips, he took a sip and felt satisfied by its strong brew. Returning his gaze to the soldier, Alexei discovered him staring unblinkingly at the sky, his life having slipped away before the nurse could return.

The old Ural soldier was also present, threading his way carefully among the wounded men with a bucket of water. Cradling each man's head as a father would cradle his son, he offered water to their parched lips. When he reached Shura, he set down his bucket and, bending over the lifeless body, closed the lids and crossed the arms. Then, after crossing himself, he picked up his bucket and resumed his work.

'This is what our army is reduced to.'

Alexei had to turn his body to see who was speaking to him. The staff captain stood by his elbow, smoking a cigarette, his handsome face contorted by a scowl and the hard glare he fixed on the wounded men. 'Our army is powerless under the German onslaught.' He pulled hard on his cigarette, blowing the smoke out with a sharp exhalation.

His inability to communicate embarrassed Alexei and added to his frustrations.

Having finished his cigarette, the staff captain immediately lit another. He was quiet for a while, deep in his own thoughts. Over the weeks, Alexei had become accustomed to the young officer's visits and felt comfortable when, on some occasions, he turned silent and reflective.

'The Germans are breaking through our lines on a wide front,' he said eventually. 'We don't have good soldiers.' Sweeping his arm at the mass of men, he said, 'Most are peasants. They have no breeding, no gallantry and are stubborn as mules. It is almost impossible to get them to follow instructions.' He drew deeply on his cigarette. 'Russia was doomed from the very beginning.'

Moving closer, he lowered his voice. 'I feel the army is betrayed by *Stavka*. Shortages have reached a critical stage. Each day, a new order comes to send men to attack the lines. And each day our attacks are rebuffed and our men end up here.' He made another sweeping motion at the rows of dead and wounded.

Alexei's gaze swept over them and beyond, to the plumes of smoke wafting over the battlefield. He nodded his head in agreement and, not for the first time, found himself questioning the army's outdated methods.

The staff captain checked his watch. 'It's getting late and I have already taken up too much of your time.' Saluting, he hesitated a moment. 'Thank you, Excellency, for granting me an audience. It's a relief to be able to voice my thoughts with a commander.'

Alexei turned to watch the staff captain's receding figure, the younger man's words echoing in his ears.

In the dining tent that evening, the mood was solemn. The attack had not gone well and the Russians had been forced to abandon several trenches. Even the local girls brought in to entertain the officers could not lift their moods.

'If Warsaw falls, there is nothing to stop the Germans advancing to Petrograd and Moscow,' a general exclaimed. 'I've already sent my wife and children to live with my parents in the Urals.'

Alexei too had sent a telegram to Emily, urging her to move to their estate in Uglich on the bank of the River Volga.

'Gentlemen, let us not be downhearted.' A young major rose to his feet. Clapping his hands loudly, he turned to the girl next to him. 'Grab us a few bottles of vodka and enough glasses for us all.' As the young woman turned to leave, the officer slapped her on the buttocks. 'Quickly now,' he urged. 'We must give our brave officers on the hospital train tomorrow a proper send-off before they leave.'

The woman hurried away, returning shortly with several bottles of apple vodka.

'To your health.' The men raised their glasses and threw back their drinks. The local women, their cheeks flushed from alcohol, shrilled and clapped. Alexei winced as the sting of alcohol hit his damaged throat. Sipping vodka was considered poor form. Pointing to his throat, Alexei waved the glass away.

'Have a drink with us, Major General,' the men insisted. 'The vodka will soon restore you to full health.'

All eyes rested on Alexei, waiting to see if he would take the drink. Not wishing to lose face, he lifted the glass to his lips and emptied it in a single gulp. His throat burnt as if set on fire.

'Does Your Excellency wish to retire?' Grigory whispered in his ear.

Alexei nodded that he did.

'I'm afraid the major general needs his rest,' Grigory announced to the group. 'We have a long journey ahead of us in the morning.'

Around the table, officers rose to their feet. Stepping forward, the staff captain saluted Alexei. 'On behalf of the men, Your Excellency, we wish you a safe journey and a speedy recovery.' Dropping his hand, he continued, 'It's been an honour and a privilege to serve with you.'

Moved by the words, Alexei motioned for Grigory to help him out of his chair. Standing to his full height, he saluted the men.

Back in his quarters, the doctor stopped by Alexei's bed on his evening rounds. 'The wounds are healing well.' He shined a torch in Alexei's eyes. 'I hear the Empress has opened Feodorovsky Gorodok at Tsarskoe Selo to accommodate new hospital beds.' He switched off the torch. 'It should make for a far more comfortable stay than what we offer you here.'

As the doctor moved to the next patient, Alexei's thoughts turned to Petrograd. As disappointed as he was to be leaving his men, he longed to return to the city in the hope of seeing Marie. He had not had a response to the letter he had written before leaving for the front and yet thoughts of her were rarely far from his mind. He saw her everywhere: in the kind gazes of nurses and in the smiling eyes of the local girls. Returning to Petrograd meant the opportunity of seeing her again.

He fell asleep then and, for the first time since returning to the front, his sleep was free from the despair that usually stirred his soul and weighed painfully upon his heart.

Eastern Front, June

Tsar Nicholas sat behind his desk in his private carriage and stared out at the scenery. Despite being shelled, scorched and trampled, new shoots sprouted from the thawing land. Budding green leaves pressed through charred stumps with a resilience Nicholas found impressive. Earlier, on his walk, he had made a point of drawing attention to the shoots to the English and French diplomats who had accompanied him to the front.

'These shoots are symbolic of the grand Russian spirit,' he had told them.

'Your Highness is quite correct in his assessment,' the Englishman had said tentatively. 'But I fear that despite the size of the Russian army, it has suffered from more setbacks than victories.'

'Since the beginning of the war, our second line of troops is greater and our entire armies are much stronger,' Nicholas retorted.

Increasing his pace, he forced the diplomats to keep up with him. 'Our men are hardened and physically and morally ready. Necessity has shown the strength and resourcefulness of the Russians. Our factories are working effectively to produce guns and munitions.' He stopped and turned abruptly to face the Englishman. 'The war, my dear sir, has not only strengthened our country's resolve but has added vigour to our ranks.'

The diplomats exchanged a look but remained silent, smiling politely. Irritated, Nicholas walked ahead of them. He had tried his best. The *Duma* had been ineffective in curbing inflation and the black market. Shortages in bread and butter had led to accusations of profiteering. To make up for the shortages in munitions from their own factories, the war ministry had placed vast orders from neutral and Allied countries. However, supplies had been slow to arrive.

Nicholas decided to write a letter to his wife. Her continued support and advice was the one bright light that lifted his mood. Russia was lucky to have an empress as warm, loving and dedicated as her, he thought. Talk of her and their good friend Rasputin meddling in the country's affairs infuriated him.

My own dear heart,

It is exactly a week today since I left. I am so sorry that I have not written to you since then. It happens that I am just as busy here as at home with endless meetings and lengthy reports to read.

I arrived to depression and despondency among the generals. Talk of retreat had naturally soured the mood and affected morale. Such talk, combined with German attacks and our terrible losses, has led to much distress. Our troops have evacuated Przemysl, the fortress we so proudly won only two months ago. How quickly the fortunes of war change!

Two diplomats with us at the front accompanied me on my walk today. I was greatly vexed by one of their remarks on the spirit of the Russian people. Meeting our troops this morning to bless them before battle, I was impressed by their resolve. The trouble now, as always, remains with the shortage of munitions – which, as I pointed out to the diplomats, is being dealt with through increased effort in our manufacturing. I take heart from the reports we receive from the German prisoners that their own efforts are also stymied by the same problems we face.

I tenderly embrace you and our children.

Nicky

P.S. I am still undecided on the question of my uncle.

22

Galicia, June 1915

Nikolai sank almost to his knees in the mud caused by the heavy rain. He had returned from his leave to find the Russian Front south of the Vistula in full retreat. Forced to evacuate, Nikolai and Ivanov received orders to return to their regiments stationed at Lemberg.

Heading in the opposite direction, new recruits, sent to slow the advance of Austro-German armies, marched to the front, singing patriotic songs. The crowd parted reluctantly to let them through.

'Poor devils,' said a soldier standing beside Nikolai. 'They don't have a hope in hell against the Germans. The army barely has enough ammunition to last us a few days.' He shook his head. 'Thirty from my village joined a year ago.' He stabbed a finger at his chest. 'And I'm the only one left.'

Once the recruits had passed, soldiers and civilians again reclaimed the road. Nikolai looked around for Ivanov and found him helping a family whose wagon was stuck in the mud. His hair, damp with sweat, stuck to his face and his skin was flushed red from pushing the heavy load. At the head of the wagon, a woman held the horse's reins.

'*Tso*.' She slapped the horse's rump. '*Tso*.' The muscles on the horse's back strained and tightened but, exhausted, it failed to shift the wagon.

Dropping his pack, Nikolai rushed to help. Pressing his shoulder against the wagon, he pushed. His boots slipped in the thick mud and he nearly lost his balance, but together he and Ivanov managed to get the wagon back on the road.

'Thank you.' The woman pressed half a loaf of stale bread into Ivanov's hands.

Ivanov shook his head, 'No,' he said, gesturing to the other occupants of the wagon. 'You should keep that for your children.'

Watching Ivanov refuse the bread, Nikolai was conscious of a stabbing pain in his stomach. For a week, they had survived only on dry biscuits the army issued.

Picking up their mud-stained packs, they joined the throng along the road.

'Why did you do that?' Nikolai asked after a while, the rain streaming down his face, soaking through his clothes.

'Do what?'

'We've had nothing but hard biscuits for days. Why did you refuse the bread?'

At first Nikolai thought Ivanov wasn't going to answer him.

'Did you see the eyes of those children?' Ivanov said eventually. 'They were hungry and that bread was most likely a day's meal for them. I thought about how my wife and children are getting along without me and I hope someone will show them the same generosity.'

The rain had started to ease. Nikolai looked up to find the heavy clouds had lifted and separated, allowing rays of sunlight to shine through. They had been marching for thirty hours with very little rest and the warmth came as a welcome relief after a night of tramping through the rain.

'That's more like it,' Nikolai began, before he heard a noise like the turning of a motor. Ivanov heard it too and they both searched the sky for the source of the sound. A biplane broke through a knot of clouds, spitting bullets at the road.

Everywhere, people scrambled for shelter. Ivanov pushed Nikolai towards the birch trees lining the road.

'Run!' Ivanov shouted, pushing Nikolai into the cover of the woods. 'Keep running!'

Nikolai stumbled. The adrenalin pumping through his veins made him forget his tiredness and he ran as fast as he could. He glanced back at the road. Dead bodies lay everywhere, tangled with crushed carts.

Ivanov and Nikolai kept running. When they could no longer hear the drone of the plane and the screams of the wounded, they stopped.

Nikolai fell to his knees. 'I . . . can't . . . go . . . any . . . further,' he gasped.

Also breathing heavily, Ivanov dropped his pack and sat on it. 'We can only rest for a short while. We must keep moving. It's too dangerous to return to the road.'

Nikolai looked around at the forest. 'Which way should we go?'

Ivanov reached for his compass and flicked open its lid. 'That's east.' He pointed. 'We head that way to the Russian border.'

As his adrenalin receded, Nikolai was overcome by a wave of fatigue. 'I'm ready to fall asleep right here.'

'No, we can't stay here . . . Listen!' Ivanov stood very still, head cocked. 'There's a river close by.'

'I can't hear it.'

Ivanov picked up Nikolai's rifle and threw it at him. 'You were raised soft.' He said it without malice. 'You've never had to survive in the forest.'

'How dare you say such a thing to a superior officer?' Nikolai retorted. 'I'll have you know I often went on hunting parties.'

'Hunting parties?' Ivanov scoffed. 'Like I said –' he pulled his pack across his shoulders '– you were raised soft.'

As the Cossack set off to the east, Nikolai followed on unsteady legs, not caring where he was stepping. Above them, the sky filled with thousands of stars. They walked until they reached the river.

Dropping to his knees, Nikolai drank from the water, greedily. Ivanov walked along the banks looking for a way to cross.

'We can grab one of these fallen logs and let the currents move us downstream to the other bank.'

'Are you crazy? We'll drown. And my clothes are only just starting to dry.' Leaning against a tree, Nikolai rested his elbows on his knees. 'We've been travelling non-stop. You can go into that river if you want, but I'm staying here.'

Ivanov looked at the water, briefly mesmerised by the reflection of the moon. He was anxious to put as much distance as he could between himself and both armies. Once they crossed the Russian border, he planned to desert and make his way back to his family. He intended to say nothing of his plans to Nikolai; when the time came, he decided, he would slip away in the middle of the night.

'I'll keep first watch,' he said and threw down his pack. 'I'll wake you in a couple of hours.'

Sitting on his haunches, he watched Nikolai gather leaves and make a bed, using his jacket as a pillow. Nikolai fell asleep almost instantly and was soon snoring softly.

Leaning against the trunk of a birch, Ivanov stared at the river, his rifle resting across his lap. The lapping of the water against the bank was as soothing as a child's lullaby and soon his eyelids grew heavy. He fought the urge to sleep, but eventually fatigue overcame him and his head dropped to his chest.

It felt like only a few minutes had passed before he was woken by a noise. Startled, Ivanov's eyes snapped open. What was it he had heard? Remaining very still, he listened to the sounds of the forest.

'Lieutenant,' he whispered.

Nikolai groaned but didn't wake.

Ivanov listened. There it was again: the sound of a branch snapping under a heavy boot.

His blood froze in his veins. The sound had come from the other side of the tree he was leaning on. He tried to scramble to his feet, but was thrown back by a punch to his face. Pain exploded behind his right eye.

'What in the world . . .' The words died in his throat. Standing in an arc around him were four German soldiers, their rifles aimed at his chest.

Reluctantly, Ivanov raised his hands above his head.

'*Aufstehen!* Get up!' one of them ordered. '*Mach schnell!*'

He rose slowly to his feet, careful not to make any sudden movements. A few metres away, one of the Germans woke Nikolai with a sharp kick to his sternum.

'Search him,' their commander ordered.

One of the soldiers threw his rifle over his shoulder and stepped forward, checking inside Nikolai's boots and socks for knives.

The soldier finished his searching and handed the few things he had found to his senior officer, who then motioned him to check Ivanov.

Ivanov's right eye had swollen closed. 'Bastards,' he breathed as the German patted him down.

Smiling, the officer took out his tobacco pouch, sat on a fallen log, rolled a slim cigarette and lit it.

In a steady voice, Nikolai asked him something in German.

The officer took his time answering. Inhaling deep into his lungs, he breathed out, his face disappearing behind ribbons of blue smoke. When at last he spoke, Nikolai recoiled at the answer.

'What?' Ivanov leant in to Nikolai. 'What did you ask him?'

Nikolai hesitated. 'I asked him what he planned to do with us.'

'And? What did he say?'

'He said we'll be joining our comrades in one of Germany's best POW resorts.'

Ivanov looked once more at the river. He had missed his chance. Turning his head away, he cursed.

23

Petrograd, August 1915

Sitting on the balcony that led off her living room, Marie heard a knock on the door but didn't turn her head. No doubt it was another invitation to an outing or supper. She would refuse it as usual, choosing instead to work an extra shift at the hospital.

The picnics, horse races, balls, concerts and theatre which she had found so exciting barely two years ago, no longer held the same thrill for her.

She heard a murmuring, then the sound of the door closing. Seconds later, Anna stepped onto the balcony waving an envelope. She looked awestruck. 'It was the palace messenger with a letter from the Empress!' she exclaimed.

Curious, Marie took it and opened the seal.

> *The Empress wishes to award all the nurses volunteering at the hospital with a certificate in a ceremony in September. Afterwards, a horse race will be run in the Empress's honour in the fields outside Tsarskoe Selo.*

'Is the messenger still here?' Marie handed the invitation to Anna.

'He's waiting downstairs.'

'I suppose I should attend.' Marie pushed her chair back. 'I can't refuse the Empress's wishes.' Stepping inside, she went directly to her writing table. 'I'll invite Darya to come with me. It might stop her from complaining that I never go anywhere with her.'

After giving her letter to Anna she returned to the balcony, and looked down at the street, busy with traffic and people. It was a mild afternoon and she considered going for a walk across the Palace Bridge but dismissed the idea. The city held too many memories. Thoughts of Pyotr and Nikolai loomed large but increasingly it was Alexei who dominated them. Once, she mistook another officer strolling in the Summer Garden for Alexei, and her pulse had quickened. Her heart sank with disappointment once she realised her mistake.

She was still thinking of Alexei when Anna joined her, carrying a tray of tea and delicate jam *piroshkies*. In the street, the palace messenger had disappeared in the direction of the Winter Palace. He passed a pair of well-dressed women and tipped his hat. Walking arm in arm, the women were chatting animatedly.

A refugee begging in the street with her child approached hesitantly and held out her palm. 'Alms for the poor,' she pleaded. 'So my child can eat,' she added when the women ignored her.

Without pausing their conversation, one of the women reached into her purse and dropped a couple of coins at the refugee's feet.

'God bless you,' the mother called after them. The women did not look back.

'I'm not hungry.' Marie handed Anna the plate of *piroshkies*. 'Take these and give them to the mother and her child.'

A few minutes later Anna crossed the street to where two refugees crouched against the wall. The woman kissed Anna's hand in gratitude before hastily gathering the buns. She handed one to her child, who stuffed it into his small mouth.

'They are from Poland,' Anna told Marie when she returned. 'The retreating Russian army destroyed their village so nothing useful was left for the advancing German army. They've been on the road ever since.'

'Where is her husband?'

'Killed,' Anna replied flatly. 'Her two eldest sons are fighting somewhere in the south-west.'

Marie shook her head sadly. 'That poor woman,' she said. 'How will they survive winter?'

The officers' hospital in Tsarskoe Selo was not far from Alexander Palace, and an hour's tram ride from Petrograd.

Alexei sat up in bed; the bandages covering his face had been replaced by smaller dressings. He was reading the latest report from *Stavka* and the news made him scowl. All along the line, the German army was forcing the Russians back.

A hot flush spread through his body and, finding the wound at his neck, made it throb. Putting a hand over the dressings further aggravated the pain and he closed his eyes.

A moment later, a doctor pulled back the curtain.

'Good morning, Excellency.' After looking at Alexei's chart, he examined his wound and the broken ribs.

'I'm happy with how these are healing,' he remarked. He held a stethoscope to Alexei's chest then frowned. 'There's still wheezing in your lungs, though, which concerns me.' He called for a nurse, who listened intently to the doctor's instructions before hurrying away. She returned a few minutes later with a form, followed closely by Grigory.

'Considering the severity of your injuries,' the doctor said, 'I'm going to recommend you be invalided from active duty.' He signed the form the nurse had given him, then put it on Alexei's bedside table. As he turned to leave, Alexei grabbed his wrist. Surprised, the doctor looked at him questioningly.

Alexei pointed to his throat. 'How long?'

The doctor sat on the chair next to the bed and regarded Alexei with tired eyes. 'Your lungs and your vocal cords have been damaged,' he explained. 'In time you will regain your speech. However, the damage to your lungs could continue to cause discomfort.'

Alexei slumped back against the pillows. He pointed to the form the doctor had signed. 'I am a soldier,' he said in a harsh voice.

'I know this must be very hard for you.' The doctor's voice sounded sympathetic. 'I'm very sorry.'

Once the doctor had left, Grigory, in an attempt to distract Alexei, held up an invitation from the palace.

Alexei barely registered what Grigory was saying. His mind was still reeling. Invalided from the army? Unthinkable. He was a professional soldier. What else could he do? His importance, his status and pride were all bound up in his identity as a commander.

'Your Excellency?'

Alexei looked up at Grigory, who was regarding him with concern. 'How would you like me to respond to the Empress's invitation?'

'Hmm?'

'The invitation, Your Excellency. To the ceremony and horse race organised by the Empress.'

Alexei shook his head. 'Send my apologies.'

'The change of scenery might do you good,' Grigory cajoled.

Alexei sighed. 'Alright. Then I will go, but have a carriage ready in case I wish to leave early.'

24

Novo-Georgievsk, Poland, August 1915

Bogoleev paced the room, tears of frustration blurring his vision. North-west of Warsaw, the fortress of Novo-Georgievsk was defended by a series of outer forts that had been modified at the start of the war to thwart a German advance on the city. For the past few weeks, the German army had surrounded Novo-Georgievsk, bombarding it with their guns.

Bogoleev ran a hand through his hair. With Warsaw evacuated, he believed the army must abandon the fortress. Cut off by the siege, the garrison of ninety thousand men was fast running out of ammunition and supplies. But Grand Duke Nicholas, the supreme commander of Russia's military, had ordered that the army defend the fortress at any cost.

Outside, a German shell exploded in a nearby building, showering Bogoleev with dirt and dust. Before he could react, there was another explosion and the floor shifted beneath him. Soot and smoke filled the room.

The door flew open and a soldier rushed in. 'The building's been hit! We have to evacuate!'

Bogoleev followed the man to the corridor and saw there was already a crowd blocking the small staircase that led outside.

The force of the next explosion threw him backwards and, losing his balance, he fell heavily. A pair of hands grabbed him under the armpits and lifted him to his feet.

'We have to get out before the building collapses.'

Bogoleev turned towards the voice but the man had already vanished in the press of people rushing to get out. Ahead of him, the thickening smoke folded around the men, giving the impression they were being dissolved into grey fog. Steadying himself against the railing, Bogoleev descended the stairs towards the prism of light. Once outside, he fell to his knees, coughing, and was momentarily blinded by the smoke. Breathing hard, he stood up and looked around at the burning fortress. Men carrying buckets of water raced to put out fires.

There was nothing more to be done, he thought. The fortress was lost. He had to find a way to save himself.

Staggering away from the wall, he stumbled towards the stables. The door had been blown off its hinges. Frightened horses neighed and stamped their hooves. Bogoleev followed a group of men rushing to rescue them. Grabbing a horse's bridle, he patted its neck. 'I'll get you out,' he said gently to the animal.

Above him orange flames had spread to the roof. Creaking loudly, the walls looked ready to buckle. As Bogoleev tugged at the horse's bridle, a section of the roof broke off and crashed to the ground close by. Startled, the horse reared.

'Easy boy.' He patted the animal's head.

Acrid smoke filled the stables. Squinting into the haze, Bogoleev looked for a way out. To his left, flames licked at a hole left by an explosion. He kicked at the hole to make it bigger. The planks, singed almost to ash, fell away easily.

'Come now.' The horse pulled its head away, reluctant to move. Bogoleev tugged harder. 'Come!' he shouted over the roar of the fire, and this time his horse obeyed, following Bogoleev through the gap.

Outside the barn, guns drowned out all other sounds. Gripping the bridle Bogoleev hauled himself onto the horse's back and urged him forward, but the guards barred his passage at the gates.

'We have orders not to let anyone through.'

'Let me pass,' he commanded. 'I am carrying an important message from the general for the grand duke,' he lied.

The guards exchanged a look, uncertain what to do.

'There's little time. I must pass!' Bogoleev shouted over the rattle of gunfire.

Relenting, the guards opened the gates.

'There are German snipers hiding,' one guard warned. Crouching low against the horse's neck, Bogoleev rode hard towards the trees, bullets whistling past him. His pulse racing in his throat, Bogoleev reached the cover of the woods and turned the horse towards the border.

Alexander Palace, August

Tsar Nicholas sat on the balcony, looking out over the garden. On the table sat the remains of the afternoon tea he had shared with his wife and her adviser, Rasputin.

The war was not going in his favour. The fall of Warsaw and the surrender of Novo-Georgievsk had rattled Russian morale. In parlours and breadlines, rumours spread of Germany's plans to invade Petrograd and the evacuation of the royal family. The growing number of dead, missing and captured men, coupled with the shortage of food, threatened to lead to mass unrest in the streets and factories. Worried, Nicholas had decided to seek his wife's counsel.

'Nicky darling,' Alexandra said, once he had enumerated Russia's troubles, 'there is no doubt that you've been placed in a very difficult position. In the matter of us leaving, you should immediately put a stop to all rumours. I have no plans to abandon my duty in the hospitals.' She gestured to the tall man sitting beside her. 'Rasputin and I are in complete agreement that you have done your very best for your country.'

Nicholas leant over and squeezed his wife's hand affectionately. 'You're the only one who truly understands me.'

She returned the squeeze with a loving smile but it quickly slipped from her face. 'However, there are certain individuals who continue to let you and Russia down. Of course I don't wish to place blame on any one individual, but –' she paused and, gently releasing her hand from his, placed it on her lap '– your uncle, for instance . . .'

'I'm in no mood to discuss my uncle. There is no one I can trust to replace him.'

'No need to get upset, my dear Nicky. I'm sure the grand duke had done his best. But one cannot deny that he is terribly unpopular with the Russian people.'

'They are ignorant. They don't know what they are talking about.'

'That may be so, but the people are hurting and they are looking for someone to blame.'

'My uncle is not a sacrificial lamb.'

'And no one is suggesting he should be. All I'm proposing . . .' She turned to look again at Rasputin, who nodded in encouragement. 'I think that much of the potential unrest would subside if you take over your uncle as the supreme commander.'

Nicholas looked from one face to the other. 'You can't seriously be suggesting that I should replace my uncle? It would be a betrayal of our relationship, of the trust I placed in him as a military commander.'

His wife nodded gravely. 'I understand how difficult this must be for you to hear, but we truly believe it will be for the good of the country.' Taking another sip of her tea, she smiled sweetly at him again. 'But of course the decision is entirely yours to make.'

25

Galicia, July 1915

The long line of Russian POWs snaked along the road. Nikolai and Ivanov marched silently side by side in the middle of the group. Raising his head, Nikolai looked at the procession of men that stretched as far as he could see. Reaching an open field, they were ordered to sit on the grass. Pressed close, the men spoke softly among themselves, each one relating the circumstances of their capture, as they waited for their names and details to be recorded on individual cards.

'Second Lieutenant Kulbas, Third Hussar Regiment,' Nikolai said when it was his turn.

'Next of kin?'

Nikolai named his parents.

'Where were you stationed?'

'I have been working behind the lines, close to Warsaw.'

The clerk looked up. 'Why?'

'I was a translator.'

'Are you a spy?'

Nikolai shook his head. 'No.'

The clerk studied Nikolai then, as if satisfied he was telling the truth, informed him, 'You will be transferred to the officers' camp,

Lieutenant. There you will have a better class of accommodation.' Raising a stamp, the clerk was about to bring it down on Nikolai's card when Nikolai interrupted.

'I have a friend. You processed him just before me. Will we be together?'

The clerk placed the stamp on the table and picked up the previous card. 'Your friend is not an officer,' he noted.

Over the past nine months, Nikolai had grown close to Ivanov; he admired his strength of character. Although they came from vastly different worlds, Nikolai found himself seeking Ivanov's company and advice in preference to most of the officers who shared his quarters. 'I'd prefer not to be separated from Corporal Ivanov,' he said.

The clerk laughed. 'You're in no position to make demands.'

'If Corporal Ivanov cannot join me at the officers' camp,' Nikolai persisted, 'then I will go wherever he is sent.'

Surprised, the clerk leant back in his chair.

'Unlike your allies, your government does not send any provisions for its POWs,' he said frankly. 'Conditions in the officers' camp are far more pleasant than those you would experience with –' the clerk checked Ivanov's card again '– Corporal Ivanov.'

Nikolai kept his face expressionless. 'I understand.'

'As you wish.' The clerk shrugged. Reaching for a different stamp, he brought it down hard on Nikolai's card.

Marienburg POW Camp, Poland, September

Nikolai watched as the rim of the sun appeared over the horizon and lit the neat blocks of huts. The Belgian and English soldiers stood at their windows and doorways, watching as the Russian POWs filed towards the gates. It had become apparent from his months at the camp that the Germans reserved the worst treatment for the Russians.

At sunrise each day, Nikolai joined his fellow prisoners in a march to the outskirts of the town, where they worked ten-hour days, digging quarries for iron ore. Toiling in the sun, the prisoners demolished houses, churches and cemeteries to get to the iron-rich soil. Removing corpses was particularly gruesome, and with each resting place disturbed, the men murmured prayers and crossed themselves. This morning, as the gates opened and they filed out, Nikolai was disappointed to find that they were headed for a cemetery once more.

Beside him, Ivanov scratched at a blister that had burst and hardened into a callus. Since arriving at the camp two months ago, Ivanov had grown increasingly quiet, staring out into the woods beyond the barbed wire with distant eyes.

Standing at the gates of the cemetery, Nikolai rubbed his arms to warm himself as he waited for his name to be called.

'Kulbas!'

He stepped forward.

Consulting his list, the German soldier handed him a shovel. 'You lot will be clearing out the graves from the children's section,' he said.

Ivanov blanched when Nikolai translated the orders, muttering under his breath as they were led to a corner of the graveyard and shown where to dig.

'They are animals,' Ivanov muttered angrily as he pushed his shovel hard into the packed dirt. 'It's bad enough that we are forced to dig up old people's graves, but the children . . .' Ivanov shook his head. 'No, these men are worse than animals.' He spat at the ground. 'Even animals would not act like them.'

Throwing down his shovel, Ivanov climbed out of his hole.

'What are you doing?' Nikolai whispered, shooting a nervous glance at the soldiers.

'I will not defile a child's grave,' Ivanov hissed defiantly.

'You two, get back to work,' came a barked command.

Nikolai resumed shovelling the earth, imploring Ivanov with his eyes to do the same. Ivanov, though, stood where he was, glaring at the soldiers who were now running towards him.

'Work!' one of the soldiers shouted at Ivanov. He pointed to the hole next to Nikolai. '*Schnelle!*'

Ivanov threw down his shovel. '*Niyet.*'

The soldier's jaw tensed. He picked up the shovel and pushed it into Ivanov's chest.

'Work!' he repeated.

Ivanov spat at the small patch of dirt between the soldier's boots.

The soldier stared at the damp stain on the ground then slowly lifted his eyes and fixed them on Ivanov. Ivanov stared back.

As Nikolai watched in horror, the soldier lifted his rifle and slammed it against the side of Ivanov's face.

Ivanov's head snapped back. Blood began to trickle from a large gash under his right eye. The soldier then rammed the butt of the rifle into Ivanov's stomach. Winded, he fell to the ground, pressing one hand to his face and gasping for air. The final blow came down hard on his back.

Breathing heavily, the soldier leant down and grabbed Ivanov by his collar. Dragging him to the edge of the grave, the soldier kicked him in and threw the shovel after him.

'Now, all of you,' he said dusting the dirt off his hands and clothes, 'back to work.'

'Lyova,' Nikolai whispered into the grave.

Two hours had passed, but Ivanov had not moved. Frightened to go to him, Nikolai called his name repeatedly, trying to get a response.

'Ivanov,' he said, a little louder. He shot a nervous look at the soldier standing nearby. 'Answer me: are you hurt?'

The soldier walked past, stopping to look down at Ivanov.

'Your friend is not such a big mouth now, is he?' he sneered. He reached into his pocket and pulled out his tobacco pouch. 'You know what your problem is?'

Nikolai did not answer.

The soldier rolled a cigarette, smoothing it between his long fingers. Placing it between his lips, he smiled at Nikolai as he lit it.

'The problem with Russians,' he said, blowing smoke through his nose, 'is that you have no discipline.'

Nikolai returned to digging the earth.

'Take your army, for instance. Your generals spend half their time arguing with one another. Instead of working together to win battles, they bicker and try to save their own arses.'

Nikolai's back stiffened. How did the soldier know what passed between the Russian generals?

Noticing Nikolai's reaction, the soldier let out a laugh. 'We've been listening to conversations between your generals for a long time. We know all about your offensives well in advance.' Bending over, he drew deeply on his cigarette then exhaled in Nikolai's face. 'And that's why Russians will never win against the mighty German army.'

Straightening, the soldier flicked the remainder of his cigarette onto the ground and turned on his heel. Pausing by the grave where Ivanov lay unconscious, the soldier unbuttoned his trousers and urinated.

'It seems the beating has made him as gentle as a lamb.' He laughed.

Nikolai kept his head down, staring at the red ember burning at the end of the cigarette. His throat ached with the need to pick it up. Snatching up the cigarette, he sucked at it greedily. With each drag, shame and humiliation washed over him. The tobacco went straight to his head, making him dizzy. He closed his eyes, letting the dizziness travel from his head down his spine. When he opened his eyes again, he saw the soldier staring at him, his mouth twisted in a cruel grin.

At the end of the day, Nikolai, with the help of two other POWs, lifted Ivanov out of the grave. Taking his shirt off, he soaked it in water and dabbed gently at Ivanov's face. The swelling over the right eye had forced it completely shut but the other was open and staring.

'Lyova.' Nikolai searched his friend's face for signs of recognition. 'Can you hear me?'

Ivanov's staring eye moved towards the voice. His lips parted, but no sound came out.

'Help me carry him back to the camp,' Nikolai said to the others.

They carried Ivanov by his arms and legs on the march back, stopping occasionally to swap men when they grew tired. The sun had dipped behind the hills and stars had filled the sky by the time the POWs reached the gates to the camp.

In their hut, Nikolai sat at the foot of Ivanov's bed, praying his friend would survive the long night.

'Lord in heaven, please hear me. Spare Ivanov his life. Let him live.' His voice cracked. 'He has a son he has never held. He has a wife and daughters.'

'Kolya.'

Nikolai opened his eyes and leant over Ivanov's cot, his heart beaing faster. Had his friend spoken?

'Water,' Ivanov croaked through cracked lips.

Cradling his head, Nikolai wet Ivanov's lips with water from his canteen. 'I saved you some soup,' he said.

'I'm tired,' Ivanov said weakly. 'I want to rest.'

Nikolai lowered Ivanov's head back on the cot. 'I'll be right here.'

Ivanov regarded Nikolai through his one good eye. 'Thank you.'

The next day Nikolai woke early. He had slept badly, his ears alert to the smallest sounds rising from Ivanov. He massaged the spot where his head ached with a dull pain.

'Lyova, are you awake?'

Ivanov moaned and turned towards his friend's voice.

Nikolai sucked in a breath. 'That guard has done a number on your face.'

'Just wait till I get my hands on that goat fucker!' Ivanov tried to lift himself on his elbows but Nikolai gently pushed him back.

'You're in no condition to talk. Let me take a better look at your face.'

Nikolai tentatively touched the swelling. Ivanov winced.

With no hope of finding bandages, Nikolai tore a strip from the bottom of his shirt. He soaked the cloth with water from his canteen, then placed it over the wound.

'This will help reduce the swelling. Keep it on your face while I go and get us some food.'

Nikolai moved to leave but Ivanov grabbed his wrist.

'Why are you doing this, Nikolai? I don't understand. You stay with me rather than go to the officers' camp. And you are looking after me now. Why?'

Nikolai shrugged. 'Wouldn't you do the same for me?'

Creases deepened around Ivanov's eye. 'I was ready to abandon you by the river and make my way alone.'

Nikolai stared at his friend. 'You don't mean that.'

Ivanov gave him a hard look that confirmed the truth of his words.

Nikolai's stomach hollowed. 'Each of us lives with our own conscience,' he said in a raw voice. 'I could not live with myself knowing you were suffering and I did nothing to help.' After a moment's silence he added, 'I once left a friend behind, thinking I was doing the right thing. I should have stayed with him,' he said, thinking of the night he left Pyotr at the field hospital. He was like a brother to me and I left him. I live with that guilt every day.' He paused. 'So you see, we are no different, you and I. Perhaps you are the better man because I *did* leave Pyotr while you stayed with me.'

26

Tsarskoe Selo, September 1915

Fifteen officers on leave from the front arrived early with their stallions in preparation for the race. All day, workmen rushed about setting up marquees while servants arranged tables, chairs and settings brought from the palace. The pavilion erected for the royal family and dignitaries was decorated with flags and flowers chosen especially by the Empress.

Trains and carriages brought visitors from Petrograd and the estates at Peterhof. Women wearing large hats and carrying parasols mingled with men in suits. The oldest grand duchesses, both dressed in white, sat together surrounded by a group of eager young officers bidding for their attention. Tsarevich Alexei, wearing a Cossack uniform, sat close by his mother between his two servants. The Empress sat beside Rasputin, with her servants and ladies-in-waiting hovering around them.

Alexei arrived in a *troika*, drawn by three horses harnessed side by side, accompanied by Grigory and several other officers from Tsarskoe Selo. On the way, they had discussed the Tsar's decision to replace the grand duke as the military's supreme commander.

'What is your opinion, Major General?'

Alexei shook his head. 'It's not for me to question the Tsar,' he said diplomatically. 'But I don't believe the grand duke deserved the demotion.'

'What do you think will happen now?' another asked.

'The Emperor will have to spend more time at the front.'

'I don't think the Empress is going to like that very much,' an officer with a heavily bandaged arm said with a laugh.

'I should think she would insist on visiting him at *Stavka* with her children,' someone suggested.

'Will we ever be rid of that *nemka* and her priest?' the first officer asked.

'I should think not. The Emperor is devoted to both of them. Rumour has it, he can't make a decision without them.'

All talk of politics ceased upon their arrival as the men became distracted by the first group of riders, who were lining up for the race. After much jostling and a few false starts, the starting gun fired and the horses took off. Around the course, spectators rose to their feet for a better view. From his vantage point close to the pavilion, Alexei followed the riders through his binoculars. As the riders turned a corner, Alexei's attention was drawn to a figure standing close to the gates. His heart nearly stopped as he recognised Marie – not just in his imagination, but right there. Dressed in a simple but elegant summer dress and broad-brimmed hat, she was the epitome of grace. As he watched, she turned and said something to her companion, a slender young blonde woman dressed in the latest fashion.

Marie's face was animated, glowing with excitement.

A horse stumbled, throwing its rider to the ground. A loud gasp rose from the crowd and they pressed forward, obscuring Alexei's view. Lowering the binoculars, he looked for her but there were too many people blocking his eyeline.

'Is there something the matter, Excellency?' Grigory stood at his side. 'If Excellency is worried about the rider, I can find out whether he's been injured.'

'No. No need,' Alexei said, scanning the crowd again for Marie. At last he spotted her close to the accident scene. Craning her neck, she was looking in the direction of the rider. The crowd reluctantly parted to allow the doctor and his assistant to reach the injured man. Marie attempted to follow them but was stopped by her companion, who pulled her away to a less crowded area.

'Hand me my cane please, Grigory,' Alexei said, without taking his eyes off Marie. 'There's no need for you to come too.' He passed Grigory his binoculars. 'I won't be long.'

He found Marie and her companion at a small table near the pavilion. It was the first time he had seen her without her nurse's habit and he thought that she had never looked lovelier. His pulse quickened and a certain uneasiness crept into his mind. Had she received his last letter? And if so, how would she react when meeting him again? He had almost decided to turn back when she saw him, and her eyes brightened with an astonished joy that lit up her face.

'Mademoiselle.' He bowed formally. 'What an unexpected surprise.'

'Excellency.' Marie offered him her hand.

Bending low to kiss it, he gave her fingers a gentle squeeze, noticing that she blushed and pursed her lips to restrain a smile.

'May I present my cousin, Mademoiselle Darya Mostovsky.'

Darya held out a gloved hand. 'Won't you join us?'

Alexei moved a chair close to Marie's. 'Are you enjoying the races?' he asked.

'I was until one of the riders had a fall. Dasha stopped me from going over to help.'

'And rightly so,' her cousin interjected. 'After all, you are not on duty and your dress would have been ruined in the mud, not to mention how inappropriate it would have looked. Don't you agree, General?'

'Not wishing to contradict you, Mademoiselle, but I can vouch for Mademoiselle Kulbas's skill from first-hand experience. The rider would have only benefited from her attention.' Alexei's throat burnt with the effort of speaking and he coughed delicately into his fist. 'Excuse me,' he said. 'Shrapnel wound.' He pointed to the purple scar snaking down his neck.

A worried expression crossed Marie's face. 'Were you badly hurt?'

'I was lucky. Another man took most of the impact.' Seeing the sad expressions on the women's faces, Alexei said, 'We should not dampen the mood with talk of war. Ah, there's a waiter. Let us have some champagne.'

As the drinks were served, Alexei observed Marie more closely. She was as beautiful as he remembered her. Her boots, her long fitted dress, the fur on her collar, her hat, and the light makeup was youthful and in keeping with the latest fashion. Yet, in contrast to so many of Petrograd's women, she was modest and reserved, and did not draw unnecessary attention to herself. Alexei found it hard to take his eyes off the heart-shaped face. He noticed a new sadness in her that showed in the strain at the corners of her grey eyes. He felt an overwhelming urge to soothe her pain, to stroke her hair and feel the smooth warmth of her skin.

She looked up and their eyes met and held for a long moment. She was the first to break contact, dropping her gaze to her lap.

'And how is your family?' Alexei asked her. 'Last time I saw you, you had received a message which greatly distressed you.'

A shadow passed over Marie's face. She stared down at the glass in her hand. 'My parents and younger brother are in Narva and are fine. As for my brother Nikolai –' her voice caught but she quickly regained her composure '– I have not heard from him in a while.' Placing her glass on the table, she absent-mindedly twisted the engagement ring on her finger. 'My fiancé is still missing. I've sent letters and telegrams to Stavka but there has been no news. It's as if he has vanished from the face of the earth.'

Leaning over, Alexei lightly touched her hand. Her fingers were soft and he longed to clasp them. 'If I can be of any assistance –' he began but was interrupted.

'Your Excellency!' A soldier with an eye patch rushed towards them. Reaching the table, he clicked his heels and saluted. 'It's a great pleasure to see you again, Your Excellency.' Turning to the ladies, he bowed respectfully before turning back to Alexei.

'At ease, soldier,' Alexei said. 'What can I do for you?'

'You don't remember me? I was in your battalion at the start of Tannenberg.'

Alexei stared at the face of the man. Although his features were familiar, he still could not place him.

'I was a gunner then,' the young man prompted. 'You saved me from a whipping when my gun failed to fire.' Turning to Marie, he explained, 'I was a nobody, a simple recruit. When my gun failed to fire at an enemy aeroplane, a sub-lieutenant threatened to make an example of me but the Colonel . . . Oh, I beg your pardon –' he nodded at the epaulets on Alexei's shoulder, 'the Major General stood up for me.'

'Did he?' Marie looked at Alexei admiringly.

'Oh, a hero!' Darya clapped her hands.

'I remember now,' Alexei said, nodding. 'What's your name, soldier?'

'Leshev, Your Excellency.'

'And what are you doing here?'

Leshev pointed to his eye. 'The gun exploded, taking my eye with it.'

'That's awful!' exclaimed Darya.

'God gave. God took back.' Leshev shrugged. 'I'm no use at the front so they sent me here to help in the stables. And you, Excellency? I heard you were shot.'

'I was. I survived it only to be invalided by a mortar shell,' Alexei said briefly, not wishing to elaborate further.

'May God look after you.' Leshev looked over his shoulder towards the stables. 'I should be going back. They're about to start another race. I hope you did not mind me coming over, Excellency. I wanted to pay my respects and thank you.' Saluting Alexei, he again turned and bowed deeply to Marie and Darya.

'What a charming fellow,' Marie said after Leshev had left.

A loose curl escaping from under her hat fell across her face. Alexei reached over and tucked it behind her ear. Marie's cheeks stained pink.

'*Mon Dieu!*' Darya exclaimed, checking her watch. 'I must be going. I promised Mama I would accompany her to the theatre. Are you staying at Tsarskoe, Excellency? Would you be a dear and escort Marie? She's due to start her shift at the officers' hospital following the races.'

'It will be my pleasure,' Alexei said a little too eagerly. Rising to his feet, he kissed Darya's gloved hand.

Once she had left, Alexei turned to Marie. 'I was not aware you are working in Tsarskoe.'

'They've been short-staffed at Feodorovsky Gorodok hospital, so they asked some of the volunteers from Petrograd to help there. I've been working in both places since the beginning of summer.'

Calling a waiter, Alexei asked for a pencil and paper. He wrote a quick note to Grigory informing him that he was taking the *troika* but would send it back for him and the other officers.

'Shall we?' He offered his arm to Marie and accompanied her to where the *troika* waited.

'I must apologise,' Marie said a little shyly as the coachman urged the horses forward. 'It was wrong of Darya to impose on you like this.'

'On the contrary, your cousin did me a great favour.' He gave her a smile that made her blush.

'I wish you would not speak like that, Major General.'

'Why do you insist on calling me by my title?'

'How else would I address you?'

'Call me Alexei. Or, if you prefer, Alyosha.'

'I like Alexei.'

'Then Alexei it is.' He moved closer, taking her hand. 'I have not been able to stop thinking about you since we first met at Petrograd. Did you receive my letter?'

She nodded. 'Please, Alexei.' She shifted away from him.

'I know you have feelings for me.' He gazed at her steadily. 'It was in your eyes when you saw me today.'

She felt the heat of a deeper flush staining her cheeks. 'I insist you stop talking to me like this,' she said sternly. 'It makes me uncomfortable.'

She tried to pull her hands away but he held on to them, tightening his grip. 'You told me once we can be nothing but friends. Surely, you must realise now how impossible that is for me.'

'Must I remind you that you are a married man? You have made a commitment to your wife.'

He sighed. 'My marriage has been dead a long time. We are only together for the sake of appearance.'

Letting go of her hands, he touched her face.

Her skin tingled from the heat coming off his fingertips.

'Marie.' The tone of his voice was serious. 'I've never felt this way towards anyone before.'

She closed her eyes, feeling a rush of emotions, wondering if it showed on her face. Part of her, touched by his words, ached to believe him, to surrender wholly to him. She was certain if he chose to kiss her at that moment, she would be powerless to resist.

'Look at me, Marie.'

She opened her eyes. 'I've already given you my answer.' Her voice sounded strange to her ears. 'We can be nothing but friends.'

He went rigid and withdrew his hand. 'Is this your final word on the matter?'

She said nothing. Dropping her eyes, she pulled absently at the fabric of her dress.

'Tell me the truth, Marie. I need to know what is in your heart.'

'I have told you.' Her voice quivered and almost faltered. 'I do not love you.'

The next day, Alexei thought of little else, other than what Marie had said. The words had hurt. But he was sure he had heard some uncertainty in her tone, as if she were trying to convince herself as much as him. And that gave him hope.

All day, he anticipated her arrival and could barely contain his disappointment when Emily appeared instead, having arrived that morning from Uglich.

'Alyosha.' She kissed him lightly on the cheek. 'We were so

worried for you. I've brought presents from the girls.' She handed him a parcel. 'They have been very busy knitting warm socks and writing letters to you.'

Alexei opened the parcel, inspecting each item carefully. Then he read the letters, smiling at the girlish sentiments they contained. Emily, meanwhile, peeled off her gloves and unfastened the clutch on her stole, letting it fall softly to her lap.

Alexei could sense her studying him as he read.

'Since Warsaw, everyone has fled to the country,' she began, her tone conversational. 'Before that you would have never known there was a war on by the way the Petrograd society carried on.' Emily wrinkled her nose with disapproval. 'Every week I received invitations to ambassadors' balls or the theatre. I came across Countess Natalya several times.' She said the name with great distaste.

'How is the countess?' Alexei asked with little interest. He checked his watch. Surely if Marie was going to visit she would have been here by now.

'Dripping in diamonds and laughing far too loud. She was hanging off the arm of a lieutenant who looked much too young for her.'

Alexei only half listened as Emily continued to talk.

He checked his watch again.

'Are you expecting someone?' She stared at him suspiciously. 'You have checked your watch several times since I've arrived.'

'Of course not,' Alexei replied, defensively.

Emily's eyes hardened. 'I must be going. I have a million things to do.' She gathered her gloves and stole. 'I shall visit you again tomorrow, Alexei. That is, unless you have made other arrangements.'

'You are welcome at any hour.' Alexei's words sounded insincere even to his own ears. 'I shall look forward to it.'

She gave a cold laugh and, leaning forward to kiss him, whispered, 'I have been married to you a long time, Alexei. And I know when you are lying.'

27

Tsarskoe Selo, September 1915

Marie did not visit him that day or the one after. He had almost lost hope when she arrived on the third evening, looking exhausted. His joy at seeing her instantly erased the anguish he had felt for the past three days. As she moved closer, he noticed the dark circles under her eyes.

'You look tired.' Nonetheless, he still thought her the most beautiful creature he had ever seen.

'The hospital train arrived today with more wounded. This is the first chance I've had for a while to sit down.'

'Have you eaten?'

She shook her head. 'I'm not hungry.'

'Did you meet the train at the station?' He was not interested in the train. What he wanted was to hear her speak, to continue looking at her.

Untying her nurse's veil, she took it off and folded it on her lap. 'We help with transporting the wounded to hospitals. The grand duchess has asked if I would accompany her on the hospital train to the front.'

'And what did you answer?'

'That I wasn't sure. I was too tired to think.'

'You should go home.' Even as he spoke the words, he hoped she would stay.

She shook her head. 'I need some fresh air.'

'Then I suggest we go for a walk.'

They walked alongside the lake. Masses of lilies-of-the-valley, growing around the Children's Island, filled the air with a sweet scent.

Alexei gazed at the water, but his thoughts were focused on Marie. He perceived a tension that stretched in the silences between them, and wished he could say or do something to break it.

Crossing a bridge, their hands brushed briefly. As if touched by an electric bolt, she moved away abruptly.

Alexei was first to break their silence. 'I was afraid I would never see you again.' He kept his eyes on the lake, fearful of what he might read in her expression. 'What made you change your mind?'

She looked down at her hands, as if weighing her answer. 'I came to apologise.'

He turned to face her. 'Apologise for what?'

'I may have misled you . . . as to my feelings.'

His heart took a leap. 'Marie –'

'Please, Alexei, let me finish,' she said, cutting him off. 'I meant what I said the other day. I'm promised to another man.'

She turned her head, her eyes flooding. 'I have to believe he is still alive and will come back one day.'

Taking a step towards her, Alexei touched her hand. 'How long do you plan to wait for him?'

She shook her head, covering her face with both hands. Moving closer, he pulled her into his arms. She did not resist, resting her face against his shoulder.

He stroked her hair, wishing he could hold her like this forever.

Breaking away, she wiped her face with her hands. 'I'm becoming ridiculous.'

He kissed the top of her head, pressing her a little closer to his chest.

She started to pull away. 'I must be heading back.'

He let her go reluctantly. 'Will I see you tomorrow?'

She hesitated a moment, then nodded. 'Yes.'

Alexei woke in the morning excited at the prospect of seeing Marie again. He called in a barber to cut his hair and trim his moustache, waxing the ends into sharp points. Holding up a mirror, he agonised over his receding hairline, thinking it made him appear older. He tried to avoid looking at the protruding scar, but involuntarily his eyes kept returning to it. The wound was healing well and the skin around it had paled from purple to a sickly yellow. Touching the wound, his fingers probed around the edges till a sharp pain made him draw back. At least, he thought optimistically, his voice was coming back, though slowly.

He waited for her on the verandah. Choosing a seat with a view of the entry, he paid scant attention to the conversations around him.

She arrived in the late afternoon, wearing a loose-fitting coat with fur trim over her uniform. He watched her for a full minute before she saw him.

'Good afternoon.' She waved, smiling.

There it was, he thought, that intoxicating smile.

'Good afternoon.' He kissed the tip of her fingers. 'I heard today the Empress has kindly opened the library. I thought we could take our tea there.'

'A marvellous idea.' She checked her watch. 'I have exactly one hour before my shift begins.'

The room was lined on three sides with books, protected behind glass doors. Walking around the shelves, they read the names on the spines aloud to each other. Subjects ranged from travel, genealogy and history to biographies of famous people and novels, as well as almanacs and anthologies.

'May I be of some assistance?'

A slight man dressed in a three-piece suit regarded them from over his pince-nez. 'I am the curator of the library.'

'His Highness has an impressive collection,' Marie remarked.

'This is one of three libraries at the palace,' the librarian informed them proudly. 'His Highness also keeps a personal collection of editions embossed with the imperial eagle. They are very special. I can show them to you, if you like.'

'Some other time perhaps,' Alexei said and, cupping a hand under Marie's elbow, led her to the other side of the room.

'I think you may have hurt his feelings,' Marie scolded him.

'I did not want to spend the short time we have together listening to the librarian,' he said irritably.

A smile fluttered over her lips and she walked with him to a quiet corner away from the curator's gaze, where they spent the remaining time reading favourite passages to each other, first from Pushkin, then Chekov.

When the grandfather clock chimed the hour, Marie jumped to her feet.

'I must be going.'

Alexei helped Marie with her coat. She was almost at the door when he called after her. She turned back to face him, her eyes earnest and expectant.

He wanted to say he could not wait to see her again; that tomorrow was too long away. He wanted her to know that he would be counting every hour, minute and second, but at the last moment his courage failed him.

'Thank you for coming,' he said instead, his words drying on his lips.

The next day he again waited for her on the verandah and they spent an hour together in the library. In between reading, their conversation ranged widely, covering theatre and art and, inevitably, the war. At first he thought she would grow bored discussing military issues, but she remained interested throughout their conversation and expressed her opinions in a clear, concise manner.

'Papa's contacts in manufacturing hold the view that compared to our European counterparts the Russian factories are outdated and inefficient.'

'Is your father not insulted by such statements?'

'Not at all.' Marie smiled, the tired creases deepening around her eyes. 'He believes it explains why we are doing so badly against the Germans.'

'I had imagined your family to be more patriotic.'

'My family *is* patriotic, but we are also realists. If our factories and railways were as efficient as the Germans', Russia would be in a far better position to defeat our enemies. With the toll the war is taking on our homeland, it will not be long before people's patience reaches breaking point.'

'The Russian character is synonymous with suffering,' Alexei said, 'and we understand that sacrifices are necessary.'

'Russian families have already sacrificed enough.'

Alexei heard the sadness in her voice and regretted his comment. Every fibre in his body wanted to reach out to her. Leaning forward, he folded his fingers over the hand resting on her lap. To his delight, she did not pull away.

His eyes drank in her features. Travelling from her broad forehead, his gaze moved to her eyes, the dark lashes, the narrow nose and finally rested on her full lips. What he would give to kiss those lips and have them return his kiss.

Marie's hand felt hot under Alexei's palm. The quickening of her pulse made it hard to breathe. 'Maybe we can read a little from Pushkin,' she managed to say.

'Of course.' His hand fell away and the breath returned to her lungs.

Moving closer to the lamp, Marie read from a volume of Pushkin's poetry. Alexei, listening intently, sat so still Marie thought at one stage he had fallen asleep. Pausing to check, she lifted her eyes, and found herself momentarily lost when their eyes locked. Clearing her throat, she resumed reading.

And where will fate send death to me?
In battle, in my travels, or on the seas?

Or will the neighbouring valley
Receive my chilled ashes?

She was aware of Alexei studying her in the dappled light. He was sitting so close that their knees were almost touching. His scent flooded her senses, and she repeatedly lost her place on the page.

He shifted in his seat and, flustered, she dropped the book.

'How clumsy of me.' She bent to pick it up. Their hands reached the volume at the same time, their fingers touching. With one hand, he grabbed the book and with the other, he took her hand. Turning her palm up, he kissed the delicate skin at the base of her wrist.

Her heart somersaulted wildly inside her chest. 'Alexei.' Her voice was hoarse.

Lowering his face to hers, their lips brushed.

'Alexei . . . please.' She could barely breathe.

His tongue, warm and moist, parted her lips. Unexpected heat spread across the surface of her skin. A soft moan left her lips when he pulled her into his arms. For a moment, she forgot everything as his kisses travelled across her face, landing like summer rain over her eyes, lashes and brows.

'I have dreamt so long about holding you like this.' His kisses moved lower to her cheeks, nose and jawline.

Marie's breathing grew shallow. 'Alexei,' she said, exhaling, knowing she must stop him and yet wanting him to keep kissing her, wanting this moment to last forever.

Then she remembered.

Pyotr.

She pushed him away. 'Oh dear God.' Her hand flew to her mouth. 'What have I done?'

'Marie.'

She could not look at him. 'This is wrong.' She felt tears filling her eyes. 'This . . . we . . . it can never be.'

'Marie, how can you say that?' He made a move to take her into his arms.

'Don't.' She saw the hurt in his eyes and almost lost her

resolve. 'Please . . . I can't see you again.' Grabbing her purse, she ran out of the room, down the corridor and into the darkening evening.

Behind her, she heard his voice calling after her in the cool night breeze.

28

Tsarskoe Selo, September 1915

Alexei did not see Marie again – or not to talk to anyway. Each day he waited in his usual place on the verandah. He saw her arriving at dusk, having caught a later train, and rushing past without turning her head to left or right. Each day he lived for the moment when she might look up to where he waited and, seeing him, smile. But even as he stood hoping, she quickened her step as if sensing his eyes on her and disappeared into the building.

Returning to his room, he would move to the small writing table in the corner and there he would stay for long periods, thinking of her. When Grigory arrived, Alexei would send him away, ordering that no one be received, and refusing dinner.

He had not imagined her kissing him back. When she parted her lips, he sensed the yearning in her, that she was opening her soul to him. And now he could not reconcile himself to losing her.

His despair was increased by the knowledge that there was no one to whom he could confess his feelings. There were plenty in society and among the officers whom he could call on to dine with but when it came to speaking candidly on matters of the heart, he had no confidant. His closest companion was Grigory, who tended to his physical needs, ensuring his uniforms were freshly laundered and his boots polished to a high shine. But even with him, their relative ranks created a barrier, so that when it came to unburdening his soul, Alexei found himself completely alone.

Emily visited him daily, bringing with her news and letters from their daughters.

'When will he be free to leave the hospital?' she enquired one day after a doctor had finished examining Alexei.

The doctor removed his stethoscope, his eyes thoughtful. 'The lungs have not yet fully recovered.'

'Yes, but how much longer is he required to stay here?'

'If his lungs continue to improve, he will be free to leave in the next few weeks.'

'And not any sooner?'

'Emily, please,' Alexei interrupted. 'The doctor has already given you his opinion. Do not press him further.'

'I thought you would be eager to be reunited with your daughters,' she said sharply.

'If Your Excellency wishes, I can make provisions to have you discharged next week,' the doctor offered. 'Of course it will not be the ideal situation, but with proper care, I see no reason why your lungs cannot continue to heal.'

'That's settled then.' Emily stood to leave. 'I'll make the necessary arrangements to have a nurse accompany us.' Extending her arm, she shook hands with the doctor. 'Thank you, Doctor, for all your help, but I feel it's time my husband came home.'

'Your Excellency must be pleased to be going home,' Grigory said when Emily and the doctor had left. Hanging Alexei's uniform, he began brushing it down with meticulous strokes.

'Hmm? Yes, I'm very glad,' Alexei replied absently.

Grigory stopped brushing Alexei's uniform. 'Is there something troubling you, Excellency?'

For a fleeting moment, Alexei considered confessing to Grigory. 'No,' he said eventually. 'It's nothing. I was just thinking about the move to Uglich.'

'The country air will be beneficial for your lungs,' Grigory pointed out.

Alexei sighed. 'I suppose you're right.'

Grigory returned to brushing down the uniform. 'Not to mention seeing your daughters again after so long.'

Rising from his chair, Alexei moved to the window. Autumn had arrived with a sudden change of weather. A howling wind thrashed at the birch trees, scattering the leaves across the path. Alexei stared at the scenery with unseeing eyes. He felt stirred by a sense of loneliness. He hated the thought of leaving Marie. Even though she avoided him, at least here in the hospital he was near her. He had to speak to her, he decided.

A nurse arriving to change the bedsheets broke Alexei out of his reverie. Turning to her, he said, 'I wonder if you could be of assistance to me, Mademoiselle? There is a nurse who has been especially kind to me but I haven't seen her for a few days. I wonder if you could tell me which ward she's been moved to?'

From his peripheral vision, Alexei saw Grigory stop what he was doing and look at him with curiosity. Ignoring him, Alexei gave the nurse his most charming smile.

She smiled back. 'What's the nurse's name?'

'Marie Kulbas,' he said, struggling to keep his voice light. 'You see I'm due to be discharged and I wish to thank her especially for her help.'

'Oh.' The nurse's smile slipped. 'I'm sorry, Excellency, but Marie won't be back for a while. She's received a transfer to another hospital.'

Alexei's stomach tumbled. 'I hope not because she was unhappy?'

'No, nothing like that. That is, I don't think so.'

'I don't understand.'

'We received a telegram from her this morning. She wishes to be closer to her residence in Petrograd.'

'I see.'

'If you wish, you could leave a message for her with the matron,' the nurse suggested.

'No, that won't be necessary,' he said, not bothering to hide his disappointment. 'It's not important.'

Uglich, September

By late September, the picturesque village of Uglich had had its first dusting of snow. Looking at the onion-domed cathedrals and the busy marketplace, it seemed to Alexei that little had changed in the riverside village. As their *troika* passed *muzhik* women with colourful shawls and wide hips, he remarked that they were better fed than their compatriots in the cities.

'They don't have to worry about the strict rationing or black-market prices,' Emily said. She pulled the fur collar of her coat tighter against the cold. 'You made the right decision sending us here. There is none of the unrest that we saw in Petrograd.'

They were approaching St Dmitry on the Blood when Emily asked the driver to stop. Capped by a dusting of snow, the church's five blue domes were vivid against the bleached sky.

'I thought we might light candles in the memory of our parents.' She removed the layers of fur from across her lap. 'It's been a while since we've both been here.'

Inside, surrounded by icons and gilded frames, Alexei lit a candle and thought about his parents. A stern military man, his father considered any outward show of affection to be a weakness of character. He had married Alexei's mother when she was in her teens and he in his early thirties, and they had had their first child, Alexei's sister, a year later. Two more – Alexei being the youngest – followed in quick succession. Alexei's mother, whom he remembered as warm and loving, had died from complications during childbirth when Alexei was only five.

Placing the candle at the altar, Alexei lit a second candle for his infant brother and prayed that his mother had found in heaven the happiness she was denied on earth.

The red bricks of his childhood home slowly came into view as the *troika* climbed the hill. When they turned into the courtyard, the front door flew open and the three girls ran out to greet them.

'Papa!' Alexei barely had time to climb down before his daughters threw their arms around him.

'Girls,' their governess scolded gently. 'What did we talk about this morning? You must conduct yourselves like ladies at all times.'

Paying scant attention to her, the girls continued to push one another out of the way to get closer to Alexei, all talking at once.

'How long will you be staying, Papa?'

'I'm learning to paint, Papa,' Vera said and pressed a folded piece of paper into his hands. 'I did a special painting for you.'

'Papa is not interested in your silly hobbies,' Irena said jealously.

'Mama! Irena is being bossy again.'

'Girls, please.' Emily motioned for the governess to remove them.

'Come now, girls.' The governess ushered them towards the house. 'Your parents have travelled a long way.'

'Wonderful to have you back home, Your Excellency.' The butler stepped forward. 'You must be tired. We have your rooms ready.' He motioned to an ageing footman. 'Take the Excellencies' trunks to their rooms.'

'What happened to our other footman?' Alexei asked as he watched the old man struggle with the heavy load. Two maids helped him to pull the trunks down and carry them inside.

'Joined the army, Your Excellency. I wrote to you about it. They say he's made corporal.'

'Yes, of course,' Alexei said absently. 'I shall go directly upstairs to change. Upon my return I wish to speak with the manager about the estate.'

The butler cleared his throat. 'I'm afraid the manager has also left, Excellency.'

'So who's been looking after the estate?'

'I've been managing it to the best of my ability.' The butler looked at his feet. 'With most of the men gone, we've had to make do with fewer staff.'

'How many have we lost?'

'We don't have enough hands to mow and plough even a third of the fields.'

'What about the orchard?'

'The footman and I have been picking the fruit,' the butler said, 'and the cook has been keeping a vegetable garden. The occasional deer along with what we have in the cellars should be enough to see us through winter.'

'And fuel?'

'There's not enough to keep the whole house warm. We've closed off some sections to save on heating.'

'Good idea. Starting tonight, we will all sleep in the front rooms. I will sleep in the study. Speak to Madame Serova to organise everyone else's sleeping arrangements. Then first thing tomorrow, Grigory and I will start chopping wood for winter.'

'But, Your Excellency,' the butler exclaimed, 'that would not be fitting for a man of your position. Not to mention the strain on your lungs.'

'My lungs will benefit from the exercise,' Alexei said firmly. It seemed a new, more austere phase of his life was to begin. And with any luck, he thought, it would drive Marie from his mind.

29

Marienburg POW Camp, Poland, December 1915

Nikolai's soul was sinking, falling a little deeper each day. He had been in the camp for nearly six months and half the men who had entered the camp with him had died, either from starvation or disease. And every day, more were lost.

The dead were buried in the mornings. When the ground was frozen, they lit small fires to warm the earth. As the bodies were lowered, men clutched their caps to their chests and sang a hymn, the wind whipping at their beards and shaggy hair. Afterwards, filing down from the burial ground, the men joined the queue to receive their breakfast.

Hunger did not give Nikolai a moment's respite. It consumed his every waking thought. Even as he stood beside the graves, thoughts of food gnawed at the corners of his mind.

Desperate to quiet the ache in his stomach, he scrounged through rubbish bins, often fighting with other men over food scraps.

This morning he had woken with a throbbing head and a new pain in his bones. Propping himself up on his elbows, he immediately fell back with dizziness. Closing his eyes, he waited for the sensation to pass. Then, sitting up, he pulled his *papakhi* low over his ears.

Picking up his boots, he inspected their soles. Held together with nails and strings, they did not look as if they would last him the remainder of winter. He checked the leather and was pleased to find it had not frozen overnight.

Looking to the far end of the hut, he saw the dark form of the small stove. Threading his way between the cots, he took care to step lightly on the creaking floorboards so as not to wake the other occupants. Outside, a howling wind thrashed the birch trees against the flimsy cabin walls. Icy air seeped through the gaps, leaving a film of frost over the walls. Blowing on his hands, Nikolai rubbed them hard against one another. He unhooked the gas lamp from the nail above the stove and lit the wick. Yellow flames grew and flickered, creating a circle of light around him.

Squeezed by a sudden sharp tightening in his chest, he coughed into his hands. When he removed his hand from his mouth, he discovered a dark stain on his palm. An uneasiness hardened in his stomach.

There was a rustling at his elbow and a shadow fell across the stove.

'You're up early.' Ivanov stood beside him, his large frame almost blocking out the light.

Nikolai wiped the stain against his pants before Ivanov could see it.

Crouching before the stove, Ivanov felt for signs of heat. 'The damn stove has gone out again.' Opening the latch, he looked inside. 'It's ice-cold.'

'What did you expect? The Germans take the thickest logs for themselves, leaving us with these thin branches.' Nikolai searched through the pile of wood in the corner. Selecting a few pieces, he broke them against his leg and fed them into the stove. Ivanov lit a match and held it close against the branches until the wood started to crackle and the flames took hold. He turned and smiled at Nikolai. 'That should soon build into a nice fire and we'll be able to have ourselves a hot drink.'

'We've used the same tea-leaves so many times there's nothing left in them to brew.'

Ivanov's smile broadened. The side of his face where the butt of the German soldier's rifle had cracked his cheekbone was dented, giving the impression of only half his face smiling.

'I have a little rum.' He winked.

Nikolai gaped at him. 'Where did you get it?'

'Never mind, I have my ways.' Throwing one of his thick arms around Nikolai's shoulders, Ivanov said, 'You just leave it to me. I'll make you a hot drink that'll put hairs on that skinny chest of yours.'

Nikolai's laugh quickly turned to a cough that racked his lungs and made him double over.

Ivanov helped him back to his cot and eased him down. Worry had replaced the laughter in his eyes and he pressed a hand against Nikolai's forehead.

'You're not well.'

'I'm fine.' Nikolai pushed Ivanov's hand away. 'It's only a head cold.'

'You're burning up.'

'I told you I'm fine.' He gave Ivanov a reassuring grin. 'At home, we had a cook who snuck us vodka when we fell sick. She swore it was the best remedy for the flu.'

Clearly not convinced, Ivanov hesitated. Thin grey light had started to filter through the dirty window, pushing back the dark shadows into the corners. The other men in the cabin were starting to stir and soon the guards would sound the whistle for roll call.

'I'll tell the guards you are too ill to go out into the fields today.'

Nikolai started to object but Ivanov stopped him. 'I don't want to hear any more arguments from you.' He lowered Nikolai gently down on his cot and threw his own blankets as well as Nikolai's over him. 'Get some sleep.'

Nikolai closed his eyes and felt the room spinning around him. His teeth chattered uncontrollably and his body shook. Grabbing the blankets, he pulled them up to his chin and fell into an uneasy doze. He was not sure how long he slept. He was vaguely aware of Ivanov sitting at the end of his cot and holding something out to him. He tried to swallow but his tongue, thick and swollen, was stuck to the roof of his mouth. Voices and images flashed by in a confused blur.

Tears mixed with sweat streaked down his face and he felt himself sinking into a dark ravine. Then, from the belly of the darkness, a light grew and a figure appeared within it. The figure was moving slowly towards him, his features hidden by the bright light behind him. He drew closer and to his joy, Nikolai recognised Pyotr.

Pyotr smiled sweetly at him. 'Kolya, brother, what has become of you?' He placed a cool hand on Nikolai's burning forehead.

'I'm so thirsty,' Nikolai confessed.

Pyotr continued to smile knowingly at his friend. 'It's time.'

'Time for what?'

'It's time you came with me.' Pyotr held out his hand.

'I don't understand.' Nikolai's brow creased. 'Where are we going?'

'Come with me. It's time to put an end to your suffering.'

'Where will we go?'

'I will take you to a place where there are never any wars, or hunger, only eternal peace.'

Nikolai shook his head. 'There is no such place.'

'There is and I can take you there.' Pyotr took Nikolai's hand in both of his. 'Come, let's not waste any more time.'

Nikolai felt his body lift effortlessly off the cot. An overwhelming sense of relief washed over him and he forgot his pain. He followed Pyotr towards the light, moving at first slowly then gradually gathering speed. As he neared the light, he saw other figures waiting to greet him.

'Who are these people, Pyotr?'

'It's been a long time, my friend. There are many of us here now.'

Holding tighter to Pyotr's hand, Nikolai moved into the light.

Ivanov shook Nikolai's limp body. He had returned from the fields to find Nikolai curled up in the cot. The few words that escaped his lips made no sense. The boyish face was red and glistening with sweat, the dark curls soaked and matted against his scalp. Ivanov touched Nikolai's hand. It was burning. Turning his friend over, Ivanov wiped Nikolai's face with a damp cloth. Nikolai's breath came out in shallow wheezes and smelt like rotting fruit. In desperation, Ivanov shook him.

'Fight, goddammit.'

A hand squeezed Ivanov's shoulder. He turned to see another prisoner.

'That won't help,' the man told him.

Shrugging the hand away, Ivanov stood gazing at the limp body.

'There's nothing anyone can do for him now,' the other prisoner said, shaking his head.

Something snapped in Ivanov's brain. Turning, he grabbed the other man by the collar. 'If you want to live to see another day, comrade, you'll keep your opinions to yourself,' he snarled. Ivanov loosened his grip and the man stumbled away. Ignoring the astonished stares of the other prisoners, Ivanov sank to his knees beside Nikolai's cot.

'You cannot die here. You must fight.' Ivanov's lips trembled. Bringing his hands together, he prayed. He sat like that for a long time, begging all the saints for the life of his friend.

When he looked down again at Nikolai, his face was calm. His head had rolled to one side and his eyes stared blankly at the corner of the hut. Ivanov touched Nikolai's hand and immediately recoiled at its coldness.

'Brother, if I survive this hell, I will go to your parents and let them know their son was an exceptional man.' Ivanov lowered the lids over the glassy eyes. 'That's my promise to you.'

30

Narva, February 1916

The carriage stopped before the large iron gates and the stable boy, Ivan, ran to open them. The carriage then moved slowly up the path to the main house.

Herman Kulbas was waiting at the top of the stairs, looking older and stooped. Valentin, looking sombre, stood beside him. Marie jumped from the carriage, ran up the stairs and threw her arms around her father.

'My child, the Lord has seen fit to test us.' Herman Kulbas's voice was thick with anguish. 'My son, your brother, is gone.' A sob escaped him and his body went limp.

'Papa! . . . Valentin, quick, help me.'

Together brother and sister escorted their father inside and eased him into a chair. Dropping his head into his hands, Herman Kulbas sobbed like a child.

'My boy . . . my Nikolai.' He turned his wet eyes to the ceiling. 'Dear God, why did you have to take away my boy, my firstborn? Oh Nikolai.' He dropped his head in his hands again. 'We can't even give him a proper burial.'

Marie's heart lurched. 'What are you saying, Papa? We will surely have a church service.'

Monsieur Kulbas shook his head. 'He is buried in some godforsaken field.'

Marie moved to put her arms around her father but he motioned her upstairs to her mother's room. 'Go . . . go to her. She's been asking for you.'

Removing her hat and coat, Marie threw them on a sofa and hurried to her mother's bedroom.

The curtains were drawn tight and except for a dim pool of light around the bedside lamp the room was dark. Marie's mother lay on her bed, clutching a photo of Nikolai.

Sitting on the bed, Marie took her mother's hand. Pauline Kulbas slowly turned her head and, seeing her daughter, smiled feebly.

'Marie, you came.'

'Of course, Mama. I came as soon as I received the telegram.'

Pauline Kulbas bit down on her lower lip and shut her eyes. Tears streamed down her fleshy face.

'It is no use. My Nikolai has been taken from me. He was just a boy, at the beginning of his life. Why must mothers send their children to war? Why did he go? Why, Marie? Tell me.'

'Dearest Mama.' Forgetting her own pain, Marie struggled to comfort her. 'Please, you must calm yourself. Would you like me to send for some tea?'

Her mother shook her head. 'He's never coming back, Marie. I will not see him marry or hold his children.' She turned her face away. 'A mother should never have to go through the pain of outliving her children.'

For the rest of the day Marie sat close by her mother, leaving her side only to eat a small supper with her father and Valentin. Still dressed in the mourning clothes she had travelled in, Marie fell asleep in a chair beside her mother's bed.

Anna woke her with a gentle squeeze of her shoulder.

'You should get some rest.'

Marie followed Anna to her bedroom, where she was helped out of her dress and into her nightdress. Exhausted, she fell instantly to sleep.

❧

Pauline Kulbas stayed in bed for over two weeks, refusing all visitors. Throughout, Marie sat by her mother's side.

On the morning of the church service, Anna laid out Marie's mourning outfit. Numb and empty, Marie stared at it dry-eyed.

'The carriages will be arriving shortly.' Anna held out a hand to her. 'You need to get ready.'

Marie took Anna's hand and allowed her to help her off the bed and into her dress.

Later, as the family waited for the carriages, the room was heavy with silence. Sitting on the couch, Marie held tight to Pauline Kulbas's hand, which was cold and limp.

Across the room, Monsieur Kulbas sat ashen-faced, smoking a pipe. A sickly yellow pallor had replaced his usual healthy glow. Valentin stood behind him, holding on to the back of his father's chair, his knuckles white.

The double doors opened and they turned at once to the butler.

'The carriages are here,' he murmured.

Emptying his pipe in the ashtray, Monsieur Kulbas was the first to rise. Marie helped her mother to her feet, holding on to her elbow to steady her. Together with Anna, she guided Madame Kulbas into her coat and pinned her hat.

'Are you ready, Mama?' Marie asked gently, dabbing away her mother's fresh tears.

Unable to speak, Madame Kulbas nodded and took her husband's arm, and the pair walked slowly out the door. Behind them, Marie and Valentin, followed by Anna and the remaining staff, filed out the front door and descended the stairs to the waiting carriages.

In the church, dark-clad mourners filled the pews. Marie paid little attention to the service. The pastor's words, the murmuring of condolences and sympathies, did not come even close to soothing the burning ache in her chest. Closing her eyes, she conjured memories of her brother as he was before he left for the front. Nikolai at ten, teasing her mercilessly, and then as the dashing young man in a dinner suit, escorting her to the theatre.

Pauline Kulbas's broken cry brought Marie back from her reverie.

All around, members of the congregation turned and looked at them with soft eyes. Oblivious, Pauline Kulbas rocked back and forth, beating her chest, her mouth set in a frozen scream. Stepping down from behind the altar, the pastor took her hand.

'Nikolai is in the arms of Lord Jesus,' he said, speaking directly into her ear, his face close. 'God, in his infinite wisdom, has taken him into his embrace.'

Aside from her lips, which continued to quiver, Madame Kulbas's body became still, and she looked back at the pastor with round, liquid eyes.

Patting her hand, he gave her a reassuring smile. 'Your son is in a better place, enjoying eternal life.'

'Thank you,' Marie said, her voice dry and brittle.

The pastor gave them both a sympathetic smile. 'I will pray for you,' he said, letting go of Pauline Kulbas's hand.

Following the service, the mourners filed out and moved slowly towards waiting coaches. Walking behind her parents, Marie watched them leaning into one another, her father's strong, reassuring arms folding around her mother, stroking her hair. Something broke inside her and, ducking behind an elm tree, she cried bitterly into her hands.

31

Marienburg POW Camp, Poland, June 1916

The camp guards moved through the huts, turning on lights and kicking the prisoners out of bed. Ivanov propped himself on his elbows, blinking the sleep out of his eyes. Moving to the window, he looked through the grimy glass at the steel-grey sky of the pre-dawn hour and cursed softly under his breath.

All over the camp, men filed outside like ghosts.

Grabbing his tin, Ivanov joined the queue for soup. It saddened him to watch the men waiting in line like schoolchildren. Hands meant for ploughing, fruit picking or harvesting cupped around tins, held out meekly for rations barely enough to prevent them from starving. Once boisterous and full of life, the men now appeared numb and indifferent to their fates. For them the war was as good as finished. Living behind barbed wire, with little contact from the country they had fought for, they felt abandoned by their emperor.

At night, raiding rubbish bins outside the kitchen, they looked for turnips or potato peelings, or crusts of bread left over from the Germans' supper. If they had anything to trade, they crossed the barracks to the fence that separated them from the outside and traded it for food from the locals. Ivanov had managed to trade Nikolai's boots for a loaf of bread and some butter.

His eyes moved to the far end of the camp, where Nikolai was buried. Close by, men were digging a new grave and beside them, the body of a man lay stretched on the ground. Someone had already removed his boots and jacket. Summer had brought with it fresh bouts of dysentery. It spread quickly through the camp, claiming victims with little effort.

Having dug a deep hole, the men lifted the dead man by his arms and feet and lowered him into the grave. As they shovelled the earth over the body, they started their mournful chorus. In the queue, men turned towards the melancholy voices. Slowly, tentatively, they raised their faces to the wind, and sang along. The wind blowing from the west lifted their voices and carried them like a long-forgotten memory across the plains to their families.

Ivanov drove the pickaxe through the soft earth. It was back-breaking work but he did not register the discomfort. For weeks, his mind had been preoccupied with devising a plan. Worried he would not survive the camp long enough to hold his son in his arms, he had resolved to escape. The warmer weather had made the guards lethargic, and as the days grew longer and hotter, they became ever more careless.

Stopping to mop his brow, Ivanov studied the dense forest surrounding the quarry. The thick foliage made flight hazardous but at the same time would provide ample cover. Over the weeks, the seeds of an idea had germinated and gradually solidified into a plan.

Dropping his axe, Ivanov waved one arm while clutching his belly with the other.

'Comrade!' he called. 'Comrade!'

The two closest guards looked up.

'What is it?' one of the soldiers barked irritably.

'Toilet . . . toilet, comrade,' he said in broken German. 'It's urgent.'

'You know the rules. You have to wait till lunchtime.'

'Please, comrade. I can't hold it.'

'Then soil your pants.'

Ivanov creased his brow as if he had not understood what the soldier said.

'Please, comrade. I am not well.' He saw the soldier hesitate and look to where the other guards stood under a shady tree. They were turned away and not paying them any attention.

'Alright then,' the soldier said. 'But be quick about it.'

'*Danke*,' Ivanov bowed his head. 'I will be very quick.'

Walking ahead of the soldier, Ivanov took a quick survey of his surroundings. As soon as he stepped into the brush, he slowed down his pace. The soldier pushed him in the back with his rifle.

'Hurry and do your business quickly.'

Ivanov stopped moving and stood still.

'What is the matter with you?' the soldier barked. 'Have you gone deaf?' He shoved Ivanov's shoulder. 'Can't you hear me? I said –'

In a swift move, Ivanov grabbed the rifle and slammed it into the soldier's face, breaking his nose. The soldier's hand flew to the injury. Before he had a chance to react, Ivanov wrestled him to the ground, strangling his breath with a hard elbow in the diaphragm.

Gasping, the man rolled on the ground, holding his stomach. Ivanov knew the soldiers all carried daggers strapped to their ankles and, pressing his large hand over the soldier's mouth and nose, he grabbed the dagger and plunged it deep into the man's jugular. The soldier's eyes grew wide with surprise. His body twitched, liquid filling his lungs, then went limp. A low gurgling sound rose from the lips and Ivanov pressed down harder to suppress it. Under his gaze, the light in the soldier's eyes dimmed and extinguished. Slowly lifting his hand he let the head drop to one side. Knowing he only had a short time, Ivanov grabbed the rifle and dagger, and ran into the woods.

He kept running for hours without stopping, determined to put as much distance between himself and the guards as possible. Panting, he eventually paused to rest his head against the trunk of a tree. His heart hammering, he took deep breaths. Standing motionless, he listened, but all he could hear was his blood pounding loudly in his ears.

Looking down at his hands, he saw his bloodied fingers and suddenly felt sick. Grabbing a fistful of dirt, he rubbed it into his palms and felt a little comforted that, with his hands dirty, he no longer could see the blood.

As his breathing calmed, his thoughts turned to Marina. He had received a postcard from her with a picture of his family. His boy, with round cheeks and a soft tuft of curls, sat upright on his wife's lap, his sisters on either side. Ivanov carried the photo in his pocket and each night, before drifting off to sleep, he kissed their faces.

Pulling out the photograph now, he traced his finger over each family member, pausing a little longer over his son.

'My son, I hope you never have to experience the terrible guilt of taking another man's life.'

Replacing the photo, Ivanov pushed himself off the tree and again started to run towards the east and, he hoped, home.

32

Russian Front, June 1916

Embers flew from the flames like tiny fireflies. As a child, Bogoleev could sit for hours staring into the fire while the rest of the world carried on busily around him. It had always helped to clarify his thoughts.

It was almost a year since he had fled Novo-Georgievsk, eventually reaching the reserves.

The Russian armies, led by General Brusilov, had been mounting a campaign to attack the Austrians across a wide front. With morale at an all-time low, the Russians needed this victory, and Bogoleev believed Brusilov was the man to deliver it.

'Captain!' An infantryman saluted and stood to attention.

Bogoleev returned the salute. 'At ease, soldier.'

'Our men have found a Russian who claims to have escaped a POW camp twenty-four kilometres west of here.'

'Where did they find him?'

'He came up to our trenches and called out to our men.'

Bogoleev considered this. 'Do you think he's telling the truth?'

The infantryman hesitated. 'He could be a deserter . . . or a spy. But I think he's who he says he is. He's in a bad way.'

Bogoleev scratched the stubble growing across his chin. He

stared into the fire for a few minutes longer before asking, 'Where is he now?'

'The orderlies have him in the infirmary. He collapsed as soon as he was pulled into the trenches.'

'Keep him there. Make sure someone is watching him at all times.'

'There's one more thing: he was carrying a German rifle and we found a dagger strapped to his waist. When they undressed him in the infirmary, there were patches of blood on his clothes.'

'His own?'

'He has minor scratches and bruises on him.' The soldier hesitated again. 'When the doctor examined him, he said the man's cheekbone had been broken, not recently but some time in the past year. The doctor thinks that the man had not received proper medical attention so the bones have not set correctly.'

'Has he told us his name?'

'Yes, Captain.' The soldier took a small piece of paper from his pocket and handed it to Bogoleev. Scratched in pencil in unusually good handwriting was the man's name, rank and regiment.

'Whose handwriting is this?'

'His.'

'What did he do before the war?'

'He claims he was a farmer, a Cossack from the River Don. His father taught him his letters.' Reaching into his pocket again, the soldier pulled out a photograph. 'We also found this on him.'

Bogoleev studied the picture of the modestly dressed woman with her three children. Flipping it over, he read the other side.

'It is from Moscow,' the soldier added.

Bogoleev read the sender's name: Marina.

'If he is a spy, then he has certainly gone to a lot of trouble to appear authentic.' Bogoleev placed the folded paper and the photo in his breast pocket. 'All the same, we must be cautious. Until we can verify this man's identity against *Stavka*'s records, keep a close watch on him. Don't let him draw anyone into dialogue about the army's plans.'

'Yes, Captain.'

'Dismissed.' Bogoleev saluted.

Alone again, Bogoleev turned his gaze back to the flames. He needed time to think. If the man was a spy, he could jeopardise the entire offensive.

Rising to his feet, Bogoleev decided to see the man for himself. Pulling back the flaps of the tent, he walked into the dressing-station. A nurse stepped forward, holding out a hand to stop him.

'I'm sorry, Captain, but we are very busy at the moment.'

'I need to speak to the man they brought in a little while ago.'

'Come back tomorrow morning after we have finished sorting through –'

'I wish to see him now,' Bogoleev insisted.

Taken aback, the nurse pointed to a cot at the far end of the tent.

The man was asleep and the soldier stationed to guard him dozed on a chair next to him. Bogoleev woke the soldier with a small kick to the heel of one boot. The soldier's eyes opened then, seeing the captain, he jumped to his feet.

'At ease, soldier.' Bogoleev saluted. 'I wish to be alone with the Cossack.'

Bogoleev sat on the chair vacated by the soldier. Studying the man by the light of the candle, he tried to decide whether he really was who he claimed. Despite the gaunt cheeks, he had the broad, strong features of a Cossack. His right cheekbone sat at an irregular angle that gave one side of his face a grotesque look.

How had he escaped the Germans? Bogoleev wondered. Leaning forward, he narrowed his eyes. Was he a spy sent by the enemy?

The Russians had long suspected that the Germans had cracked their codes and intercepted telephone calls. However, suspicion that the information was passed to Germans through a network of spies had never been ruled out either. Leaning back in his chair, Bogoleev pulled out the folded piece of paper with the soldier's name and opened it.

'Leo Nicholaevich Ivanov.' Bogoleev read aloud.

At the sound of his name, the man's eyes opened.

'Good evening, Corporal,' Bogoleev said amiably.

The man's face turned towards him.

'Water,' he said hoarsely, and ran his tongue across his lips. 'I need some water.'

'Nurse! This man needs water.'

The nurse gave Bogoleev a dark look but did as he asked. Propping up Ivanov's head, she brought the cup to his lips.

'Thank you.' Ivanov closed his eyes as the nurse lowered his head back to the cot.

'How do you feel?' Bogoleev asked.

'Like I've been put through a meat grinder.'

Bogoleev nodded once. He wondered if it was too soon to interrogate him. Deciding that Ivanov – if that was his real name – was more likely to trip when tired and not thinking straight, Bogoleev decided to ask him a few questions straight away and study his reaction.

'They tell me you escaped from a POW camp.' Bogoleev kept his voice light to avoid arousing the man's suspicions.

Ivanov nodded without opening his eyes.

'How did you escape?'

'I killed a German.'

The words came out flat but Bogoleev noticed Ivanov's body tense as he said them.

'How did you do it?'

Ivanov slowly opened his eyes and Bogoleev was surprised to see them brimming in the candlelight.

'I plunged his own dagger into his throat.' Ivanov paused, then added in a softer voice, 'He choked on his own blood.'

'That was a courageous act. You deserve a medal.'

'I did what I had to do. I place no pride in taking another man's life.' Ivanov turned his face fully to Bogoleev. 'The army can reward me by letting me visit my family.'

'In time. Right now, we may be on the cusp of a major victory.'

Ivanov gave a hollow laugh. 'Victory or defeat, Captain, I've had enough of bloodshed. I'll be happy just to see my family.'

At that moment, Bogoleev was certain Ivanov was who he claimed to be. If a spy, he'd be eager to boast about his heroic deeds and push to learn more about the upcoming offensive. Instead, he showed little interest in either. There was still a possibility that he was a deserter and, having got lost, had stumbled back into the Russian trenches. Bogoleev thought he'd try a different tactic. He showed Ivanov the paper with his details.

'Is this your hand?'

Ivanov nodded.

'It's unusual for a farmer to have such beautiful handwriting.'

'My father insisted that his children, including his daughter, learn their letters.' Ivanov let out a chuckle. 'He made us practise writing them every night. I was just good at it. And a lucky thing, too, because it helped me land a job behind the lines as a clerk for a while.'

Pulling the photograph from his breast pocket, Bogoleev pretended to study the faces. In his peripheral vision he could see Ivanov watching him silently.

'You have a handsome family.'

The words seemed to unhinge Ivanov. 'I've never held my son.'

'Your family is from Moscow?'

Ivanov shook his head. 'No, we come from the steppes. My wife and children moved to the city with her sister during her third trimester.'

'How are they faring?'

'They are struggling, same as everyone.' Ivanov coughed; the strain of talking was making him weaker.

'I'll leave you to rest.' Bogoleev rose to his feet. 'We'll talk some more tomorrow.'

'May I ask a question?'

Bogoleev stopped. 'Of course.'

'Why do I need someone guarding me?'

'It's just a precaution.' Bogoleev waved a hand as if it was of no importance. 'You have been through a lot and with the nurses and doctors run off their feet we want to make sure you're not forgotten.'

He called the guard over. 'Be sure he is well looked after.' He could tell his answer did not convince the Cossack.

'Captain?'

'Yes, Corporal?'

'May I please have my picture back?'

Bogoleev handed it to him, hesitating briefly to cast a last look at the family. 'If I had a family as beautiful as yours, I'd try to escape and return to them.'

Ivanov said nothing, not looking up from the picture.

33

The Brusilov Offensive, June 1916

Thick clouds of smoke hung low over the trench-marked plain. For the past few hours, the Russian army had been pounding the Austro-Hungarians with their artillery as part of a coordinated effort to break through the enemy's lines. Lowering his binoculars, General Brusilov handed them to Bogoleev.

'What news?' Brusilov asked, walking briskly to where several commanders crowded around a map.

'Early reports are promising. Our troops have broken through the first line of trenches.'

Brusilov nodded, pleased. 'And the Austrian reserves?'

'Taken by surprise; they've been stretched and are opening up huge gaps.'

The generals moved to allow Brusilov to study the large maps. Bogoleev waited at a respectable distance behind them. The field communicators from the four points of battle continuously reported their advances and the results were dutifully marked on the maps. Brusilov looked down at the table. Little red dots marked the advance of the five Russian armies.

'Gentlemen . . .' Brusilov raised his eyes. 'I believe victory may be at hand.'

At dusk, Bogoleev stood before his assembled men. He had already inspected them to ensure all guns were properly cleaned and ammunition pouches were full.

'This is an important day,' he began. 'Yesterday our guns silenced the Austrians' artillery, breaking through their first line of defence. Today, it's our turn. Moving through the tunnels, we wait for orders to attack the trenches.'

Bogoleev paused, searching for words to inspire his men.

'We are close to achieving a major victory for our beloved Russia.' Taking a breath, he concluded, 'As sons of Russia this is the definitive moment in our lives. This is our chance to bring honour to ourselves and glory to our motherland. This will be our finest hour!'

Standing shoulder to shoulder, the men held their rifles poised over the lip of parapets. Above them shells howled through thick, soupy air. With each explosion, the sky glowed red then settled into black. Having lost any sense of time, Bogoleev could not remember how long they had been waiting in the trenches. Since the guns had begun their thunder, the noise had grown until it seemed like a single dull roar. He knew the shelling would gradually slow to individual bursts, indicating the time for the infantry's attack.

His men waited silently alongside him. Shells landing close to the trenches made nervous recruits jump. One of them, sensing Bogoleev's eyes on him, dropped his head in embarrassment.

'What's your name, son?'

'Igor Alexandrivich Andropov, Captain.'

Another shell exploded, throwing dirt and ash over their heads. Bogoleev put a hand out to steady himself. Andropov, his body pressed to the wall, crossed his arms over his head.

'It's alright.' Bogoleev placed a hand on the young man's shoulder. Cocking his ear to the sound of the artillery, he added, 'I think the guns are starting to slow down.'

Andropov looked down at his feet with an agonised stare.

'Captain!' The voice came from down the trench. Faces turned to the lieutenant squeezing his way between the men. 'The order has come.' The lieutenant saluted. 'We are to attack.'

The sky was a trace lighter by the time the men prepared to climb the parapets. Bogoleev waited with tense fingers curled around his rifle. His senses, at their sharpest before a battle, felt as if they were balanced on a knife's edge. He wiped at the sweat on his brow.

Suddenly, officers along the line blew on their whistles. Torrents of men poured over the parapets and ran at the Austrian trenches. Behind them, Russian guns pounded the enemy, the explosions shooting up walls of fire in the trenches. Sporadic gunfire rattled from the Austrian lines, white sparks glowing against the darkness and the smoke.

'Take cover!' Bogoleev threw himself into a crater. A body slumped next to him but he had no time to see who it was. Leaping to his feet again, he charged, spearing a man with his bayonet as he jumped over. Before long, his men had secured the first line of trenches.

Joined by a second regiment, Bogoleev's men stormed another line of enemy trenches, trapping the Austrians within.

By the time the sun had worked its way up the sky, the fields were quiet. Bogoleev took stock of his men. Half had fallen. Stretcher-bearers carried the worst of the wounded back to the field hospital. The remaining wounded leant against the walls, waiting for their turn.

Bogoleev was on his way to the kitchen when he saw Andropov being stretchered to the field hospital. The young face was bleached grey and his eyes were closed. The bearers lowered the stretcher to the ground next to a long row of casualties. Kneeling beside Andropov, the medic cut away at the bandages to inspect the wound.

'How is he?' Bogoleev asked.

'He took a bullet through the knee,' the medic responded without taking his eyes off his task. 'He's lost a lot of blood.'

Bogoleev looked at Andropov's pale lips and felt a twinge of sadness.

'Will he walk again?'

The medic gave Bogoleev a sidelong look.

'Not on two legs,' he said and moved to the next patient.

In the hospital, news of Brusilov's victory was celebrated with bottles of vodka. The nurses rationed it among the patients, who passed the bottle around, taking turns to swig at the neck.

'To Brusilov!' The man in the bed next to Ivanov raised the bottle.

The sharpness of the alcohol made Ivanov's throat and chest burn. Once the pain subsided, the alcohol's steady warmth spread through his body, relaxing the tension in his muscles. He stretched his legs, luxuriating in the crisp white sheets. He had been transferred from the field hospital to one further behind the lines, from where he would be transferred to Moscow on the hospital train.

At a nearby village, the Grand Duchess Vladimir's hospital train waited at the station. Throughout the afternoon and early evening, wounded soldiers were brought on carts and wagons, and officers arrived in motor-ambulances.

It had been raining steadily and there was no cover over the platform, which was packed with stretchers carrying the wounded. After several hours of waiting, Ivanov's clothes and thin blankets were soaked.

At last nurses in Red Cross uniforms began to help the wounded to board the train. Ivanov was to share a cabin with ten other men.

'Thank you, nurse,' he said to the young woman who showed him to his bunk. There was something familiar about her. It was nothing he could pinpoint; more like a feeling that hovered just beyond the reach of his consciousness. Sensing Ivanov's eyes on her, the nurse reddened and ducked her head.

'You look familiar,' Ivanov said by way of explanation.

The nurse lifted her grey eyes and smiled self-consciously.

He was about to ask the nurse her name when the door of the

cabin opened and in stepped an elderly lady with steel-grey hair. The nurses straightened and stood to attention.

'I am the Grand Duchess Vladimir,' she told the men. 'My train will transport you to Moscow where you will be admitted to hospital. My nurses will see to it that your needs are fully met.' She smiled unexpectedly. 'Each one of you is a hero in our eyes and we hope to repay a small part of our immense debt to you by ensuring you have a safe and comfortable journey.'

'What utter garbage,' one of the soldiers muttered after the grand duchess had left. 'While we die in the trenches and our families starve at home, them lot eat caviar and compete over which one of them is working the hardest for the war effort.'

'Don't complain,' said the soldier in the bunk below him. 'For the next two days, we'll be resting between clean sheets and eating proper food.'

Ivanov rolled onto his back and stared at the ceiling. He could not shake the thought that somehow he knew the nurse. He was still thinking of her when the train jolted and left the station. Soothed by the carriage's rhythmic rocking, he soon fell asleep.

Marie followed the grand duchess out of the cabin, letting the door close softly behind her. She had agreed to join the hospital train in the hope that looking after the soldiers would help take her mind off her grief. Transferring from the officers' hospital at Tsarskoe Selo had been no use. She felt Alexei's presence everywhere. On a rare visit, she stopped at the library and spent a wretched hour staring at the same page without comprehending a single word. The one time the librarian approached her, she had burst into tears, frightening the old man. Staying in Petrograd or escaping to Narva also proved futile. Every stall, street corner, theatre and building reminded her of Nikolai and Pyotr's absence.

Finally, she had contacted the Grand Duchess Vladimir and volunteered to join her train. She had thought her volunteer work at the hospital would have equipped her for what she was going to find at the front, but as soon as she stepped off the train and looked at the ghostly faces, she knew nothing could have prepared her. More than anything, she found the way the soldiers stared at her so openly disconcerting.

She remembered a piece of advice the grand duchess had given her as they readied the carriages to receive the soliders. 'These men have been separated from their sweethearts for a long time,' she'd said. 'It's only natural that the first young girl they meet is going to remind them of their lover. Be kind, but brisk.'

Marie hadn't detected any lust or love in the Cossack's eyes when he stared at her, but still, the scrutiny had made her uncomfortable.

34

Moscow, June 1916

Clouds of steam rose from both sides of the train, briefly obscuring those waiting on the platform.

'We're here!' one of the soldiers said excitedly. 'Moscow!'

Pressing his face against the small grimy window, Ivanov searched the crowd outside.

The grand duchess entered the cabin, followed by two of the nurses.

'Gentlemen, you will be alighting shortly. There are carts and carriages waiting to transport you to the hospital.'

Stepping off the train, Ivanov sat down midway along the platform with his back against a wall. Orderlies and nurses with Red Cross armbands rushed about, lifting and carrying the worst of the wounded to the waiting motor-ambulances. Scanning the faces rushing past him, Ivanov wondered anxiously whether Marina had received his letter in time. He saw the grey-eyed nurse, who had come into his carriage on the first day, help a wounded officer off the train. He had only seen her that once, yet he still felt that he knew her from somewhere. He watched as she helped the officer to a wheelchair and placed a blanket over his lap.

Puzzled, he shook his head and looked away, his eyes falling on a slim woman walking among the wounded. Wearing a printed scarf and clutching a toddler to her chest, she stepped carefully between the outstretched limbs, her eyes scanning each face hopefully.

Marina!

A well of emotion surged inside him, pressing at his chest. He whispered her name. 'Marina.'

At the same moment, the woman's body went rigid and she turned her head. It was impossible that she would have heard him yet as if by instinct her eyes sought and found his. A cry burst from her lips and she rushed towards him, not so careful any more where her feet landed.

'Lyova!' Dropping to her knees, she showered his face with kisses. 'Lyova, Lyova, Lyova!' She repeated his name with every kiss. 'My love, my heart. I was so worried I would never see you again.' Tears pooled in her eyes as she traced the scar on his cheek. Taking her wrist, he brought her fingers to his lips and kissed them.

Pressed between the two adults, the little boy started to protest. Pulling away, Marina turned him around and, for the first time, Ivanov beheld his son. The boy had inherited his mother's brown almond-shaped eyes. Sitting on his mother's lap, he stared shyly at his father.

'I named him after you,' Marina said, then murmured to her son, 'Meet your papa, Leo Leonovich.'

The toddler wriggled in his mother's arms. Marina placed his small feet on the ground and the child took a few steps then fell onto Ivanov's leg.

'Careful you don't hurt Papa,' Marina said with a laugh and gathered the child back into her arms. 'Where will they take you?' she asked.

Ivanov shrugged. 'I think they said Golitsyn Hospital.'

'I've been doing a little volunteer work there. I'll be able to visit you.'

'What about the children?'

'You've been away nearly two years. The children have grown. Tanya is almost a woman. She's been a great help.'

'We will have to start considering a suitable match for her,' Ivanov teased.

'There will be plenty of time for that after the war.' Her smile dropped and her face grew serious. 'For now we need to concentrate on getting you back to health.'

Around them, those men who could walk were summoned to the transport that would take them to hospital. Walking beside him, Marina held tight to Ivanov's hand. When they reached the wagon, she stood on tiptoe and kissed him.

'I love you,' she whispered against his lips, and sealed her words with a second, longer kiss.

Marie saw the woman holding the child kiss the soldier a second time. Watching them, a spark of jealousy flashed through her. She felt her chest tighten and immediately regretted it, chastising herself for wishing another couple's happiness for herself.

She had never felt so alone, needy for someone with whom to share her thoughts. And secrets. And desires. She longed to be held, to feel strong arms around her. To be kissed.

She wanted Alexei.

She could not forget him. As God was her witness, she had tried. Riddled with guilt, she tried again and again to push him out of her head. Yet despite her struggles, her thoughts steadfastly held on to him. Throughout the day, she kept up the pretence to herself that he meant little to her. But in the bewitching hour before sleep, when her defences were at their lowest ebb, she couldn't hold back her thoughts, and the memory of their kiss blazed through her like a firestorm. His scent returned to flood her senses. She felt the touch of his moist lips and grew weak against the pressure of his hand pulling her face towards his.

While Alexei grew more alive in her mind, images of Pyotr dissolved like snowflakes. It alarmed her how quickly he was fading from her memory. She was already forgetting certain details: the exact colour of his eyes or if his chin dimpled when he smiled. But even as the edges faded, she clung to the final threads, worried he might never return should these last strands be set adrift.

Having been helped onto the back of the wagon, the Cossack soldier was now sitting in a corner. Marie searched her memory for the soldier's name. Maybe he had never offered it and she, unsettled by his scrutiny, had never asked. It did not matter now, she thought. They came from different worlds and were unlikely to meet again.

As the wagon pulled away, Marie saw the woman carrying the little boy step off the kerb and, ignoring the protests and shouts of drivers, stand in the street waving after the wagon until it had vanished from view.

35

Petrograd, January 1917

Katya stood among a crowd lining the bridge, staring down at the frozen Neva River. A handful of policemen hovered over a hole in the ice into which a diver had disappeared a few minutes ago. A chilling wind was blowing but no one wanted to move. All eyes were fixed on the frozen expanse of the river and the black figures that stood in the middle of it. Finally, the diver emerged and was helped onto the ice by the policemen. He was holding one end of a thick rope, which he passed to the policemen and the crowd gasped as the men pulled on it and dragged up a body from the freezing water.

'It's the Tsarina's holy man, Rasputin,' someone whispered, and the words spread through the crowd.

'May his spirit burn in eternal hell,' a woman spat.

'And same goes for his German whore,' muttered another.

The words were uttered just loudly enough for those standing close by to hear.

Katya turned to leave. Hurrying, she weaved through the traffic to the other side of the street. She was already late to make the breadline and did not look forward to the prospect of spending the remainder of the morning standing in the queue only to be turned away when the bread ran out. Quickening her step, she felt irritated with herself for wasting time at the bridge.

They had never made it to Warsaw. When the Germans invaded the city, Katya and Fyodor had again joined the exodus of refugees, this time to Petrograd, arriving at the start of winter. They found lodging in a squalid single room run by an elderly widow. Though she looked fragile, Madame Ozerova was a shrewd woman who insisted on prompt payment. Having very little money, Katya begged her to give them an advance on their rent until she could find a job.

'The city is full of refugees and all of them looking for a place out of the cold,' Ozerova told her. 'Why should I grant you an exception?'

'You don't have to,' Katya said. 'The boy and I have come a long way. We've lost everything. We don't expect handouts, we're willing to work for our lodging.'

The widow had looked at the two of them speculatively.

'Alright,' she said finally. 'I'm too soft, that has always been my curse.' She raised one hand to show Katya the knotted fingers crooked with arthritis. 'These crippled hands are not much help to me any more.' She buried them again in the folds of her thick shawl. 'They always feel worse in winter.'

'I have some ointments that can help relieve the pain.'

'I don't want any of your gypsy witchcraft,' Ozerova retorted. 'First thing tomorrow morning, you empty the chamber-pots, then you scrub the staircase. As for the boy, my legs don't hold up standing in the breadline all day. He needs to be at the queue by six, otherwise there will be none left by the time his turn comes. Do you understand?'

Fyodor nodded.

'What's the matter with the boy?' Ozerova looked Fyodor up and down. 'Is he mute?'

'He's very quiet,' Katya said quickly. 'You'll have no problems with him.'

'You'd better be right, because the first sign of trouble and I'll throw both of you out into the street.' Taking her cane from where it leant against the wall, Ozerova walked to the stairs. After labouring up a few steps she turned and, seeing that they had not followed, shouted, 'What's the matter with you? Have you turned into a pair of statues?'

She showed them to a room with a single cot covered by a thin mattress and a small table that listed to one side. A window looked down on the busy street. In the corner, a stove sat cold.

'In this wretched city, the only people who can afford to keep a warm stove are the aristocracy and the bourgeoisie,' Ozerova said bitterly. 'The rest of us have to scrape and beg for a handful of coal.' She handed Katya the key. 'There's a spare chamber-pot downstairs if you want it.'

Gathering her courage Katya asked if the widow could also spare them some food. 'We've had nothing to eat all day,' she pleaded.

'I'm not running a charity,' Ozerova snapped, but when Fyodor went downstairs with her to retrieve the chamber-pot, she gave him a small parcel wrapped in newspaper. Upstairs, they opened the bundle to find a large slice of bread, a stick of salami and some cheese.

Katya turned the corner and cursed to find the line already snaking around the block. She looked up and down for Fyodor. When she couldn't spot him, she joined the queue and was surprised to find news of Rasputin's death had already reached those ahead of her.

'I heard the Emperor finally woke up to the fact his wife was that swine's mistress and ordered his execution,' a woman said.

'Bah!' said another, waving a dismissive hand. 'The Emperor is too busy with the war. My Vadya wrote in his last letter that things are deteriorating in the trenches. They have now lost all the territory they won during the Brusilov Offensive.'

The women tutted and shook their heads.

'While our men eat bullets and suffer from frostbite, we starve behind the lines,' said the first woman. 'People are fed up.' Lowering her voice, she checked to see that she would not be overheard. 'We've been on a strike in our factory for several days and it looks as if we'll remain that way for some time to come.'

Standing among them, Katya remained silent, offering no opinion.

'I've seen you around Vyborg,' the second woman said abruptly, turning to face Katya. 'You're often walking with that boy.' A few other women turned and looked at Katya as if noticing her for the first time. 'Do you work in one of the plants?'

Katya nodded, feeling her cheeks turning red at having so many eyes on her.

'You have started only recently.' The woman's eyes narrowed with suspicion.

'We are new in Petrograd,' Katya explained, confused as to whether the woman's last comment had been a statement or a question.

The eyes lingered on Katya's face as if deciding whether she could be trusted. Suddenly a youth with his cap pulled low darted forward and began pressing pamphlets into the women's hands.

'Stop the imperialistic tyranny,' he said in a low hurried tone. 'Join the workers' Soviet.'

Katya waited in the line until it became clear that the bread had run out. The women's disappointment at having to leave empty-handed spilled into anger at the baker, accusing him of hoarding the flour. Arguments broke out and someone threw a rock at the shop window, shattering the glass. Katya left as the police arrived to disperse the crowd.

Walking back to her flat, Katya hoped Fyodor might have had better luck. She ran up the stairs, taking them two at a time. Behind her, the widow's voice bellowed from the bottom floor. 'Where have you been? The boy has not given me my bread. You wretched thief, you are trying to rob me of my meagre rations.'

Closing the door behind her, Katya found Fyodor at the stove, feeding something into it. A single loaf sat in the centre of the table. Katya covered the space between the door and the table in three quick steps and cut a large slice of bread as Madame Ozerova's heavy fist banged loudly on the door.

'Open the door this minute. I know you are trying to hide from me. Shame on you, robbing an old woman of her last morsel of bread.'

Katya opened the door and, before the old woman could say another word, pressed the bread into her hands.

'I'm sorry, Madame Ozerova, but I arrived late and missed out. Please, this is half of what Fedya managed to get with our coupons.'

'I heard you leave before the sun was up.' Madame Ozerova's face wrinkled into deeper creases. 'Where did you go?'

'I saw a crowd gathered along the Petrovsky Bridge and was distracted. I'm sorry, it won't happen again.'

'Stay away from them revolutionary types,' the old woman warned, misunderstanding the reason for the gathering on the bridge. 'No good will come of them.'

Katya closed the door behind the widow, letting out a small sigh. Turning, she looked at Fyodor, who looked back at her with a mischievous smile.

'What is it, Fedya?' she asked, the corners of her lips lifting also.

'I met a revolutionary coming back from the bakery,' he said, still smiling. 'He gave me five rubles to distribute these pamphlets for him.' Bringing his hands from behind his back, Fyodor showed Katya the bundle of papers he carried.

'Fedya, if the police catch you with those, you'll be arrested and charged with treason.'

'I did not hand out a single one,' Fyodor said quickly. Motioning to the stove with his chin, he added, 'I fed them to the stove instead.'

For the first time, Katya noticed the warmth wafting from the stove. 'Fedya!' she said, laughing. Remembering she still carried a pamphlet herself, she reached into her pocket. Too frightened to read it in the open, she had carried it home to read in private.

'*Join the workers' Soviet*,' she read aloud, '*and put an end to the imperialist war that has bled our country, killed our men, starved our women and made orphans of our children. Bring glory back to Russia! Join the workers' Soviet!*'

Katya was aware of the Soviet meetings from overhearing whispers at the plant, but she had never attended one. Reading the pamphlet a second time, she felt a stirring of emotion begin to swirl. Folding the paper carefully, she slipped it back into her pocket.

'I am sick of having my children go hungry every day.'

The women working turned from their machines to look at Larissa. Standing with her hands on her hips, Larissa's usually laughing eyes flashed with anger.

'Two days in a row I've missed out on bread. How am I going to feed my family?'

'I don't have two sticks to rub together to fend off this freezing cold,' said another.

'I say we should go on strike until the government gives us bread,' Larissa said.

'And coal,' added a third voice.

'I say we go on strike now!' Larissa punched her fist into her open palm.

'Strike! Strike! Strike!'

As more and more women joined the call for a strike, Katya remained rooted at her post, torn. Part of her wanted to join with them, but who would look after Fyodor if she was arrested?

'Let's head to the men's factory,' shouted Larissa over the noise.

The doors were pushed open and Katya, caught in the press of women, had no choice but to follow. Outside the icy air whipped at her arms and legs. Taking shelter in a doorway, she watched the women march across the courtyard to the men's section. Throwing snowballs at the windows, they beckoned the men to come outside. Among the faces pressing against the window, Katya spotted Fyodor. A few minutes later, he came out, following a group of young men holding aloft a red flag.

The chanting, which had started with, 'We want bread! We want coal!' soon turned to 'Down with the imperialistic regime!' and 'No more war!' Moving through the factory gates, the crowd headed down the street.

'Fyodor!' Katya called, worried, but the boy didn't hear her.

Katya followed the crowd, keeping her eyes on Fyodor and trying to push through the crush of people to reach him. A few times, she lost sight of him and her heart hammered in panic. The crowd continued to swell, and more people stood between her and the boy. Someone started to sing 'La Marseillaise' and the crowd joined in.

Up ahead, the crowd came to a stop. Craning her neck, Katya saw soldiers blocking the road. As more people also noticed them, the singing died away.

'Turn around and go back,' the commanding officer shouted to the crowd.

'We want bread, we are starving,' a woman shouted back. 'Our children are freezing. We have no coal.'

'There is a war on.' The officer squared his shoulders. 'We all have to shoulder the burden.'

'We're tired of war. We want peace.'

Katya started to squeeze through the crowd towards Fyodor.

'If you don't disperse immediately, I have orders to shoot,' the officer warned.

Grabbing Fyodor's arm, Katya pulled him towards her. 'We need to get out of here.'

Fyodor shook his head. 'I'm not leaving.'

'Soldiers, take aim,' called the officer.

A deathly silence descended.

Nobody moved.

All eyes were focused on the raised weapons. Surely the soldiers wouldn't fire on unarmed citizens?

'Fedya!' Katya tugged at the boy's arm. 'We must leave *now*.'

'I'm not leaving,' he replied tersely. 'I can look after myself.'

'FIRE!'

Katya shut her eyes, her right hand flying across her body in the sign of the cross. A long second passed before Katya realised nothing had happened. Opening her eyes, she saw the soldiers still in position, their rifles aimed at the crowd.

'I said FIRE!' shouted the officer, his face turning red.

Still nothing happened. The crowd started to stir.

Pulling out his pistol, the officer pressed it against the temple of the nearest soldier.

'Did you not hear me, soldier?'

Katya used all her strength to pull Fyodor behind her into a side street.

Crack!

The guns fired into the crowd.

'Run, Fyodor!' Katya pushed him ahead of her, not letting him turn to see what was happening to the crowd. Behind them, bullets were fired into the screaming throng.

36

Petrograd, February 1917

The early morning sun lit the tips of St Isaac's domes. Marie sat at her table close to the French doors, oblivious to the view, her tea growing cold by her elbow. The temperature had dropped sharply but inside they had a warm fire. The coal shortage had forced them to grow frugal, and they only lit the fire for a few hours in the morning and again in the evening, while for the rest of the day they wore deerskin coats to keep warm.

Outside, the faint sound of people shouting grew louder. Lifting her head Marie listened. The angry voices, partially muffled by the thick glass panes, came from the street directly below.

Anna appeared in the doorway and walked over to the balcony door. Marie stood to join her. As she opened the door, a blast of cold air rushed at them, making their eyes water.

Strikes and demonstrations had become part of daily life. The security police and the Petrograd garrison had initially managed to disperse the demonstrators but, more recently, the soldiers had refused to fire on women and children. Stepping out onto the small balcony, Marie looked down at the angry mob.

'The revolution has started,' the people below cried to the faces appearing at the windows. 'All power to the workers! Down with the imperialist regime!'

'What's happened?' a neighbour called out.

A man was about to answer when shots rang out and the crowd scattered, swallowed by the narrow side streets.

Anna's fingers fastened around Marie's arm. 'We'd better go inside.'

Marie, mesmerised by the scene, didn't move.

'Please,' Anna persisted, tugging at Marie's arm. 'It might get dangerous.'

Marie allowed herself to be pulled inside and Anna closed the doors, turning the large key in the lock. 'Do you suppose it's true?'

Detecting the quiver in Anna's voice, Marie placed an arm around her narrow shoulders.

'Don't worry,' she said. 'This will soon pass.' But even as she spoke the reassuring words, Marie struggled to believe them.

Pskov, March

Tsar Nicholas sat behind the desk in his private carriage. Travelling from the military headquarters in Mogilev, his train was detained in Pskov, less than a day's journey from Petrograd.

Since the murder of Rasputin, Alexandra had taken to bed, grief-stricken. Unable to leave her side, Nicholas had not returned to the front, spending his time at their palace in Tsarskoe Selo instead. He was aware of the mounting disorder in Petrograd but had hoped people's wartime patriotism would eventually triumph over any revolutionary sentiments.

Pale yellow light from his lamp spilled over the telegrams strewn across a map of the eastern front. Picking up pages at random, his shoulders gave an involuntary shudder at the repeated requests for his abdication. He reread the telegram from his uncle, the Grand Duke Nicholas.

I beg you on bended knee to avoid bloodshed and abdicate the throne.

He dropped the telegram back on top of the pile of papers. Grief squeezed his throat. He stood and paced the carriage. Pausing at the window, he looked blankly at the stretch of densely packed pine and cedar trees, capped with snow. On the horizon, the pale sun sank, taking with it the last of the day's warmth. Watching the sky change, Nicholas chewed absently at the inside of his lip.

He checked his watch. It would not be long now. The air in the carriage felt stale yet he did not move to open the window. Pulling at his collar, he tried to relieve its noose-like grip on his throat but eventually gave up and slumped on the chair by the window, waiting for the end to arrive.

It was dark when the second train slowed and stopped. Two figures, wrapped in heavy coats with their heads bent against the cold bite of the night air, alighted and walked hurriedly towards the royal train. Watching them approach, Nicholas recognised Guchkov and Shulgin, members of the state Duma. Returning to sit at his desk, Nicholas felt the heavy hand of dread closing around him. He took a breath and readied himself for what was to come.

Guchkov and Shulgin entered the carriage and for a moment stood nervously, as if wondering whether they should bow. The Tsar saved the men from their embarrassment by waving them over.

'Gentlemen, let's get this over as quickly as possible.'

Picking up his pen, Nicholas signed the papers the men placed before him. And although his expression was set, he could feel the pinpricks of tears stabbing at his eyes.

37

Petrograd, March 1917

Marie sat across from Princess Maria, staring mutely into her teacup. Since Pyotr had been declared missing, Marie had called on the princess regularly, though Pyotr's absence loomed large in the silences between them and their conversations were invariably strained and awkward.

Today, the princess had sent for Marie to inform her she was leaving Petrograd.

'With the Emperor abdicating, our future here is uncertain.' She stirred her tea slowly. 'Things seem to be a little better in the south. I've left instructions with the staff to notify me if there is . . . well . . . in case there is any word from Pyotr.'

Marie nodded, her throat constricting.

The princess reached across the table and touched Marie's hand.

'It's been almost three years since we last heard anything from him.' The princess dropped her chin. 'Maybe we should consider the possibility that he's not coming back.'

Marie felt the room spin around her. 'How could you say such a thing?' She pulled her hand away.

Flinching at the harshness of Marie's voice, the princess retreated to her seat. 'Don't for one minute assume that I feel no pain. I carried that child inside me and felt him grow. I rejoiced in his every turn and kick and prayed that God would grant him a long and happy life.' She dabbed at the corner of one eye with a handkerchief. 'The day he introduced me to you, I thought all my prayers had been answered. I would give my life to have him back. But it seems that when it comes to war, God is on no mother's side.' She looked at Marie earnestly. 'You are still so young, Marie; don't throw away your chance to find happiness with someone else.'

Marie immediately thought of Alexei and blushed.

'Maybe you have met someone already,' the princess remarked.

Unable to hold the princess's watchful gaze, Marie's eyes dropped.

'There's no need to feel ashamed,' the princess said, a hint of sadness creeping into her voice. 'Seeking happiness is never something to be ashamed of.' She sighed. 'I am sure it is what Pyotr would want,' she added.

Leaving the palace, Marie politely refused the offer of a carriage. She needed to think and decided she would walk. The sky was bright and clear and everywhere the streets were quiet, but the roadblocks, barricades and charred remains of buildings were reminders of the city's tensions. Wrapping her coat around her, she walked along the footpath, the princess's words echoing in her head. Maybe Pyotr's mother was right. Maybe it was time to stop grieving and start living.

Arriving home, Marie headed straight to her room. Taking off her coat, she sat before her dressing table, staring at her reflection. Then, opening one of the drawers, she pulled out Pyotr's diary. Her heart somersaulting, she turned to the back, where she kept his last letter. Marie's eyes filled with tears as she read his final words to her.

Together again, we would never part. I beg you to wait for me.

Tides of emotion swirled and drove against her chest. She lowered her head, one hand resting on the diary. She was still sitting there, anchored to her seat by grief, when Anna came in to help her get ready for dinner.

Once dressed, Marie held out the diary to Anna. Hesitating,

Anna took the small leather-bound book and flicked through the pages. 'This is Pyotr's.'

Marie lifted her eyes. 'I want you to take it away.' She spoke the words softly, her voice caught and pulled by an invisible force from within.

'Are you sure?'

Marie nodded, tears flooding her vision.

'What do you want me to do with it?'

Marie's shoulders slumped. She dropped her eyes. 'Do what you think is best.'

'Marie . . .'

'Anna, please.' She bit down on her fist. 'Take it away before I change my mind.'

Anna placed a hand on Marie's shoulder. 'Maybe it's for the best,' she said.

A quiver passed through Marie. 'Yes,' she said. 'I think so too.'

'Is there something I can do for you?'

Marie shook her head, not able to speak and not able to look Anna in the eyes. For a moment, she considered confessing, to unburden herself from the guilt she carried. But even as her eyes turned to Anna, her throat clamped. She couldn't do it. Anna would not understand.

'What is it, Marie?' Anna's look was full of concern. 'Would you like me to send your apologies to your uncle? Tell them you are not well?'

'No,' she said. 'I just need a few minutes on my own.'

After Anna had gone, Marie again opened her drawer, this time to retrieve a letter she kept in a bundle between other letters from her family. Untying the ribbon, she found the one she was looking for. Her heart sped at the sight of Alexei's handwriting. Holding the envelope close to her face, she inhaled, but any scent the letter once may have held had long disappeared.

Unfolding the single piece of paper, she read the few lines.

Dearest Marie,

Her body ached to hear him whisper her name again.

> *I know this is an impossible dream, the mere infatuations of a foolish man . . . How I wish I was ten years younger. I would have fought to win your affections.*

She wondered if he still felt the same way, or if he had long forgotten her. She read the words again – *fought to win your affections.*

'This is foolish!' she said aloud. 'You know what officers are like, Marie. Besides, he's a married man. You must forget him!'

But even as she uttered the words, her heart unhinged at the hope of meeting him again. Memories of their days in Tsarskoe Selo slipped across her mind like scenes from a dream.

An exhausted sigh escaped her lips. 'That's all it is,' she told herself, 'a dream.'

Feeling hollow, she stared at her reflection in the mirror. Slowly, a stern look hardened around her eyes.

'It's time you grew up,' she told herself.

Getting to her feet, she reached for the shawl Anna had laid out on the bed. Hesitating at the door, she inhaled then, stepping through, shut it decisively behind her.

38

Moscow, April 1917

Once discharged from hospital, Ivanov joined his family at Dmitry and Tamara's apartment. His family slept in the tiny living room, while Dmitry and his wife had the bedroom. On his first weekend home, Tamara and Dmitry treated the children to an afternoon in the park, leaving Marina and Ivanov to be on their own.

In the afternoon light, Marina stood before him as he sat on the bed. With her back to him, she pulled out her hairpins, then shook her head so that her hair cascaded over her shoulders in a river of gold. Ivanov suddenly felt shy as his wife unbuttoned her shirt and then her skirt and let them drop to the floor. She turned and his gaze moved down the length of her, pausing at the dark shadow between her legs.

'You've gone grey,' she remarked. 'It makes you look distinguished.' Moving closer, she traced the silver strands growing at his temple, then ran her fingers lightly, gently down to where the broken bones caved into his face. And her smile disappeared.

Removing her hand, Ivanov brought it to his lips and kissed each finger in turn. He had spent countless nights dreaming of her, recalling the press of her fingers as she held him close, gripping his back like her life depended on it. Wrapping his arms around her, he thought back to the long lonely nights when all had seemed lost. It was thoughts of returning to her, to her warm, welcoming arms, that had sustained him and given him strength. Without even knowing it, she had saved him. Because of her, he had wanted to live. Nuzzling his face against her neck, he inhaled the sweet lavender scent of her soap on her skin.

She took his hand and placed it over her left breast. He could feel her heart beating in her ribcage like a trapped bird. He kissed her, first tenderly on the lips and then urgently, moving his mouth down to her throat and breasts. He bit gently at the taut nipples and she moaned, clawing at his curls, pulling him closer.

He drew her down to the bed and lowered himself on top of her. As he entered her, he heard her breath catch. The tiny gasps made him want to weep in gratitude. He held her tight, showering her with kisses, needy and possessive of her.

Afterwards, they held one another. Resting her head on his shoulder, she caressed the length of his chest with the tips of her fingers.

'Lyova?'

'Hmm?' His voice was groggy with sleep.

'Now that you are released from the army, will we be returning to our village?'

'We have little to go back to. We have no livestock, and with no one tending the fields they would have all gone to weed.'

'We can't stay here. Dima has been more than generous, but we must find a place of our own.'

Ivanov had been thinking along the same lines. 'Dima has found me a job at his munitions plant as a machine operator. We'll start looking for our own place as soon as I am earning money.'

'With so many refugees in Moscow, it will be hard to find anywhere decent.' She lifted herself on one elbow. 'Can't we somehow go back to our village?' She kissed his chest. 'Back to the steppes?' Ivanov groaned as her lips moved lower. 'To our home by the Don?'

Ivanov's breath became shallow as Marina's warm lips reached his torso. 'What are you doing to me, Marishka?'

Lying flat on top of him, Marina brought her face level with his. 'I don't want to stay in Moscow any longer.'

Cupping her face, he kissed her lips. 'Why do you say that? My pay at the munitions plant will be more than what we earned from the farm – and I'll work hard. Things will get better, just be patient.'

'I wouldn't be so sure, if I were you!' She rolled off him. Taking her wrist, he tried to pull her back. 'Listen to me, Lyova.' Twisting her hand, she freed her arm and reached for her blouse. 'Things will not be getting better any time soon.'

'Why do you insist on talking about this now?' he sighed. 'Come, Marishka . . .' He smiled suggestively. 'Show me again how much you missed me.'

'I'm serious.' Stepping into her skirt, she fastened it and reached for her shirt. 'Every day there is a new strike. One day the trams don't run. The next day the garbage is overflowing. The shops along Arbat don't have anything to sell. And even if they did, they are so expensive we couldn't afford to buy it. There is no coal. No bread. Every morning Toma and I line up for hours for bread. I don't dare send the girls on their own in case others steal the bread from them.

'As for the factory, according to Dima the workers are deliberately sabotaging the equipment. And when the foreman and owners yell at them, the workers feign ignorance, and blame the interruptions on faulty equipment.'

'People are sick of the war. Things will settle down.'

She gave him a level look. 'Get dressed, Leo. It's getting dark. They will be home soon.'

Although he was sympathetic to the workers' grievances, Ivanov avoided their meetings. Keeping his head down, he worked diligently at his station.

'Afternoon, comrade.'

A couple of paces away stood a tall, handsome, dark-haired man. 'You are new here.' The man thrust his hand out. 'I saw you walking to the plant this morning with Dmitry. I'm Mikail Aleksandravich Bazarov.'

Ivanov took his hand. 'I know who you are.'

Bazarov smiled. 'So you are familiar with the Bolsheviks?'

Ivanov turned back to his machine. 'I know of them.'

'Dmitry is a member. Maybe you'd like to come to our next meeting.'

'I prefer to keep to myself.'

'Times are changing. The workers of Russia need to unite to bring about progress.'

Ivanov said nothing. A foreman approached and Bazarov pretended to be helping Ivanov.

'What are you doing away from your station, Bazarov?' The foreman, a large potbellied man, glared at them suspiciously.

'I was just helping the new operator with his machine.'

Ivanov gave Bazarov a stony look.

'Do what you have to do quickly and get back to your own work,' the foreman said sharply. 'And if I find you are stirring trouble –' he pointed a fleshy finger at the two men '– I'll throw you both out.'

As soon as the foreman left, Ivanov turned to Bazarov. Grabbing the other man's collar, he hissed into his face, 'I can't afford to lose this job.' He tightened his grip. 'You understand me?'

'Calm down, comrade.' Bazarov held up his palms.

Ivanov let go of Bazarov's collar. 'Stay away from me.' He gave him a small shove.

'Fine, I'll leave you alone. But just in case you change your mind, we are holding a small memorial in honour of the Petrograd workers.' Bazarov slipped a folded pamphlet into Ivanov's coat pocket. 'You have heard about the fate of the bread rioters, haven't you?'

'Of course I have,' said Ivanov tersely.

'Then I hope to see you at the meeting.' Touching his cap, Bazarov walked back to his station.

The changes promised by the Provisional Government formed after the abdication of the Tsar were slow to arrive but Ivanov remained hopeful, reasoning that problems caused by years of war and mismanagement could not be resolved overnight.

Walking with Dmitry to the plant the next morning, they passed several stalls selling revolutionary books. Dmitry stopped to browse at one with a banner reading SOCIALIST REVOLUTIONARY PARTY. Ivanov lit a cigarette and watched as Dmitry haggled over the price of a book with the vendor.

'Which party do you belong to, comrade?' asked a young man with a dusting of hair over his upper lip, who was standing behind the stall.

'I don't belong to any party,' Ivanov said gruffly.

'You can join ours,' the youth said excitedly. 'The Socialist Revolutionary Party is the most democratic of all the parties.'

Ivanov groaned and turned his back on him. 'That's funny – that's what the Mensheviks and the Bolsheviks say about their parties.'

Leaving the stall, Ivanov and Dmitry fell into step. Tucked under his arm, Dmitry carried the latest edition of *Pravda*, a revolutionary paper with columns in it written by a man named Lenin.

'I like this Lenin.' Dmitry pointed to a picture of a scowling, nearly bald man.

'Who is he?'

'You don't know Lenin? He is the leader of the Bolshevik Party and currently living in exile. There are rumours he'll be returning soon.'

Ivanov shrugged. 'I don't know much about these things.'

Dmitry changed the subject. 'I heard you met Bazarov.'

'I suppose he told you of the reception he received from me.'

'He's telling everyone you welcomed him with open arms.' Dmitry laughed. 'Are you coming to the memorial?'

'I'm thinking about it.'

'The Provisional Government has announced the First Congress of Soviet Deputies,' Dmitry said. 'After we remember the Petrograd workers we plan to nominate a representative to attend the congress on our behalf.'

'On whose behalf?'

'Our behalf – yours and mine.' Dmitry looked at Ivanov incredulously. 'The Bolshevik Party.'

'I'm not a member.'

'You can join at the meeting.'

'I don't know.' Ivanov sighed.

'Listen. I've been approached by some of the men.' He placed a hand on Ivanov's shoulder. 'They want you to represent them at the meeting.'

'Why me? I'm not even a member. Why don't you nominate yourself?'

Dmitry shook his head. 'The men like you. You fought at the front and escaped a POW camp. You have earned their respect. And trust.'

'But I don't know the first thing about politics.'

'There's not much to know.' Dmitry nodded a greeting to the guard at the gate. 'All you have to do is attend the congress and put forward our grievances.'

'You should find someone else.'

'The men want you. And you owe it to them to represent them.'

'I don't owe them anything. I've paid my dues. I fought for my country.'

'Then do it for your fallen comrades.'

Ivanov thought of Nikolai. 'I suppose you are right. I will do it for them.'

At the meeting, Ivanov was one of three nominated. He stepped anxiously to the platform.

'Comrades.' Nervous about standing before his peers, Ivanov paused. Clearing his throat, he started again. 'Before the war, I was just a simple Cossack.'

'We can't hear you,' a voice interrupted from the back. 'Speak up.'

'I have a family,' Ivanov continued, louder this time. 'A wife and three children. We had a small plot of land by the River Don, a home made of mud walls and a thatched roof. I knew little of the world outside our village.' As he saw that the men were listening intently, he grew more confident. 'When the war began, I joined the army. I pray my son will never have to witness the horrors I saw at the front. Captured by the Germans I spent months in a POW camp. And do you think the Tsar cared? The English and French governments sent parcels, but not ours. They forgot about us.' Ivanov stopped, choked by a lump growing hard in his chest. 'So many men, good honest Russian men, lost their lives in the camps.'

Around the room, heads nodded.

'Life was not much better for my wife and family. Pregnant with our third child, my wife could not tend our land. There were no men to help her. Forced to sell our livestock, she moved to Moscow to live with her sister. And what do you think she found here?'

'No bread,' came one response.

'No coal,' came another.

'Black-market prices.'

'No proper accommodation.'

Ivanov held up his palms for quiet. 'You are all correct. She found the same hardships as your families have been suffering. This war, started by imperialists who care little about their people, has bled Russia dry. As your representative, I will tell the congress that as the men died at the front, their families starved and froze through the long winter months. I will tell them that the Bolshevik Party demands an immediate end to the war.' The more he spoke, the more Ivanov warmed to his task. Feelings of anger and hurt he had kept locked in his chest rushed through him. Clenching his fist, he brought it down against his open palm. 'We demand an end to the butchery. We demand an end to the suffering of the Russian people. We demand an end to the WAR!' he shouted.

Around the room, loud applause broke out.

When the votes were counted, it was declared that Ivanov had won with a convincing majority.

'Congratulations.' Dmitry shook Ivanov's hand. 'You will make a great representative.'

South-Eastern Front, May

Silence had descended across the front. His binoculars pressed to his eyes, Bogoleev scanned the enemy's trenches from the top of a hill. Since news of the abdication, the men had little stomach for fighting.

To his left the Russian trenches stirred with early morning activity. Men gathering for roll call moved at a lethargic pace, and when an officer walked by, few greeted him with the appropriate salute.

News of uprisings in Petrograd started whispers circulating that the Provisional Government was under pressure to end the war. Each day, more soldiers went missing as men deserted the front in droves. Even the threat of the firing squad did little to stop the exodus. Tired and fed up with army life, those who remained showed little inclination to follow orders and reports of growing unrest and mutiny filtered daily through the wires. Watching the soldiers file in, Bogoleev wondered how many more had fled overnight.

Growing up, Bogoleev had always dreamt of joining the army elite, and as soon as he was eligible he had signed with the infantry, seeking adventure and a better future than the one offered by his working-class family. His initial enthusiasm gave way to disillusionment as his requests to attend officers' school were ignored. When eventually accepted, he had to work twice as hard as those men from a higher social standing. He held his tongue when less-deserving candidates received promotions and medals that rightfully belonged to him.

The Tsar's abdication in March came as a surprise. He could not conceive of a time when Russia would be without a monarch as its head of state. But once the shock wore off, Bogoleev found he was not averse to the end of the monarchy.

Below him, a sergeant read the roll call. As Bogoleev suspected, more had defected. The remaining men shifted on their feet and answered to their names with little enthusiasm.

Bogoleev sighed. It was disheartening to see men look so dispirited.

About to join his men, Bogoleev's attention was drawn to the sound of an approaching car. It stopped a few metres away from the line and a passenger got out. He approached the sergeant and exchanged a few words. One of the soldiers stepped forward and, together with the visitor, walked towards Bogoleev.

Rising to his feet, Bogoleev slapped the dirt off his pants, all the time keeping his gaze on the visitor.

'I'm Vasily Mishkin and I represent the Soviet Deputies.'

Squinting slightly into the sun, Bogoleev shook hands with the visitor, his eyes darting to the envelope Mishkin carried in his hand.

'I have an urgent message from Petrograd,' Mishkin said, glancing at the soldier.

'That will be all, Private,' Bogoleev dismissed the soldier.

'An All-Russian Congress of Soviet Deputies is to be convened in Petrograd,' Mishkin began. 'Each division is to elect a representative to attend the congress.' He handed the envelope to Bogoleev.

'What is the purpose of this congress?'

'It is to give ordinary men the chance to voice their grievances and concerns before the new government. It is the opportunity to put forward ideas for a more democratic society.'

Bogoleev opened the envelope and read the first couple of lines.

'I can tell you exactly what each and every man here wants,' Bogoleev said, lifting his eyes from the page. 'An end to the bloodletting.'

'Of course we all want a speedy end to the war,' Mishkin conceded. 'But Russia signed a contractual agreement at the start of the war and we have a duty as a nation to honour our promise to our allies, especially now that the Americans have joined the war on our side.'

'It says here,' Bogoleev noted, pointing to a line in the letter, 'that the new Provisional Government has a duty to its people.'

'Our leaders are working very hard to achieve a better future for our nation.'

'And meanwhile men continue to die in the trenches.'

'We are aware of these difficulties,' Mishkin stammered. 'That is why we have established the congress. Our leaders are eager for working-class Russians to voice their opinions.'

'I will organise a meeting.' Bogoleev folded the letter and slipped it back into the envelope. 'You will have your representative from our division.'

Bogoleev escorted Mishkin to his car and watched as its trail of dust receded down the road. He absent-mindedly tapped the letter Mishkin had given him against his leg. The idea of a congress at which ordinary Russians could have their say intrigued him. Motioning to a corporal, he waved him over.

'Inform the men there is to be a meeting this afternoon and I want everyone to be present.'

39

Petrograd, June 1917

The foyer of Mariinsky Palace swarmed with delegates attending the congress. It was the first time Bogoleev – who had been elected as a representative – had entered the great foyer and he stood in the middle of the parquet floor for a few seconds, stunned by the opulence.

Resuming his progress, he browsed the stalls, stopping occasionally to scan the spines of books and read the brochures. In one corner, a crowd of men had gathered in front of a stand with a large red banner on which the words SOCIAL DEMOCRATIC BOLSHEVIK PARTY had been written in bold letters. Curious, Bogoleev moved closer.

A tall man with a thick mop of dark curly hair and small round glasses stood in the middle of the group, talking animatedly.

'What we stand for is the immediate end to the war.' Despite his boyish features, the speaker's voice emanated confidence.

'Who's that?' Bogoleev asked one of the men nearby.

'That's Trotsky. He's a close comrade of Lenin's.'

'Rumour has it,' another man added, 'Lenin will be speaking today at the congress.'

'Our enemies accuse our leaders of being German spies,' Trotsky's voice shrilled. 'They ridicule our demands for peace and redistribution of land. But my comrades and I are here to give you our solemn promise that with the last breath in our bodies we will fight until this imperialist war comes to an end and our peasants, whom we believe are the legal custodians of the land, are compensated for centuries of servitude.'

A cheer went up, followed by a press of bodies as men reached out to shake Trotsky's hand.

In the auditorium, Bogoleev took his place in one of the first few rows. In his breast pocket he carried the speech that he was scheduled to deliver before the congress. Pulling out the folded paper, he smoothed out the creases and was reading over the words he had prepared when he became aware of whisperings from the back of the auditorium. He turned to see what was happening.

'Lenin is here.'

Walking swiftly through the crowd, a short, stocky man with a high forehead and serious eyes made his way to the podium to speak privately to the chairman.

The chairman turned to the leaders. 'Due to his very busy schedule, Monsieur Lenin, the leader of the Social Democratic Bolshevik Party, asks to speak out of turn.'

Shouts of, 'Let him speak! We want to hear Lenin speak!' rose from the crowd.

Stepping behind the rostrum, Lenin waited for the cheering to die down. Once he had everyone's attention, he leant forward.

'The time has come for the Russian people to stand united. We, the Bolsheviks, believe that all ownership of the land must be redistributed to the peasants. I ask you: whose blood soaked the fields during this war? And whose families suffered while their men fought in the trenches? Was it the aristocracy? Or the bourgeoisie? Or the rich landowners?

'It was none of them. It was the blood of the hard-working people; their souls used as cannon fodder to serve an imperialist, capitalist war. Furthermore, our economy, crippled by this brutal, imperialist war, is on the brink of ruin. There is no flour or coal and our people are hungry and cold. On behalf of the Russian workers, the Bolshevik Party demands that the Provisional Government and their leader, Monsieur Kerensky, declare an immediate end to all hostilities.'

Raising his fist, Lenin's voice hit a high pitch. 'While our men continue to fight, our women and children starve and freeze during the long winter months from the lack of bread and coal. On behalf of the working people, I denounce the Provisional Government in their continued support of the Russian war effort. They have betrayed our revolution. This war is nothing but a tool to aid the wheels of capitalism, to serve the egos of imperialist tyrants.' He paused, gathering his breath.

'I demand an immediate end to the war. An end to the butchery. And an end to the suffering of the Russian people. I demand that power be restored equally to all Soviets. No longer should our peasants suffer at the hands of the few capitalist landowners. All estates must be expropriated. All land must be nationalised. And all peasants must have the right to dispose of the land as they wish.'

Lenin's voice was drowned out by cheers from the crowd. A chant started at the podium and gathered momentum until everyone was caught up in it.

'All power to the Soviets!'

'Down with the capitalist war!'

Lenin's lips curled into a smile. He raised his fist above his head and the audience responded with even louder cheers.

'Land, peace and bread for the peasants and workers!' he shouted above the noise of the crowd.

A shiver ran across Bogoleev's skin. He stood and joined the chorus, drowning calls for order from the chair.

Stepping down from behind the rostrum, Lenin acknowledged the cheering crowd with a triumphant wave.

'What did you think, Leo?' Dmitry asked Ivanov, following Lenin's address to the congress. He and Bazarov had accompanied Ivanov to the congress. 'Did you not find it inspiring?'

Ivanov was moved by what Lenin had said, but still felt some reservations. 'I'm all for peace and the redistribution of land, but I'm not sure about taking the land by force,' he said hesitantly.

'Your problem is that you are too idealistic.' Bazarov slapped a hand on Ivanov's shoulder. 'The gentry are not just going to hand over their land. We need to take it from them.'

'Look over there: there's a crowd gathered at the Bolsheviks' stand.' Dmitry craned his neck. 'I wonder if Lenin is still here? Come on, let's see if we can shake his hand.'

Lenin was not there but in his place was a short, thickset man with a pock-marked face and dark wiry hair. He introduced himself as Joseph Vissarionovich Stalin.

'I've read your articles in *Pravda*,' Dmitry said. 'You supported Lenin when he broke away from the Mensheviks.'

Stalin smiled, clearly pleased to be recognised. 'How are you enjoying the conference, comrades?'

'We thought Lenin was an inspiring speaker,' Dmitry said. 'We came over in the hope of meeting him.'

'Comrade Lenin had to race off to another engagement,' Stalin explained. He handed the men a flyer each. 'But we are having a meeting later today. Comrade Lenin will be giving a speech. You might like to join us?'

'I'm not sure we can make it,' Ivanov said. 'We are catching the overnight train back to Moscow.'

'Speak for yourself, Lyova.' Dmitry took Ivanov's flyer from his hand and stuffed it in his pocket. 'I'm not giving up the chance to shake Lenin's hand.'

'Our comrade here –' Bazarov motioned with his chin to Ivanov '– does not agree with Comrade Lenin's suggestion of taking the gentry's land by force.'

Stalin nodded his understanding. Bending his head close to Ivanov's he said, 'None of us wants bloodshed, but there are times when force is a necessary evil in the quest for greater good. The Kerensky government is nothing but a puppet for the captialists. That's why they insist on continuing with this imperialist war. As for the landowners growing fat on the sweat of the peasants, they will not easily renounce their power. In the end, neither they nor the government really care about ordinary Russians.' Pulling his face away, he studied Ivanov's scar. 'Tell me, comrade, were you in the war?'

Ivanov nodded.

'And how did you receive your injury?'

'In a POW camp.'

'And while you were away, did the government look after your family? Did your children have enough food to eat and coal to keep warm?'

A dark shadow passed over his face. 'No, comrade, they did not.'

After that, Ivanov found himself nodding to all of Stalin's suggestions, and by the time he'd left the palace, he had agreed to join the Red Guards.

Moscow, June

Convincing Marina to move to Petrograd was not easy.

'What will we do there?' she asked incredulously. 'Why do you want to pack us off to Petrograd?'

Taking her hand, Ivanov said, 'I have joined the Red Guards.'

'You've done what?' She snatched her hand away. 'Did you not experience enough bloodshed in the trenches?'

'It's not the same. I agree I was misguided in joining the imperialist war . . .'

'Listen to you – imperialist war!' Marina snorted. 'You even talk like them now.'

'Oh, Marina, I wish you'd been there. I wish you had heard Lenin speak. He understands the grievances of the common people.'

'Bah! I do not have the time to attend meetings.' Turning to the stove, she lifted the boiled kettle and emptied its contents into a copper tub. 'I've got children to feed and laundry to wash. I rise at dawn and wait in the breadline for hours and pray it does not run out before it's my turn.'

'The Bolsheviks are trying to change all that.'

Placing a hand on her hip, she gave him an appraising look. 'Alright. I'll come with you. We'll move to Petrograd. But not before you promise me we will have a place to live.'

Wrapping his arms around her, Ivanov kissed her neck. 'I promise. You won't regret your decision, Marina. The Bolsheviks are going to change everything. Just wait and see.'

Pulling herself free, she turned back to her laundry. 'Do me a favour, Lyova . . .' She kept her eyes fixed on her task. 'Stop making promises you cannot keep.'

40

Tsarskoe Selo, August 1917

At Alexander Palace, Nicholas Romanov walked along the rows of turned earth, stopping at intervals to pull out a weed or check on the first shoots of a new plant.

Since his abdication, the former Tsar and his family had been under house arrest. Arriving in Tsarskoe Selo in late March, Nicholas had found his wife greatly distressed as the events in Petrograd spiralled out of control. With all five children sick in bed with measles, Alexandra felt she had no choice but to remain in the palace rather than join the exodus. Since then, countless letters to his cousin, King George of England, asking for asylum, had gone unanswered.

With little to do, Nicholas spent the first few weeks wandering through the empty halls. Selecting titles from his vast collection of books, he read aloud to his children in their rooms, or silently to himself in the library. He also turned to physical activity. He shovelled snow and went on long walks around the compound.

The guards spoke to him with an open hostility that initially confused and puzzled Nicholas. Upon meeting one of his jailers for the first time, Nicholas had offered the man his hand.

The guard, an unkempt man with leathery skin, chewing on a large wad of tobacco, retorted, 'Not for anything in the world.'

'But, my dear fellow, why? What have you got against me?'

The guard did not answer and instead spat at the ground, his tobacco-stained saliva landing just short of Nicholas's boot.

In May, the family received permission to start a kitchen garden in the palace grounds. Grateful for a project to occupy their time, Nicholas and his daughters threw themselves into the task of planting, weeding and tilling the land for their crops. Not far from them, embroidering in her wheelchair, Alexandra kept a protective eye on her family.

'Where do you want this, Papa?'

Panting slightly, Olga and Tatiana carried turf, the load suspended at each end on parallel wooden bars, their skin glowing with the effort.

'Put it over there.' Nicholas pointed to a section of the garden where he planned to plant a row of cabbages.

As the girls struggled to lower the load, Tatiana's hat fell off, revealing her bald scalp.

'Look at her, stripped of all her charm and graces she's as ugly as a crow,' someone called.

Nicholas looked at the group of people, their heads pressed through the bars of the ground's gates. Each day they gathered to shout abuse and insults. The guards did nothing to stop the jeering and at times even encouraged the crowds further by joining in with the taunts.

The girls' hair had begun to fall out when they were ill, and Alexandra had ordered them shaved to help the regrowth.

Her cheeks crimson, Tatiana snatched up her hat, pulling it tight over her ears. As she walked past, Nicholas reached out a hand to comfort her.

'I don't understand, Papa. They always used to cheer when we went past in the carriages.' Her green eyes glistened. 'What happened for them to hate us so much?'

The former Tsar had no answer.

Sitting at the head of the dining table that evening, Nicholas led his family in giving thanks for the food they were about to receive. The maid moved slowly around the table, serving ladlefuls of potatoes and lentils. Accompanying the imperial family at the table were the last of their loyal supporters, who had joined them in house arrest.

Alexandra kept her head high, not making eye contact with anyone. Her lips tightened when the maid served her the food.

'What . . . no meat again?'

'I'm sorry, Your Highness. That's all the guards allowed the cook.'

The meal passed mostly in silence, occasionally broken by stilted conversation and the soft clanking of cutlery against china. They had almost finished eating when the door to the dining room opened and the commandant entered. A soft-spoken man in his late thirties, Colonel Kobylinsky was a professional soldier who had served in the Imperial Guard regiment and was now working with the Provisional Government.

'I'm here to inform you that you are to be transported to a new location in the morning.'

Stunned, the family looked to Nicholas for answers.

'Where are we being sent?' Nicholas asked, rising from the table.

'I'm afraid I'm not privy to that information,' the colonel replied. 'But I would suggest you pack furs and warm clothing.'

After the colonel left, silence again stretched through the room. The girls began to weep quietly, their narrow shoulders shaking under their thin cotton blouses. Pacing the room, Nicholas stopped and held his head in his hands.

'Papa,' Anastasia's pale eyes fixed on her father, 'are we being sent to Siberia?' The look in her eyes cut Nicholas so deep he thought his heart would splinter into pieces.

'My darling girl.' He embraced her. 'We have no choice. We must place our trust in our captors.'

'I'm frightened, Papa,' she said. 'I don't want to leave our home.'

'I know, but as long as we are together, I will not let anything happen to you.'

❧

The imperial family and their entourage were ordered into waiting cars just before dawn. Alexandra had been up all night supervising the packing of their belongings. She sobbed bitterly for the entire fifteen-kilometre journey to Alexandra Station, where a carriage disguised as a hospital train was waiting for them.

Before leaving the car, Nicholas reached over and lightly touched Alexandra's knee.

'Alex dearest,' he said, wishing he could find the words to comfort her, 'I am sorry.'

'You have nothing to apologise for.' Alexandra straightened her back. 'You are the Tsar of Russia and, as far as I'm concerned, you have performed your duties admirably.'

Stepping out of the car, she refused the offer of her wheelchair and, leaning on Nicholas's arm, walked to the platform.

In the east, the sun rose, painting the clouds in rose and gold. But Nicholas saw no beauty in the morning, only its part in the desolation of his family.

Uglich, September

Sitting by the window, Alexei read the newspaper.

The Germans had pushed back the Russian army to Riga.

The United States of America had entered the war in April 1917 and, in order to prove Russia's commitment, Kerensky staged a summer offensive. The result was a collapse of the Russian lines, and further plummeting of morale, sending even more Russians into the arms of the Bolsheviks.

Across the regiments, a spirit of revolt was sparked in war-weary men.

The speed of the Russian army's collapse left Alexei bewildered and apprehensive about the future. He took to spending long hours locked away in his study, poring over newspaper reports with a permanent scowl.

In response to his growing agitation, a wariness descended over the household. When he entered a room, his family grew rigid, conscious that the slightest irritation could provoke his anger. Busying themselves with their chores, the staff stole nervous glances in his direction and took pains to move silently through the house, lowering their voices to whispers when they passed his room.

His days, shaped by a series of routines, grew tiresome for him. Waking early, he dressed and together with Grigory he went riding for an hour to exercise the horses. In the afternoons, he took walks, accompanied by Grigory or one of the two eldest daughters. His days grew interminable, adding to his irritation and restlessness.

'I have decided to visit Petrograd.' Alexei announced to Emily over supper one evening. 'I'll be leaving in the morning.'

'You can't be serious, Alexei.' Emily looked surprised by the announcement. 'You know better than I it is not safe for you there.' Her eyes moved to their daughters, who had stopped eating and were watching the exchange between their parents. Leaning forward, she said in a low voice, 'You cannot abandon us at such a time.'

'You are perfectly safe here.' Alexei avoided Emily's gaze.

'How can you say that?' She lowered her voice further. 'You have heard the rumours of soldiers deserting the front and arriving with their guns to seize the land from nobility.'

Alexei shifted uncomfortably in his seat. 'Of course I have.'

'And you still wish to leave us unprotected?'

'I will only be gone for a few days. I need to find out for myself what's happening in the capital.'

Tonya's small chin quivered. Unable to hold her emotions in check, she burst into tears. Next to her, Irena draped an arm over her sister's shoulder, murmuring soothing words in her ear.

'Where will you stay?' Emily asked in a voice turned cold.

'At our apartment. Irena.' Alexei turned abruptly to his eldest daughter. 'Take your sister to her room and calm her.'

Irena flashed her father a severe look. Motioning to one of the servants, she asked for their meals to be brought to their room.

'May I be excused too, Papa?' Vera asked.

'Yes, yes, go join your sisters.' Alexei waved her away.

'Is there anything I can do to change your mind?' Emily asked in a softer voice once the girls had left.

Alexei shook his head. 'My decision is final.'

Emily leant back in her seat. 'Alexei, I know you've been restless ever since your arrival and all this talk of mutiny must surely weigh heavy on your thoughts. But what good will it do to return to Petrograd now? What could your visit possibly achieve?'

Alexei slammed the table hard with his palm, knocking over his wine glass. 'Enough! My decision is final!'

The room fell still, as if all the air had been sucked out of it. When Emily lifted her head to look at Alexei, her eyes had turned hard. She signalled to the butler, who promptly pulled her chair out for her. Rising to her feet, she left without another word, leaving Alexei alone at the table.

41

Petrograd, September 1917

With the growing unrest in the capital, Monsieur Mostovsky had decided to move his family south to the Caucasus. Marie descended the curved staircase, passing the large windows and gilded mirrors all covered with white sheets. Servants and valets hurried from room to room, their arms loaded with sheets, speaking in hushed voices. Directly before her, workers were busy covering the large chandelier. The crystals trembled like tiny bells under the white sheet before eventually falling silent.

Marie found Darya and her parents in the grand hall, going over last-minute details. This was where she had attended her first ball, she thought sadly. Covered in sheets, the room had none of its former dazzling appearance and instead had taken on a melancholy feel.

Dressed in a navy blue travelling suit and matching hat, Darya watched the goings-on forlornly from a corner. Her face brightened when she saw Marie.

'I've come to say goodbye,' Marie said.

'Come with us,' begged Darya.

'I can't.' She took her cousin's hand between her own. 'I will never be able to repay you for all your kindness.'

'Where will you go from here?'

'I received a telegram from my parents urging me to return to Narva. I'll be leaving as soon as I can.'

'But Narva is no longer safe.'

'The Germans are still over two hundred kilometres away.'

'I suppose.' Then, struck by a new thought, Darya asked, 'What will you do about your studies?'

Marie gave a defeated shrug. 'There's nothing I *can* do. I just have to hope I'll be able to return to them once the political situation is resolved.'

'Promise you will write to me, Marie.' Darya squeezed her hand, then impulsively threw her arms around her.

'I will,' Marie said, her voice raspy with unshed tears.

The stifling atmosphere in the train carriage made Marie long for fresh air. The featureless landscape stretched endlessly on all sides. Standing, she opened the window slightly and pressed her face against the cold rush of air. Passing a village, the cinder from the outdoor stoves and the dry dung of domestic animals mingled into an aroma that assaulted her senses. Shutting the window, she sat back down.

There was a time I used to look forward to travelling through this countryside, she thought, wrinkling her nose. Now everything is dull and devoid of charm.

Her grim mood was not abated by her arrival in Narva. Marie was acutely aware of the heaviness that hung over the family, especially at mealtimes. She avoided looking at Nikolai's empty seat at the dining table, while across from her, dressed in her mourning black, Marie's mother ate with little enthusiasm.

Passing her mother's room earlier, Marie had looked through the half-open door to see her curled on top of the bed, clasping Nikolai's photo to her breast, crying into her pillow with loud hiccupping sobs. Frightened by her mother's anguish, Marie stepped back into the hallway, closing the door behind her.

Now she searched her mother's face for signs of her earlier tears. Pauline Kulbas had made a feeble attempt to mask her pallor by applying a dusting of rouge over her cheekbones. Her puffy eyes, however, betrayed her grief.

Reaching across the table, Marie touched her mother's hand and a look of understanding passed between them. Taking Marie's hand, her mother gave it a gentle squeeze.

Marie caught her father watching them from over the top of his round glasses. Despite his best efforts, he was ill-equipped to deal with his wife's grief. His attempts to offer words of comfort, no matter how well-intentioned, often came across as clumsy and did little to ease her pain. Marie gave him a small smile to let him know she understood how he felt and did not judge his shortcomings. He smiled back.

'We've heard rumours,' he said, breaking the silence, 'the situation in Petrograd is becoming perilous. Many of the palaces have been confiscated and several grand dukes are imprisoned in Peter and Paul Fortress.'

'The rumours are true, Papa. Since the abdication, the soldiers have been ransacking palaces while the owners look on, helpless,' Marie confirmed.

'Barbaric!' Monsieur Kulbas shook his head.

'The whole of Petrograd is in a frenzy to rid itself of its imperial past,' Marie continued. 'Students tear down eagle crests from the top of shops, and fly revolutionary flags from every post.'

'Why don't they call the guards?' her mother asked.

Marie turned to her. 'They did, Mama, but the garrison soldiers sent to restore order mutinied and turned on their commanding officers.' Marie shuddered, remembering the long nights she'd been kept awake by the chatter of guns. 'There is no order anywhere. Along Nevsky Prospect almost every shop has been vandalised and looted.'

'I heard that red cloth is draped over the Romanov eagles at the gates of the Winter Palace,' Valentin said.

Marie nodded. 'A revolutionary flag now flies in the palace square.' Dropping her gaze to her wine glass, she continued. 'Strikes keep everything at a standstill. There are days where no post is delivered and the garbage piles up at the side of the streets.'

'If it weren't for Rasputin, Russia would not be in this mess,' Valentin declared hotly. 'That so-called holy man had the Tsarina under his spell and together they destroyed any chance Russia had of winning the war.'

'That is enough, Valentin,' his father warned. 'That is no way to speak about the Empress.'

'We've all heard the rumours,' Valentin persisted. 'Marie, tell Papa what everyone is saying in Petrograd.' He did not wait for a response and continued, undeterred. 'And now, with the Russian army in disarray and the Germans in Riga, there's little to stop them from making it all the way to the capital.'

'Valentin Kulbas!' Pauline Kulbas's face flushed with fury. 'I will not hear another word about Russia losing this war. Your dear brother, God bless his departed soul, never questioned his duty and paid for it with his life. That Lenin –' she spat out the name as if ridding herself of a terrible taste '– is a snake and a traitor to his country, conspiring with the Germans who smuggled him back into Russia so he can spread his poison. As for Kerensky . . .' Pushing her chair back, she stood abruptly. 'The government is made up of opportunistic thieving thugs bent on an orgy of blood and alcohol.'

Valentin opened his mouth to respond but a warning look from his father made him close it again.

'If you'll excuse me, I have a headache and wish to retire.' Without waiting for a response, Madame Kulbas left the room, leaving the rest of the family to finish their meal in silence.

Following lunch, Marie joined her father in the study.

'Papa, is it not true that only a stretch of open country separates Narva from the German line?'

'I know what you are thinking, Marie, but you have nothing to fear. The Germans are still a long way away and the Russian troops will stop them before they get anywhere close to Narva.'

'What happens if they do reach us?'

'Pray they don't,' Herman Kulbas said, lighting his pipe. 'Conquerers have never been kind to the conquered.'

❧

Arriving in Petrograd late in the evening, Alexei walked into the drawing room of his residence and headed straight for the cabinet where he stored his vodka. Taking a crystal glass, he half filled it. None of the reports had prepared him for the scenes that had greeted him as he travelled through the city. At the Winter Palace drunken sentries stood around bonfires, or shot at targets set up near the colonnades. Some of the bridges were blocked by barricades. As his carriage negotiated its way around upturned carts and wooden boxes, the soldiers and civilians standing guard stared in at him. None of the soldiers flinched at the sight of Alexei in his military uniform and they waved him through without the proper salute.

'I have taken care of your luggage,' Grigory said, entering the room. 'Do you need me to do anything else, Excellency?'

'You can join me in a drink,' Alexei said, pouring a second glass of vodka. He held it out. 'We have known each other for a long time, but have never drunk together.'

Grigory hesitated for the briefest moment before accepting. 'Thank you, Excellency.' Taking a couple of sips, he placed his glass on the side table. 'Forgive me, Excellency, but I am not much of a drinker.'

Alexei laughed dryly. 'It seems the formal deference to superior officers is a thing of the past.' He raised his glass to Grigory. 'You are the last of your kind.' Taking a sip, he grimaced and touched the scar on his neck. 'Damn this wound!' Swirling the liquid once in the glass, he swallowed it in a single gulp. Wincing, he reached for the bottle again.

'What will become of us?' He emptied his glass a second time. 'Our country, the people?' He placed his empty glass on the table. 'The Provisional Government doesn't seem to have any control over the army or the masses. It all seems so lost.'

'The Lord works in mysterious ways, Excellency.'

'That, my dear man, sounds very much like something my wife would say.'

Grigory gave a wry smile but offered no comment.

'You know my marriage has all but ended. Oh, do not look so shocked, Grigory. I was never faithful to her.' Alexei's voice grew reflective. 'I never loved her the way a man should love a woman. Soldiering was all I was ever good at.'

'My father used to say, "Living life is not like crossing a meadow." Your family knows you have done your best for them, despite the difficulties.'

Alexei let out a sigh. 'If I am ever lucky enough to have another woman love me,' he said, his thoughts wandering to Marie, 'I swear to love her for all my remaining days.' He waved a dismissive hand and reached for the bottle again. 'Don't let me bore you with my talk. Have one last drink with me before bed.' He refilled both their glasses.

'*Za zdorovie*.' He raised his glass. 'To your health.'

In the inky darkness of pre-dawn, Alexei woke to the sound of loud knocking at the door. Groggily, he picked up his watch from the nightstand. Four o'clock. The knocking became more urgent before abruptly stopping, followed by the sound of many men talking at once. Among the voices he recognised Grigory's, but could not make out what he was saying. Opening the drawer of his nightstand, he reached for the silver Luger and managed to conceal it beneath the covers a split-second before the door flew open. Soldiers barged in, followed by an ashen-faced Grigory carrying a candelabra.

'What is the meaning of this?' Alexei demanded. He reached for his dressing gown at the foot of his bed.

'I'm terribly sorry, Your Excellency,' Grigory said. 'I tried to convince them to come back later in the morning but they insisted . . .'

'Be quiet,' one of the men barked at Grigory. Stepping forward, he announced, 'We are here to search the premises and confiscate all weapons.'

'On whose authority?'

'On behalf of the Soviet citizens.'

The man motioned to one of the other soldiers, who moved swiftly to where Alexei's sabre hung from the wall. Pulling it out of its sheath, the soldier grinned as he took in the quality of the craftsmanship. Close to the sabre, Grigory had hung Alexei's uniform. In a swift move, the soldier ripped the epaulets from the shoulders.

Grigory jumped forward but was beaten back by the butt of another soldier's rifle. Winded, he fell to the floor, gasping for breath.

Under the bedsheets, Alexei's fingers tightened over the gun. Getting up slowly, he hid the gun in the folds of his dressing gown.

The search took just over an hour and as well as Alexei's two rifles and a handgun, the soldiers took several bottles of wine and vodka. While they searched the apartment, their leader – a wiry man with black curly hair and a beard trimmed to a point – remained in Alexei's room, helping himself to cigarettes.

'You've heard of Lenin?' he asked casually, in between blowing smoke rings.

'I've heard of him,' Alexei replied coolly.

'He's a great man.'

Alexei said nothing.

The soldier looked over at Grigory who, having recovered, was sitting by Alexei's side.

'You, comrade – have you heard of Lenin?'

'I've heard he's a German spy,' Grigory said defiantly.

'Vicious lies spread by the puppet bourgeois government. Mark my words –' the soldier pointed his cigarette at Grigory '– the Bolshevik Party will one day rule the country. And when they do there'll be no more war, or hunger, or shortages. We shall live in Utopia. The peasants will no longer have to pay taxes to rich landlords.' He leant back in the chair. 'The people who work on the land will have full ownership of it.'

Grigory glared at the soldier.

'What is it, comrade? Cat got your tongue?' With a satisfied smile, the soldier placed his boots on Alexei's desk.

When the search was over, the leader turned to Alexei. 'Now

I must ask you to accompany us to the garrison, where you'll be held for questioning.'

Alexei kept his expression neutral even as his stomach dropped like a stone. His grip tightened around the gun still concealed by the dressing gown.

'I need a moment to dress.'

'Be quick about it.' The soldier was unsteady on his legs. 'I don't have all morning to wait for you.'

When the soldier had left the room, Alexei hid the Luger under the mattress.

'As soon as the soldiers leave, take my gun,' he told Grigory, 'and return to Uglich.'

'I can't leave Petrograd without you,' Grigory protested as he helped Alexei into civilian clothes. 'Where do you suppose they will take you, Excellency?'

'I don't know. Most likely, the Peter and Paul Fortress.' He placed a hand on Grigory's shoulder. 'There's little you can do for me here. You must return to Emily and the girls. Find a safe place you can take them at the first sign of danger.'

A heavy hand rapped loudly on the door. 'Hurry up in there.'

'I am trusting you with my family,' Alexei said, and for the first time the two men embraced.

42

Petrograd, October 1917

The cold spoke of more snow to come. And although the wind had died down, the icy air bit into the men's toes and fingers, and burnt the exposed skin of their faces. Kneeling on the ground behind the pedestal of Alexander Column, Ivanov had his gun levelled at the walls of the Winter Palace. Next to him, Dmitry blew on his hands, curling and uncurling his fingers around his rifle.

'God help us,' Dmitry groaned. 'We'll freeze before this siege is over.'

From the River Neva, the guns of battleship *Aurora* faced the palace, trapping Kerensky and several of his ministers inside the palace walls. With the sky fading, triangles of light streamed from the gilded windows over the snow.

Since moving to Petrograd and joining the Red Guards, Ivanov had attended many Bolshevik meetings, where increasingly the talk had turned to seizing power from the Provisional Government. People continued to suffer as inflation bit into their meagre wages. Shortages in raw materials and fuel, transport difficulties and falling demand had forced many factories to close down. Finding cheap accommodation was almost impossible. Only through their Red Guards connections had Dmitry and Ivanov found a three-room apartment which they shared with their families.

Meeting at the back of factories, Ivanov and Dmitry joined hundreds of workers to hear delegates speak. Many workers, angry at losing their jobs, blamed the government. Marina and her sister rarely attended the meetings but tonight, at their husbands' beckoning, they had agreed to join them at one of Lenin's appearances.

'The March revolution is not finished,' Lenin bellowed from his lectern. 'The Bolshevik Party, not the Provisional Government, is the true representative of the Russian people. Kerensky and his ministers have been ineffective in putting bread on the plates of the people. They continue to support this imperialist war. And meanwhile, our men are still dying, our children are still hungry and with winter almost upon us there is not sufficient fuel to warm our stoves.'

The room smelt of the cheap tobacco the workers smoked. The hazy yellow lighting made the faces appear slightly jaundiced. Ivanov stole a look at his wife. The printed dress she wore was frayed at the hem, and her hair was tied back in a faded kerchief. Leaning against the wall, she had her arms crossed over her chest and was staring intently at the stage. Sensing his eyes on her she turned, fixing him a look that made him drop his gaze.

Meanwhile, Lenin was reaching the end of his speech. 'We, the Bolshevik Party, will fight to ensure the ordinary families take back what is rightfully theirs.'

The room erupted in an ovation that went on for several minutes. Ivanov joined in the applause, cheering enthusiastically. When he turned to look for Marina, she had gone.

He found her outside, sitting on a bench. 'Why did you leave?'

'I had heard enough.'

He sat down beside her. 'Comrade Lenin makes a lot of sense.'

The lines around her eyes creased with tension. 'You think so? You think his policies are going to put bread on our table?'

'Yes I do. He listens to the people. He is demanding change. You heard what he said, the revolution is not over.'

'There's been enough blood shed in the trenches, Lyova.'

'Who's talking about bloodshed?'

She levelled him a look. 'How do you think your comrade Lenin and his Bolshevik Party are going to seize power? Do you think the Provisional Government would just hand over power to the Bolsheviks?'

'If that's what the people are demanding, then –'

'Don't be naïve!' she snapped. Looking over her shoulder, she lowered her voice. 'There's only one way the Bolsheviks can take power, and that's through armed uprisings.'

Ivanov stared at his hands. 'It might not come to that.'

Marina touched his forearm. 'You know I am right, Lyova. There will be an uprising. And it will not be bloodless.'

They did not have to wait long for Marina's words to be proved right. A few weeks later, a demonstration erupted into riots that came close to resulting in a coup. Soldiers loyal to Kerensky dispersed the crowd with machine-gun fire. Ivanov and Dmitry narrowly escaped by hiding under a bridge, listening to the chaos of the crowd scattering in terror. They emerged from hiding only once the streets had grown quiet. With the white summer nights, it was difficult to keep to the shadows. Ducking between side alleys, they made their way back to their apartment.

Marina and Tamara greeted them at the door. 'Where have you been?' Marina threw her arms around Ivanov's neck. 'We were worried sick.' Pulling back, she studied him for signs of injury.

'I am fine.' He kissed her brow. 'Just tired.'

Stoking the fire in the stove, Marina brewed tea and served it to them with bread. Ivanov sat down to eat, but Dmitry and Tamara took their supper to their bedroom.

Sitting by Ivanov's feet, Marina rested her head against his legs. 'Some of the men from the party came looking for you. They wanted to know if you made it.' She spoke softly, her voice rasping. 'I don't know what I would have done if you had not made it home tonight.'

Finishing his supper, Ivanov put down his cup. 'I'm here now.'

She nuzzled closer. 'Maybe now we can go back to our village.'

'That's not possible.'

'Why?'

'Our job here is not done.'

'But the party is finished. And so are the Red Guards.'

Ivanov gave her a confused look.

Marina tilted her head to one side. 'You have not heard?'

Ivanov felt his bowels liquefy. 'Heard what?'

'Lenin,' she said. 'He's fled the capital.'

'How do you know?'

'The men from the party told me. They think he's heading for Finland. The afternoon papers are calling him a traitor, a German spy.'

A lump hardened in Ivanov's throat. 'They're just vicious lies.'

Marina threaded her fingers through his. 'That's not all. Trotsky is under arrest.'

'On what grounds?'

'Treason.'

Despite the arrest of the Bolshevik leaders, disillusionment with the Provisional Government to bring an end to the war led more Russians to join the party. Reports filtered through from the trenches, bringing news of men deserting the front in droves.

'Troops openly refuse to participate in offensives,' a soldier, recently defected, told the group of Bolsheviks who had gathered at Ivanov's apartment. 'Skirmishes planned by those still loyal to Kerensky sometimes manage to cut through enemy lines. But without the rest of the men willing to follow, any territory gained is quickly lost to counter-offensives.'

Dmitry handed the soldier a glass of vodka.

The soldier raised his glass. He was missing half his index finger. '*Za vas.*'

Around the room the men emptied their glasses.

Dmitry refilled them. 'Is it true Kerensky has reintroduced capital punishment for men who refuse to join the offensives?' he asked.

The soldier nodded. 'That son of a viper! Kerensky has ordered the officers to turn their guns on us if we refuse to fight. But it's no use. We're still refusing. I saw three men shoot an officer after he pulled his gun at one of the soldiers.'

A murmur rippled through the group.

'The army can't continue like this,' Ivanov said. His speech had started to slur.

The soldier held out his glass to be refilled. 'Change is on the horizon, comrade. It will come.'

'The question is, what is Kerensky planning to do?'

'Word is, he is blaming the generals for their failure to assert discipline. He's already replaced General Brusilov with General Kornilov as Commander-in-Chief.'

Ivanov shook his head. 'Kerensky has made a mistake replacing Brusilov. He was a great general.'

'His decision might yet backfire on him.'

'What do you mean?'

'Kornilov is an ambitious man. He was overheard at the front boasting about plans to overthrow Kerensky.'

'Could he do that?'

The soldier shrugged and downed his glass. 'Anything is possible.'

At the end of August, troops under the command of General Kornilov marched on Petrograd to call for the resignation of the government and the handover of power to the Commander-in-Chief. Having heard of Kornilov's plans, Kerensky turned to the Red Guards to help protect the city.

On the morning of the coup, Ivanov and Dmitry were woken by knocking at the door.

'What is the meaning of waking us at this hour?' Ivanov asked the messenger.

The boy handed him an envelope. 'It's a message from the Petrograd Soviets, comrade. You are to meet at the Palace Square.'

'What for?'

'I don't know.' He rocked impatiently on his heels. 'I have to go. I have many of these messages still to hand out.'

Ivanov followed the boy out to the top of the stairs. 'Who gave this to you?'

'A man at the Smolny Institute,' the boy said, looking back over his shoulder. 'The order has come overnight from Lenin.'

'You think it's a trap?' Ivanov later asked Dmitry.

Dmitry shrugged. 'I'm not sure, but I think we should be careful entering the square.'

'The boy said the order has come from Lenin.'

'Do you think it could have something to do with Kornilov's threats to overthrow Kerensky?'

Ivanov scratched the back of his head. 'Why would Lenin want to support Kerensky?'

'I guess we'll know soon enough.' Dmitry checked his watch. 'We are expected there in an hour.'

At the Palace Square, Ivanov and Dmitry were surprised to find thousands of men already there. Troops stood shoulder to shoulder with workers. Ivanov spied groups of young cadets and women dressed in military uniforms, all of whom were armed with rifles.

Standing on an upturned box, Kerensky's skin appeared sallow. When it was time to address the crowd, he squared his shoulders and puffed out his chest.

'Today, our great city is under threat. Presently, General Kornilov marches on Petrograd to make himself military dictator of Russia. This is a blatant attempt by the bourgeoisie to crush the revolution. Citizens and comrades! Listen to me! I know the past years have not been kind to you. But we must look beyond our grievances! We must pool our resources to defend our revolution! Railway workers loyal to the Petrograd Soviets are halting the soldiers' progress.

We have reports that trains are being diverted, lines blocked and rails removed, making it impossible for the general to transport his troops to the capital.

'The Bolshevik leader, Vladimir Lenin –' at the mention of Lenin, the workers let out a loud cheer. Kerensky paused to let the applause die down. 'Comrade Lenin has also agreed to halt the ambitions of General Kornilov.'

Another loud cheer.

'Citizens,' Kerensky continued, 'we must protect our city. I ask you, on this historic day, to join forces, to put aside our differences and as comrades to fight against our common enemy.'

'How are we supposed to halt the advance of armed forces when we are unarmed ourselves?' Dmitry yelled out.

'That's a good question, comrade,' Kerensky replied. 'We will issue a rifle to every man and woman who will defend the capital. Workers will be organised into defence squads and stationed at strategic locations around the outskirts of the city.' He stopped and took a breath. 'Today,' his voice boomed across the square, 'the future of our great revolution rests on your shoulders.'

Following Kerensky's speech, rifles were handed out and each faction was assigned an area of the city.

Ivanov and Dmitry were allocated the southern border of the capital. They remained all day at their post without firing a single shot. They returned to their apartment when they received news that the government had repelled Kornilov's advance.

'The coup failed,' Ivanov told Marina. 'There was no bloodshed.'

'Thank the Lord.' Marina crossed herself. 'Where did you get those?' she asked in alarm when she saw they were carrying rifles.

Wrapping them in a blanket, Ivanov hid the weapons at the back of a cupboard. 'We were issued these by the government. With all the excitement, no one asked for them back.'

Tamara helped Dmitry with his jacket and boots. 'What will happen now?'

'By agreeing to defend the city against Kornilov,' Dimitry said,

'Lenin proved that the Bolsheviks are not traitors to the revolution. Kerensky has no choice but to release the Bolshevik leaders.'

'And what about Lenin?'

Dmitry smiled. 'He will return from exile a hero.'

The following month, the Bolshevik leaders, including Trotsky, were released. After their liberation, an All-Russian Soviet of Workers' and Soldiers' Deputies congress was held at Tauride Palace. The large auditorium was bursting with delegates, many of whom were forced to stand in the aisles. Plumes of cigarette smoke hung low over the crowd like a fog, choking the room of oxygen. At the conclusion of the elections, Trotsky was voted president of the Petrograd Soviet. Speaking before the delegates, Trotsky announced that his first task would be to neutralise the Petrograd Garrison troops.

Ivanov and Dmitry stood close to where Trotsky was speaking.

'I don't think it's going to work,' Ivanov whispered to Dmitry.

'It will.'

Ivanov was doubtful. 'How?'

'The troops hate the Provisional Government as much as we do.'

'That doesn't guarantee they will not take arms. There are three hundred and fifty thousand of them, and only ten thousand of us.'

'Think about it, Leon. Every one of those three hundred and fifty thousand men is fearful of only one thing.'

'What?'

'To be sent to the front. And that's exactly what the Provisional Government has planned for them.'

'So, if Trotsky promises to keep them at Petrograd . . .'

'They will not take arms against the Bolsheviks in the event of a coup.' Dmitry finished the sentence.

A chill shuddered through Ivanov. 'A military coup?'

Dmitry turned so they were face to face. 'What else?' Checking over his shoulder he dropped his voice. 'I heard a rumour today: Lenin is returning with immediate plans for a military takeover.

This time, nothing will be left to chance. The coup is going to be stage-managed.'

In October, the same rifles that were issued by Kerensky's government to protect the city against General Kornilov, now faced the palace where the prime minister and his cabinet were meeting. Sporadic exchange of gunfire was followed by long periods of silence. Finally, as the night's velvety cloak blanketed the city, the Red Guards broke through the barricades. The few remaining defenders protecting the palace offered little resistance.

Ivanov and Dmitry, carried along by the wave of rushing feet, were swept in through the right-hand entrance. Once inside the palace, men fanned out. Ivanov and Dmitry followed a group running down the stairs, where they found huge packing cases lined up along the walls. Using their rifles, soldiers prised the lids open.

'This must be the cellar,' Ivanov said, looking around at the piles of carpets, linen and dinnerware strewn across the floor.

'Get some of this into you,' a guard said, pressing a bottle of wine into Ivanov's chest. Ivanov took a swig and felt it flood his shivering limbs with warmth. Perching himself on one of the upturned crates, he watched proceedings, taking regular sips from the bottle. Everywhere soldiers were busy stuffing the contents from various crates into their coats and tunics. Finding an ostrich feather, Dmitry stuck it in his hat.

'Stand straight, you worthless scum,' Dmitry said, imitating an army officer. 'You are a poor excuse for a soldier.'

'Stop, comrades! Put everything back. This is the property of the people.' A Red Guard commander shouldered his way through the men. 'Don't take anything,' he ordered. 'We are not thieves and this is the property of the people.'

Across the room, other soldiers took up the cry. 'The commander is right. Put it back, comrades. These don't belong to us.'

Ivanov, having already drunk most of his wine, was allowed to keep the bottle but everyone else returned their spoils. Dmitry looked crestfallen as he handed back the set of plates he was carrying.

'Well, at least we have this wine to enjoy,' he said, taking the bottle from Ivanov. 'Come now, Lyova, let's explore the palace.'

Together they strode along the corridors, peering into the rooms. The old servants in their blue, red and gold uniforms mumbled nervously, 'You are not allowed in there.' Neither Ivanov nor Dmitry paid them any attention. At the door to one chamber, a guard blocked their way. 'You can't go in there, comrades.'

'Why not?' Dmitry asked.

'We've got Kerensky's ministers in there.'

'And where's Kerensky?'

'He escaped,' the guard said sheepishly. 'He must have slipped out a side door. But don't worry, comrades, we'll find him.'

Upon reaching the main entrance, Ivanov and Dmitry climbed the Jordan Staircase, staring in open wonder at the white marble floors, blue colonnades and gold baroque trimmings.

'Look at this chandelier,' Ivanov said when they reached the top of the stairs. 'It probably cost more money than you and I could earn in a lifetime. And to think, there are probably hundreds like it in this palace alone.' With his head reeling from the wine, he steadied himself against the railing. 'It's not right,' he muttered. 'The aristocracy should not be allowed to have so much.' He turned to Dmitry. 'The Bolsheviks must win power,' he said passionately. 'Only then will the workers and peasants have equality.'

They continued to walk through the corridors for some time longer, stopping occasionally to look inside a room. Eventually, they followed a group of guards carrying furniture and heavy cases to waiting trucks and wagons.

'Where do we go?' Dmitry asked a Red Guard commander who was recording and marking the cases.

The Red Guardsman looked up with tired eyes. 'Where are you stationed?'

'We share an apartment with our families.'

'Then go home. Get some rest.' He smiled. 'You did well tonight.'

Walking back across the Palace Square, Ivanov was in a relaxed mood. A youth climbed over the barricade and ran towards them.

'Comrades,' the boy called out, breathless with excitement. 'Have the Bolsheviks won?'

'Yes, young comrade,' Ivanov said, placing a hand on the boy's shoulder, 'we won.'

From across the road, Katya saw Fyodor rush over to the soldiers and exchange a few words. One of the men placed a hand on the boy's shoulder, making Fyodor beam.

She had tried to keep him away from the revolutionary groups, fearing for his safety, but in the last few months he had started spending most of his spare time with a group of young radicals from the factory. Katya no longer felt she had any hold over him, and it worried her. Fyodor became increasingly secretive, often disappearing for hours at a time and refusing to tell Katya where he had been. Pointing a crooked finger at Fyodor the day before, Madame Ozerova had complained he was shirking his chores and threatened to throw them out.

'You're an old capitalist fool and one day soon we'll make you pay for your actions,' Fyodor retorted.

It had taken Katya an hour and several cups of chamomile tea to calm the old woman and persuade her not to evict them.

The next day had started unremarkably. Fyodor had left before Katya was out of bed. After emptying the chamber-pots and brewing tea for Madame Ozerova's breakfast, Katya left to join the breadline.

Wind lashed at her face like icy needles. Gathering her cloak about her, she walked at a brisk pace, paying little attention to the soldiers milling in the streets. Passing one of the barricades, she nodded a curt greeting to the sentry.

As soon as she reached the breadline, she realised something was wrong by the restlessness of the women.

'What's happened?' she asked the woman ahead of her in the queue.

'The second revolution has started. The Bolshevik Red Guards have taken over the telegraph and post offices. The garrisons and the train stations are all under rebel control.'

Katya's heart dropped to her stomach. Abandoning the line, she set off in search of Fyodor. Twice she went to the factory and both times found the gates locked. Noon cannons had boomed from the Peter and Paul Fortress when she followed a crowd to the Winter Palace.

'Lenin's Red Guards have surrounded the Winter Palace,' a man told her. Around her, crowds waved red flags. Walking through the crush of people, Katya found Fyodor among a group of boys she recognised from the factory.

Grabbing him by the elbow, she swung him to face her. 'Where have you been? I've been worried sick.'

Fyodor wrenched his arm free.

'I'm fine. I can look after myself.'

'Why didn't you tell me where you were going?'

Fyodor said nothing. Flashing her a dark look, he pushed his way deeper into the crowd. For a moment, Katya considered following him, forcing him to return with her back to the safety of their room. In the end, she decided to make her way to the back of the crowd and wait.

Later, as the crowd thinned, Katya's eyes darted from one end of the square to the other, searching for the thin figure of Fyodor. She could not see him and was growing worried until the moment she saw him run across the road. Moving into the shadows, she watched his face light up with pure joy. He left with his friends, waving a red flag and singing 'The Internationale'.

This is the final struggle
Let us group together, and tomorrow
The Internationale
Will be the human race.

Katya stepped out of the shadows and leant against the building. Looking up at the sky, she felt a new heaviness weighing upon her heart.

'Keep him safe,' she whispered to the moon, 'he's only a boy,' then hurried home.

43

Narva, December 1917

Gauzy mist spread across the fields and settled in an icy film over the grass. Above the mist, the sky was as clear and pale as blue porcelain. Wearing heavy winter boots, Marie walked beside her father, struggling to keep up. They would normally use the motorcar or the carriage for the trip to the factory, but declaring that he 'fancied a walk', Monsieur Kulbas had asked Marie to join him.

Buoyed by the popularity of the Bolsheviks, the workers at the plant had threatened to go on strike for a number of weeks. Herman Kulbas had heard rumours that a meeting was being organised, and hoped to reason with the workers and convince them not to strike. On reaching the plant, Marie and her father found the gates chained and a banner declaring the factory to be the property of the Soviet workers.

'The audacity of those . . .' Monsieur Kulbas's lips clamped over the profanity that threatened to explode out of him.

He marched towards the back gates, Marie hurrying after him.

'To think,' he grumbled, 'after all I have done for them, they betray me like this.'

'Please, Papa, calm yourself. Things will settle down. The whole empire is in turmoil.' She caught his arm to slow him. 'Everything will work out.'

'I don't think so, Marie. Not this time.'

At the back gates, they saw the keeper. A stooped man with a bushy beard and fading blue eyes, Lomtev had been working at the factory longer than anyone could recall.

'Monsieur Kulbas, thank heavens you are here!' Lomtev shuffled forward.

'What's happened?'

Lomtev glanced over his shoulder nervously. 'Those good-for-nothing thugs surrounded me this morning and took away my keys. May the devil take them, they nearly broke my arm.' He rubbed at a spot above his right elbow. 'But old Lomtev was one step ahead of them.' Grinning, he tapped his temple with his wrinkled finger. 'I have a second set and took them out as soon as they left me.'

Lifting his shirt, he showed them the keys he had pinned to his waistband.

'Good man.' Monsieur Kulbas looked around them to make sure they were not being watched. 'Hurry and open this door.'

'They are having the meeting on the factory floor.'

The factory, comprised of three two-storey grey buildings with angled rooftops and blackened chimneys, was surrounded on all sides by tall fences.

Marie and her father followed Lomtev past the first building.

'We should go through the back,' Lomtev suggested. 'They probably have someone guarding the front.'

It started to snow as they ducked between the buildings. Stopping at the back door, Lomtev pressed his ear to the wood, listening. Satisfied it was safe, he tried his key in the lock, working it back and forth, loosening the latch that had grown stiff with frost. It took Lomtev several attempts to unlock it. Once inside, he ushered them to the canteen where the meeting was already underway.

'What is the meaning of this? Who has authorised this meeting?'

Marie had never heard her father raise his voice at his employees. A dozen heads turned in surprise.

Monsieur Kulbas turned to the closest man. 'I asked a question. Have you all gone mute?'

A tall, blond youth stepped forward. 'We are on strike against you and your family who have been living in luxury off the proceeds of our sweat and toil.'

Turning crimson, Monsieur Kulbas trembled with rage. Squaring his shoulders, he faced his accuser. 'I have never taken a kopek that did not belong to me. And I challenge any man who thinks otherwise to prove it.' Thrusting his chin forward, he glared at the workers. Some looked at their feet, not willing to meet his eyes, but others met his stare boldly.

'I have lived my life honestly,' he bellowed, 'and lost a son in the war.' His voice wavered slightly. 'No one can ask any man to do more.'

'Workers, don't be fooled by his words.' The blond youth addressed the assembled men. 'His family is rich because they have exploited people like us for generations. He speaks of hardship and honesty but they are just words to him. I say let's put the strike to a vote.'

'Vote if you must.' Monsieur Kulbas looked each man in the eye. 'But don't vote blindly. Think about what you are doing. Most of you have been working for me for years. We built this factory together. Don't throw away all that we have achieved on a whim.'

But his plea fell on deaf ears and the members of the factory's Soviet of Workers voted to go on strike.

Forced to leave, Monsieur Kulbas looked shrunken as he walked through the factory gates.

'It's over.' He disentangled his arm from Marie's. 'They have won.' Increasing his pace, he did not turn to see if she was following.

Marie watched his disappearing figure, wishing Nikolai was there to counsel her on how to help him. After the devastating loss of his son, Herman Kulbas had attempted to distract himself through work. Now that too had been taken from him, and Marie feared her father would descend into deep despair.

Back at the house, Marie unlaced her boots by the front door.

'How did the meeting go?' Anna was waiting with a pair of silk slippers.

'The gates were locked,' she said in a quiet voice. 'When we did finally get in, Papa could not stop the men from striking.' She could hear her parents' muffled voices coming from the drawing room. 'He is awfully angry.'

'Those revolutionary hooligans!' Anna helped Marie with her coat and hat. 'Now all the workers feel they can behave as they wish.'

Marie ran a hand over her clothes and hair. 'I think I'll join my parents.'

'Zoya just went in with a fresh pot of tea.'

Entering the room, Marie went directly to sit beside her mother.

'Oh, Marie, your father has been reading me the most dreadful news. First the Tsar and his family were forced to leave their home, and now these radicals have attacked the Winter Palace.'

Marie exchanged a look with her father. It was obvious he had not told his wife about the strike at the factory.

Zoya placed a glass *estekan* beside Marie and took Pauline Kulbas's empty one to refill it from the *samovar* in the far corner of the room.

'The papers say that the women's battalion sent to defend the palace was massacred.' Madame Kulbas blew her nose delicately into a handkerchief. 'That Lenin is an animal.' She paused to accept a fresh glass of tea. 'There's nothing he will not do. His Red Guard thugs cause havoc wherever they go, putting wrong ideas in the workers' heads.'

Marie glanced again at her father. He was staring out the window. The paper, with the bold headline THE BOLSHEVIKS' REVOLUTION, lay on his lap.

'You seem lost in thought, Herman,' Pauline Kulbas remarked. 'What are you thinking?'

'Hmm?' Herman Kulbas blinked. 'Well . . .' He picked up the paper and flicked through it until he found the article he was looking for. 'It appears Lenin wants to sign a peace treaty with the Germans.'

'That spineless villain! But I suppose an end to the fighting can only be a good thing.'

Monsieur Kulbas regarded her with a defeated expression. 'Lenin might be wanting an end to the war, but he won't be putting an end to the hostilities. With the war no longer a concern for them, the Bolsheviks will be free to push forward with their policies of seizing land and nationalising the factories.'

'That man is a traitor and a spy. To think we lost our precious Nikolai just to end up . . .' Madame Kulbas could not go on.

'Come now, Mama.' Marie rubbed her mother's back. 'Maybe you should rest for a while.' She helped her mother to her feet. At the door, Marie took a last look at her father.

Herman Kulbas, having removed his glasses, held them at the end of his fingers like a man about to be hanged and was staring blankly at the tangle of trees just outside the window.

44

Narva, March 1918

From the moment the Bolsheviks seized power, Lenin pressed his newly appointed war commissar, Leo Trotsky, to sign a peace treaty with Germany. In November, Trotsky travelled to Brest-Litovsk, a town close to the trenches, to negotiate the terms of the treaty. As negotiations continued, German demands grew and Trotsky argued with Lenin over signing a treaty that would be humiliating to Russians. In January 1918, the Germans gave the Bolsheviks an ultimatum.

Trotsky stalled, still refusing to sign.

On 18 February 1918, the Germans broke the truce, attacking Russian territory. Virtually unopposed, the German army entered Estonia. In one of life's ironies, the previous day the Estonian National Council had issued a Declaration of Independence, declaring Estonia to be a neutral and independent state.

Caught between the retreating Red Army and the advancing Germans, Narva endured days of relentless shelling. Exploding shells shook the earth and rattled the nerves to the point that the citizens thought they might go mad. As a precaution, Herman Kulbas ordered his family to sleep in the two large rooms downstairs.

On the morning of March 4, Marie woke with a start. The room was still pitch-black and it took a moment for her eyes to adjust to the darkness. Eventually she could make out the shape of her mother sleeping beside her.

'Mama.' She shook her shoulder. 'Listen, the shelling has stopped.'

Running to the bay windows, Marie pulled back the heavy curtains.

'What's going on?' Valentin asked, his voice groggy with sleep.

Across the room, Pauline Kulbas sat up stiffly.

'Herman?' She turned to her husband. 'Herman, wake up. The shelling . . . it has stopped.'

Suddenly alert, Herman Kulbas sat upright then sprang up to join Marie by the window. Father and daughter stared into the quiet expanse of the morning mist carpeting the fields. After weeks of continuous shelling, the silence was almost unnerving.

'What do you see?' Pauline Kulbas asked.

'Nothing,' her husband replied. By now, Valentin too was standing by his father's side.

They were startled by loud knocking at the front door and, soon after, a knock at the drawing room door. Zoya, her face flushed and looking as if she had dressed in a hurry, walked in.

'Sorry to disturb you, Madame,' she said with a curtsy, adjusting a woollen shawl over her shoulders. 'There is a messenger here with an urgent letter for Monsieur Kulbas.'

'It's from the mayor, Monsieur,' Zoya said as he pushed past her.

Marie, still in her nightgown, followed.

'What have you got for me, young man?' Monsieur Kulbas addressed the tall youth waiting for him at the landing.

Reaching deep into the pocket of his winter coat, the young man pulled out a white envelope. 'From the mayor, Monsieur.'

Having known the mayor for many years, Herman Kulbas immediately recognised the handwriting. 'Why didn't the mayor call me on the telephone?'

'The phone lines are all down after last night's shelling.'

Ripping open the sealed envelope, Monsieur Kulbas read the brief note, his grip tightening into a fist when he reached the end.

The messenger shifted nervously from one foot to the other. Thinking the youth was waiting for a tip, the butler stepped forward with a few coins.

The messenger stepped back, shaking his head. 'No, Monsieur, thank you all the same but I was told by the mayor to wait for the Monsieur's response.' He turned shyly to Monsieur Kulbas. 'He said it was urgent.'

Monsieur Kulbas nodded his understanding. 'Zoya,' he said, 'take this young man to the kitchen and make him some breakfast.' He turned back to the messenger. 'Have the butler bring you to the library when you have finished eating. I will have your response to the mayor then.'

Marie waited for the messenger to leave with Zoya, before stepping forward. 'What is it, Papa?' She touched him lightly on the forearm. 'What did the mayor say?'

'Narva has surrendered to the Germans.'

Pauline Kulbas, who had come to stand by Marie's side, drew in a sharp breath. Herman Kulbas walked over and pulled his wife into his embrace. She whimpered into his chest, her round shoulders quaking under the wrap she had hastily flung around herself.

'Now, now, my dear, stop this nonsense,' he soothed. 'As long as we cooperate with them, they will leave us be.' He kissed her forehead. 'It will be like having house guests.'

Marie tensed. 'What do you mean "house guests"?'

Her father's face grew serious. 'The Germans will billet their soldiers and officers among the city's residents.'

'Can they do that?' Valentin asked. 'Just march into people's homes?'

Herman Kulbas let out a hollow laugh. 'They are the victors, my son. They can do whatever they like.'

Spring had always been Marie's favourite season. After the dark winter months, the longer days, new green shoots and the migration of birds never failed to lift her spirits. Today, however, looking out from her bedroom window, the blossoming of spring did little to lift her sombre mood.

Hearing footsteps, she turned to see her father and Valentin walking rapidly along the gravel path towards the shed. Wearing heavy winter boots, her father carried a spade in one hand and a satchel in the other. He waited outside the shed for his son, who emerged a few minutes later pushing a cart.

There was a knock at the door and her mother entered.

'What's Papa up to?' Marie asked.

Madame Kulbas joined her daughter at the window. Together they watched as Monsieur Kulbas crossed the open field with Valentin and disappeared into the woods.

Reaching into the folds of her dress, Pauline Kulbas produced a velvet bag of the deepest shade of green. 'I need you to listen carefully,' she said in a low voice. 'Get your most precious pieces of jewellery and place them in this bag.'

'What will you do with them?'

'Your father is burying them in the woods in waterproof bags.' Taking her daughter's hands between her own, she warned, 'You must not speak to anyone about this. The Germans will suspect we have buried our gold and they will bribe the servants to find out where.'

'Surely our servants would not betray us,' Marie cried. Most of the household's staff had been with the family for years.

'My child,' Marie's mother looked at her sadly, 'these are desperate times. In a few hours, the whole of Narva will be swarming with German soldiers. Who's to say who can or cannot be trusted?'

Looking into her mother's face, Marie saw the deep lines of worry around her eyes and agreed to do as she had asked.

Going to the jewellery box on her dressing table, she chose a few pieces, mainly ones with sentimental value, and placed them in the bag.

'Here you are, Mama.' She handed over the bag.

Madame Kulbas touched Marie's wrist, her fingers cold as ice. 'These are dark days, Marie. Pray they will not last long.'

Once her mother had gone, Marie returned to the window in time to see Valentin leave the woods alone and run to the stables. He had no sooner disappeared from view than Marie became aware of the noise of approaching cars.

Valentin emerged from the stables. He paused a moment, his face turned to the sound of the engines, before he started running towards the house. Still some distance away, it was clear the cars were moving fast, their engines shredding the stillness in the air. The sound of running feet reached her door.

'Marie, come quick.' One hand on her chest, Anna was panting for breath. 'The Germans. They will be here soon.'

Marie's eyes darted to the woods. Papa!

'Get my boots,' she said to Anna, her eyes searching the edge of the thicket.

'Marie, the Germans . . .'

'Do it now.' Marie cut her off. 'Quickly!'

Outside, Marie ran to where her father had entered the woods. She hadn't stopped to put on her coat and the chill wind cut through her thin layer of clothing.

'Papa!' she shouted when she reached the trees. 'Papa!'

Her lungs burning, Marie leant one hand against a tree.

'PAPA!'

'For heaven's sake, Marie. Stop this racket.' Herman Kulbas stepped from behind the bushes.

'Didn't you hear me?' Marie asked. 'I've been calling and calling.'

'Of course I heard you. I'd be surprised if the whole German regiment didn't hear you.' He walked towards her with unhurried steps. She noticed he no longer carried anything.

'What did you do with the cart and the spade?'

'I don't know what you are talking about.' He wiped his hands on his trousers.

'I saw you go into the woods with them.'

Herman Kulbas straightened and looked at her as if considering how much he should tell her. 'I hid them,' he said eventually.

'Oh, Papa.' She handed him a handkerchief. 'You've got mud all over your pants.'

Herman Kulbas cocked his head to one side. 'Stop fussing over my pants.' He took her handkerchief and wiped his hands. 'What are you doing out here anyway? You'll catch your death dressed like that.'

'I was worried for you.' She was still slightly out of breath. 'The Germans are almost here.'

A look of worry passed over Herman Kulbas's face but he quickly regained his composure and gave Marie a confident smile. 'In that case, let's not keep our guests waiting.'

Back at the house, they found two wagons and a motorcar parked by the front steps.

'We'll go through the front door,' Marie's father whispered, offering her his arm.

Keeping her head high, she walked past the Germans. Braving a glance at the wagons' occupants, she was surprised by how young most of them looked. Their coats hung off their thin frames, giving them the appearance of children dressed as soldiers.

The household staff carried buckets of water to the soldiers, who took it in turns to fill their canisters. As Marie passed, a few of the men called out words that made her blush.

At the top of the stairs, a group of German officers in long woollen coats and *Pickelhauben* stood beside Valentin and a pale-faced Pauline Kulbas.

Together, Marie and her father climbed the stairs slowly. The nearest officer took off his spiked helmet, tucking it under one arm. He stepped forward, clicked his heels and gave them a short bow. 'I am Captain Klaus Greenhauser. My men and I are to be stationed here.'

Next to Marie, her father returned the officer's bow with a tilt of his head. 'I am Herman Kulbas and this is my daughter Marie. I see you have already met my son and wife.'

'They greeted us in your absence.' The captain looked pointedly at Herman Kulbas's trousers.

'You must excuse my attire,' Marie's father said apologetically, and motioned for them to go inside. 'Let us all move into the drawing room. We will be far more comfortable out of this cold.'

The officers made no move to go inside. Marie noticed the captain was now staring at her muddy boots, frowning.

'May I enquire as to why you were in the woods, Mademoiselle?'

'My daughter and I always enjoy an invigorating walk first thing in the morning.' Herman Kulbas looked down at his pants. 'I'm afraid I tripped,' he said lightly, but no one smiled.

'Indeed.' Captain Greenhauser's gaze lingered on Marie a moment longer. 'You must have left in a hurry, Mademoiselle,' he observed. 'You didn't even stop to put on a coat.'

Marie's heart skipped inside her chest. Had the captain guessed what her father had been doing?

'Captain, we have refreshments prepared for you.' Despite her smile, Marie detected a tremble in her mother's voice.

With a small nod, the captain, followed by the other officers, walked after Pauline Kulbas to the drawing room and Marie hurried upstairs to change.

Descending the stairs a few minutes later, after having changed out of her muddy clothes, Marie found the cook, Lara, and Zoya standing with their ears pressed to the closed doors. Seeing Marie, the two stepped back quickly, dropping their eyes.

'What are they talking about?' Marie asked in a low voice.

'I'm not sure, Mademoiselle,' Lara said, staring at her shoes. A pink flush rose from her neck to her face. 'We only just got here.'

'Thank you, you may go,' Marie told them.

They hesitated, seemingly reluctant to leave.

'What is it now?' Marie rolled her eyes.

'It's the soldiers, Mademoiselle. They are hungry.'

'So why don't you feed them?' Marie asked, frustration creeping into her voice.

'There's not enough food.' The cook wrung her hands nervously.

'I sent the stable hand, Ivan, to see if the baker had any bread he could sell us. He came back empty-handed looking white as a ghost. Isn't that right, Zoya?' She looked to Zoya who nodded her head vigorously.

'Tell her about the baker,' Zoya prompted.

Lara looked over her shoulder at the closed doors and lowered her voice further. 'Ivan found the baker sitting outside his shop with a big gash across his forehead. The soldiers had beaten him with their rifles for resisting when they robbed him of all his bread and several sacks of flour.'

'They're going to starve us to death,' Zoya whimpered.

'This is no time to fall apart,' Marie said sharply. Seeing Zoya recoil, she added in a softer voice, 'We'll manage. I assure you my father will take care of us.'

Zoya blew her nose loudly into a handkerchief.

Lara said, 'The Germans have posted a notice in the middle of the town square ordering all residents to take soldiers into their homes. Ivan said some people have chosen to leave instead, but the Germans are only allowing them to take one suitcase and everything is searched to make sure no one has packed any valuables. This lot –' she pointed to the wall, beyond which the soldiers had already started to pitch their tents '– are only marginally better. I've given them all our bread and cooked them what eggs we had and they threw their dirty uniforms at me to wash.'

'Some of them have broken into Master's wine cellar and are passed out drunk on the lawn.' Zoya shook her head. 'Savages. God help us all.'

'That's enough,' Marie snapped. 'We must not let them see us in despair. Zoya, you get started on the uniforms. And Lara, take Ivan with you to the cellar and see how many potatoes we can spare. Maybe you can make the soldiers a broth for later.'

Marie's decisive instructions stirred the two women into action. 'Yes, Mademoiselle.'

They hurried off and Marie rapped on the drawing-room door,

waiting a moment before opening it wide enough to put her head through.

'Come in,' her father beckoned and, together with the German officers, stood when she entered.

She walked over to the settee where her mother sat with a straight back.

'Naturally all livestock and food reserves will be confiscated by the army,' Captain Greenhauser was explaining to her father.

'What will we eat?' asked Herman Kulbas, visibly taken aback.

'You will receive rations.' Leaning back in his chair, the captain continued. 'My officers and I will live in the house. You and your family will share the servants' quarters with your staff.'

Madame Kulbas threaded her fingers through Marie's, squeezing them tightly.

'No need to upset yourself, madam.' The captain smiled. 'As long as you cooperate, you'll find us quite civil.' His smile didn't reach his eyes. 'Now if you will excuse us, my officers and I need to discuss private matters of importance.' And with those words, the captain signalled an end to the conversation, dismissing the Kulbas family from their own parlour.

45

Fortress of Peter and Paul, Petrograd, June 1918

The only light in the crowded prison cell came from a single window set high in the wall.

Dampness pressed at Alexei's chest. He slept badly, coughing and shivering with the cold. During the day, he spent hours watching the sunlight shifting along the wall and tried to think about how people in the city's crowded streets were spending their day.

Today he watched the patch of light through a hazy filter. His head, burning like a furnace, rolled from side to side.

He was dimly aware of men moving about him, occasionally kneeling before him and staring into his face with concerned looks. In his weakened state, the voices all sounded muffled and distorted and he looked back at the faces with little comprehension.

Falling into fitful dreams, he imagined himself in a bright sunny room. Marie was there, in the dress she had worn to the races. Smiling, she looked at him with her warm grey eyes. She offered him a glass of water and when she bent over, gently cupping his head in one hand, the light caught the small gold cross dangling from her neck. Alexei woke feeling parched, his breath shallow in his lungs.

A commotion outside distracted him from his discomfort. Men's shouts mixed with the sound of heavy footsteps running down the corridor. The gates flew open and guards carrying torches entered, yelling and pulling men to their feet.

'Get up, old man.' A large guard kicked Alexei's boot. 'You are all to move to the courtyard.'

Hooking a hand under Alexei's armpit, the guard lifted him to his feet and, sensing Alexei was too weak to walk on his own, kept his hand there, propelling him forward. In the corridor, the guards used their rifles to push the prisoners into lines.

Led out into the public square, Alexei, accustomed to many days in the dark, blinked in the sunlight. Shielding his eyes, he shuffled into the middle of the square, where the guard who had been supporting him threw him to the ground. Two prisoners helped him back to his feet and held him upright, which was when Alexei saw that they were facing a mob of guards. As he watched, one of the guards stepped forward and, without warning, raised his pistol and shot the first prisoner in the head. Stepping over the crumpled figure, the guard shot the next prisoner.

The man beside Alexei murmured his last prayers. Alexei, too, consigned his soul to God and silently said goodbye to his family. As a third, fourth and fifth man were executed Alexei focused on the image he carried in his head, wanting his last thoughts to be of Marie.

'Halt! What is going on here?' A man with straw-coloured hair shouldered his way to the front. The guards reluctantly parted to let him through.

One of the guards stepped into the man's path. 'Papers?' Reaching into his jacket the man pulled out a folded piece of paper, which he offered to the guard. After studying the papers, the guard stepped aside. 'My apologies, Comrade Commissar.'

'What is the meaning of this?' the commissar asked when he saw the dead bodies.

'These men are officers from the imperial army and enemies of the revolution,' one of the guards replied.

The commissar frowned. Raising his voice, he said, 'Comrades, listen to me. My name is Sergei Bogoleev and I am a commissar with the Red Army. We need to stop these executions. We must show the Russian people that we are not mindless killers.'

'These men have grown fat from sucking the blood of people like us,' replied a guard. Behind him, other soldiers nodded and pressed forward.

'This one here –' the executioner kicked a lifeless body '– enjoyed humiliating us. He called us worthless stupid *muzhiks*. He deserved to die like a dog.'

Bogoleev raised a palm to pacify them. 'Comrades, you are not like them.' He pointed to the trembling, ragged men. 'I hate them as much as you, and, once trialled, they will pay for their arrogance and greed. But for now, we must put emotion aside and maintain discipline.'

The guards grew quiet, as if considering Bogoleev's words, though some continued to throw hate-filled looks at the remaining prisoners.

'Guards, escort these prisoners back to the dungeon,' Bogoleev ordered.

As the men filed past, his eyes fell on a man carried by two others. Stepping forward, he stuck out an arm to stop them. Bogoleev looked into the prisoner's face. He motioned to one of the guards. 'This prisoner needs medical attention. Take him to the hospital.'

The guard looked at Alexei with hard eyes. 'The man is an enemy of the revolution. He deserves to rot in a cell.'

Anger flared in Bogoleev's chest. 'If you don't do as I say, you'll be replacing him in the prison cell.' Drawing close to the guard, he smelt the scent of his unwashed skin and the nicotine on his breath. '*Now*, comrade,' he said coolly. 'Do I make myself clear?'

'Yes, Comrade Commissar.'

The guard motioned for another guard to move Alexei from the line. A stretcher was called and Alexei was lifted onto it.

Bogoleev looked into Alexei's face. A layer of film clouded Alexei's eyes and he looked around with incomprehension. As the men lifted the stretcher, Bogoleev grabbed the guard's arm. 'I want our best doctors to look after him.'

The guard opened his mouth to object then closed it. 'Yes, Commissar.'

'One more thing: I want a guard to be stationed outside his room. No one other than the doctors or nurses must be allowed to see him. Not without my permission.'

The guard nodded. 'Yes, Commissar.'

Yekaterinburg, July

Buoyed by their rapid success in Petrograd and Moscow, the Bolsheviks began a campaign to enforce their rule over the rest of the country. They were opposed by the White Army, which was fiercely against the Bolshevik revolution. The White Army commanders used the humiliating terms agreed to by the Bolsheviks at Brest-Litovsk to rally support. With Tobolsk, where the royal family was held, threatening to fall into the hands of their enemies, Lenin ordered their evacuation to Yekaterinburg, in central Russia.

On their arrival at Yekaterinburg's train station, the guards led the Romanovs into two open cars and drove them through the streets at walking pace. Crowds that were packed onto the sidewalks jeered, calling out lewd remarks.

'Keep your head up, dear,' Alexandra instructed Tatiana. 'Don't let them forget who you are.'

A large peasant with a full beard broke away from the crowd and, eyes blazing with hatred, spat into the car.

'German whore,' he hissed.

Alexandra kept her eyes straight ahead, resisting the urge to wipe the saliva off her face. Next to her, Nicholas rested a sympathetic hand on her knee and gave her his handkerchief.

Their cars came to a stop before a nondescript building hidden from the street by tall wooden gates. Red Guards stood watching as the family struggled with their luggage to the foyer.

'Before we let you move to your rooms,' a guard said, blocking their way, 'we need to inspect your baggage.'

'Whatever for?' protested Alexandra. 'You have already taken everything of value.'

Pushing past her, the guard broke the lock on the first trunk and began rifling through the clothes.

'What exactly are you looking for?' Nicholas asked.

Opening Alexandra's trunk, the men pulled out her medical bag, sniffing and sticking their fingers into every vial and ointment.

'This is an outrage!' she shouted, close to tears.

'Shut your mouth!'

Nicholas stepped forward, squaring his shoulders. 'Sir, I demand you apologise to my wife.'

Rising to his feet, the guard stood over Nicholas. 'You are not at Tsarskoe any more. You demand and receive nothing. And if I hear you open your mouth again, you will be sentenced to hard labour.'

Turning back to the trunk, the guard gave it a sharp kick, spilling more of its contents over the floor. 'Take your vile things away.'

Walking behind two guards, the Romanovs made their way to the back of the house, where they were assigned two bedrooms, a toilet they shared with their guards, and a large living room with an arched doorway.

Within a few days, a second wooden fence surrounded the house and more sentries were posted every few metres.

'You would think this place was a fortress given the number of guards assigned to it,' Alexandra commented one evening. She was sewing a necklace into the hem of Olga's skirt. Her own corset had several brooches and rings sewn into its lining. She shifted in her seat to reposition one that dug into her ribs.

'Should God permit,' Alexandra told her daughters, 'this jewellery will see us through in exile.'

On the morning of his fiftieth birthday, Nicholas drew back the curtains to find that his window had been nailed shut.

'Papa!' he heard Tatiana scream. Rushing to his daughters' bedroom, he found them huddled in a corner as a guard whitewashed the windows outside.

Rapping his knuckles on the glass, he demanded angrily. 'What is the meaning of this?'

The guard shrugged and mouthed, 'Orders.'

Stricken, Nicholas stood back and watched as the last of the blue sky disappeared behind the white paint.

Refused contact with the outside world, the family remained ignorant of the civil war between the Red and the White armies. Had the Romanovs known, it might have brought them some comfort to learn that the White Army had fought the Reds almost to the perimeters of Yekaterinburg.

Worried that the presence of the royal family might provide extra motivation to the Whites, Lenin gave the orders that sealed their fate.

Waking early, Nicholas climbed out of bed, careful not to disturb his sleeping wife. Walking to the lavatory, he avoided eye contact with the guard posted outside. The man leered and as Nicholas moved past him hissed, 'Don't forget to look at the drawings.'

Nicholas ignored the comment. The guards had pasted on the walls pornographic drawings of Alexandra with Rasputin. After the first time he saw them, Nicholas took pains not to let his eyes wander over them a second time.

Later, strolling through the garden with his daughters, he heard artillery fire coming from the direction of the woods. Faces turned to the sound, they listened, trying to judge the distance to the fighting.

'Who are they shooting at, Papa?' Tatiana asked.

'They might be just practising their drills,' he replied, not wishing to alarm them even as he noticed the guards all held their rifles with white-knuckled grips.

Upon returning inside, Nicholas found Superintendent Yurovsky waiting for him in the family's living room. Alexandra, who had been sitting at the table, stood stiffly when she saw him.

'I was arranging the medicine when the superintendent dropped by with a gift for Alexei.'

Nicholas understood that Alexandra's reference to medicine meant she had been removing jewellery from frayed hems. Rattled by the unexpected visit, her movements were jumpy and agitated, leaving Nicholas to wonder if she had managed to hide what she was doing without rousing suspicion.

'I brought some eggs for your son.' The superintendent stepped forward, showing Nicholas the basket of fresh eggs. 'I heard little Alexei has been unwell and thought these might help increase his strength.'

'That is kind of you.' Nicholas's words came out flat, without gratitude.

'Well, I shall not bother you any longer.' The superintendent turned to leave but before he reached the corridor, he stopped. 'One other thing: there's been some gunfire in town and we might be obliged to move your family at short notice.'

'I'm sure you will decide what's best for us.' Nicholas kept his voice even despite the hollow feeling in his stomach.

'Good day to you.' The superintendent gave them a small nod. 'And my apologies for disturbing you unannounced.' He glanced to where Alexandra kept her basket.

'Not at all.' Alexandra smiled thinly.

'Oh, Nicky, do you suppose the superintendent suspected me?' Alexandra asked, her words spilling out in a rush as soon as the superintendent was out of earshot.

'I don't know, but we must be more vigilant.' He looked at the archway through which the superintendent had disappeared. 'I do not trust that man.'

It was well past midnight when the family physician, Dr Botkin, woke the Romanovs.

'I apologise for disturbing you, Your Highness, but I have just been informed by the superintendent that there has been some more fighting in the town. For your safety they have decided to evacuate the family from the building.'

Thirty minutes later, the Romanovs were washed, dressed and ready to leave. Alexandra and her daughters wore corsets with jewellery sewn into the bodices and carried pillows that had jewels hidden in the stuffing.

Carrying Alexei in his arms, Nicholas led his family down the stairs and out of the house. They crossed the courtyard and entered a long hall that took them to a small basement room.

Finding it empty of furniture, Alexandra turned to the closest guard and asked, 'May we not even have a chair?'

Two chairs were brought in and Nicholas, still carrying Alexei, sat close to his wife. After a tense wait, during which no one spoke, the doors opened and the superintendent strode in, followed by several guards. A lone light cast a thin circle in the middle of the room. Standing just outside the circle, the superintendent's features were partially hidden, giving him a menacing air.

'*Nicholas Romanov, in the interest of our glorious revolution*,' he read aloud from a yellow telegram, '*you and your family have been sentenced to death*.' Lifting his gaze, he looked Nicholas straight in the eye. 'I have orders to shoot you all.'

'What?' Nicholas jumped up. Behind him, Olga and Tatiana screamed and clung to each other. Alexandra hurriedly crossed herself just before the first bullets were fired.

Nicholas was the first to fall, staggering backwards. Behind him, Alexandra, shot through the head, was thrown to the floor, a dark stain spreading like a red halo around her head. The guards, bunched in the doorway, fired wildly into the room, none of them able to get clear shots over one another's shoulders.

The girls proved harder to kill, with the bullets ricocheting from their bejewelled corsets.

'Hold your fire!' the superintendent shouted and the guns fell silent. Drifts of smoke filled the room. Although the screaming had stopped, three of the girls, still breathing, whimpered on the floor.

'Finish them off,' Yurovsky ordered.

Moving from one sister to the next, the guards silenced each girl with a bullet to the temple.

Taking small shallow breaths, Alexei's fingers still clutched at his father's jacket. The last thing he saw was the barrel of the superintendent's gun as he fired at close range.

In the still, cool darkness of the early morning, the bodies of the Romanovs were carried on stretchers to a truck waiting at the front of the house.

Holding a bag of jewels stolen from his victims, the superintendent watched the tail-lights fade into the distance. Mopping the sweat from his brow, he joined the group of guards passing a bottle of rum between them.

'Well, comrades,' he said, taking a long swallow from the bottle, 'I think our job here is done.'

46

Petrograd, August 1918

Alexei's continuous coughing fits tore the air from his lungs, leaving him exhausted. Next to his bed, two candles flickered in the necks of empty bottles. Closing his eyes, he concentrated on steadying his ragged breathing, while his heart drummed irregular beats. His bones and muscles ached. Inhaling, he doubled over as a fresh bout of coughing overcame him. When it finally passed, he straightened and looked around at the bare whitewashed walls.

He had been in hospital for eight weeks recovering from typhus. He spent his days with little to do. Allowed only the Bolshevik-sponsored newspapers, he refused to read them, despising the Soviet glorification in its articles. He tried to think back to the day in the courtyard, but his memory of the events was sketchy and disjointed.

'You were brought here on the orders of a high-ranking commissar,' the nurse tending to Alexei told him. 'The sentry posted outside your door has strict orders as to who is allowed in and out of your room.'

'And what news of the war?' Alexei asked.

'Lenin is promising supplies of food to soldiers who join the Red Army,' she whispered while pretending to adjust his pillow. 'He has made Trotsky the new war commissar. Trotsky now makes regular trips to the front in his armoured train, giving long speeches on the importance of victory against the White Army.'

She took Alexei's pulse. 'Of course, I'm not familiar with army politics but it seems to me an army confident of victory should not need to go to such lengths to rally the support of its troops.'

Straightening, the nurse smiled sweetly at the sentry hovering a few metres away. A silent Cossack with broad shoulders and dark wavy hair, he might have been handsome if not for the injury that deformed one side of his face.

With each passing day, Alexei's health improved. As he regained his strength, he was allowed to spend the mornings in the garden. Accompanied by his silent sentry, Alexei's repeated queries about his family and the length of his stay in hospital went unanswered. Then one day he was told a commissar would be visiting him.

The sun had already begun its descent in the west when the door to his room opened and Bogoleev walked in. Alexei's initial surprise at seeing him soon turned to suspicion when he noticed the red armband and realised Bogoleev must be the commissar.

'You are looking much better than the last time I saw you.' Bogoleev smiled and dropped a copy of *Dien*, one of the Bolshevik newspapers, on Alexei's bed. 'I believe this is the second time I have saved your life.'

Alexei started to speak but Bogoleev stopped him. 'There's no need to thank me.'

'*Thank* you?' Alexei snorted. 'For making me your prisoner?'

'I thought you might be a little more grateful.'

'You saved me from your own guards. They were behaving like animals.'

'What do you expect?' Bogoleev replied coldly. 'For three years, the officers treated those men as cannon fodder. They degraded and humiliated them, then packed them off to be slaughtered. Did you expect the men to then turn and bow before them?'

'You know very well not all officers behaved as you have just described. Besides, what about you? Last time we met, you had been made a captain.'

Bogoleev's jaw tensed. 'I had to work twice as hard for every one of my promotions than most officers. More than once, I was passed over in favour of men who turned up their noses at me because my father was a teacher and not a nobleman.'

'Is that why you joined the Red Guards? To get revenge?'

Bogoleev was silent for a moment. 'Is that what you think?'

'So why did you join the Reds?'

'I heard Lenin speak.' He said reflectively. 'His reasoning made sense. Kerensky's army was in disarray and his provisional army was powerless to turn the country around. Soldiers were leaving the front in droves. It was obvious the war was as good as lost. So yes, I joined the Reds. They need men who can lead, men who are able to develop policies and organise troops. Men like me.' He walked around Alexei's bed and leant over him. 'And men like you.'

Alexei laughed contemptuously. 'You must be mad. I will never join your army of ruffians.'

Bogoleev straightened. 'Be careful what you say, Serov. You are no longer in charge.'

'I'd rather face a firing squad.'

'That can be arranged,' Bogoleev said sharply. 'But what about your family? Are you willing to risk their lives as well?'

Alexei's mouth went dry. 'What do you mean?'

'We know they are living in Uglich.'

'You wouldn't dare.'

'I do whatever is necessary.'

'What happened to you, Bogoleev? You are not the man I remember.'

Bogoleev stared at Alexei. 'The war happened,' he replied coolly. 'The war left its mark on all of us.'

'You should have let those hooligans shoot me.'

'Despite what you think, that's not what the Red Army is about. We believe in equality between people, regardless of their background. We stand for the people.'

'You are deluded, Bogoleev. The Red Army is a bunch of thugs. It's only a matter of time before the White commander crushes you.

Trotsky has no military experience and the Allies will never support the Bolsheviks now that they've signed the peace treaty with the Germans. The Red Army is doomed.'

'We have the support of the people.'

'The Whites have the support of the imperial commanders and the Allied forces.'

'There are plenty of imperial commanders who have joined us.'

'Hardly enough to help you win. It's only a matter of time before the Tsar –'

'The Tsar is dead,' Bogoleev said flatly. 'And so is his family. The Romanovs are no more.'

'The whole family?' Alexei looked at Bogoleev in disbelief. 'Why?'

Bogoleev's lips pursed into a thin line. 'It was a necessary step towards the greater good of the revolution.'

'Surely you don't believe that.'

'We are at war.' Bogoleev's voice raised an octave. 'And the Tsar and his family posed a threat. They needed to be –' he faltered. '– removed. There was no other choice.'

'The Russian people will never stand for it.'

'The Russian people hated the Romanovs, especially that German woman.'

Alexei pointed an accusing finger at Bogoleev. 'And you want me to join your gang of murderous criminals?'

'I'm warning you, Comrade Serov.'

'If this is your bargain with me, than you should have let them shoot me.'

Bogoleev studied his fingernails. 'There were very few commanders in the imperial army whose opinion I respected.' Looking up, he met Alexei's eyes. 'I saved your life that day because I knew you'd be an asset to the Red Army.'

'I will never join.'

'I'm going to ignore your comments for the last time.' Bogoleev picked up his hat and coat. 'Remember what I said about your family. I will return in two days for your answer.'

The sentry stood to attention when the commissar stepped into the hallway.

'At ease, comrade.' Bogoleev stood staring at the closed door, weighing a thought in his head. 'Have you been the sentry during these past weeks?'

'Yes, Comrade Commissar.'

'And during this time has Serov had many visitors?'

The sentry blinked. 'I was told he is not allowed visitors. His aide came by a few times but I refused him entry.'

'Very good.' Bogoleev eyed the sentry, taking the man's measure. There was something familiar about him. 'What is your name, comrade?'

'Ivanov, sir.'

'I know you. Did you fight at the front?'

'Yes, Comrade Commisar. I had escaped a POW camp and you were the captain of the battalion that rescued me.'

Bogoleev smiled in recognition. 'Of course, I remember you now.' Leaning forward, he placed a hand on the Cossack's shoulder. 'If the aide returns, allow him to visit but keep the door open and listen closely. I will return in two days. When I do, I want to know everything that was said in that room. Do I make myself clear?'

'Yes, Comrade Commissar.'

After months of almost no news from his family, Alexei was surprised when, the next day, the guard opened the door and stepped aside to let Grigory in. When Grigory tried to close the door behind him, the guard held out his hand.

'The door stays open.'

'I don't know how much time they are going to allow us,' Grigory whispered as soon as the guard turned away. 'I tried several times to visit you in jail and again here in hospital but I was refused each time.' He handed Alexei a parcel. 'It is from your family, but the sentry outside said he would have to go through the contents before you can have them.'

Alexei gestured for Grigory to sit down. 'I had a visit from Sergei Bogoleev. You've met him. He was the captain I was speaking to on the morning I found the Luger gun. He is now a political commissar and wants me to join the Red Army.'

Grigory fell silent as he slowly absorbed this surprising piece of information. 'What will you do?'

'Bogoleev is leaving me little choice. He is coming back tomorrow for his answer.'

'There must be something you can do. Maybe you could escape and go into hiding?'

Alexei shook his head. 'He knows Emily and the girls are staying at our estate in Uglich. He has threatened to go after them – but there still may be a way.' Alexei's eyes flickered to the sentry. 'I would need your help.'

Grigory leant forward. 'I'll do whatever you ask.'

It seemed only a few minutes had passed when the sentry announced that visiting time was over. Grigory left, promising to send a telegram to Emily on Alexei's behalf. After he was gone, the sentry motioned for Alexei to move to one side and wait as he checked his parcel. Alexei stood with barely restrained anger as the Cossack rummaged through the contents and opened his letters.

'Those are personal letters from my family,' he protested.

'I have my orders,' came the reply, but his tone suggested he was taking no pleasure in his task. Returning the letters to their envelopes, he placed them neatly back in the parcel. 'I will leave you to read your letters in private.'

Alexei was surprised by the unexpected show of respect. 'Thank you,' he said.

Taking his parcel, he carried it to the garden and sat under a large birch tree. A faint breeze, subtle and welcoming, moved through its branches. Among the letters and gifts his family had sent, the girls had packed his copy of *The Lady with the Little Dog*. Marie had held this very copy and read aloud from it. He noticed a bookmark. Opening the volume to the marked page, he read the first line.

> *And only now, when his head was grey, had he really fallen in love as one ought.*

A quiver passed through him. The words reflected his own heart. He had thought himself in love before, but it had never felt like this. Marie was water to his parched throat. His need for her went deeper than anything he had experienced before.

He stared at the cover. Tentatively, longingly, his fingers hovered over the surface her hands had touched. Bringing the book close to his face, he hoped to catch a scent that reminded him of her. It held the musty odour of old books, but beyond that, there was something else, a floral feminine fragrance, that took him back to the gardens of Tsarskoe Selo.

'Marie,' he whispered. 'Do you think of me?'

As promised, Bogoleev returned the next day for his answer.

'I'm pleased to hear you have accepted my offer.'

'You have left me with little choice.' Alexei kept his face blank. 'However, I do have one request. I would like to return to Uglich to visit my family.'

Bogoleev considered the demand. 'What guarantee do I have you will not flee?'

'Where would I flee? You know very well I will not put the lives of my family at risk.'

Uglich, August

'How long do you have?' sitting in the library, Emily's eyes glinted in the glow radiating from the fireplace.

'Three days.'

'Is that all?' Anxiety shadowed her features. 'That hardly leaves us any time.'

'That's all Bogoleev would allow me.'

'I don't think I can do it.'

'You must; we have no other choice,' Alexei said sharply.

Shrinking, she turned away, hiding her face behind her hand.

Regretting his tone, Alexei turned her towards him. 'I know the past few months have been hard on you.'

'You have no idea what I've been through.' She wiped her eyes. 'How much I worried. You should never have gone back to Petrograd. If only you had listened and stayed away, none of this would have happened.'

'Calm yourself, Emily. There may still be a way. If you only listen to my plan.'

She shook her head. 'I can't go through with it. The woods are full of partisans. They'll slit our throats if they get half a chance.'

'I'll protect you.'

'No,' she said decidedly. 'I won't risk our daughters' lives.'

'Whatever happens, you cannot stay here.'

'What are you saying?' Her face turned pale, despite the warmth of the fire. 'You told me we'd be safe here.'

Unable to say the words, Alexei looked directly into her eyes, letting her know the truth.

Rising from her seat, she began to pace the length of the room. 'How could you do this to us? This is all your fault, Alexei. You have put our lives in danger!'

'That's enough!' Alexei barked, fearing she was growing hysterical.

Startled, Emily stopped pacing and stared at him.

'Emily,' he said in a gentler tone, 'I know I have placed us in an impossible situation. I'm sorry. That was never my intention.' He took a step towards her. 'I have a plan but I need your help to make it work.'

Emily's chest rose and fell with every breath. 'I don't think I have it in me,' she said.

Gripping her shoulders, he brought his face close to hers. 'Emily, we have no other choice.'

Dressed in simple peasant clothing, they loaded a few essential belongings onto a small wagon, ready to leave under the cover of darkness. It was agreed that Grigory would remain behind, to avoid arousing suspicion. Once they reached Latvia, they would send word for him to join them.

'Do not pack anything of value in your bags,' Alexei warned. Emily had sewn three of Alexei's medals and several of her jewels into the hems of the dresses she and the girls wore.

Alexei kept to the road but at first light he turned the wagon towards the woods, following a narrow, rarely used trail. Going around a tight bend, they came across a group of men carrying a log to create a roadblock. Others, carrying torches, stepped into their path. When they got closer, they saw the men were Bolshevik partisans. Emily pressed close against Alexei.

'State your business,' demanded one in a gravelly voice. A thickset man, his moustache covered the whole of his top lip.

'We are travelling west to visit my wife's sick mother.'

Using his torch, the Bolshevik looked inside the wagon and saw they were carrying very little. 'Why do you not take the road?'

'We thought it would be safer going through the back roads. We didn't want to get caught in the fighting.'

Scratching the stubble on his chin, the guard turned and nodded to the others. 'Let them pass, comrades.'

The men had started to remove the roadblock when they were startled by the sound of galloping hooves.

'Halt!'

They turned to see two riders racing towards them.

'Don't let them pass!'

The men carrying the log dropped it and drew their guns. As the riders came closer, Alexei recognised Bogoleev and the guard from the hospital.

'This man is escaping the Red Army.' Bogoleev pointed to Alexei.

'My family is innocent. Tell these men to give them a free passage,' Alexei demanded.

'You are in no position to give orders here, Serov,' Bogoleev retorted. He motioned for the men to search the wagon.

The thickset Bolshevik, clearly put out by Bogoleev's authority, stepped forward. 'I give the orders around here. Who are you?'

Bogoleev pulled out his papers.

'I'm sorry, Comrade Commissar,' the partisan said stiffly when he had inspected them. Turning to his men, he bellowed, 'You heard the commissar – start searching the wagon.'

'You must have thought me a fool to let you go without sending someone to spy on you,' Bogoleev told Alexei.

'Surely you cannot in good conscience expect me to leave my family to fend for themselves. Let me see them safely to their destination and then I promise –'

'You will do no such thing!' Bogoleev interrupted. 'You will leave immediately with us.' He gestured to two of the Bolsheviks, who jumped into the wagon while Ivanov pointed a rifle at Alexei's chest. Grabbing Irena and Vera, the Bolsheviks held a knife to each of their throats.

'I beg you, don't harm them,' Emily pleaded.

'If you want your daughters unharmed, madam, your husband must join us and vow to fight the imperial White Army.'

In the back of the wagon, the Bolshevik soldier pressed the tip of his knife against Irena's throat, piercing the skin. A drop of blood trickled down her pale neck.

'Please let them go,' Emily sobbed. 'I beg of you.' She unfastened a gold bracelet she had hidden under her sleeve and held it out to them. 'Take this in exchange.'

The soldier took the bracelet, studied it in the dim light then dropped it into his pocket. He turned to Emily. 'You cannot buy me with your gold and fancy clothing.' Then he smiled, revealing several teeth missing. 'All the same, the Red Army appreciates your generosity.'

'Enough.' Alexei turned to Bogoleev. 'Do I have your word you will let my family go?'

Bogoleev nodded to the partisan and he eased the pressure on Irena's neck, motioning for his comrade to do the same.

'You have my word,' Bogoleev said.

Alexei's shoulders sagged. 'Then I will do as you ask.'

'You have made the right choice, comrade.' The partisan returned his knife to its sheath. Irena and Vera sagged to the floor of the wagon in relief. Tonya looked up at Alexei, her eyes swimming with tears.

'Papa . . .' She placed her small hand over his. 'What will we do without you?'

Alexei bent and kissed her forehead. 'You must be brave and do exactly what Mama asks of you.' He then embraced each girl in turn, pressing them against him.

'Send word to Grigory once you are safe,' he whispered in Emily's ear. 'He will look after you.'

'You've done the right thing.' Bogoleev patted Alexei's back. Turning to one of the men, he ordered him to hand over a horse. 'Just remember,' he told Alexei, 'as long as you remain loyal to the Red Army, your family will be safe.'

Mounting the horse, Alexei felt the sentry's gaze on him. Turning his head, their eyes met and held for the briefest second, and in that moment, before Ivanov's expression went blank, Alexei saw empathy in the other man's face.

47

Narva, September 1918

The chickens were the first to be killed to feed the army. Marie helped Lara collect wild mushrooms, goutweed, stinging nettle, sorrel and thistle for soups for the family. But these did little to quell the ever-present pangs of hunger.

From the food supplied to prepare meals for the Germans, the household received little more than tea and bread. Lara pilfered what she could, hiding it in the folds of her clothes. Later, sharing the few morsels with the rest of the household, she entertained them with tales of how she had managed to get the food past the Germans. 'Those flea-bitten German boys are too busy scratching themselves to pay proper attention.' Her large breasts bounced with her laughter. 'It's like stealing food from a baby.' One night, when she had failed to return to the servants' quarters at her regular time, Anna and Zoya went looking for her. They found her under a tree, her face badly bruised and cut. Helping her back to their quarters, they lay her on a cot close to the fire. Dabbing gently at the cuts, Marie cleaned Lara's face and stayed by her side, soothing her back to sleep when she woke screaming.

When Anna and Zoya went to the kitchen to work the next morning, Marie was still by Lara's side.

Lara slept fitfully, her head thrashing against the pillow. Her hair, matted with sweat, stuck to her scalp, and her eyes burnt with feverish brightness. Marie placed cold compresses on the bruises and gently brushed back her hair. Slowly, Lara regained some of her strength and was able to tell them what had happened.

'After I'd served their dinner, one of the soldiers followed me back to the kitchen. He managed to corner me behind the stable.' Lara's skin flushed at the memory. 'He made advances. I slapped him and tried to get away.' A single tear slid down her cheek. 'He got angry. He was strong and threw me to the ground. Then he lifted my skirt . . .' Her voice faltered.

'It's alright, Lara.' Taking her hand, Marie tried to comfort her. 'You don't have to tell us.'

'No.' Lara shook her head determinedly. 'In a funny way, God was watching over me. I managed to free myself and I ran back to the kitchen, but a piece of cheese I'd hidden in my bodice fell out. Two of them dragged me out of the kitchen and beat me.' Tears streamed unchecked down her face. 'I begged them to stop. I thought they would kill me.'

'They have an armed guard in the kitchen now to watch us,' Zoya told Lara.

'An armed guard in my kitchen?' Lara raised herself into a sitting position.

'It's too soon for you to be getting up.' Marie tried to push her back down.

A defiant look crossed Lara's face. 'I'm fine, thank you, Mademoiselle. With your permission, I'd like to return to the kitchen first thing tomorrow.'

'Your cuts and bruises have not healed yet,' Marie argued.

'I'll tolerate another beating if I have to but I will not tolerate a German soldier in my kitchen.'

The beating had not cowed Lara, and she continued to steal food from the kitchen the moment the guard's back was turned.

In the main house, soldiers rummaged through the Kulbases'

belongings, looking for valuables. Once the rooms and cupboards had been searched, they ripped up the parquet.

The captain ordered a search of the woods, where they found the cart and the spade but nothing else. That night, the captain summoned Herman Kulbas to join him in the parlour. Pouring them each a finger of whisky, he said, 'Let's be frank with each other. I know you have jewels hidden somewhere in the woods.' The captain gave Herman Kulbas a tight smile. 'I will eventually find them, with or without your help.' He pointed to Monsieur Kulbas with his glass. 'You can help your family by telling me where you've hidden them.'

'You are mistaken, Captain. There are no hidden jewels.'

The captain smiled. 'I understand there was an unfortunate incident involving your cook.'

'There was no justification for your soldiers to beat one of my staff.'

'We cannot have the household staff stealing food. They had to make an example of her.'

'It was a small piece of cheese and she stole it because you allow us little more than stale bread.'

'I can change that.' The captain moved closer to Monsieur Kulbas. 'I can either increase your ration or reduce it further – it all depends on how much you're willing to cooperate.'

Herman Kulbas kept his face passive, meeting the captain's stare. 'There is nothing hidden in the woods.'

The captain's smile disappeared. 'I don't believe you are fully appreciating the gravity of the situation. I can make it very unpleasant for you and your family.'

Herman Kulbas placed his untouched drink on the coffee table. 'I've already told you everything.'

'Very well,' the captain said. 'Suit yourself. Starting tomorrow, your ration will be reduced. There will be two armed soldiers stationed in the kitchen to make sure nothing goes missing.'

Herman Kulbas dropped his eyes for a moment to control his emotions, then forced himself to look back into the captain's face.

The smile that greeted him chilled him to the core. 'If there are no more issues you wish to discuss, captain,' he fought to keep his voice steady, 'I'd like to return to my family.'

'As a matter of fact, there is one more matter. My men suffer from lice. Their clothes need to be boiled.'

'We have large copper pots the men can use.'

The captain's smile widened at the same time as his eyes turned a shade darker.

Understanding the meaning behind the smile, Monsieur Kulbas retorted, 'My household staff have enough to do with cooking and chopping wood for your men.'

'This might be a good opportunity for your children to participate.'

'Surely you are not suggesting my son and daughter be engaged in doing your men's laundry?'

The captain downed his drink. 'That's precisely what I mean.'

In the laundry, Marie and Anna, with the help of Valentin, stoked fires and boiled water in large copper pots. Their skin slick with sweat, their faces flushed as they stirred the uniforms with long sticks. Taking a load out to dry on the lines, Marie was approached by a soldier.

'My uniform needs mending.' The man held out a torn collar to Marie.

'I don't know how,' she said matter-of-factly and went back to hanging the wet uniforms on the line.

Grabbing her arm, the soldier spun her roughly and pushed the uniform at her.

'I want this mended by tonight or none of you gets to eat tomorrow.' His eyes blazed with fury. 'Do I make myself clear?'

Marie nodded, not trusting herself to speak without her voice breaking. The soldier held on to her arm a little longer, squeezing it tighter. 'By tonight,' he warned again, then walked away, his boots crunching on the gravel.

Marie stood frozen on the spot with her eyes shut, fighting back tears. She did not notice Anna approach and prise the uniform from her clenched fist.

'It's alright, Marie,' she soothed. 'I'll look after this for you.'

Marie opened her eyes and tears of gratitude and humiliation spilled down her face.

That evening Marie sat close to Anna, watching as Anna threaded a needle then made small, even stitches. Marie then attempted to do a few on her own.

'It's a good start.' Anna smiled encouragingly.

Bending her head close to the uniform, Marie compared her irregular stitches to Anna's straight, even ones and laughed. Her parents looked at them curiously and smilingly shook their heads at the sight of two of them holding a uniform between them and laughing. As for Marie, a smile played about her lips as she struggled with the next few stitches and, for a fleeting moment, her amusement helped drown the gnawing ache in her belly.

Each day posters with the latest announcement flapped in the wind as if impatient to fly away. Marie and Anna joined a crowd of people in the town centre, craning their necks for a better look.

'What does it say?' a person at the back of the group called out.

'The Germans are demanding that each household volunteer two members to grow vegetables for their troops.'

'Outrageous,' a man next to Marie hissed under his breath. 'We hardly have enough time to tend to our own gardens, and even those vegetables we do manage to grow they take from us.'

Arriving home exhausted one evening, his hands blistered from handling the hoe all day, Valentin said, 'The Germans have put up a new announcement today.' He warmed his hands by the fire. 'If any family is not contributing enough, a family member will be taken by force and held until their family complies.' He paused and blew on the bowl of broth Lara handed him.

'My nerves can't stand any more,' declared Pauline Kulbas.

Marie put a protective arm around her mother. 'Let's do something more cheerful. Do you want to play a round of cards?'

Madame Kulbas shook her head. 'No, I'm too tired.'

Sitting her mother on the bed, Marie undid the hair coiled at the back of her mother's neck and ran a comb through the thick locks.

'You've grown so thin, Marie.'

Surprised by her mother's sudden remark, Marie's hand froze for a moment. 'We all have,' she said, carrying on with her combing.

'I worry about you, Marie.' Pauline Kulbas looked up at her daughter. 'Your father and I are at the end of our lives; we have tasted both the sweetness and the bitterness of its fruit. But you, child –' she cupped a hand under Marie's chin '– you are still at the beginning. I don't want to see the spark in you slip away. Don't let this war beat you. Life has a way of healing your wounds, but you need to keep yourself open to all its possibilities.'

Marie gently pulled her mother's hand away. 'You must rest.'

Pauline Kulbas searched her daughter's face for a little longer before dropping her eyes.

'Goodnight, Mama.' Marie kissed her mother's cheek. 'Don't worry about me. I'll be fine.'

Pauline Kulbas's hand tightened around Marie's wrist. 'One day you will be a mother,' she said, sadly. 'And you'll realise that a mother never stops loving or worrying about her children.'

48

Western Russia, October 1918

Bogoleev walked into the mud dugout, removing his fur *papakha*. He went straight to the map spread across the table, ignoring Alexei and Ivanov, who had been waiting for him for the past thirty minutes. Taking a gas lamp, he placed it at the centre of the table.

'The lines have been cut.' He pointed to a series of markings on the map. 'The English are pressing from the south-west and the White Army is closing from the east.' He raised his head to meet the other men's eyes. 'We're surrounded.'

'We can't fight on two fronts.' Alexei stepped into the light. 'Our best chance is to take a defensive position and then flee once it is dark.'

Bogoleev gave Alexei a long look, considering his advice.

'No,' he said finally. 'We will stay and fight.'

'That would be suicide.'

'I don't see an alternative,' Bogoleev said in an abrasive tone. 'You know as well as I do that if Trotsky hears we have fled, he'll drag us all before a firing squad without a moment's hesitation.'

Alexei leant over the table. 'You have a responsibility to the men under your command.'

Bogoleev took a step closer to Alexei. At his full height, he stood almost a head taller. 'Don't lecture me on responsibility. For years, our esteemed generals threw away soldiers' lives without a second thought. The men out there –' he jabbed a finger towards the trenches '– know what they are fighting for and they are willing to lay down their lives for it.'

Alexei held Bogoleev's gaze a little longer before dropping his eyes.

Satisfied, Bogoleev turned to Ivanov. 'Prepare the troops for battle.'

The men stood to attention, watching their commander. As Bogoleev spoke to them about victory, some eyes travelled to the white skies, then down to the mud on their boots before eventually returning to rest on Bogoleev. The dull thundering of cannons, not far away, sent small tremors through the soles of their boots, making the men shift nervously.

'Comrades, today we fight for Soviet socialism. Today we fight the enemies of the revolution. We must put an end to the tyranny and the oppression that has plagued the hard-working peasants' lives throughout Russia's history.'

Pausing, Bogoleev stared into the distance. When he spoke again, his voice was softer and the men had to lean in to hear him.

'You have proved yourself worthy soldiers. Our leaders in Moscow have noticed your efforts and rewarded you accordingly with better rations and promotions. Today, I will stand beside you to fight our common enemy. Side by side we will fight to right past injustices, for the glory of our revolution and freedom for our children.'

As snow fell steadily, dusting coats and *papakhas* in white flakes, the men blew on their hands, waiting to see whether the enemy would mount the first attack.

Alexei stood between Bogoleev and Ivanov, one eye pressed against the viewfinder of his rifle. The icy air squeezed his lungs, making his breath wheeze inside his chest. He hated fighting for the Reds and twice had tried to escape. After he was captured a second time, Bogoleev warned him he would be shot on sight if he tried to escape again.

Surrendering or defecting was also out of the question. With the unspoken understanding that neither side took prisoners, Alexei's only choice was to continue with the Reds.

Somewhere across no-man's-land a bugle sounded. White Army soldiers in long dark coats, *papakhas* pulled down over their ears, ran across the snow-covered fields. Having dug into the hill, the Reds held the higher ground and immediately opened fire on the advancing army. In between exploding shells, the chatter of machine guns and the screams of the wounded, a military band played a marching tune as men fell around them.

Pressing his back against the trench wall, Alexei reloaded his gun, drew a breath to steady himself and took aim. His first shot missed but the second hit a soldier in the kneecap. The man reeled and collapsed to the ground, grabbing his knee with both hands. Eyes wide with pain, he looked around for a place out of the firing range. Spotting a crater, he crawled towards it, dragging himself on his elbows. He was almost at the mouth of the crater when a bullet hit him in the head and he fell, still, to the frozen earth.

A shell exploded to Alexei's left and he threw an arm over his head to protect himself from the shower of metal fragments.

'Come with me.' Bogoleev tapped first Alexei and then Ivanov on the shoulder. Holding his rifle in front of him, Bogoleev climbed the ladder to a platform where a machine gun was mounted. Last to climb the ladder, Alexei reached the gun just as Bogoleev and Ivanov were pulling the two operators from behind it. One, still alive, opened and closed his mouth, gasping for air. Blood foamed at his lips and trickled down his chin. Kneeling over him, Alexei made the sign of the cross.

'Leave him,' Bogoleev barked. 'Help me operate the gun.'

The machine gun's legs were bent and half buried under debris. Pulling the trigger Bogoleev sprayed bullets into the air at random.

'Keep it steady,' he yelled.

Taking the stand, Ivanov kept the gun from jumping.

'Serov, feed the bullets.'

Alexei was about to rise when a faint pressure on his hand made him stop. The soldier's blood oozed out of the hole where the shrapnel had embedded itself. Looking straight at Alexei, the soldier moved his mouth, struggling to form words. Alexei placed his ear close to the soldier's lips.

'P-pray for . . .' The noise of the battle drowned out the rest of the words. Alexei waited a few more seconds, and when he heard nothing more lifted his head in time to see the soldier shudder then grow still.

'Serov!'

Alexei jumped to his feet. He had only taken a step when another explosion threw him off the platform into the trench. Dazed, he lay on his back staring at the pale sky and struggling for air.

'Comrade Serov!'

Still struggling for breath, Alexei pushed himself to a sitting position and looked back up to the platform.

Ivanov, his jacket splattered with blood, leant over the edge. 'I need your help. The commissar is hit.'

Slinging the strap of his rifle over his shoulder, Alexei climbed back up the ladder. He found Bogoleev, bloodied and unconscious, slumped over the machine gun.

Laying him on the ground, Ivanov pulled out his field medical pouch and, after applying iodine, bandaged the wound to stop the bleeding.

'Help me lift him.'

Hooking Bogoleev's arms around their shoulders, Alexei and Ivanov carried him between them. At the field hospital, they placed him on a stretcher and stepped back to allow the doctor to examine the wounds. Cutting the bandages, the doctor carefully peeled them back to look at the raw flesh. A nurse stood at the doctor's elbow.

'There's nothing more you can do for him,' she said when she saw Ivanov and Alexei still waiting. Seeing Ivanov's hand bleeding, she lifted it to take a better look. 'That looks as if it might need stitches.' She pointed to a single chair at the front of the tent. 'You'd better wait over there until the doctor can see you.'

'It's only a flesh wound.' Ivanov pulled his hand away.

The nurse shrugged. 'It's your choice. I can bandage it for you but come and see me if it gives you any trouble.'

Katya watched the soldiers leave, their bodies hunched against the wind. Aside from the odd exploding shell, the battlefield had fallen quiet, catching its breath before the next instalment. Stretchers carrying the wounded arrived at a steady pace. Several times, she stopped to look at the mangled bodies, praying that she would not find Fyodor among them.

Fyodor joined the Red Army after having lied to the recruiting officer about his age. Mortified by his decision, Katya followed him, volunteering as a nurse. He was not pleased when he found Katya had also volunteered and even less pleased when she was assigned to the same regiment as he. Before moving to the front, Fyodor had made Katya promise she would not embarrass him by repeatedly asking after him.

Sucking air through her teeth, she joined the doctor still bent over the wounded commissar. The officer's light hair was matted and his skin, covered in blood, was almost translucent. Using a wet cloth, Katya dabbed at his face, pushing the hair away from his eyes.

'There is shrapnel lodged in his skull,' the doctor said without looking up, 'and there's some more above his knee.' He pointed to Bogoleev's right leg. 'I can pull out the pieces in his leg but the one in his head . . .' He let his voice trail off. Standing up he stretched and wiped his brow with the back of his hand. He looked at the row of stretchers, all bearing men who wore the same expression of twisted pain on their faces, and sighed.

'We raise them, send them to war, patch them up when they are injured and send them out again only to receive them back broken again.'

Katya ducked her head, trying to keep her emotions from spilling over. The doctor squeezed her arm as he moved past her to his next patient, leaving a bloody imprint on her sleeve.

Sitting outside his dugout, Alexei stared into the flames, nursing his rum. Beyond the fire's halo, the night was inky black. A shell exploding in the distance lit up the sky before darkness closed in again. Alexei considered his options.

It was unlikely Bogoleev would pull through and this provided Alexei with an opportunity. On the other hand, Bogoleev had vowed to have Alexei shot if he tried to escape again. Reaching a decision, he threw the remainder of his drink into the fire and, keeping to the shadows, made his way to where he had a satchel hidden.

Back in the dugout he shared with Ivanov, Alexei lay awake in the dark. Ivanov was a light sleeper and bigger than Alexei; he could easily overpower him in a hand-to-hand struggle. Alexei listened to the sound of Ivanov's breathing. The rhythm had slowed, the breaths growing deeper. Stepping lightly, Alexei moved briskly to the dugout opening.

'Where are you going?'

Alexei's hand stilled on the thick flap. He turned to face Ivanov.

'I couldn't sleep.' Alexei kept his voice casual. 'I thought I'd step out for some fresh air.'

There was a long silence and Alexei's pulse quickened, fearing Ivanov might be suspecting something. Finally the Cossack grunted and said, 'Don't be long.'

Leaving the dugout, Alexei knew he had to move quickly. He drew his collar against a bitter cold wind blowing from the west. Spying the dark shape of the sentry leaning on his rifle, he made his way towards him. A light rain had started to fall, and the mud underfoot was deep, slippery and clinging.

'Do you have a match?' Alexei approached the sentry, a cigarette between his lips.

The sentry shifted his feet. 'I don't smoke.' He kept his eyes fixed on the dark horizon.

Patting his pockets Alexei found a match and lit it against a log that secured the mud walls of the trench. A faint light flickered into life and he studied the sentry's features.

'How old are you?'

'Old enough,' the sentry snapped back.

Alexei held up his palms. 'I'm sorry, comrade. I did not mean to offend.'

'I look younger than I am.'

Alexei nodded. 'You must be freezing. I have just the thing to warm you up,' he said amiably. 'It will put some hair on your chest and replace the smell of your mother's milk on your breath.'

The young sentry frowned but let the comment pass.

'I have some distilled vodka stashed away in a burnt-out shell of a tree just to the left of the trenches.'

The sentry stiffened. 'I can't let anyone pass.'

'Oh, come now, comrade.' Alexei draped an arm over the boy's shoulders, giving him a friendly squeeze. 'I will only be a few minutes.' Cocking his head to one side, he asked, 'You do drink, don't you?'

'Of course.' The reply came a little too quickly.

'Good man.' Pulling on the last of his cigarette, Alexei stubbed it out under his boot. 'What's your name, comrade?'

The sentry gave Alexei a suspicious look. 'Fyodor.'

'Well, Fyodor, I promise to only be a few minutes.' And before the boy could object, Alexei moved past him into the darkness.

Away from the trenches, Alexei hastened towards the woods, conscious that he only had a short time before Ivanov or the sentry raised the alarm.

Naked branches of trees threw distorted shadows as Alexei climbed over rocks, weaving between the trees. His boots squelched loudly in the mud. He stopped a few times, listening for the sound of approaching voices. Hearing nothing, he continued, careful not to trip over anything in his path.

Heading north-west, Alexei followed the railway tracks. He walked all night without stopping. By mid-morning the next day, he emerged from the woods and began his journey across a plain dotted with the occasional tree. Away from the shelter of the woods, the wind was harsher, blasting icy snow against his skin. The exertion of dragging his feet through the snow made his lungs burn and he had to pause every now and then to rest.

In a satchel he carried under his coat was a crust of bread and some pork fat saved from the previous night's dinner. He removed the small bundle and, taking the ration of pork fat, bit off a chunk. Chewing slowly, he wrapped the rest up again and replaced it in the bag.

He had lost track of how long he had been walking. Stopping to rest his head against a birch tree, his eyes drifted to the branches above him. Prisms of light reflected through icicles hanging from the limbs. The bright colours seemed out of place in the frozen white expanse and, in his fatigue and desperation, Alexei thought he discerned a divine message. Bringing his palms together, he knelt before the grey, watery sky.

'Dear Lord.' He paused, not sure how to continue. 'I have not been a faithful subject, but if you can hear my prayer, take pity on my soul and lead me to safety.'

Kneeling in the snow, his eyes looked to the skies, waiting for a sign his prayer had been heard. When no sign came, he rose stiffly to his feet and, with one last look at the pale sky, resumed his journey west.

It was dark when he came across a line of abandoned carriages, and he thought he detected shadowy figures darting between them like scurrying rats. Approaching one, Alexei listened for movement and, hearing nothing, slid open the door. Hungry and weary, he huddled in a corner, pulling his coat tightly around him. His fingers wrapped around the handle of his dagger, he fell asleep.

It felt like only a few minutes had passed before his eyes flew open. He listened, heart thumping in his chest. Somewhere in the distance, a lone wolf howled and had its call returned by others.

Then he heard it again, the sound that had woken him: a soft hollow moan.

Alexei's fingers tightened around the dagger.

As his eyes adjusted to the dark, he made out the shape of a man lying curled on the floor in a corner of the carriage.

His dagger held against his thigh, Alexei rose silently and moved towards the figure. The floor of the carriage creaked and the man turned his head slightly.

Alexei held his breath.

The figure remained curled in a foetal position, barely moving.

'Water.'

Alexei froze by the outline of a soldier in a Red Army uniform.

'Water,' the soldier whimpered, as if sensing the other man's presence.

Alexei reached for his canteen and brought it close to the soldier's lips, but even as he did he saw a veil draw over the eyes and they became lifeless.

Alexei walked for days, through storms and blizzards, careful to hide at the first glimpse of another traveller. At night he took refuge in abandoned carriages or deserted villages, where he scavenged for food.

He was no longer conscious of time passing. He fell asleep to the sound of wolves baying at the moon, not caring any more how close they might be. Days blended into night as he grew weaker, and yet he willed his legs to take him forward. He focused only on getting to the west, to Latvia and his family: to freedom and survival.

49

Narva, November 1918

When the Germans evacuated Narva, the bells in town rang all day. The Kulbas family and their staff woke that morning to find the soldiers gone and the house ransacked, presumably in a manic last-minute effort to find anything of value.

In town, the streets were lined with people celebrating.

'Praise the Lord, they are gone,' a woman said, embracing Marie then her mother. 'That coward, the Kaiser, has abdicated, fleeing to Holland. Germany has lost the war!'

'Mama!' Marie grabbed her mother's hand. 'Did you hear? The Germans have lost.'

'I . . . I'm . . .' Her mother looked at the faces around her in confusion.

'Marie.' Anna waved them over from across the street. Marie and her mother crossed to her, stepping around people drinking and carousing.

'Oh, Marie.' Anna was beaming. 'It's over, the war is over.' She stopped, looking at Marie's face curiously. 'What's the matter? Aren't you pleased?'

'Of course,' Marie said with a laugh, though in truth she wasn't sure how she felt. She couldn't help but think of all that had been lost, how much had changed. The time before the war seemed as removed as an alien world. She thought back to how she was then; so young, so full of hope and optimism. She saw her reflection in a shop window, noticed for the first time the new lines around her eyes and the slightly deeper ones at the corners of her lips. She no longer recognised in the reflection the girl she had been. She turned back to the people celebrating in the square. Her gaze drifted to the clock tower as it chimed the hour. She smiled. Nikolai always set his watch to the clock's chime. At the thought of him, a faint vibration trembled her heart. She missed him, and Pyotr. And what of Alexei? She wondered where he was now, whether he was safe, if he had survived the war or if he, too, was lost to her. She squeezed her eyes to hold back the tears.

Her mother, as if sensing something of her daughter's thoughts, rubbed her back affectionately. 'The war has left us with heavy hearts,' she said gravely. 'But it is over now, and we must look to the future.'

Red Army soldiers arrived soon after the Germans had left, rolling through the town gates in their hundreds. Initially, the residents of Narva were happy to welcome their liberators. Gathering what little food they had, they took it to the town centre to feed them. The hospitals and makeshift infirmaries set up to receive the soldiers quickly became overcrowded. In between applying bandages and serving food, Marie sat with the soldiers, asking about their experiences, their homes and the families they had left behind. Some spoke frankly about their longing to return home. Others stared back at her with empty eyes that seemed uncomprehending.

'We were dispensible,' one man told her. Sitting slightly apart from the other soldiers, he had a bandaged arm. 'We lost so many men, we barely had time to bury or count them, let alone remember them. Lenin is right to call it an imperialist war. None of our commanders cared whether we lived or died. The war's only purpose was to fatten bourgeois wallets at the cost of the peasants' lives.'

'Surely you don't believe that,' Marie said, taken aback by the remark. 'Plenty of nobility and merchants also volunteered and lost their lives defending –'

'The nobility barely noticed the war, sitting with full stomachs in their fine warm palaces,' the soldier said bitterly. 'That's the way it has always been in Russia. That's why we had a revolution. Ordinary Russians proved to oppressed people everywhere that they have the power to bring about change. It will only be a matter of time before the wealthy around the globe feel the sting of the peasant's knife.'

Marie paled. 'You have no understanding of what you say.' Standing abruptly, she buttoned up her coat. 'I wish you a speedy recovery, soldier.'

'That's an expensive coat, comrade.' The soldier sneered.

'Good day to you.' She gave him a cold look.

'The Bolsheviks will win,' the soldier called after her. 'Mark my words.'

'I don't think the Russians will turn out to be the liberators we had hoped for,' Marie confided to her father.

Herman Kulbas, sorting through the books in the library, didn't even look up. 'I'm missing several volumes. I do hope the Germans didn't use them to build fires. Some of those with the Italian bindings are irreplaceable.'

'Papa, did you hear what I said?'

'Hmm?'

'I said I don't think the Russians are going to be the liberators we were hoping for.'

'I heard you the first time, Marie,' her father replied evenly. 'It was naïve of you to think otherwise.'

'What do you think will become of us, Papa?'

Looking up from his books at last, Herman Kulbas's face was grave. 'I'm not sure, Marie. They have already taken the factory. All we have left is this house. Let us hope they don't take that too.' He smiled sadly.

'I can't imagine living anywhere else.' Marie's voice was close to breaking. 'This is my childhood home, where Nikolai and I spent our summers from school. All my happiest memories are tied to these walls, these grounds. I could not bear to think we might lose it.'

'No need to worry yourself yet.' He patted her knee. 'We will manage. Somehow.'

Latvia, November

To the Latvian police who arrested Alexei, he seemed little more than a wild man. Having traded his warm coat at a nearby village for food and a night's accommodation, he wore only a grimy blanket, black with dirt, over his Red Army uniform. His bushy beard was streaked with grey. When the Latvians saw his uniform, they mistook him for a Bolshevik and threw him in jail, laughing at his claim to be a commander in the imperial army.

'You are nothing but a Bolshevik pig,' the Latvian captain spat at him.

'The Bolsheviks threatened to kill my family if I did not join them,' Alexei pleaded. 'My wife and daughters will testify to it.'

Reluctantly, the captain agreed to contact Emily, who had moved to Tallinn following Estonia's liberation. They received a telegram the next day informing them of her forwarding address.

A few days later, they received a second telegram from Tallinn.

> *I testify to my husband Alexei Serov's identity STOP Not possible for me to travel at present STOP I will pay for all his expenses STOP.*

A third telegram from a Countess Golytsyn, claiming to be a close friend of Emily, provided further confirmation of his identity.

Alexei was released from his freezing cell. Weak and exhausted, his legs could not bear his weight and he collapsed on taking his first step. As he lost consciousness, he heard a distant voice say, 'Take him to the hospital.'

Alexei remembered little of his first days in the infirmary. Burning with fever and struggling to breathe, he slept fitfully and often woke from his dreams covered in sweat and panting for air.

'Pneumonia.' He heard the word uttered but his confused mind could not be sure if it was referring to his own state.

Even as Alexei's fever began to subside, his lungs continued to burn. Nurses placed warm towels on his chest and propped him up with pillows but still he struggled to breathe.

Emily finally joined him in late February. Released into her care, he was still too weak to travel, so she rented an apartment and hired a private physician to visit him daily.

'Just as soon as the Germans left, the Red Army moved in.' Sitting close to his bed, Emily spoke in a low voice, a light tremor betraying her otherwise calm demeanour. 'They took the food the Germans had hoarded in the sheds, leaving us without any provisions to see us through winter.

'Almost immediately the local Bolsheviks announced new laws. Many were denounced.' Her teary eyes shone in the light. 'And lost their lives.' She blew her nose delicately into her handkerchief. 'We started hearing rumours of fighting between the Estonian troops backed by the White Army, and the Reds. The Whites pushed the Bolsheviks back across the border. That's when I received the telegram you were in Latvia.'

'Have you any news of Grigory?'

'Yes, he made it to Tallinn, bringing with him photos and a few of your possessions, including your remaining medals and the Luger.' Emily lowered her head. 'He said he wanted to return to Uglich to bring back some of the gold rubles he had buried. That's when . . .' She stopped and bit down on her lip.

Alexei placed a hand over hers and gave it a reassuring squeeze.

'I tried to stop him but he wouldn't listen.' Lifting her face, she met Alexei's eyes. 'He was loyal to you till the end.' Her eyes were full of tears as she continued, 'It was another month before I finally heard what became of him. They found his body not far from the house with bullet wounds to the back.'

50

Tallinn, March 1919

Marie's dark curls were swept off her face in a carefully arranged coiffure.

'Thank you, Anna. I'll manage the rest.'

Hearing the door close behind Anna, Marie was glad to be alone finally. The family was invited to Countess Golytsyn's house that night for a dinner to celebrate the liberation of Estonia in February.

Following their defeat by the combined Estonian and White armies, the Red Army immediately launched fresh attacks in an effort to recapture Narva. Although they failed to take back the city, a great number of the residents were left homeless after the heavy bombardment.

Pauline Kulbas, her nerves frayed by the continuous fighting, took to her bed. Fearing another attack, Monsieur Kulbas had decided the family should move west, away from the fighting, and made urgent plans for their relocation to the capital, Tallinn.

Marie stared at her reflection. It had broken her heart to leave Narva. To leave their home. In Tallinn, she was a stranger, a refugee. The handsome apartments her father had secured on Toompea Hill, with views of the medieval town centre, did little to lift her spirits.

By day, she managed to mask her unhappiness, but at night, alone in her room, she gave in to despair.

What did the future hold for her? All the girlish interests she had before the war, belonged to a carefree former life, one full of hope, before Pyotr and Nikolai were lost to her. She no longer cared about attending balls, dinners or the ballet. But if she was truthful, there was more to the source of her pain. Her most bitter and recurrent memories were of the autumn days in Tsarskoe Selo, and Alexei. She knew, even if he had survived the war, she had lost him when she had fled from him. She would give anything to bring back that time, to explain her feelings. The intensity of their kiss had frightened her and, confused by the depths of her emotions, she had run. Her shoulders slumped. These are the best years of my life, she thought sadly, and they're slipping by, completely useless. And all because I have been too cowardly.

A knock on the door broke her reverie.

'Marie?' Pauline Kulbas pushed the door open. 'Why, child, you are still not ready. The car is waiting outside.'

Pauline Kulbas was dressed in a simple evening dress with her hair arranged in a loose knot at the nape of her neck. Since arriving in Tallinn, she had regained some weight and her skin now had a healthier glow. But even as she tried to hide the evidence of her suffering behind a painted smile, the strain showed in the deep lines around her mouth.

'I'm almost ready, Mama.' Picking up her powder puff, Marie applied powder to her face.

Pauline Kulbas placed a small jewellery box by Marie's elbow. Inside, wrapped in a silk cloth, lay a necklace of jade and a matching brooch.

Smiling at her daughter, she warmed the cool stones in her palm before stepping behind Marie and fastening the necklace around her neck.

'The stones bring out the green in your eyes.' Straightening, she studied her daughter's reflection in the mirror.

'What is it, Marie?' Her mother's expression was worried. 'You're as pale as a ghost.'

Marie tried to put on a cheerful smile, overwhelmed by the darkness that had taken hold of her. She faltered and her face crumpled.

'Oh, Mama, I wish I knew what was wrong with me. I can't seem to shake this unhappiness that has settled over me.'

'Oh, child,' Pauline touched her daughter's hand 'You must put your faith in our Lord to give you the strength you need.' Lifting her chin with the tips of her fingers, she turned Marie's face to her.

Marie dropped her head to hide her tears. 'Pyotr is not coming back.'

'Have faith, Marie.' Pauline Kulbas kissed the top of her daughter's head. 'The Lord works in mysterious ways.'

In Countess Golytsyn's drawing room, a cluster of men, including Marie's father, had gathered around an American general. Sent to help the White Army, the American officers had become a fashionable addition to dinner parties. Marie walked past the group to join her mother beside their hostess.

'The Red Army forced him to join by threatening to kill his family,' Countess Golytsyn was telling her audience. 'What could he do? He had no choice. After all, look what those animals did to our poor Tsar and his family.'

The women shook their heads and crossed themselves.

'Who are you discussing, Mama?' Marie whispered in her mother's ear.

'Countess Golytsyn is telling us about a general who escaped the Reds.'

'His wife and three daughters made it to Latvia dressed as peasants and eventually made their way to Tallinn. It is a miracle they arrived here unharmed.' Countess Golytsyn fanned herself lazily with her delicate silk fan.

'Major General Serov's wife has been a dear friend of mine since we were girls,' the countess continued. 'Poor Emily has been through a harrowing journey with no one to help her.'

Marie had only been half listening to Countess Golytsyn's story, but at the mention of Alexei's name, she stiffened. Next to her, her mother gave her a questioning look.

'Do you know the Serovs?' Pauline Kulbas whispered.

'Not really.' Marie blushed. 'I met the general at the officers' hospital.'

'Twice before he had tried to escape the Reds and was captured,' Countess Golytsyn was saying. 'He walked for days through knee-deep snow. He was exhausted and starving when he reached the Latvian border. It was unfortunate he was still wearing his Red Army uniform. The authorities in Latvia took one look at him and threw him into jail.'

The women gasped.

'The poor man,' said one. 'How did he secure his release?'

Countess Golytsyn, looking pleased with the effect her story was having on her audience, smiled. 'Emily came to me, desperate for help. I felt it my duty to send a telegram to the authorities vouching for the general.'

The women nodded their approval and congratulated their hostess for her generosity of spirit.

'They are in Tallinn now,' the countess finished.

'The general is living here in Tallinn?'

Around the group, curious eyes turned to look at Marie.

'Yes,' the countess responded with a questioning edge to her voice. 'Do you know him?'

Marie, her heart full of conflicting emotions, found herself unable to speak. Fortunately, they were interrupted by the butler informing them that dinner was about to be served.

On the way home, the Kulbases talked about the evening, exchanging news. Staring out at the dark street, Marie was lost in thought and barely listened to her parents' conversation.

'You are very quiet, Marie,' her father remarked.

'Countess Golytsyn told us of a Major General Serov who recently escaped the Red Army.'

Despite her best efforts to disguise her feelings, traces of excitement must have betrayed her interest because her mother asked suspiciously, 'Why this curiosity regarding Major General Serov? How well do you know him?'

Marie said nothing, twisting a silk handkerchief around her fingers. Her mother took her daughter's fingers and held them still.

'I'm not sure if I should be telling you this but years ago, when the major general was a lieutenant in Narva, there were rumours . . . scandalous rumours.'

'That was just idle gossip, Pauline.' Herman Kulbas turned to Marie. 'I met Serov when he was stationed in Narva. His family owns a large estate in Uglich, north of Moscow. He comes from a long line of highly regarded professional soldiers.'

'He met his wife when he was a lieutenant,' Pauline Kulbas recalled. 'According to Countess Golytsyn, even back then, the general was unfaithful to his wife. One affair even resulted in an illegitimate child.'

Marie guessed her mother's acute sense of perception had noted the excitement she had felt at the mention of Alexei, and worried about it.

'That sort of behaviour might be acceptable in Petrograd,' Pauline Kulbas concluded, 'but in Narva, it caused quite a scandal.'

Herman Kulbas lit a pipe and puffed at it for a few seconds. 'Countess Golytsyn has little talent besides gossiping,' he said irritably. Turning to Marie, he added, 'Don't pay too much heed. In my experience, women's talk is ninety per cent fiction, ten per cent make-believe.' He winked.

Marie gave a forced smile. The mention of the illegitimate child had tightened a knot in her stomach.

'All the same, Countess Golytsyn has told me in confidence that Emily suspects her husband is having another affair.' Marie's mother settled back in her seat, resting her head against the soft leather. 'Some men are simply not capable of remaining faithful to their wives.'

That night in bed, Marie tossed and turned. Finally, realising that her attempts to sleep were futile, she gave up and stared at the ceiling, allowing her thoughts to roam freely. She thought of her afternoons with Alexei at Tsarskoe and an unexpected smile of pleasure settled on her face. Then she recalled her mother's words, and her smile faded. Was it true that some men were incapable of remaining faithful? Her mother had mentioned his wife suspected him of another affair.

Over three years had passed since he had kissed her in the library. And yet the thought of Alexei with another woman caused an invisible hand to squeeze her heart. Her fingers clasped the small cross at her throat. 'Our Lord in heaven, help me to understand what I'm feeling. I have not seen him in so long and yet the mere mention of his name sends tremors through me. Help me, Lord, for I am lost.'

51

Tallinn, March 1919

Absorbed in his book, Alexei barely noticed Emily enter the room, nor did he look up when she moved past him. She sat down, holding a small volume of Pushkin on her lap, and waited patiently for him to finish reading. Lately it had become their habit to meet in the library after supper, reading for a period before each retired to their respective rooms.

'Anything the matter?' he enquired politely, sensing an agitation in her.

Lifting her head, Emily met Alexei's gaze. He thought her eyes were moist but it could have been merely a reflection of the light. She shook her head, breaking eye contact.

'It's nothing,' she said with a forced smile. 'I just have a lot on my mind. Nothing for you to concern yourself with.'

Alexei's eyes lingered on her questioningly for a little longer.

Emily let out a slow breath. Rising from her seat, she moved to the sideboard where she poured herself a glass of sherry and a vodka for Alexei.

She offered Alexei the drink.

'Thank you.' He placed the glass on the table next to him without taking a sip.

Emily took her own drink and stood close to the fireplace, watching the flames.

'Alexei, we need to talk.'

He leant back in his chair and looked at her expectantly.

'I want a divorce.' She blurted the words out hurriedly.

Stunned, it took a moment for Alexei to regain his speech. Closing his book, he placed it beside his glass. 'Why this sudden request?' he asked, even as he suspected the answer.

'Our marriage has been dead for a long time.' Her voice sounded choked. 'I loved you once and even though I always knew I was never enough for you, part of me hoped you would learn to love me back.'

Alexei began to object but she stopped him with a motion of her hand.

'There is no use denying it. I have been a disappointment to you. I . . . I bore you.'

'Emily,' he began, but she stopped him again.

'Please, you must let me speak.' There was a tremor to her voice as if her resolve might break at any moment. 'I have disappointed you by not giving you an heir. In my heart, I was happy I had daughters. Deep down I wanted to punish you for the shame and hurt you caused me. So I prayed every night that God would deny you the one thing you desperately wanted.' Pulling out her handkerchief, she pressed it to her nose. 'Now that I have confessed, you must think me wicked.'

Rising from his seat, he took her by the shoulders and held her. 'Your confession changes nothing. You have been a good mother to our daughters and a loyal wife to me. I could not ask for more.'

'And yet it was still not enough to make you love me.'

He tried to deny it but she knew him better.

'I'm a woman, Alexei.' She gave him a sad smile. 'You look at me, you dine and sit quietly with me, but your thoughts are somewhere else, with someone else.'

He understood what she meant and did not try again to deny it. 'Where would you go?'

'I wish to join my sister in Paris.'

He nodded in understanding.

She hesitated then said, 'There is something else. I want custody of the girls, including Tonya. Although she's not my biological daughter, Tonya has only known one mother.'

'It would be too cruel to separate Tonya from her sisters,' Alexei agreed, his insides tightening.

'Then you consent to let me take the girls?'

'Why Paris?' He felt the possibility of not seeing his daughters drop through him like a stone. 'You could still stay here. You could have your own apartment in Tallinn.'

'The girls need a proper education.' Emily moved out of his arms. 'In Paris I will be able to find suitable schools for them. Besides,' she continued in a softer voice, 'there will be no chance of us constantly running into one another, if I move away.' Looking up into his face, her eyes pleaded with his. 'I need your permission to start making the necessary arrangements. I hope to leave as soon as possible.'

Alexei dragged a hand through his hair. Grief squeezed at his throat like a fist.

Emily took a last sip of her sherry and placed the empty glass on the mantelpiece. Hesitantly Alexei took a step towards her, intending to take her by the shoulders, to caress her, to make her rethink her decision. She stepped back and in that moment, he saw his reflection in the mirror above the fireplace. His hair, thinning at the temples, was almost grey. The once youthful face had lost the smooth strong lines of its earlier years. He stood, transfixed, wondering why he had failed to notice the changes before now.

Moving away from him, Emily walked to the door. 'Please consider my feelings when giving me your answer.' Before leaving the room, she turned, her hand resting on the brass handle. 'It's time for both of us to make a new start, Alexei.'

Alexei bowed his head. 'If you really wish to go, I won't stand in your way.'

Emily smiled. 'Thank you, Alyosha. I'm sorry it had to come to this.'

'So am I,' Alexei murmured, knowing in his heart that it was his fault and that, painful as it was, Emily had made the right decision: they were not meant to be together. Unbidden, an image of Marie came to him. A familiar feeling washed over him and, just as on previous occasions, he allowed himself to sink into the memory.

A week later, he watched from the upstairs window as the luggage was carried from the house in a long procession of chests and suitcases. His interview with the priest regarding the divorce had not gone well. After reprimanding Alexei for breaking a bond ordained by God, the priest mentioned several repairs needed by the church, which could be fixed by a large donation. Alexei offered to pay for them and in return secured from the church permission to divorce his wife.

'Are you just going to stand there?'

Irena stood inside the doorway, her arms folded across her chest, her voice laced with reproach. 'Aren't you going to at least try to stop her?'

When told of her parents' decision, Irena had taken the news badly, locking herself away in her room.

He walked over to her. 'I know this is very difficult for you, but your mother and I have grown apart.'

'I don't understand.' Irena's eyes pooled with tears.

He reached for her but she shrugged his hand away.

'You are still too young,' he said with a long sigh. 'In time, I hope you will learn to understand and forgive me.'

With a sob, she buried her face in his chest and he wrapped his arms around her.

'I need you to remain strong for your mother and sisters.'

The corners of Irena's lips began to lift in a brave smile but, failing, fell again.

'Go now.' Alexei kissed her wet cheek. 'Go, my darling girl. And promise you will write often.'

'I promise,' she said hoarsely.

He walked Irena to the front door and watched her descend the stairs to join the others, waiting in the car. Pausing, she turned and gave a small wave.

As the car vanished up the street, Alexei, his heart sinking, walked back into the empty house and locked himself away in the library, where he remained for the rest of the day, refusing food or visitors.

Tallinn, June

The wheels of the car crunched loudly over the gravel and came to an abrupt stop. A footman hurried out and opened the door for the passenger. A strong gust of wind greeted Alexei as he stepped out of the car and walked quickly up the stairs. The front door already stood open to receive him, spilling a triangle of light across the landing.

'Good evening, Your Excellency.' The butler helped Alexei out of his heavy coat and took his hat, handing them to a waiting servant. He then stood back and waited as Alexei checked his reflection in the mirror, smoothing a hand over his hair.

Nodding to the butler that he was ready, Alexei followed him through the marble foyer. 'The countess is receiving her guests in the parlour.'

The butler opened the large double doors and, with a discreet cough, announced Alexei to the small crowd.

'At last!' Countess Golytsyn stood to receive him with outstretched arms.

Clicking his heels, Alexei bowed and kissed the tips of her silk glove. 'Please forgive me for my lateness.' Straightening, he offered her his arm and she placed her hand on the crook of his elbow.

She smiled sweetly at him. 'Everyone is dying to meet you. I hope you will forgive me for telling them all about your daring escape.'

'Madame, you flatter me unnecessarily.'

'Nonsense, you are being too modest.'

They stopped by a waiter carrying a tray and each took a glass of champagne.

'To your health,' he said, raising his glass to her.

She inclined her head coquettishly. 'How are Emily and the girls? Are they enjoying Paris?'

'Emily has been very busy interviewing French tutors for the two younger girls. They have left her sister's place and have moved to their own apartment in Saint-Germain.'

Countess Golytsyn turned her head slightly to study Alexei's profile. 'And your eldest, Irena, has she joined Parisian society?'

'Her aunt gave a ball for her. From all reports she was a great success.'

'I have no doubt she will receive many invitations. May I be perfectly frank, Alexei? Your daughter is – how shall I put it? – a free spirit. Emily would do well to keep a close eye on her.'

'You are very kind,' Alexei murmured, even as he felt irritated by the countess's opinion.

They had drifted towards a group of men gathered by the fire.

'Gentlemen, this is the general I have been telling you about.' The countess did a quick round of introductions and the men shook hands. Turning to Alexei, she added, 'You have a reputation as a hero among our circle.'

Alexei blushed, embarrassed.

'Don't be shy, General.' Countess Golytsyn patted Alexei on the arm. 'They have heard me retell your story but I'm sure they would enjoy it much better told in the first person.' She excused herself to receive more late-arriving guests.

'Is it true that you fought alongside the Reds?' a stout man with a thick bushy moustache asked.

'I was forced to join,' Alexei responded, offended. 'They threatened my wife and children.'

'Come now, gentlemen,' said a portly man who had been introduced to Alexei as the mayor. 'Countess Golytsyn has already explained the unfortunate circumstances by which the general found himself fighting for the enemy.' Pulling out a silver case, he offered cigarettes around the circle. A servant standing in the corner stepped forward to light them, and a haze of smoke began to curl above their heads.

'Maybe you can help settle this argument for us.' The mayor blew smoke into the air. 'Having fought alongside them, what is your opinion of the Red Army? Do you think they have any chance against the White forces?'

Alexei considered his response. 'Trotsky lacks experience and knowledge in military matters.'

Around him, the men nodded, as if this confirmed their own views.

'With the British, French and now Americans all fighting with the White Army, the Reds' days are numbered,' the mayor declared.

'That's not what I said.'

'But you just admitted their war commissar has inadequate experience.'

'True, but they have recruited many officers from the imperial army who do possess the necessary expertise.'

'Surely these officers would use any opportunity to sabotage the efforts of the Reds.'

'It's not that simple, Monsieur Mayor. Some of the officers joined the Reds because their lives were threatened. Trotsky has imposed a strict regime of punishment for those judged to be disloyal.' Alexei paused to draw on his cigarette. 'The peasants and workers join voluntarily, lured by the promise of better food and supplies. I've seen Trotsky visit the front in his armoured train, reinforcing the warning that a loss for the Red Army will mean a return to serfdom.'

'I heard that General Brusilov has joined them,' offered the mayor.

'I heard the same rumour,' said another.

'That traitor!'

'Brusilov joined after his son was executed by the White Army,' said a man with a handlebar moustache. Turning to Alexei, he asked, 'Do you suppose the Bolsheviks will try crossing into Estonia again?'

'Bolshevik propaganda has already found its way across the border. They need men to fight and there is already widespread support for their movement among the peasants. There is every chance Estonia could fall into the hands of the Reds.' Alexei waited for the gravity of his words to sink in.

A butler's bell announcing the serving of dinner cut short conversations around the room. Men offered their arms to women and followed Countess Golytsyn and her husband to the dining room.

Standing at the back, Alexei exchanged a few words with a Finnish merchant who was visiting Tallinn. Having avoided society since arriving in the city, Alexei found he was enjoying himself.

He had just turned to say something further to the merchant when he saw her, and his heartbeat raced as if shot with adrenalin. She was thinner than he remembered, and paler, but still her beauty hit him like a gust of wind, rendering him speechless. Her shining eyes, framed by thick dark lashes, were gazing at him with a look of surprise he felt sure must be mirrored on his own face.

For the longest moment, they stared at each other without speaking.

Alexei's heart skipped a beat. 'Marie,' he whispered.

'You are surprised,' she replied, the sentence sounding like a statement rather than a question.

'I . . . I was not expecting to see you.' He could not take his eyes off her. 'You look beautiful.'

Her lips curved into a smile. 'Thank you.' She offered her hand to him.

He kissed her fingers, holding her hand a little longer than necessary.

She blushed and dropped her head. Then, as if sensing she was being watched, she turned to look over her shoulder.

Alexei saw an older woman in a dark silk dress with large feathers in her hair. She returned his gaze, her grey eyes regarding him with a warning look. Guessing she was Marie's mother, he let go of Marie's hand and stepped away.

'Do you know how long it's been since Tsarskoe?' He stared at Marie, not quite believing his eyes, not wanting to leave her side.

She looked away without answering.

'Three years and nine months,' he said. She slowly turned her eyes back to him. 'And each day I thought of you.'

52

Tallinn, June 1919

Although they did not speak through the first few courses, Marie and Alexei stole glances at each other, smiling shyly when their eyes met. To both their surprise they found themselves ushered to seats next to each other. Alexei spent some time speaking to the elderly princess sitting to his right. An old woman with dark eyes and thin lips, she spoke loudly of having once travelled to Moscow in the same carriage as his wife, Emily. He then turned to speak to the man on Marie's left, brushing her bare arm with the elbow of his jacket as he leant across her. Her skin grew hot and she reached for her serviette, hiding her blush behind it.

When she had heard the butler announce Alexei's name, she had thought that it must be her mind playing tricks on her. But when she saw him in the doorway she had almost cried out. She thought of approaching him and was still hesitating, undecided, when the bell had rung for dinner. Around her, voices grew muffled and indistinct as she watched him cross the room after the countess. She had followed her mother to the dining room in a state of agitation. She'd been determined to appear serene and composed when he saw her, but when at last he'd turned and their eyes had met, her heart had almost stopped. As he'd bent to kiss her hand, she'd felt the blood rush to her face and had had to look away, afraid of how much her expression might have revealed.

She could barely believe he was sitting beside her now and she kept stealing glances at him to be sure she hadn't imagined his presence. Up close, she noticed changes she had missed at first. His hair was lighter and thinner; a new hardness had matured his features and the faint lines on his face had deepened. But his confidence remained, and the quick intelligence in his eyes.

As the plates from the last course were removed, Alexei leant over.

'I almost did not come tonight,' he said. His eyes were playful and she could not help smiling. 'If not for the debt of gratitude I feel I owe Countess Golytsyn, I would have declined the invitation.' He paused, his eyes drinking in her beauty. 'And that would have been a tragedy.'

'Why a tragedy?' Marie asked, trying to conceal the joy she felt at hearing his words.

'Because I would have missed seeing you look so lovely.'

She beamed, then glanced nervously at her mother. Pauline Kulbas seemed to be engaged in deep conversation with her neighbours, but Marie was sure she was nonetheless aware of every small change in her daughter's expression.

'I need to know something.' Alexei turned his whole body towards her. 'I notice you're not wearing a ring on your left hand.'

Marie's gaze instinctively dropped to her finger. 'We never learnt what became of Pyotr.'

'And your brother?' His voice was tender and genuine in its concern.

Marie shook her head. Feeling her control over her emotions slipping, she pushed back her chair. 'If you'll excuse me, I think I . . .'

In her immediate vicinity the men half rose from their chairs before Marie motioned with her hand for them to stay seated. Alexei grasped her arm. 'Please don't go. I didn't mean to upset you.'

'I'm fine,' she assured him. 'I just need to . . .' She faltered. 'I'm fine,' she repeated. 'Truly.' She smiled, resting a hand on his arm. 'Please, don't worry. I'll be back shortly.'

❦

'She's lovely,' the princess said into Alexei's ear as soon as Marie was gone. 'She was engaged before the war. The poor boy went missing and was never heard of again.' She took a sip of her wine. 'She also lost a brother in the POW camps. They say she was very close to him. Ah, their poor mother.' The old woman tutted, her eyes moving to Madame Kulbas. 'She has never really recovered from the loss of her eldest son.' She shook her head in sympathy. Turning to Alexei, she gave him an appraising look. 'They say Marie, too, is heartbroken, but a young heart, even a broken one, is capable of mending. And she still has her whole life in front of her.'

Alexei followed Marie with his eyes, his gaze lingering on the double doors as she slipped through them.

'Please excuse me, Your Highness,' he said, bowing to the princess. 'I've just recalled a matter that requires my urgent attention.' He moved briskly and a servant hurried to open the doors for him. In the vestibule, he spied Marie turning down a corridor and hastened to catch her.

'Marie,' he called softly.

She stopped, but did not turn to face him. When he came closer, he noticed her shoulders trembling under her thin shawl.

'The princess told me about your brother,' he said gently. 'I'm sorry.'

'You weren't to know.'

'It must have been very hard for you, losing both of them.'

She turned to look directly at him. 'I miss both of them terribly.' In the light of the corridor, her eyes shone brightly. 'But . . .'

Alexei waited for her to finish but instead she dropped her eyes, covering her mouth with her hand.

'But what?' Moving even closer, he lifted her chin so he could look into her face. 'Tell me.'

When she finally met his gaze, he noticed her eyes were moist.

'I . . .' A single tear ran down her cheek and he brushed it away gently with his fingers.

Finally she said, 'I miss my brother dearly. And I miss Pyotr.

Not a day goes by that I don't think of them, that I don't wish them safely back home.' She stopped and took a breath. 'But I have missed you more.'

Staggered, it took Alexei a moment to react. Cupping his hands around her face, he brought it close to his. She looked back at him, her eyes large and brimming with tears.

'If you only knew how long I've dreamt of hearing you say those words.'

'Oh, Alexei, I love you. I've always loved you but . . .'

He did not let her finish. Her mouth parted as his lips closed over hers, kissing her, pouring into the kiss the years of separation and longing.

He pulled back and held her close. 'I can't believe I'm holding you. I keep thinking I'm dreaming and will wake to find you gone.' His lips touched the soft skin of her throat.

A quiet moan escaped her and she gripped his jacket. Tightening his embrace, he covered her neck and shoulders with kisses.

'I want to kiss all of you, explore every part of you.' His hands roamed down her back and across her hips.

'Alexei.' She struggled feebly in his arms.

'Don't ask me to stop,' he pleaded as his lips returned to brush hers. He felt dazed by the scent of her, the feel of her. 'I love you, Marie.'

Marie's breath caught in her chest as Alexei's kisses kindled a fire in her belly, making her body go weak.

She pushed against him with little strength. 'Please stop.'

Alexei loosened his grip and she stepped back, the air returning to her lungs.

'I can't do this,' she said, even though every inch of her screamed to return to his arms. 'I will not be your mistress.'

'What are you saying?' He moved closer, touching her face. 'I haven't been able to look at another woman since I met you.'

'Please don't come any closer.' She pushed his hand away. 'I will not enter into an affair. I won't be used for your amusement.'

'You are speaking in riddles. What amusement? I adore you.'

'But you are a married man,' she said.

'Marie.' He took her hand, his thumb tracing slow circles on her skin. 'My marriage has been over for a long time. Emily has asked me for a divorce. She has moved to Paris with our daughters.' Turning her hand over, he kissed the palm. 'She suspected that I did not love her.' He drew closer. 'That I am in love with someone else.' He brushed her fingers with his lips. 'And she was right. I've been in love with you since we first met in Petrograd.'

Goosebumps covered her arms and shoulders.

'You are trembling.' He pulled her shawl higher over her shoulders.

'Alexei,' she murmured in a faint voice, 'are you telling me the truth?'

He smiled warmly then, lifting her hand, pressed it against his chest. 'Can you feel that?'

'Is that your heart?' She leant closer. 'It's beating so fast.'

'Because of you.'

Hearing a sound, they stepped away from each other. The butler came through the servants' door carrying a canister on a silver tray. Not noticing them, he hurried in the direction of the dining room.

'They are serving dessert,' Marie said, suddenly anxious that their long absence might be noticed. 'We must go back.'

She walked down the corridor ahead of him, feeling his eyes on her, and entered the dining room. He followed a few minutes later, brushing a hand over his hair as he took his place beside her.

They did not speak for the remainder of their time at the table. Shortly after, the women retired to the drawing room.

Alexei bowed to the ladies then, taking Marie's hand, bent to kiss it. 'It has been the most charming evening,' he said, pressing her hand before letting it go. She smiled, suppressing a laugh at his formality.

'I must see you again,' he whispered in her ear.

'Tomorrow,' she replied. 'My parents receive callers from eleven.'

Alexei's eyes shone. 'Till tomorrow, then . . . Marie.' He drew out her name as if it were the most precious word in the Russian language. She smiled back, tiny wings fluttering inside her.

53

Western Russia, June 1919

Fyodor's fingers, stiff from having to hold the same position for too long, shook against the rifle.

Spring had been slow to arrive but quick to make way for summer. The attack they had been predicting that morning had never materialised but the troops had kept their position. The sun baking his back, Fyodor shifted his rifle slightly to adjust its weight on his shoulder.

A hand clapped his shoulder, startling him.

'A little jumpy, aren't you?' Andrei Nikolaievich said.

'It's all the waiting,' Fyodor confessed. 'It always makes me nervous.'

'Don't worry, little Fedya.' Andrei elbowed him in the ribs good-naturedly. 'You will soon be put out of your misery.'

Despite being only two years older and not much taller than Fyodor, Andrei had insisted on calling him 'little Fedya' from the very beginning. Soon everyone in his regiment called him that, despite his protests. While on sentry duty, Fyodor had allowed a soldier, a former major general from the imperial army, to pass without the proper papers. When the soldier didn't return Fyodor had raised the alarm, but it was too late. The search parties sent to bring the deserter back had failed and Fyodor's reputation as a youth still a little wet behind the ears had stuck.

'Company ready?' An order rang out through the ranks.

Fyodor's fingers tightened around his rifle.

'Fire!'

The peace of the open fields was shattered by the rattle of gunfire. Cannons boomed, creating craters where a moment ago there had been green grass.

As one of the first line of men, Fyodor cleared the parapet and ran up the sloping hill. Jumping into a crater, he covered his head with his hand as a shell landed with a loud explosion. The air, thick with gun smoke, curled around him in a soupy swirl. He coughed into his sleeve then, lifting his head, tried to get his bearings. One of the officers to his left shouted instructions to his men over the noise of the gunfire, but his orders were cut short as a bullet tore open his chest and he fell to the ground, where he lay unmoving.

Dropping his head again, Fyodor pressed himself flat against the dirt. Breathing hard, his heart hammered wildly in his ribcage.

From behind him, he heard shouts and looked up to see Red Army soldiers running back to their trenches. Springing up, he ran after them, fearful of being left behind. A grenade exploded close to him and pain ripped through one leg as he fell hard on his side. Shocked by the sight of so much blood, Fyodor let out a loud moan and clutched at his leg with both hands. Around him, bullets whizzed and sang through the air at a relentless pace. It was strange that the thought which occupied Fyodor at that moment was not whether he would survive, but whether he would recognise his mother if he met her again. Conjuring up her image, he felt a moment of panic when her features did not fix themselves in his mind. As his mother's face faded, it was replaced by Katya's concerned eyes the day he had told her he'd joined the Red Army. At that moment, Fyodor looked up to see the long barrel of a rifle. His eyes grew round as a bright light, followed by a loud crack, exploded from it.

Katya was busy applying iodine to a soldier's wound when something made her look up at the men bringing in the bodies for burial. It might have been the colour of the hair reflected by the late afternoon sun or the small stature of the figure carried on the stretcher. Whatever it was, it caused Katya's heart to jump and, ignoring the calling of the other nurses, she ran to catch up with them.

By the time the stretcher-bearers had lowered the lifeless body to join the row of dead men, Katya was already pushing the men out of her way so she could look at the face. What she saw stilled the breath in her lungs.

Fyodor – motionless, his skin translucent, his mouth open to one side – looked so peaceful that for a brief moment Katya thought he might only be sleeping.

'Fyodor.' She shook him by the shoulders. 'Wake up.'

His features seemed younger; more like the child who had once followed her everywhere than the youth who wanted to fight.

'It's Katya, Fyodor,' she said, pushing past the lump in her throat. 'Open your eyes and look at me. Fedya, please.'

Tears rolled down her cheeks, dripping onto Fyodor. She moved to wipe his face. The clammy skin felt like clay under her fingertips and the shock of it made her draw back her hand. Grabbing his thin frame, she pressed him against her.

Her cry of grief was that of a wounded animal, causing soldiers leaning on shovels, ready to bury the dead, to look to the heavens or down at their boots.

Oblivious to them, Katya rocked back and forth, holding Fyodor's body tightly against her. One of the soldiers stepped quietly behind her and placed his hand on her shoulder.

Katya felt the pressure of the man's fingers. She heard a gravelly voice telling her it was time to let go, but the meaning of the words did not sink in. It was only when a second pair of hands moved to lift her to her feet that she understood they wished to separate her from Fyodor. Wrenching her arms free, she threw herself back over the boy's body.

The men sent for the doctor and it was he who finally convinced

Katya to let go. Her face awash with tears, Katya leant heavily on the doctor's arm as the men lifted Fyodor and lowered him into the ground.

'I found him lost and bewildered,' Katya sobbed into her hands. 'He held my hand with such trust, it broke my heart.' She watched as the men poured dirt into the grave.

'I cannot imagine I could love a son more than I loved Fyodor. He was like my own flesh and blood.'

The doctor patted her back, then led her away from the graves to a cluster of grey tents. She did not resist as he sat her on a cot, unlaced and removed her boots, and lowered her head to the pillow. For the first time since she was a child herself, a gentle hand brushed away the loose strands of hair and pulled blankets up over her shoulders. Depleted, Katya did not turn her head to thank the doctor, but contined to cry till there were no more tears left to shed. Only then did she fall into a sleep of sad, meaningless dreams.

54

North-West Russia, August 1919

Soft warm raindrops ran down the windows in tiny streams. Pulling back the heavy curtain, Bogoleev looked out across the vast manicured gardens. Ribbons of blue cigarette smoke trickled from his mouth and nose.

Not far from where he stood, a man was slumped on a chair with his hands tied behind his back. Hair damp with sweat fell over his face. His top buttons were torn, revealing dried bloodstains on the white undershirt. Moaning softly under his breath, he ran a tongue over the fresh cut above his lip.

'I swear to you I am innocent,' he mumbled and his shoulders started to quake. 'I know nothing of the crimes you accuse me of.'

Bogoleev half turned to the man. 'There are quite a few witnesses who have testified against you.'

'They are lying,' the prisoner cried desperately. His right eye was swollen shut and he had to turn his head slightly to look at Bogoleev through his good eye. 'I have nothing but admiration and complete loyalty for our Comrade Lenin.'

Bogoleev smiled from behind the blue smoke. 'Of course,' he said sympathetically, shrugging one shoulder. 'Misunderstandings do occur.'

'Yes! Yes, Comrade Commissar, that's exactly what's happened . . . just a misunderstanding. I've been wrongly accused of speaking against our leader.' The prisoner strained his neck, looking up at Bogoleev with a watery smile, grateful to have met with a little understanding.

'These things do happen.' Circling the chair, Bogoleev tutted amiably and nodded. 'And so with a clear conscience you claim never to have spoken a single word against our revolutionary leaders? And you have not tried to rally support for the White Army?'

'I swear this has all been a great misunderstanding.'

Bogoleev stared coldly at the slumped figure. He motioned to one of the soldiers at the back of the room. Stepping forward, the soldier struck the prisoner hard across the cheek, splattering the parquet with fresh blood. Grabbing a fistful of hair, Bogoleev lifted the man's face to his.

'I hate liars,' he hissed.

The prisoner's Adam's apple bobbed at the base of his throat.

Unfastening his gun, Bogoleev pressed it against the fleshy part of the prisoner's chin. A low moan broke from the man's lips. 'Please, Comrade Commissar,' he begged. 'I promise to be a better citizen.'

Standing by the door, Ivanov shifted his weight to the other foot. He had slipped in unnoticed part way through the interrogation with some important news for Bogoleev. Watching the cruel game played out with the accused man made him wish he had waited outside. He was about to leave when Bogoleev, as if sensing his presence, looked up and saw him.

Ivanov could not understand the change that had come over Bogoleev since he had emerged from the coma. The doctors had deemed it too risky to remove the shrapnel embedded in his skull, so they had left it there, hoping Bogoleev was strong enough to pull through. Ivanov was fighting at the front again when he heard that Bogoleev, having survived his injuries, had been promoted by

Trotsky. A month later, Ivanov received a telegram from Bogoleev inviting him to join his unit.

Lenin had established the Bolshevik secret police, *Cheka*, to hunt out opponents to the regime. Ruthless and unyielding, they were granted greater powers by Lenin after a failed assassination attempt on his life.

Invalided from the Red Army, Bogoleev now led one of the units and, free to choose his team, had asked Ivanov to join him. Despite having heard the rumours circulating about the group's activities, Ivanov knew its members enjoyed privileges that were not available to the average citizen. Within weeks of joining, Ivanov had moved his family to a four-room apartment with increased rations for food, fuel and clothing. In return, Ivanov set up a network of spies who reported on individuals who spoke out against the revolution. The man before Bogoleev now was a low-ranking officer in the imperial army who had been found hiding in his *dacha* outside Petrograd. Denounced by a neighbour, he was overheard telling a friend that 'it was a pity the bullet had not finished Lenin off'.

Watching the icy blue eyes, Ivanov questioned whether Bogoleev was still of sound mind. There was madness behind those eyes, a shiftiness that had not been there before. He suspected the commissar drank excessively. More than once, he had found Bogoleev sitting behind his desk, one hand supporting his head while the other was wrapped around the neck of an empty bottle.

Tears trickled down the accused man's cheeks and he began to weep softly. Circling his victim, Bogoleev's eyes shone with malice as he made him beg and plead.

Ivanov turned away, looking towards the door.

Bogoleev knew he had emerged from his injuries an altered man. The doctors had warned him the shrapnel lodged in his brain might lead to complications. The migraines had started almost immediately, drumming behind his temple, robbing him of any peace. The pain ate away at his brain, gnawing at his nerves. He began drinking to dull the ache.

The zeal with which he sought out traitors grew as the pain in his head increased. Confused at first by his growing lust for violence, he soon ceased to care about its source, but allowed it to guide his actions. His position in *Cheka* gave him the authority to act on his urges. He took particular pleasure in hunting men who had looked down on him in the past and had overlooked him for promotions because of his background.

Bogoleev smiled thinly at the accused man. 'Is it true you were an officer in the imperial army?'

'I was a second lieutenant with the Ninth Sibirski Regiment,' the accused man cried. 'Please, I swear to you, I have done nothing wrong.'

Looking at the snivelling, pathetic man begging for his life, Bogoleev felt nothing but contempt. 'It is true, is it not, that your parents are landowners?'

Not raising his head, the accused nodded, his weeping growing louder.

Lifting his gun, Bogoleev rested the barrel above the man's brow. 'By the order of the Soviet people, you are found guilty of treason.'

'No. Wait . . . Please.' A dark patch spread across the front of the man's trousers.

Bogoleev's eyes hardened. As his fingers tightened over the trigger, an almost sexual pleasure filled him, and his face twisted in a grin. 'And condemned to death.'

'No!'

The room echoed with the sound of the gunshot. The man's head slumped to one side, his open eye round with shock. A pool of blood slowly seeped and spread over his hair and clothes.

Bogoleev cleaned the specks of blood from his gun with a handkerchief. The adrenalin racing through his veins made his hands tremble. Reaching into his breast pocket, he pulled out a silver flask and, unscrewing the top, took a long pull, wincing at the sharp taste. After a moment, the deep creases lining his face relaxed.

'What news have you for me?' he asked Ivanov, who was standing behind him.

'We've found him.'

Bogoleev turned sharply. 'Serov? You've found him? Where is he?'

Ivanov referred to a page inside the folder he was carrying. 'Tallinn.'

'Estonia?' Bogoleev grabbed the folder. 'Let me see that report.' His eyes scanned the contents. 'Do we have people we can trust there?'

'There is a strong Bolshevik presence among the workers,' Ivanov said, 'even with the Estonians fighting for their independence since last November.'

'I want you to head this investigation.' Bogoleev handed the folder back to Ivanov. 'Keep a close eye on Serov and track his movements.'

'What if he recognises me?'

'Keep a low profile but find out everything you can about him: who he associates with and where he frequents. Find out who the Red sympathisers are and befriend them. Do not let him out of your sight.'

Ivanov hesitated for a moment. 'You've been chasing Serov ever since you've left hospital. Is it really worth expending all these resources for just one man?'

Bogoleev gave Ivanov a long look. He liked Ivanov, trusted him, had offered him a position in his team, but despite all that, Bogoleev felt Ivanov had never appreciated the importance of this assignment. Out of all the men Bogoleev had hunted, Serov was the most important to him. He had given Serov a chance to redeem himself, to join the Reds, and had been betrayed by him.

Bogoleev stabbed a finger at the folder. 'Serov made a fool of me. Twice he escaped and twice I let him go with a warning when, by law, I should have shot him. He must pay for his treachery. I'll get him if it's the last thing I do.'

55

Tallinn, September 1919

Alexei sat in a pool of light. Outside, the clouds turned indigo as light drained from the sky.

A package addressed in Emily's handwriting had arrived with the morning post. Three crisp white envelopes sat on top of a bundle of old photos, held together with a velvet ribbon. Alexei placed the envelopes on the coffee table and eased out the photographs. A note from Emily read:

I found these and thought you might like them back. E

He undid the bow and the photos spilled across his lap.

Picking up each picture, he took a moment to study it before letting it drop. He paused at the photo of himself at the start of the mobilisation. Self-assured, he stood erect with one hand resting casually on the hilt of his sword. His hair, oiled and parted in the middle, was already showing signs of thinning. Next to him Grigory, dressed in civilian clothes, looked straight at the camera, the flash from the bulb giving his eyes an eerie ghost-like look.

Opening the letters, he read each one in turn. The first two were from his younger daughters. A light smile touched his lips reading the frivolous carefree details. Opening Emily's letter, he expected more of the same but, as he read, a knot tightened inside him.

> *Dear Alexei,*
>
> *I trust this letter finds you well. The girls and I have finally settled in our new apartment in a quiet street in Saint-Germain.*
>
> *I'm pleased to report that I have found an excellent school for Tonya. Irena and Vera are enrolled in a ladies' college but I'm afraid they are more concerned with fashion and young men than their studies. They are seldom home and refuse chaperones. I am especially concerned for Irena, who has become increasingly secretive. To make matters worse, my sister came to see me yesterday with some disturbing news. She was having coffee with a friend who casually mentioned rumours of Irena walking arm in arm with a married man. When I confronted Irena, she laughed it off. I am at a loss as to what to do. I beg you, write to her and make her see sense.*

Alexei frowned. In the past year, Irena had blossomed into a beautiful young woman. Still largely inexperienced with men, and without the protection of her father, she would be easy prey for those wishing to take advantage of her. At the thought of his daughter's reputation being compromised, blood rushed to his temples.

He found a photo of his three daughters amongst the ones Emily had sent. Standing between her two sisters, Irena looked into the lens demurely. A weary sadness settled over Alexei. He missed his daughters.

Returning the photo to the pile, he checked his watch and was surprised to find it was past midnight. Ringing for his valet, he prepared for bed, his thoughts turning to Marie and her invitation to join her for a picnic the following day.

The past few months, he had been a regular visitor at the Kulbases' apartment, spending long afternoons in Marie's company.

When he was with her, his heart felt light and he smiled warmly at all those with whom he came into contact. Even Madame Kulbas's cold reception hadn't dampened his spirits. Ultimately, even she had accepted him, on his last two visits inviting him to join the family for dinner.

The next morning, Alexei arrived at the Kulbas residence at the appointed hour. Marie flung the door open before he rang the bell.

'I saw you from the upstairs window,' she said. An attractive glow bloomed over her cheeks. 'I have the perfect place in mind for our picnic. I hope you're not averse to long walks.'

With a picnic basket packed with salted herrings, cheese, pickled cucumber and rye bread, they set off to a forest on the outskirts of Tallinn.

'I love this time of year when the air is still warm, and no rain or grey skies spoil the day,' Marie said happily as they walked along the path.

Reaching a clearing, she spread out their picnic blanket. Alexei lay beside her, his head resting on his hand, and watched her.

'There's something troubling you, Alexei. You seem a little distant today.'

Alexei sighed. 'It's Irena. I fear she may have a little too much of her father in her.'

Marie laughed. 'Surely that can't be a bad thing.' She offered him a plate with a selection of herrings and dressed salad.

'I fear she might be having . . .' He paused, unsure how much to tell her.

'You can trust me, Alexei.' She placed a hand on his arm. 'I won't judge.'

'Irena might be having an affair with a married man.'

'I see.' Her eyes dropped to her hands. 'And you are worried about her reputation.' Marie's face grew reflective, leaving Alexei to speculate on whether she was still talking about Irena.

'Marie, you know that's not how it is between us.'

'My position is not much different from Irena's.' A cloud passed over her eyes. 'You were married when we first met.'

Alexei wrapped an arm around her and pulled her close. 'I don't know how else I can assure you.' Lifting her face, he kissed her, first lightly and then fully on the mouth. He felt the strong beat of her heart pulse through her shirt and held her tighter.

'I love you, Marie,' he whispered. 'and will continue loving you till the end of my days.' Shifting his weight, he knelt before her and, taking her hands between his own, kissed her fingers. 'Marie,' he said softly, 'will you marry me?'

She stared at him with wide eyes, saying nothing, and Alexei felt his stomach hollowing. 'I take it your silence means you do not accept me.' He smiled weakly, the words burning a hole in him.

'Alexei . . .' She rested her gaze on his face. 'These past months with you have been wonderful.'

Warmth returned to his skin. 'I feel the same.' He squeezed her hands. 'When I'm with you, I feel as if everything is right with the world.'

She bowed her head and murmured, 'I just don't know if I'm ready to be married. The war has left its scars. And my memories are like heavy stones, difficult to move.'

'The war has left its effects on all of us and there's nothing anyone can do to change the past,' Alexei said, taking her hand. 'But, Marie, we have a chance to start afresh. Don't throw away our happiness because of the war.'

Seeing tears spring to her eyes, the hollow feeling returned to his stomach. 'Marie, will you accept me as your husband?' He looked into her eyes, searching for the answer. 'You said you loved me. Do you still feel the same way?'

'I . . . I don't know.'

'You don't know?'

'I mean, this is all so sudden.'

'It's a simple question, Marie. Do you love me?' He uttered the last two words with difficulty, his voice becoming thick.

When she failed to answer, his gaze slipped away from her face and desolation clamped at his chest. Letting go of her hand he rose to his feet.

'I will not embarrass you further by calling on you again. Please give my regards to your family.'

'Where are you going?' Her voice was panicked.

'I can't stay knowing you do not share my feelings.'

She grabbed his hand. 'That's not what I said.'

'You don't have to. That much is obvious. I will make immediate plans to leave for Paris.'

'Paris?'

'If nothing else, I must settle the situation with Irena.' He gave her a clipped bow. 'Good day, Mademoiselle.'

Jumping to her feet, she ran after him. 'Alexei, wait! When will you come back?'

He continued walking with quick strides. 'There's nothing for me to come back to.'

'No. Please don't do this.' Grabbing his arm, she pulled at his sleeve. 'Please don't go away.'

'What do you want from me, Marie?' he said forcefully. It was the first time he had raised his voice at her and the shock of it made them both freeze. 'You've made it obvious you don't love me,' he said in a croaking voice. 'I cannot stay in Tallinn while you are also here. Don't you see? I cannot breathe knowing you are close but don't care for me.' He turned away from her, his heart tearing into pieces. 'There's no other way.'

'No! Please, Alexei – wait!'

He stopped and turned to face her.

'What?' he snapped impatiently.

Her lips parted into a smile. Of *course* I accept you.'

'What game are you playing now, Marie?'

'I'm not playing any games.' She stepped closer. 'I love you,' she said slowly. 'And I cannot think of anything better than to spend the rest of my life by your side.'

Alexei's mouth went dry. Not trusting his ears, he remained rooted to the spot, staring at her in disbelief.

'Do you have nothing to say?' she asked with a teasing smile.

Alexei studied her face, needing assurance she was speaking the truth.

'Marie, please don't say it unless you really mean it.'

She moved beside him, taking his hand. 'I love you, Alexei. I love you with all my heart.'

Alexei was speechless. When he eventually spoke, the words fell from his lips so softly, she had to lean in to catch them.

'You have made me the happiest man in the whole of Tallinn.'

Impulsively, he took her into his embrace and with his chest filling with joy, he held her against him and kissed her.

56

Tallinn, September 1919

Marie tapped the tip of her fountain pen against her lower lip impatiently as she scanned the catalogues.

'I think I like the lace with the tiny white ribbon rosettes.' She wrote down the order number, then promptly scratched it out. 'Or maybe I should have the patterned lace with the beading.' She looked up at Anna, who returned her look with a calm smile.

'You're not being much help,' Marie complained.

Anna laughed. 'You should be helping your mother with the final arrangements for tonight's dinner.'

Marie groaned. 'Alexei and I wanted an intimate family dinner to announce our engagement; instead, Papa has invited everyone we know.'

'Can you blame him? His only daughter is engaged.' Anna pinched Marie's arm good-naturedly. 'To a major general, no less.'

Marie pouted and turned back to her catalogue. 'You make me sound ungrateful.'

Anna shook her head and smiled. 'Show me these laces you are talking about.' She leant over the catalogue.

'I prefer the rosettes,' Anna said decisively. 'They seem more . . . elegant.'

'I think I'll keep my veil simple with scalloped edgings and a garland of flowers.' Marie clapped her hands in excitement.

The curtains moved gently in the light breeze coming through the open window. Marie heard the clattering sound of hooves come to a stop outside. Hoping it was Alexei, she rushed to the window. Craning her neck, she saw a stranger with dark curly hair climb off a chestnut horse.

'Who's that?' she asked Anna, who had joined her at the window.

'I'm not sure. I've never seen him before.'

The man ran lightly up the stairs, stopping briefly at the landing to straighten his jacket and run a hand through his hair.

'I've seen him before,' Marie said, 'but I can't think where.'

The stranger turned his face and Marie saw one side was deformed.

'Pull your head back in,' Anna urged, 'before we're caught spying.'

Marie frowned. 'He looks familiar.'

'He might be a business associate of your father's,' Anna suggested.

'His clothes are far too modest for him to be one of Papa's associates.'

Marie went back to the catalogues but her thoughts kept returning to the stranger.

'Sorry to bother you, Mademoiselle,' Zoya said as she entered Marie's bedroom a few minutes later, 'but your parents are asking for you to join them and a guest in the drawing room.'

Marie quickly changed into a new lavender dress with a dropped waist. She checked her reflection in the mirror then, satisfied, walked briskly to join her family.

She found the visitor and Valentin sitting at either end of a double settee, while Monsieur Kulbas sat in his favourite armchair, holding the hand of her mother, who sat alone on the second settee.

Letting go of his wife's hand, Monsieur Kulbas stood, took his daughter's elbow and led her to the visitor. Marie saw that he had a kind face, despite the deformity. His suit was old, judging by the frayed cuffs, and he seemed ill at ease, looking around the richly furnished room with wide eyes.

'Monsieur Ivanov, may I introduce you to my daughter, Marie.'

'You look familiar, Monsieur, but I can't remember where I know you from,' Marie said after taking a seat beside her mother.

'I had precisely the same feeling when you walked in,' the visitor said with a rueful smile. 'You look just like Nikolai.'

Marie's heart jumped at the mention of her brother's name. 'You knew Nikolai?'

'Monsieur Ivanov was with Nikolai in the POW camp,' Monsieur Kulbas explained. 'He was with him when he passed away.'

'He talked about you all the time.' Ivanov looked at each of them in turn. 'Nikolai loved you all very much.'

Pauline Kulbas began to weep softly.

'I'm sorry to upset you, Madame,' Ivanov said. Placing his glass on the table, he stood to take his leave.

'No, please stay and have supper with us,' Monsieur Kulbas insisted. 'We are having a small gathering to announce our daughter's engagement.'

Ivanov gestured to his clothes. 'I'm not suitably dressed.'

'I can lend you some of . . .' Valentin stopped and glanced at his mother. Ivanov, too big to fit into Valentin's clothes, would have to choose from Nikolai's wardrobe. Pauline Kulbas smiled kindly at her son to show she wasn't upset by his suggestion.

Ivanov shook his head. 'Thank you, but I will not impose on your hospitality any longer.'

'What line of business are you in, Monsieur Ivanov?' Monsieur Kulbas stood to shake hands with his guest.

'I work in a factory.' Ivanov's eyes shifted nervously.

'I hope you're not one of those Bolsheviks.'

'No, Monsieur. I'm a simple man. I don't have any understanding of such things.'

'And what brings you to Tallinn?'

'My wife's family has distant relations in Estonia,' Ivanov explained. 'I enquired after your family in Narva and they told me you had moved to Tallinn. I hope you don't mind me calling on you without writing first. I had made a promise to Nikolai that I would.'

'Not at all. And if there is anything we can do for you, please don't hesitate to ask.'

Marie, too, shook hands with their visitor. 'It's such a pity you will not stay for supper. My fiancé was also in the war and he'll be disappointed to have missed you.'

Together the family escorted Ivanov to the door. Taking Ivanov's hand in both of his, Herman Kulbas shook it warmly. 'Thank you for coming. It has given our family great comfort to know Nikolai spent his last days with . . .' His grip weakened and he let go of Ivanov's hand.

Ivanov grasped the older man's arm and gave it a light squeeze. 'Your son was a good man. He saved my life in the camp. My greatest regret is that I wasn't able to do the same for him.'

A week later, alone in his study, Alexei paced the room. Stopping at his desk, he rang the brass bell.

'Please get my coat and hat,' he told the valet.

Outside he looked up and down the narrow laneway before making his way to Raekoja Plats, the city square. For days he had had the feeling he was being watched. His paranoia intensified when Marie told him of the unexpected visitor on the evening of their engagement.

'The man might be a Bolshevik,' Alexei warned. 'What if he learns of my escape from the Red Army?'

'That's nonsense. He was here to visit relatives.'

'How do you know he wasn't lying?'

'I don't.' She half turned to him. 'But I know that the man I met was gentle and polite and, above all, he was a friend to my brother.'

Marie's assurances did little to soothe Alexei's agitation. Walking along the cobbled streets, he thought he heard footsteps behind him. His pulse started to pound loudly in his ears. Pretending to look in a shop window, he scanned the street behind him in the glass's reflection. Seeing no one, he continued down the main street to the jeweller where he was to meet Marie, but the sense of unease remained, like a cold chill across his back.

'Darling, you worry too much,' Marie said when he told her of his concerns. Choosing one of the shiny gold rings the jeweller had arranged on the velvet cloth, she slipped it over her finger and, holding her hand at arm's length, gave it a critical appraisal.

'Mademoiselle certainly has an eye for quality,' the jeweller flattered her. 'The ring is eighteen-carat rose gold and the amethyst at the centre is of the highest grade. May I show you a matching necklace?'

'I have an uneasy feeling about the whole thing,' Alexei whispered in her ear. 'The Red Army is getting closer. It's becoming too dangerous for us to remain here.'

'What are you suggesting? That we leave Tallinn?' Marie asked. 'Alexei, have you lost your senses? What about the wedding?'

She slipped off the ring and returned it to the tray. 'I can't decide. Could you please send a selection to the apartment?'

'As you wish,' the jeweller replied with a tight smile. Motioning for his apprentice to hold open the door, he bowed as Alexei and Marie left the shop.

'We can bring the wedding forward,' Alexei said when they were in the street.

'Alexei!' He could hear exasperation creeping into her voice. 'We have two hundred guests attending, including your daughters, who are travelling from Paris. Can you imagine the chaos changing the date would cause?' She checked her watch and, spotting her driver, waved him over. 'I'm late for an appointment with my seamstress.' Placing a gloved hand on Alexei's arm, she leant close to kiss his cheek. 'Be reasonable, Alexei.' Cocking her head to one side, she smiled. 'What's a few more months, hmm?'

Following Marie's departure, the prickling uneasiness continued to nag at Alexei's senses. He had heard there were men who forged identity papers and wondered if he should secure papers for himself and Marie in case the Bolsheviks closed in.

Glancing in a shop window, he thought he saw a shadow melt

behind a building and his unease increased. Entering the shop, he watched the footpath outside, waiting for the figure to emerge.

'May I help you, Monsieur?'

A sales clerk stood by his elbow. 'Would you like me to show you something from the window?'

Alexei pointed to a small blue and white vase in the display cabinet. 'I'll take that.'

'That is an excellent choice. It is handcrafted Chinese porcelain dating to the Yuan Dynasty. The blue pigment is from the finest Persian cobalt.'

'Yes, yes.' Alexei said impatiently. 'Here's my card. My valet will make the necessary arrangements for payment.'

'Of course and if I can assist in any other –'

'You can assist by leaving me alone.'

The clerk stared back uncomprehendingly. 'As you wish, Monsieur.'

Out in the streets, darkness had gathered around the buildings, turning them steel grey. Alexei was aware the clerk and the shop owner were watching him but he continued to look up and down the street from behind a large oriental statue.

'Will there be anything else, Monsieur?' the proprietor asked hesitantly.

They must think me eccentric, thought Alexei. 'No thank you.' Pulling out his wallet, he handed the clerk a generous tip. 'You have been very helpful.'

Walking away, Alexei was again gripped with the suspicion he was being followed. Quickening his step, he turned into Viru Street. Ahead of him, two towers marked the entry into the city's medieval centre. Hailing a cabriolet, he gave the driver his address. As the cab pulled away, Alexei risked a glance through the rear window and saw a man run between the towers and fade into the darkness.

On reaching the heavy doors of his building, he fumbled with the large brass key in his pocket. He shot a look up the dark street and saw a man, hands deep in the pockets of his coat, walking briskly towards him. There was something familiar about him.

Alexei pushed the key into the lock but it wouldn't turn. Behind him, the footsteps grew closer. He tried again, rattling the key in the lock.

The footsteps were almost upon him. A cold drop of sweat ran the length of his back. His heart hammering, he looked around for something he could use as a weapon. Finding nothing, he filled his lungs and turned to face the street. If his assailant came at him with a knife, he knew how to fight him.

He watched the dark figure move past his building with no more than a cursory look.

Alexei waited for a few more minutes before slowly expelling the air from his lungs. Turning to the door, he tried the key again, and this time it turned easily.

Upstairs he took a few moments to collect himself. A large fire warmed the library. Pavlov, his valet, brought in the afternoon post on a silver tray, then waited for Alexei to dismiss him.

'That will be all, thank you, Pavlov,' Alexei said.

Pavlov dipped his head in acknowledgment. A few minutes later, Alexei heard Pavlov close the door to the apartment behind the last of the staff. Out of the staff of six, only Pavlov and the cook had quarters in the apartment. The rest left in the evenings and returned at six in the morning.

Rifling through his mail, Alexei noticed the yellow paper of a telegram and pulled it from under the pile.

It was from Emily.

Opening it, he read the few lines. Heat spread from his neck to the roots of his hair.

'Irena,' he muttered in frustration, 'how could you?' Crumpling the telegram, he threw it in the fire, watching as the edges of yellow paper curled and blackened before being consumed by the flames.

To end Irena's affair, Alexei had suggested sending her on a cruise to the southern hemisphere in the company of a chaperone. But despite the close supervision, Irena had jumped ship in Sydney and run off with a cabin boy.

Lighting a cigarette, Alexei moved to the window and looked down at the deserted street. It had started to rain and a young couple, their bodies linked under a single umbrella, hurried along the footpath. The woman's peals of laughter echoed down the street.

Temporarily forgetting Irena, Alexei smiled at the lovers who had taken shelter in a doorway, laughing and kissing. Startled by something behind them, they suddenly stopped, then stepped back into the rain and disappeared around the corner.

Alexei detected a slight movement in the space they had vacated. A figure shifted and moved then a man emerged from the doorway, walking away in the opposite direction from the couple.

Stopping under a streetlight, he turned and looked up at Alexei's building.

Alexei's throat went dry as he recognised the coat and hat of the stranger who had had passed him earlier in the evening.

57

Estonian Border, November 1919

In the officers' tent, Bogoleev studied the map. Red marks showed the advance of the Red Army across the border into Estonia. Having only recently gained independence, Estonia now faced the possibility of losing it again to the Bolsheviks. Bogoleev smiled. Victory was close at hand and he would soon take his revenge against Serov.

He should have had Serov shot the first time he tried to escape, he thought angrily. Instead, Bogoleev foolishly gave him another chance. How smug he must feel, believing he has outwitted me, Bogoleev thought. How he must mock me to his fancy friends.

To have him killed by an assassin would not be enough, Bogoleev decided. He wanted to see Serov humiliated, to see the fear in his eyes as he begged for mercy. Then, if he was lucky, Bogoleev would put him out of his misery with a bullet through the head.

Reaching for his flask, he unscrewed the top and took a long draught. Then, turning from the map, he faced the group of soldiers drinking vodka around the table. Red-rimmed eyes stared back at him. In the distance the faint rumblings of enemy artillery continued.

'Comrades,' Bogoleev began, 'Russia will soon be united under Soviet power.' His fingers brushed lightly over the shrapnel scar where a dull ache throbbed. 'Our brothers stand united before a disorganised and leaderless White Army.'

The men nodded in agreement. Bogoleev smiled but his eyes remained cold. The pulsing ache at his temple grew more intense.

'The American and French troops are pulling out,' he pressed on, 'leaving the White Army to fight on its own.' Walking around the table, Bogoleev took a glass and filled it with vodka. 'It presents us with an excellent opportunity to defeat the White Army once and for all.'

'*Za vas*.' Raising his glass, he downed its contents in a single gulp and, as the men cheered, held it out to be refilled.

Later the same evening, Bogoleev sent a telegram to Ivanov.

Events progressing as hoped STOP Keep close watch on our friend STOP.

Tallinn, December

The café bustled with late-afternoon trade. Moving to a table at the back, Ivanov chose a seat that gave him a clear view of the street. All around him the talk was of the battles between the White and Red armies.

Two men hunched over a backgammon board paused to discuss the latest news.

'To think, our army almost pushed the Bolsheviks back to the gates of Petrograd,' one man said. 'If they had only persevered a little longer.'

His friend shook the dice in his big hand then threw them onto the board. 'Personally, I don't trust those lying aristocratic Whites any more than I trust the Reds.'

Outside, a mother holding tight to the hand of a young child hurried across the cobblestone lane and disappeared behind the walls of a courtyard. Ivanov thought of Marina hurrying home with their son and daughters to prepare the evening meal, and a knot tightened around his throat. Little Lyova would have changed in the months he had been away. In her last letter, Marina wrote that he was learning his alphabet.

Ivanov ached with his whole body to be with them. He decided he would ask Bogoleev for leave once his assignment was over.

At the table next to him, one of the backgammon players was recounting to his friend the plight of a refugee woman he had met.

'The Red Army took everything from her. And when she resisted, she said that they beat her and her family.'

Ivanov turned his head away, not wishing to hear any more. It was proving harder each day to convince himself that such force was necessary. It was one thing to take from the gentry, another to take from the hands of the peasants. Opening the telegram he had received that morning from Bogoleev, he read the message. Over the months, he had sent several reports on Serov, each time stopping short of mentioning Marie. He could hardly believe his eyes when he saw them enter the jewellery shop together. Enquiring after them, he was told the couple were there to select an engagement gift for the young lady but had left without a purchase following some disagreement.

Ivanov had gaped at the jeweller. 'You mean to tell me she plans to marry that man?'

'Go in peace, my son.' The jeweller had smiled kindly, mistaking Ivanov's reaction to that of a spurned lover. 'God is closest to those with broken hearts.'

The bell above the café door jangled and a young man with dark hair walked in. For a fleeting moment, Ivanov thought he was looking at a ghost. The man's gait and the easy smile with which he greeted the other patrons reminded him of Nikolai. Ivanov stared at the man's back as he removed his hat and jacket. Sensing Ivanov's eyes on him, the newcomer turned and gave him a friendly nod before making his way to a table of young men engaged in an animated discussion on Estonia's future.

Ivanov's heart cut loose inside his chest. He missed Nikolai. To the Bolsheviks, the interests of the party came before friends or family. But Ivanov could never adhere to that demand. Nikolai had been like a brother to him. Since learning of Marie's engagement to Alexei, Ivanov had spent nights tossing in his bed, debating whether he should warn the Kulbas family of the danger they were facing. To warn them, he would betray Bogoleev and the Party. To stand back and do nothing would be a betrayal of Nikolai. Increasingly unpredictable, Bogoleev was capable of ordering the execution of the whole family, including the elderly parents.

He needed time: time to think and to consider his options. But time was a luxury that was fast running out. With the Reds in Narva, it would not be long before Bogoleev made his way to Tallinn.

Reaching a decision, Ivanov pulled a notebook from his satchel. Tearing out a page, he scribbled a few words then folded the piece of paper and put it in an envelope. Placing some coins for his coffee on the table, he hurried to the post office.

Zoya arranged the morning's mail along with the daily newspaper on a tray next to two cups of tea and a plate of fresh pastries and carried them to Pauline and Herman Kulbas.

Sitting in his armchair, Monsieur Kulbas read the newspaper, stopping at intervals to read aloud from articles his wife might find interesting. Similarly, his wife shared news and gossip gleaned from the letters or asked her husband's advice before responding to invitations.

'This one is addressed to you, Herman.' Pauline Kulbas turned the envelope over. 'There's no sender's name or address on it.'

Herman Kulbas took the envelope and opened it.

'It's anonymous.' He swallowed, colour draining from his face. 'It says, *Cheka* has been hunting Alexei since he deserted the Red Army. As a consequence, it adds, Marie's life is also in danger!'

'What?' Taking the letter, Pauline Kulbas read the few lines. 'Who would write such a letter?'

Herman Kulbas's shoulders sagged. 'I don't know.'

'Do you think we should take the warning seriously?'

Herman stared at the ceiling as if looking for an answer. 'Yes,' he said finally. 'I think it's serious.'

An hour later Alexei and Marie joined her parents in the parlour and Herman Kulbas showed them the letter. Marie read it first, then, trembling, she passed it to Alexei. 'Who do you suppose has sent it?' she asked.

Her father shrugged. 'There was no return address on the envelope.'

'I was afraid this may happen,' Alexei said in a low voice.

'What should we do?'

Alexei looked at them each in turn. 'I must leave Tallinn,' he said. 'By staying here, I'm putting all your lives in danger.'

Marie's fingers folded over Alexei's. 'If you go, I will come too.'

Aside from the family, the household staff and a few friends, the church was nearly empty. A hasty letter to the guests explained that, due to the uncertainties caused by the civil war, the wedding had been brought forward.

Holding her father's arm, Marie looked elegant in a white silk dress. The veil, a gauzy layer of embroidered lace held in place by a garland of flowers, fell in a long train behind her.

Waiting for her at the altar, Alexei wore his full military uniform.

His two younger daughters sat in the front pew. Emily had declined the invitation but had sent a delicately crafted Chinese porcelain bowl as a wedding gift.

Alexei smiled at his bride. Radiant under her veil, a gentle smile played on her lips and her grey eyes were bright with happiness, showing, without a hint of reservation, how she felt.

The ceremony was brief and simple. The small choir sang psalms and the priest read prayers blessing the couple.

At the end, Alexei offered Marie his arm and led her out of the church.

'I have never seen a bride as beautiful as you,' he whispered in her ear. 'Marriage becomes you.'

❧

Later that evening at Alexei's apartment, Anna helped Marie as she prepared for her first night with him. Most of the room lay in shadow, with the only light coming from the candles on the nightstand and the large fire in the hearth. Marie's heart raced so that she could barely breathe.

Helping her undress, Anna offered her reassuring words, 'All women are nervous on their wedding night. It is nothing unusual.'

Taking the new satin and lace nightgown, Anna laid it on the bed.

'I don't know what to do,' Marie cried desperately. 'What if I behave all wrong?' A new thought made her eyes grow large with alarm. 'What if he is disappointed?'

'Don't talk nonsense. The general adores you.'

Dabbing a little perfume on Marie's neck and elbows, Anna then slipped the gown over her head. The light fabric clung to her curves, accentuating her figure.

'This is far too revealing.' Marie blushed at her reflection.

Anna smiled. 'You look beautiful.'

There was a knock at the door and Anna moved forward to open it.

Alexei stood on the threshold.

'Good evening, Excellency.' Anna stepped aside to let him in then, giving Marie a final reassuring look, slipped out, closing the door quietly behind her.

They stood for what seemed a long time, looking awkwardly around the room, nervous about making eye contact.

'Would you like a glass of port?' Marie asked, going to the table holding the carafe and six small crystal glasses. Filling two glasses, she offered one to Alexei. 'It's a gift from Papa. He had it especially imported from Portugal.'

Accepting the drink, Alexei took small sips, studying Marie over the rim of his glass. Her face grew hot as his eyes travelled down her neck to the tops of her breasts just visible above the neckline of her gown. Taking her unfinished drink, he placed both glasses on the table. Slipping one hand around her waist, he pulled her towards him and smiled at her sharp intake of breath as he closed his lips over hers.

Pulling his head away, he kissed her face, laying soft tender kisses on her brow, eyelids and cheeks. Moving his lips down, he nuzzled the base of her throat.

With every kiss, she felt the stirring of desire grow more urgent. His hands slid lower and the moment he slipped the nightdress over her shoulders, she moaned softly.

Lowering her onto the bed, he whispered, 'This might hurt a little. I'll be as gentle as I can.'

She stiffened, frightened and excited in equal measure. Caressing her breasts, he kissed between them, then licked at the pink tips until they were erect. A whimper rose in her throat as warm wetness swelled between her legs. Shivering, she parted her thighs as she threaded her fingers through his hair.

When he entered her, the pain was excruciating. Biting hard on her lower lip, she stifled a scream. Shifting his hips, he guided himself deeper into her and, this time, she could not contain her cry.

She could not believe anything so painful could ever be pleasurable.

'Try to relax,' he said, then moved deeper inside her.

This time the pain was much less and she lifted her body off the bed to meet his rhythm. At first slow and tender, his thrusting gradually quickened. He moaned into her hair, cupping her buttocks with both hands. Reaching climax, he tensed and, with a final shudder, fell still.

Breathless, they lay pressed against each other, listening to the drumming of one another's hearts, the crisp sheets tangled between their legs. Unexpectedly a sob escaped from her lips and, pushing away his arms, she sat up and drew her knees to her chest. Soon her sobbing was so intense, her face was flooded with tears.

Surprised, Alexei looked at her uncertainly. He made a move to gather her in his arms then hesitated.

'What is it darling?' he murmured, drawing her to him. 'Why are you crying?'

Confused by the sudden cascade of emotions, Marie shook her head, not sure how to answer him. Burying her face in his chest, her sobs eased.

'Marie,' Alexei said quietly, 'speak to me. What have I done?'

She shook her head.

His chest was wet where her tears had been.

'I don't know. I can't explain it.'

'Hush now.' Kissing the top of her head, Alexei tightened his embrace. 'I'm here for you.'

Comforted by the pair of arms folding around her, the pain she had carried locked in her chest receeded to a faint throb before disappearing altogether. She calmed, as if cleansed by her tears, and fell into an exhausted sleep.

That night, Pyotr and Nikolai visited her in her dreams.

Gazing on her with kind, understanding eyes, they spoke softly to her.

'I'm glad you have found happiness,' Pyotr told her.

'You are not disappointed in me?'

'Of course not.' He was surrounded by a halo of brilliant light. 'We are happy for you.'

Before receding into the shadows, Pyotr turned and smiled at her. 'I wish you a long and happy life, Marie.'

In the morning, Marie gazed into Alexei's sleeping face. She kissed his lips softly and felt joy at his smile.

'Hmm,' he moaned groggily, opening his eyes. 'Don't tell me you're one of those women who wakes at the first hint of light.'

'I am actually.' She giggled. 'But until now, I've always slept alone so I had no need to stay in bed for long.'

'What are you suggesting, Madame Serova?' He raised an eyebrow.

She smiled shyly. 'Well, let's see if you can convince me it would be worth my while to stay in bed a little longer.'

A week later, Marie stood before the mahogany bookcase in her parents' study, the tips of her fingers brushing the spines of the books. She had her back to her mother, who sat on the couch, head bent over her needlework. Dropping her hand, Marie turned to the corner of the room where more trunks were stacked ready to be loaded into the car to be transferred to Alexei's apartment.

'What's troubling you, Marie?' Pauline Kulbas asked without looking up.

Marie sighed. 'How can you tell?'

Smiling, Pauline Kulbas lifted her gaze. 'I've known you since I felt the first kicks of your tiny feet inside my body.' She patted the space next to her on the couch. 'Come, sit next to me.'

Marie sat down beside her mother. 'You know that Alexei and I must leave Tallinn soon.'

'I do.' Madame Kulbas took Marie's hand.

'I don't want to leave you and Papa. I'm not sure when I will see you next.'

'You are a married woman now, Marie,' her mother reminded her. 'Your place is by your husband.'

'I never thought you liked Alexei.'

'I had my reservations,' Pauline Kulbas confessed. 'And who could blame me? He is almost twice your age, with grown children and a reputation . . . These were not qualities I had hoped for in a son-in-law.'

Marie opened her mouth to protest, but her mother lifted a finger to stop her. 'Let me finish. On the positive side, Alexei is from a good family. But –' she shrugged '– none of that matters if you are in an unhappy relationship.'

'He loves me.'

'I know he does.'

'How can you tell?'

'It's in the way he looks at you, as if you are the most important person in the room. It's in the tender way he brushes the hair off your face or holds your hand or leans close to whisper in your ear. He loves you deeply, and it is wonderful to behold.'

Throwing her arms around her mother, Marie hugged her. 'I'm going to miss you terribly.'

'Child, the Lord blessed me with three children, each a jewel in my life.' She stroked Marie's dark hair. 'My darling girl, you used to cry on my lap like this when you were a little girl and your brother teased you.' Lifting Marie's chin, she touched her cheek. 'Do you love Alexei?' she asked.

'With all my heart.'

Pauline Kulbas nodded as if confirming something to herself. 'Then you must go with him. You have my blessing and, if it is God's will, you'll return to us some day.'

Marie kissed her mother's palm. 'I promise it will not be forever.'

Tallinn, December

'Where's Serov?' Bogoleev snapped. Leaving the front two days earlier, Bogoleev had hastened across the country to Tallinn. 'Why have you not been keeping me up to date?'

'There has been little to report,' Ivanov said, keeping his voice impassive. 'I have been following him for weeks. His routine hardly changes.'

Bogoleev narrowed his eyes. 'Does he suspect he is being watched?'

'I don't think so. I have been especially careful.'

'What about his circle of friends? Who does he socialise with?'

'He regularly calls on Countess Golytsyn. She is a friend of his ex-wife's.'

'Does he have a mistress?'

'There is a local girl, originally from Narva.' Ivanov wiped his brow with his sleeve. 'I have seen them together a few times.'

'Who is she?'

'Her father had a factory in Narva.' Ivanov tried to keep the panic out of his voice. 'She moved to Tallinn with her parents. She is of no importance.'

'They are bourgeoisie?'

'The father is well respected. They lost a son in the war.'

Bogoleev stared at Ivanov through narrowed eyes. Ivanov kneaded his palms over his knuckles, suspecting that Bogoleev's instincts told him he was hiding something from him. Placing an arm around Ivanov's shoulder, his eyes remained cold.

'You've been away from your family for a long time,' he said. 'Maybe you should take a break, return to Petrograd.'

'What about Serov?'

'Leave him to me,' Bogoleev said flatly.

Ivanov swallowed. A sharp pain tightened in his stomach. 'And what do you plan to do with the girl and her family?'

'They are not important.' Bogoleev gave him a thin smile. 'I'm only interested in Serov.'

58

Tallinn, December 1919

Alexei and Marie stopped at a café on Pikk tanav, the long street that ran from the town hall all the way to the harbour. Choosing a table close to the window, they sat in silence for a while, watching the passing parade of well-dressed couples.

'I've met someone who can help us secure tickets to Australia,' Alexei said when the waitress had taken their order.

'Is he trustworthy?'

'I believe so. An acquaintance of Countess Golytsyn introduced him.'

They paused when the waitress returned with their coffees and a selection of colourful marzipans.

'He will provide us with false identity papers in case we are stopped by the Bolsheviks. We will travel to London where we'll board the TSS *Themistocles* to Cape Town and then Australia.' He reached for a sweet.

'When do we leave?'

'Tomorrow.'

Marie's mouth fell open. 'So soon?'

'Marie . . .' leaning across the table, he lowered his voice. 'This is our best chance. The Red Army has already crossed the border. If we are to escape, we must do so straight away.'

She fell silent, staring into her cup.

'You're right. It's too dangerous for you to stay in Tallinn,' she said at last. 'But why Australia? It's so far away. Mama has never recovered from losing Nikolai. And for me to go to the other side of the world . . .'

'Irena writes that the sun in Sydney is so bright, it makes the horizon shimmer,' Alexei said. 'She writes that the Pacific Ocean is the colour of turquoise, stretching as far as the eye can see.' His eyes shone in wonder. 'It must be a sight to behold.'

'But it's so far away,' Marie repeated. 'Why can't we stay in Europe?'

'We will not be safe anywhere in Europe,' Alexei replied, his voice tight. 'We need to get as far away from the Bolsheviks as possible.' He took her hand. 'I would never forgive myself if any harm came to you. We will be safe in Australia. *Cheka* cannot reach us there. I promise you, it will only be for a few years. And then we'll return.'

She stared at a spot on the table, unable to meet his eyes. 'And what if the Bolsheviks win?' she asked. 'What if it's never safe for us to come back?'

'That will never happen,' Alexei scoffed. 'They will never win. Never!' An elastic silence stretched around them. Alexei was first to break it. 'Marie, I will not go without you.'

Marie smiled, the sadness that had settled across her eyes clearing. 'I know you won't.'

By the time they left the café, a light breeze had sprung up, fresh and fragrant.

'Let's take a walk by Kadriorg pond,' Marie suggested.

Entering the park, they found a bench by the icy pond and watched couples skating arm in arm.

A few metres away, a man knelt to tie his shoelace.

A tingling sensation on the back of Alexei's neck made him give the man a second look. But having tied his laces the man stood and continued on his way.

Marie moved closer, nestling against Alexei for warmth. 'I wonder what it would be like waking up to a hot Christmas Day,' she mused. Her fingers played absently with the gold cross at her throat.

The couple on the bench hadn't noticed the figure watching them from behind an ancient alder tree. In any case, Bogoleev was almost unrecognisable beneath his bushy beard. He had spent three days surveying the address Ivanov had given him, but had not seen Alexei. Gradually, the realisation had sunk in: Ivanov had betrayed him.

It was only by chance that he had noticed the couple leaving the café. He had recognised Serov immediately.

Rising from their bench, the couple began to walk towards the park gates. Bogoleev's heart was racing. Should he do it now? No, he cautioned himself. There were too many people about.

Serov and the young woman crossed the street and hailed a cabriolet. Bogoleev quickly stepped into the next cabriolet and ordered the driver to follow them.

He had the driver drop him at the top of the street where Alexei's cabriolet had stopped. The sun had set behind the buildings and the street lamps' faint glow grew stronger. Keeping to the shadows, Bogoleev moved to an alley opposite the building Alexei and his companion had entered.

He looked down at his hands. They were shaking.

He needed a drink.

Touching his face, he felt pain throbbing in his skull. It was time to act. Pulling out his revolver, Bogoleev held it by his side.

'Drop your gun.'

Bogoleev's throat went dry. 'Who's there?'

Ivanov stepped out of the shadows.

Bogoleev relaxed, 'What are you doing here?' Then he saw the gleam of metal in Ivanov's hand. 'What's the meaning of this?' His grip tightened around his revolver. 'I can have you shot for pulling a gun on me.'

'I don't care any more.' Ivanov's voice shook. 'I have stood by and watched too many people die at your hands.'

'Each one of them was an enemy of the revolution.'

'Not all of them. The women and children who were murdered. How were they the enemy?'

'I'm not discussing this with you.' Bogoleev's skull felt ready to explode.

'Let them go.' The trembling in Ivanov's voice was replaced by a strong, authoritative tone.

'Who?' Bogoleev coughed a laugh. 'Serov? Are you mad? You know better than anyone how long I've been hunting him.'

'I'm telling you again: let him go.' Ivanov's voice was steady.

Bogoleev's face turned dark. 'Serov betrayed me.'

'How did he betray you? You forced him to join the Red Army. You threatened his family in front of him.'

'I SAVED HIS LIFE!' Bogoleev's head was pounding. Closing his eyes, he touched his scar. 'I should have shot him myself, but I let him live and he escaped. The man is a traitor.'

'He thought you were dead. We all did.'

'What's Serov to you anyway? Even if you don't care about yourself, think of your family,' Bogoleev warned. 'Once the Party finds out you have turned traitor, they'll be thrown out into the street. Or, worse, sent to Siberia. You are willing to sacrifice them for Serov?'

'I have my reasons.' Ivanov took a step closer. 'This is your last chance, Commissar. Let them go. Forget about Serov.'

'I told you, I can't do that.' Bogoleev raised his gun.

The sound of gunfire shattered the peace of the quiet neighbourhood. From across the street, a footman saw a man run out of the alley clutching his arm.

A balding man with a round face raced out of the next building, hastily shrugging a coat on over his shirt. 'What's going on?' he called out to the footman. 'I thought I heard gunshots.'

'Not sure, sir,' the footman said, scratching his head. 'I heard two shots and when I came out, I saw a man run out of that alley. I'll call the police.'

The footman had turned to go back inside when the bald man said, 'Wait,' and gestured to the alley. A figure was crawling along the road, dragging himself on his elbows. Reaching the gutter, he collapsed and lay motionless. The two men rushed to him, turning him over. Blood gurgled in his mouth and his eyes stared in shock. Opening his jacket, they saw the man's shirt was soaked with blood.

'I'll call the ambulance.' Jumping to his feet, the footman ran back to his building.

The bald man leant over and said, 'Help is on its way.'

The wounded man's wide eyes moved towards the voice. The lips moved, but no words emerged.

By the time the footman returned, the rasping breath was coming louder. Then the man's body twitched and, with a final gasp, fell still.

59

Tallinn, December 1919

Marie huddled close to Alexei as medics lifted a body onto a stretcher while police officers interviewed residents and passers-by.

Alexei called the footman over. 'We heard gunshots. What happened here?'

'There was a shooting in the alley,' the footman said, still visibly shaken. 'A man was killed.'

'Did they find who did it?' Alexei asked.

'He was hiding behind a tree, shot in the arm. The police took him away.'

'Did you get a look at him?'

'It was dark so I didn't get a proper look. I saw the police take him away. Maybe they'll be able to help you.'

Alexei approached one of the policemen. 'Who's in charge here?'

The policeman pointed to an officer barking orders at the mouth of the alley. 'The inspector.'

'The suspect has been taken into custody,' the inspector told Alexei.

'Did you learn the man's name?'

The inspector shook his head. 'He wouldn't talk. In any case, he's not from around here. Probably a pair of drunk communist agitators. Those men have no discipline. They are just as likely to turn their guns on their own comrades.'

Back in their apartment, Alexei was quiet, staring at the street below from behind the curtain. Who were those men? Were they communist agitators as the inspector had suggested? Was it just a coincidence that the shooting had happened outside his apartment?

Alexei shook his head. None of it made any sense.

'It's late, Alexei,' Marie said. 'Come away from the window.'

He did so reluctantly, still troubled by the unanswered questions.

The next morning, the street sweepers washed the dark stains off the pavement. Marie and Alexei climbed into the waiting cabriolet stacked with their trunks. As the cab pulled away from the kerb, neither turned to look back at the dark alley wreathed in grey morning mist.

Epilogue

Sydney, February 1921

The Pacific Ocean stretched out before him, waves crashing and sending foam almost to the tip of his shoes before retreating. The hot sun beat down, blinding him with its glare.

Distracted by a tugging at his pants, Alexei glanced down to see the round smiling face of his granddaughter looking up at him. At six months, Nina was chubby and content, with golden hair and eyes the green of shallow water. She squealed when Alexei lifted her, legs kicking the air in excitement.

'Oh Nina, leave your grandfather alone.' Reaching for her daughter, Irena took Nina from her father's arms. 'She'll wear you out if you let her, Papa.' She pinched the fat rolls of her baby's legs in mock reprimand. 'I've got a feeling she's going to be a handful when she grows up.' She smiled adoringly at her daughter.

As daylight faded, the crowds trickled away, leaving the beach to catch its breath. In the early twilight, the ocean changed from blue to silver, and stars pricked the sky.

Alexei gazed at the horizon, picking out the Southern Cross. Even after a year of gazing up at the stars, their configuration in the

Southern Hemisphere still left him confounded. Oh, the vertigo of a displaced life, he thought sadly. It robbed him even of the simple joy of looking at the heavens to find them unchanged.

He did not hear the soft tread of footsteps on the sand until they were almost upon him.

'Nina has fallen asleep.' Marie laced her fingers through Alexei's. 'Irena and Thomas are taking her home.' Caressing the small swelling of her stomach, she smiled, then was silent for a while, looking out to where the ocean kissed the sky.

'How long do you think before we see our family again?' She kept her voice neutral, but Alexei understood the meaning behind the question.

'When it's safe for us to return.' He wished he could sound more optimistic.

Marie exhaled, wrapping a protective arm around her stomach. She felt the fluttering of the baby's movements and took it as a good sign that their baby was strong and healthy. 'I hope it's a boy,' she said. 'We should call him Grigory.'

Alexei's eyes grew soft. 'Grigory would have been pleased to know I named my first son after him. He might have been alive today, if not for me.'

Marie's palm felt soft and cool against his. He gave her hand a gentle squeeze.

'I love you.'

Resting her head against his chest, she replied, 'And I you.'

Author's Note

The Russian Tapestry remembers those who have come before us. Drawn from anecdotes recited at family dinners, it is the imagined history of the Serovs' journey, blending legend with fact and make-believe with truth. It is the bringing together, unlocking and sharing of the stories that bind us.

It took two revolutions to bring my husband and me together. The Russian Revolution in 1917 was the catalyst that prompted his grandparents, Marie and Alexei Serov, to flee to Australia. Over half a century later my family, similarly, escaped their homeland following the Islamic Revolution.

Marie Kulbas was the daughter of a rich Estonian merchant, studying law in St Petersburg. Engaged before the war, her fiancé went missing in action and never returned. She had three brothers, two of whom died from cholera during the German occupation of Estonia. The family later moved to Tallinn, where Marie and Alexei met.

Alexei Serov came from a prestigious family, which boasted court painters and conductors in its midst. A major general in the Imperial Army, Alexei had fought on the eastern front. He was the father of two daughters with his first wife, Emily, and a third, younger, daughter, who was illegitimate but who also lived with them. Infirm and unable to return to the army, he was later forced to join the

Reds (as the Workers' and Peasants' Red Army was known), but managed to escape, travelling through blizzard conditions to reach Lithuania.

The parallel lives that preceded my husband's and my union fascinated me. Like me, Alexei and Marie possessed migrant hearts. They travelled halfway across the world to start life anew in a foreign land, with little more than their hopes and dreams to sustain them. Unlike for my family in Iran however, their lifestyle in pre-war Russia was one of glittering balls, the ballet and horse races. As a long-time lover of Russian literature, I started imagining the world they inhabited, their first meeting and their eventual love affair. As their story started to take shape in my mind, I was swept away by the romance of the period and the tragedy of the war that followed it.

Starting out, I had little to guide me other than their obituaries, a few dusty photos and Alexei's three surviving medals; their diaries had all been lost or destroyed over the decades. Nevertheless, supplemented by my own research, these treasures provided me with a skeleton upon which I was able to flesh out my story. At times, in the interest of storytelling, I took liberties with the truth, bending it slightly to suit my purpose.

My supporting characters – Ivanov, Bogoleev, Katya and Fyodor – were born from my imagination and are not based on any real people, dead or alive.

Each of us has a story we carry silently within us, protected in our soul. Australia is the sum of all her stories. As custodians of these narratives, it is our duty to keep alive the memory of our ancestors for the benefit of future generations. In *The Russian Tapestry* I attempted to echo and recreate some of these migrant tales to bring alive the past. In telling their story, I hope to have done justice to the memory of Marie and Alexei Serov.

Acknowledgements

This book owes much to the collaborative efforts of many people. My most ardent thanks go first to my publisher, Bernadette Foley, for championing my writing and believing in it from the beginning. Special thanks to Ali Lavau, whose amazing editorial guidance transformed the initial manuscript into a tighter, stronger book. To Professor Roger Markwick for cross-checking the accuracy of the historical and military terms. And Kate Ballard for her patience and advice as the manuscript went through its second, third and fourth drafts. Many thanks to the team at Hachette Australia – from editors, to designers, to publicity and the sales team. Every book benefits from the collaboration of many people and without you, *The Russian Tapestry* would not be what it is today.

To my friends – you know who you are – who supported me every step of the way. Your encouragement was the tonic that spurred me onwards when I felt like giving up. A special thanks to Vassiliki and John, for the loan of their eleven-volume encyclopaedia, which proved to be an invaluable resource.

Finally, to my parents, my husband, our boys, my in-laws and our siblings; your love sustains and nourishes me. I would especially like to thank my father-in-law, Oleg, who has generously allowed me to write about his parents. I love you.

Banafsheh Serov was born in England but spent her childhood in Iran, from where she fled with her family during the Iran–Iraq War to eventually resettle in Australia. She is the author of *Under a Starless Sky*, the true story of her family's escape from Iran. She lives in Sydney with her husband and sons, and owns and manages a chain of bookshops. *The Russian Tapestry* is her first novel.